A Room Full of Killers

Michael Wood is a freelance journalist and proofreader living in Sheffield. As a journalist he has covered many crime stories throughout Sheffield, gaining first-hand knowledge of police procedure. He also reviews books for CrimeSquad, a website dedicated to crime fiction. *A Room Full of Killers* is his third novel.

@MichaelHWood
/MichaelWoodBooks

Also by Michael Wood

Outside Looking In
For Reasons Unknown

Short story
The Fallen

A Room Full of Killers

MICHAEL WOOD

A imprint of HarperCollins*Publishers*
www.harpercollins.co.uk

Killer Reads
An imprint of HarperCollins*Publishers*
1 London Bridge Street
London SE1 9GF

www.harpercollins.co.uk

This paperback edition 2017
1

First published in Great Britain by
HarperCollins*Publishers* 2017

A catalogue record for this book is
available from the British Library

ISBN: 9780008222406

Set in Minion by Palimpsest Book Production Limited, Falkirk, Stirlingshire

Find out more about HarperCollins and the environment at
www.harpercollins.co.uk/green

To Woody
26/05/04 – 09/06/16
The best writing companion I could ever ask for. A true friend, and now, a genuine Golden Star.

PROLOGUE

I was in agony. The pain was immense. I couldn't believe it. I looked across at the alarm clock and saw that it was just after 1:30 a.m., and I hadn't been to sleep yet. How could I when all I wanted to do was vomit everything I'd ever eaten.

I managed to roll out of bed and practically crawled to the bathroom. I made it to the toilet just in time. The sick was never-ending. I honestly thought I was going to bring up an organ. There was so much of it. It was like that scene from *The Exorcist*.

I must have woken my sister, Ruby, because I looked up to wipe my mouth and she was standing in the doorway. She had her hands on her hips and a serious look on her face like she was going to tell me off. If I hadn't felt like I was dying I would have laughed. How could she try and look mean and threatening when she was wearing Hello Kitty pyjamas?

'Could you be any louder about it?'

'Sorry, Ruby, did I wake you?'

'No, I always go for a walk around this time.' She looked at her wrist as if there was a watch there.

1

'Sorry. I don't think I should have reheated that curry I had for my tea.'

'Have you made yourself sick so you don't have to go to school in the morning?'

'No. Why would I do that?'

'Because I heard you telling Dad you hadn't done your science homework.'

'I've not made myself sick, Ruby. Go back to bed.'

I managed to pick myself up off the floor, although I felt dizzy and the sweat was pouring off me. I had to steady myself against the wall. I was shaking and hot but I felt cold at the same time. I had no idea a chicken korma could cause such agony.

'Do you want me to wake up Mum and Dad?'

'No. It's OK. I think I'll go downstairs and see if we've got anything to settle my stomach.'

'OK.'

'Are you going back to bed?'

'Yes,' she said, folding her arms.

'Go on then.'

'I'm waiting until you've gone downstairs. I don't want you to fall.'

I went to go downstairs and kept looking back at Ruby, who wasn't moving. I knew what she was going to do. I would have made some kind of sarcastic remark but I was frightened of opening my mouth and being sick again, because Dad had just polished the floorboards. He'd kill me if I splattered regurgitated korma all over them.

I was halfway down the stairs when I heard Ruby tap on Mum and Dad's bedroom door. 'Mum, I had that dream again. Can I come in with you and Dad?'

I smiled to myself. Ruby had promised that she'd sleep in her own bed all through the night. It was her New Year's resolution yet she'd broken it within three days. She hated sleeping on her own, God knows why.

As soon as I opened the door to the kitchen, Max jumped out of his basket, tail wagging, and thought I wanted to play with him. He started jumping on his back legs. As much as I loved the little dude, playing with a Fox Terrier at two o'clock in the morning was not my idea of fun. He ran over to the back door so I let him out.

I left the door open while I looked for something to take. Dad suffered really badly with his stomach. He only had to look at a jar of beetroot and he got indigestion. He was bound to have something that could stop my stomach doing somersaults.

I found a small tub of Andrews Salts and made myself up a glass. I swigged it back in one gulp and shuddered at the taste. It was nasty.

Max came running back into the kitchen with a tennis ball in his mouth and dropped it at my feet. I wasn't going outside to play fetch in the garden. It was bloody freezing out there. I made him go back to his bed, locked the back door and went into the living room. I didn't have the strength to walk up the stairs.

I curled up on the sofa, pulled the blanket around me and tried to get comfortable. Whatever was in that medicine seemed to be working as there was no gurgling sound coming from my stomach. I wasn't shaking as much either.

I was shattered. I looked at the clock – 02:15. I'd never been up this late before in my life. I was just nodding off when Max came in and licked my face. He lay down in front of me on the floor. He could tell I was ill and was looking after me, bless him. He was snoring in seconds. I wish I could fall asleep so quickly.

04:50

Max started licking my hand and barking. I briefly opened my eyes but, as it was still dark, I nudged Max away and pulled the blanket over my head. If he wanted to go out again he'd have to wait. I was finally warm and comfortable.

Another bark. This time he was nuzzling my hand and trying to pull the blanket off me with his teeth. He may be a cute dog and able to get away with a lot of things, but there was no way I was getting up for him now.

'Max,' I whispered loudly. 'You'll wake everyone up. Go to sleep. Now!'

I waited. I heard him groan, walk around in a circle a few times then drop to the floor. Thank God for that.

05:05

It seemed like only minutes later that he started fussing me again. He was yapping, barking, tugging at the blanket, and licking my face. I threw the blanket off me and stood up to turn on the living room light. I can't remember what I was saying to Max but as soon as the room lit up I saw exactly why he'd been behaving so oddly.

There was a leak coming through the light fitting in the middle of the room. It didn't make sense. The bathroom was above the kitchen, not the living room. My eyes adjusted. Shit! It wasn't water pooling on the coffee table. It wasn't water dripping and splashing all over the cream carpet. It was blood. I looked up at the light; the surrounding ceiling was a mass of blood. It was dripping down, splattering against the glass, bouncing off and soaking the carpet. This wasn't real. It couldn't be. I was having a nightmare caused by my fever, surely.

Max barked. I looked down at him and he was speckled with blood. His paws were covered in it. Oh my God. This wasn't happening. Surely, I was running a fever from all the vomiting and having a nightmare.

I ran out of the living room and up the stairs, two at a time. 'Mum, Dad, wake up,' I called out. It was pitch-black and still early so my voice echoed around the house. I didn't care if I woke up the whole street.

I knocked on their door but didn't wait for a reply. I grabbed the handle and pushed. I flicked the light switch on.

'Mum … '

That was the moment everything stopped. My life ended right at that second as I looked into my parents' bedroom and saw a scene of horror. All I could see was red. The walls, the ceiling, the floor, everything was covered in red. Huge sprays of blood covered every surface.

I could feel my heart pounding hard in my chest as if it was about to erupt. No. This wasn't happening. It couldn't be real.

I walked further into the room and looked at the bed, trying to make sense of what my eyes were seeing, but my brain hadn't caught up yet. The bed was a tangled mess of limbs and everything was dripping. It was like a scene from a torture porn film. I didn't know if anybody was on the bed or not. Then I saw it. Dad had given Mum a really expensive watch for Christmas, just a week or so earlier. She'd loved it and spent most of Christmas Day staring at her wrist. She was still wearing it but the face was smashed. Her arm was covered in blood, but it wasn't attached to her body. I swallowed hard to keep the bile from rising in my throat. I saw Dad's leg with the Manchester City football shield tattoo. Like Mum's arm it was splattered with blood. And there, in the middle of the bed, I saw the worst horror of all: the blood-stained white face of Hello Kitty winking at me.

ONE

According to the satnav it would take three hours and nineteen minutes to drive from Norwich to Sheffield. Add on traffic jams, roadworks, and fuel stops, and they would easily make the Steel City in four hours.

The seven-seater people carrier was waiting outside the back entrance. It was parked as close as possible to the door. The windows in the Citroën were tinted; the locks from the back doors had been removed, and there was a security grill between the front and back seats.

In the front passenger seat was Craig Jefferson, his extra-large uniform straining at the seams. He checked the glove box for provisions: boiled sweets, three cans of Red Bull, and a Sudoku puzzle book. Behind the wheel sat Patrick Norris. This was Patrick's first run. He knew the route; he had been studying the *A-Z* all afternoon, but the worried expression on his face was for his charge, not his driving ability.

Time ticked slowly by. They should have left by now.

'What's taking so long?' Norris asked, fidgeting in his seat.

'Red tape probably. Just when you think you've filled in all the forms you find another batch that needs signing.'

'They do realize Norwich are playing at home today, and it's a late kick-off. We're going to get caught in the traffic.'

'They don't care about that. Once they close that door their job is done. It's down to us then. They don't care if it takes us three hours and nineteen minutes or nineteen hours and three minutes. Mint imperial?' He held out the packet.

'How many of these runs have you done?'

Jefferson sighed as he thought. 'Too many to count. I don't go to Sheffield very often though. In fact, I can't remember the last time I went. You know it's bad when you're given a run to Sheffield.'

'Do you think there's some kind of hold up?' Jefferson asked, craning his neck and looking out of the back window at the dormant building. 'Maybe it's been cancelled.'

'Trust me, it won't get cancelled. They're as keen to get rid of him as we'll be to drop him off. Are you any good at Sudoku? I'm not sure if that should be a three or a five.'

The steel door creaked open and two burly men in similar uniforms to Norris and Jefferson came out. They towered over the young man between them.

His face was gaunt and pale. His hair had been recently shaved which added to the emaciated refugee look. He was a slight build, short for his age, and had the appearance of an innocent man heading for the gallows.

While one of the men secured him to the back seat, the other tapped on the passenger window. Jefferson lowered it.

'What took you so long? It's freezing out here.'

'If you must know, we had a hard time saying goodbye. He's such wonderful company.' His reply was laced with sarcasm.

'Well you can join us if you like?'

'Tempting offer but I'm clipping my toenails tonight. Here you go.' He handed over a clipboard with the required paperwork to be signed once they reached Sheffield. It was like delivering a washing machine.

'Off we go then, Patrick. Head for the A17 and no stopping under any circumstances except for fuel for me and the car.'

Shackled in the back of the car was fifteen-year-old Ryan Asher. Norwich born and bred he was about to leave the city for the first time, and he was never coming back.

His left leg jiggled with nerves. He had been told what was happening to him, where he was going, and what his final destination in approximately three years' time would be, but it was the unknown he was scared of. A new city and new people, where the only things they knew about him was what the newspapers had reported. Nobody knew the real Ryan Asher anymore. Nobody wanted to know.

In the middle seat of the car, he sat back and looked out of the window at the darkening Norwich landscape. He was born here. He played with his friends here. He went to school here. He murdered here.

A three-hour journey with nobody to talk to, no radio, nothing to read, and a wall of darkness outside the window to torment his troubled mind. He couldn't get comfortable and kept adjusting himself. He bit his bottom lip and could taste blood. He wondered how fast they were travelling? Was Sheffield far from Norwich? He hated not knowing. They could be taking him anywhere. Maybe he wouldn't make it to Sheffield. The driver kept gazing at him through the rear-view mirror. His look was sharp and scared. What did he think Ryan was going to do? He was a fifteen-year-old boy who looked twelve, not Hannibal Lecter.

The driver and the front seat passenger didn't speak much. The odd banal comment on the amount of traffic and how dark it had become, but that was it. They would probably save their conversation for the journey back when it would be just the two of them. Ryan could guess what the main topic of conversation would be – him.

Ryan let out a deep breath he didn't know he had been holding and closed his eyes. The first image that came to mind was the look on his mother's face the first time he saw her after their world had been torn apart. She didn't look like his mum anymore. Gone were the bright blue eyes, the cheery smile, and the dimples – replaced with a look of horror, fear, and loathing. She had brought a monster into the world. She had given birth to evil and stood back while her son destroyed lives.

'I'm sorry,' he said when he looked up at her. 'I'm really sorry.' It was baseless but it was all he could think of.

Belinda Asher didn't reply. She couldn't reply. She was using every ounce of energy to keep herself standing. Her legs were shaking uncontrollably. She was freezing cold, yet sweat was pouring from every pore. Her mouth was dry as she looked at her only son's face. Her eyes were full of tears that refused to fall.

'Mum. I'm really sorry. Where's Dad? Is he coming?'

'I want to go.' The words fell out of her mouth to the female detective who was holding her up. No words were exchanged. The detective slowly turned her around and led her across the room.

Ryan was crying. 'Mum, don't leave me. I'm sorry. I'm sorry. I didn't mean any of it. Mum, please. I'm so sorry.'

At the door, Belinda Asher turned around and a heavy shroud of silence fell over them all. Somewhere, a clock was ticking, high-heeled shoes were clacking down a corridor, planets were formed, stars died and, all the while, mother and son were locked in a battle of immense will-power.

'Don't call me that,' she said. 'I have no idea who you are.'

Ryan opened his eyes and stared out of the car window. A tear fell which he didn't wipe away. He had never cried as much as he had in the past few months. At first, he was embarrassed by his tears. Now, he didn't care who saw.

Why was he crying? For the pain and emotional distress that he had caused his family; for the life he had lost; for his victims?

He no longer knew. All he did know was that he had ruined the lives of so many people, including his own, and, for that, he felt incredibly sad.

The car pulled into a service station. The fat one in the front passenger seat struggled to get out. Ryan watched as he waddled to the toilets then into the small kiosk shop.

'Are we nearly there?' Ryan asked, looking at the reflection of the driver in the rear-view mirror. He didn't get a reply. Ryan was the enemy. He was not to be engaged with.

The fat one tested the suspension as he eased himself back into the car. 'I needed that. Red Bull might give you wings but it goes straight through me. I bought you a Twix. They didn't have any granola.'

'Not much bloody difference, is there?'

'If you don't want it, I'll have it.'

'And listen to you moan about being borderline diabetic? No, thank you.'

Ryan wasn't acknowledged. He wasn't asked if he wanted anything from the shop, or if he needed the toilet. To them he was a tumour – difficult to ignore and impossible to forget.

Three hours and forty minutes after they left Norwich they arrived at their destination in Sheffield. Off a main road and down a long bone-shaking track, they came to a set of electronic gates with razor wire on the top.

The driver lowered his window and leaned out. He pressed the call button on the intercom, and the small screen above lit up. The face of a man loomed out at them in black and white.

'Yes?'

'We have Ryan Asher with us.'

'Drive up to the second set of gates and turn off your engine.'

The screen went blank, and the gates slowly opened. They drove through and stopped when they reached a second set of gates. The first set closed behind them. They were trapped in a small rectangle with high fencing on all four sides and barbed wire tightly coiled along the top. Nothing happened.

'What's going on?' the driver whispered to his colleague.

'We're being filmed and photographed from every conceivable angle.'

After a few long minutes of silence, the second set of gates opened. Norris turned on the engine and continued driving along the pothole-lined track until they reached the entrance to the imposing nineteenth-century building.

Ryan remained in the back of the car as it pulled up. The driver opened the door and looked at the frightened teenager.

'Out you get.'

As Ryan was led out of the car he looked up at the terrifying building casting long shadows from the full moon directly above it. He was mesmerized by the imposing façade; the massive bay windows; the severe leaded panes of glasses. It was something out of a classic Hammer Horror film.

The front door opened and a large barrel of a man waddled down the steps. A yellow glow from the lighting behind enveloped him.

'Ryan Asher?'

'Yes.'

'Welcome to Starling House.'

TWO

DCI Matilda Darke's morning routine had changed beyond all recognition over the past month. The alarm clock was set for six o'clock, though she was usually awake and up before it sounded. She no longer dragged herself out of bed; she threw back the duvet and hopped out.

She headed for the conservatory where a newly acquired treadmill waited for her. She plugged her iPod into it – a little bit of David Bowie to start the day – and began a five kilometre jog. Matilda had only been doing this routine for a few weeks but she was sure her thighs and calves were getting tighter. Her bum certainly felt firmer and, maybe she was kidding herself, but her black jacket didn't seem as figure-hugging. It would be a long time before she could wear the size ten Armani suit hiding away in her wardrobe but she was getting there – slowly.

It had been the idea of her friend, Adele Kean, to get in shape. Maybe it would make her feel better, not just physically, but mentally too – give her something else to focus on rather than grieving for her late husband, James. Adele was a member of Virgin Active and managed to drag Matilda along with her. However, fifteen minutes into her first session and Matilda knew a gym was most definitely not for her.

She looked at herself in the floor-to-ceiling mirror and didn't like the wreck staring back at her. The whole open-plan gym felt like a zoo; preening and presenting body-beautifuls – not so much working out as auditioning for God only knew what. The stains some people left on the equipment reminded Matilda of animals scent-marking their territory. The selfie-obsessives would never welcome Matilda into their den with her neurosis and baggy sweaters – not that she wanted them to.

So she treated herself to a treadmill and a couple of kettlebells and turned the conservatory into a make-shift gym. She wasn't sure James would approve, the conservatory was his pride and joy, but as long as Matilda was well and functioning normally he would be looking down on her and smiling, especially that time when she caught her headphone wire on the treadmill handles and fell off.

The five kilometre jog took her thirty-two minutes. She was desperate to get it under thirty and promised herself she would jog at a faster pace tomorrow morning. She had a quick shower, breakfasted on a high-fibre cereal and black coffee and was ready to leave the house.

Today was a rare day off for DCI Matilda Darke. She could have spent it relaxing at home and flicking through the many channels of trash TV, but one look at her wedding photo would bring a flood of memories to the surface and, before she knew it, the whole day would be lost to her depressive state – why hadn't she met James sooner? Why hadn't they had children? Why had he been taken so early? Besides, she had promised her parents to call in for a long-overdue visit and she had errands to run.

Matilda opened the front door, took in a lungful of autumnal air and stopped dead in her tracks. On the doorstep at her feet lay a large padded envelope. She looked around but there was nobody about. She picked it up. On the front was her name in large capital letters. It had been hand delivered. She took it into the house and closed the door firmly behind her.

The package felt heavy. She sat on the sofa and slowly pulled open the tab.

'Oh God, no.'

Matilda pulled out a thick hardback book. The picture on the front was of a smiling blond-haired, blue-eyed, seven-year-old boy. The title of the book, *Carl*, in big red letters at the top, and the author's name, 'Sally Meagan', at the bottom. This was the official version of the disappearance of Carl Meagan, as seen through the eyes of his heartbroken mother. Carl would forever be on Matilda's mind; the boy she failed to rescue from his kidnappers and return home to his doting parents. And now there was a book. The whole world would read about her failings.

Matilda opened the front cover and saw it had been personally signed:

'Matilda, an advanced copy just for you. May it give you as many sleepless nights as it's given me. Sally Meagan.'

Carl

by

Sally Meagan

Introduction

I had never had a night away from my only son before. Any holidays and business trips we had, Carl always came along too. However, on this particular occasion, the event in Leeds was at night and Carl had school the following morning. Now he was getting older it was harder to take him with us. I didn't want him missing his education.

My mum, Annabel, had looked after Carl hundreds of times. He loved his ma-ma, as he called her, and she loved him. She lived close to us in Dore, Sheffield, and often called to take him to the park or shops. She had never looked after him alone overnight before. However, she was my mother. I had nothing to worry about.

The event in Leeds was for Yorkshire Businessman of the Year. It was Philip's first time nominated for anything so we knew we had to attend. Mum came to our house for a light tea and brought plenty of provisions for her and Carl. They had planned a night in front of the TV watching DVDs and playing games. I think my mum was more excited than Carl.

At six o'clock, I kissed Carl goodbye. I gave him his instructions to be a good boy, not to answer back to ma-ma, and to go to bed when she told him to. He looked at me with those big blue eyes and smiled. I knew he would behave but I also knew he would cause great mischief for my mum. She would love it, though. I kissed my mum too. I thanked her once again and we left. They stood on the doorstep and waved us off. That was the last time I saw either of them …

Matilda couldn't read on. She knew what was to follow. She had lived and breathed Carl's disappearance for eighteen months. She knew the case inside out; evidently, though, not from the point of view of his distraught mother.

The Meagans blamed Matilda for not returning their son home to them, and the book was going to be a scathing attack on her, her abilities as a detective, and South Yorkshire Police as a whole.

The Meagans were a wealthy family who owned a chain of organic restaurants throughout the region. It wasn't long after Carl's disappearance that a ransom demand for a quarter of a million pounds was made. It wasn't easy, but Philip Meagan managed to get the money together and a drop-off point was arranged. Matilda, leading the investigation, was designated the courier.

In a cruel twist of fate, Matilda's husband, James, lost his battle with a brain tumour on the same day as the drop-off had been arranged. Neither wanting sympathy from her colleagues, nor the case to be taken from her at such a crucial stage, she told nobody of James's death and continued with her duties.

Those around her noticed Matilda was quieter than usual but put it down to the mounting stress of the case. Everyone was working under exceptional circumstances.

By the time night fell Matilda headed for Graves Park alone. A bag containing two hundred and fifty thousand pounds in cash sat next to her on the front passenger seat. She waited. Ten o'clock came and went and there was no sign of the kidnappers. Eventually, her mobile burst into life.

'Where the fuck are you?' It was the angry, accent-less tone of the kidnappers.

'Graves Park, where we agreed.'

'What car are you in?' The voice was muffled as if the kidnapper had something covering the mouthpiece of the phone.

'Black Seat. I'm flashing my headlights.'

'You lying bitch. There's no other car in the car park.'

'Car park?'

'By the animal farm.'

'We said by the tennis courts.'

'Do you want us to kill this kid?'

'No. Give me five minutes.'

Matilda grabbed the bag from the seat and jumped out of the car. She ran. She ran as fast as she could. A montage of faces went through her mind: the innocent face of a petrified seven-year-old, missing his parents; Sally and Philip Meagan, agonisingly waiting in their living room for a phone call from Matilda saying she had their child back safe and well; the painless image of her husband in his hospital bed, finally at peace, and the look of horror and disappointment on the faces of her colleagues when they found out how she had messed the whole thing up.

Matilda ran past the eerie concrete tennis courts and up the hill to the wooded area of Graves Park.

'I'm coming,' she said under her breath. 'I'm coming, Carl.'

Her legs ached as she pounded the solid ground. She was in the wrong shoes for running. Her lungs struggled to cope with the heavy breathing, and the cramp in her side was forcing her to slow down. She couldn't. She had to plough on through the pain.

She pulled a torch out of her pocket and flicked it on. A brilliant white beam lit the path ahead. She made it through the woods and out the other side, past the toilet block and the café and eventually reached the car park.

She stopped. She stood on the edge, torch held aloft, and throwing the beam all around her. The car park was empty. The kidnappers had left, taking Carl Meagan with them.

'Carl?' she called out, her shaking voice resounding around the open space. 'CARL!' she screamed, but her cries just echoed, answered by no one.

She could smell the cold night air tinged with burning car fumes. She had missed them by a matter of seconds.

THREE

Kate Moloney was a tall woman with long black straight hair which she wore in a severe-looking ponytail. Her skin was deathly pale and smooth. The red lipstick she always wore was striking and gave her a vampish air of power. She looked at least a decade younger than her forty-three years. She was curvaceous and wore long dresses or sensible trouser suits, yet made sure they were all figure-hugging to show off her natural assets. Her shoes were painful to wear but were part of her power outfit – impossibly high heels which echoed around the corridors as she walked with a straight back and her head held high. She was a woman on a mission.

Her office on the ground floor of Starling House was elaborate and necessary. The large mahogany desk with hand-carved detail dominated the room. The dark-red painted walls and cream-coloured carpet were expensive but a warranted luxury. The office made a statement to Kate's position. She deserved everything in this room and had worked hard to get it.

Surveying her office, she stood with her back to the window, arms firmly crossed. A knock came on the door and brought her out of her reverie. Despite the fact she wasn't doing anything, she waited a moment before telling her visitor to enter.

The door opened and Ryan Asher was led inside by an overweight man with greying hair, a pockmarked face, and grease stains on his shirt. He didn't enter the room. He showed Ryan in and quickly closed the door without saying a word.

'Ryan, nice to meet you. Please, sit down.' Kate gestured to the uncomfortable-looking wooden chair in front of her desk. She waited for Ryan to sit before she sank into her high-backed leather seat.

Kate leaned forward on her desk and interlocked her fingers. Her nails were sharp and painted a vivid blood red. 'Firstly, I'd like to welcome you to Starling House. I know it wasn't ideal for you to arrive at the time you did last night, but we do that for security purposes. And for your own safety too. I hope you managed to get some sleep in the holding room. It's draughty, I know, but I don't like the accommodation block interrupted once everyone is asleep. Now, you're going to be with us until you're eighteen, at least; it could be longer. From here you will go to Wakefield Prison where you will serve out the remainder of your sentence. I'm sure you've already had all this explained to you.'

Ryan's face looked blank. His brown eyes were wide and he wore a heavy frown, which suggested he was petrified of the nightmare he had found himself in. He nodded.

Kate dropped her voice for a softer tone. 'Ryan, I know this is frightening. You're away from home and your family. However, I know you're fully aware of the circumstances that led you here. I will, of course, make your stay as comfortable as possible and, if you ever need to talk about anything, I am always available. OK?' For the first time, she smiled. It wasn't a reassuring smile, more of a threatening gesture – your time will be comfortable here, providing you don't step out of line.

'OK.' His voice was high-pitched and it quivered.

'Good. Now, I'm going to show you around – introduce you to some of the staff and the other boys. After lunch you will have a meeting with Dr Klein who will assess you for any specific needs you might have. Shall we?'

Starling House was a Victorian building on the outskirts of Sheffield. Formerly owned by boxing promoter, Boris Wheeler, it was bought by Sheffield City Council in the late 1980s, following Boris's death. Unfortunately, maintenance and upkeep of the building ran into hundreds of thousands of pounds every year, and the Heritage Trust soon found themselves with a costly white elephant on their hands.

After years of wrangling, it was eventually sold cheap to a private organization who were able to adapt Starling House into what it is today – a secure home for some of the most violent boys in Britain.

Before it was due to open in 1996, almost every resident of Sheffield had signed a petition and staged protests outside the Town Hall demanding the council not allow it. The people of Sheffield boycotted Starling House. Nobody applied for a job there, so staff had to be drafted in from elsewhere and live on the premises.

During the summer months, when trees were in full bloom, Starling House was invisible from the main road running past it, and people could pretend it didn't exist. When autumn came, and the leaves had died and fallen, Starling House could be seen through the barren branches for miles. It was difficult to avoid, and the imagination was left to fester and mutate and come up with all kinds of stories of what was going on behind those thick stone walls.

Kate Moloney had been at Starling House since it eventually opened in 1997; starting as a junior officer before working her way up the promotional ladder. She was the only original member of staff left. It wasn't easy to keep people as many found it diffi-cult to be surrounded by such evil on a daily basis. There was the odd security officer who had stayed longer than two years, but the majority moved on just as Kate was getting to know them.

Kate showed Ryan around Starling House personally. She wasn't afraid to be left on her own with the teenage boys, despite the tabloid newspapers labelling them as the most disturbed children in the country. By the time Kate saw them they all had the same look – frightened, nervous, worried, petrified, and wishing they could travel back in time to undo their violent deeds.

She stole a glance at Ryan who, at first, dragged his feet with his head down, but eventually looked up and was either impressed or scared by the imposing building. High ceilings and ornate stonework adorned every corridor and room. Any removable original features had been taken out long before it became a home for teenage murderers – the sweeping oak staircase, the stained glass windows in the atrium were all gone. It was a bland, dull, lifeless building with very little character and charm. Depressing, cold, and stark, it was a building with no redeeming features.

The first stop on the tour was the gym. Kate didn't linger too long in here. There was a damp problem which was getting worse; the smell was an assault on the nose. The library and computer room were adequately equipped but nothing was state of the art. Even the books looked like they belonged at a jumble sale. As they went from room to room Kate tried to engage Ryan in conversation: did he like computers? Did he read much? Was he a fan of the gym? Each question was answered with the same monotone grunt or shrug of the shoulders.

The recreation room was a large space with a pool table, table tennis and football tables, as well as worn sofas surrounding a widescreen TV with DVD player and games consoles attached. At the side of the room there was a bar (without alcohol). There were patio doors leading out into the grounds but these were securely locked and alarmed.

'Most of the boys like to come in here when they've finished their lessons for the day,' Kate said. They stood in the doorway.

At the top of the room four boys were standing around the pool table wearing the identical uniform of navy combat trousers and grey jumper. They weren't close enough to engage in conversation. The four stopped their chatting and looked at the new inmate about to join them, then went back to what they were doing.

'Craig,' Kate called to one of the boys at the pool table and beckoned him over. 'Craig, this is Ryan Asher. He arrived last night. Could you introduce him to the other boys – show him around the rec. room?'

'Sure,' Craig shrugged.

'Excellent. Thank you. Ryan, it's almost time for lunch. Afterwards, I'll talk you through the timetable we have for your lessons then I'll introduce you to the staff.'

'OK.'

Kate smiled and left the room, closing the door behind her.

She made her way back to her office. It was difficult to take an impression of Ryan Asher. He had barely said a dozen words to her. She thought of herself as a good judge of character and hoped Ryan wouldn't cause too much trouble.

'Richard, you haven't seen Oliver anywhere have you?' she asked the fat guard who had shown Ryan into her office as she entered the main hallway.

'He's in the rec. room,' he replied in his usual flat burr.

'I've just come from there.'

'No idea, then,' he shrugged and went on his way.

'Charm personified,' she said to herself.

Craig walked slowly over to Ryan and eyed him up and down, taking in everything about him from his shaven head to his battered Converses. They were almost toe to toe, and Craig was still staring.

'So … where you from?' Craig asked. He had stale bad breath and his teeth were brown.

Ryan thought it best not to flinch from the smell. His fellow murderer may take offence.

'Norwich,' he replied with a catch in his voice.

'Oh. I've never been there.'

'It's nice.'

'Maybe I'll go one day then. You could show me around.'

Ryan gave a nervous laugh, thinking Craig was joking. The look on Craig's face told him he wasn't. 'Erm … OK.'

'Well, let's show you what's what.' He pointed to the various items. 'Pool, football table, table tennis table. You know what they're for. TV with PlayStation One and a Wii, for some reason. The DVDs are in the cupboard, but don't expect any of the new releases. And, we've only got Freeview.'

'OK,' Ryan replied.

'Let me introduce you to the other lads. You're number eight, and they're not all here at the moment as some are doing extra lessons. Anyway, playing pool is Lee and Jacob. Lee is the blond one. Thomas is sat reading as always—'

'What's going on?'

The door behind them opened and in walked Callum Nixon. Tall, well-built, heavy brow and swagger.

'Just showing the newbie around.'

Callum circled Ryan, having a long, lingering look at the skinny young boy. He slammed his arms down, grabbed him around the shoulders and marched him off to the centre of the room.

'Let me guess. Craig's been pointing out all the features like he's selling a house on one of those shit programmes on Channel 4. I'll show you the real Starling House. This is the rec. room, which is our only private place. You'll notice there's no guards in here. That's because this is our room. If you see a guard in here, you know there's been some shit going off somewhere. I'm Callum. I'm from Liverpool, and I sit on the recliner next to the sofa. If I catch you sitting in it, I'll gut you. Understand?' Callum's face remained stoic – he wasn't joking.

With wide, frightened eyes, Ryan nodded.

'Good lad. Now over there we've got Jacob. He raped and murdered his girlfriend. Next to him is Lee. He set fire to a caravan while his parents were sleeping in it. Killed them both. Craig killed his parents too, didn't you, Craig?'

Craig gave Ryan a small smile which twitched at the corners.

'Thomas, sitting down reading, as always, hacked his entire family to death with an axe, including his eight-year-old sister.'

'Why don't you tell him what you did?' Jacob called out.

'I don't need to tell him what I did.' He leaned in to Ryan and whispered in his ear, loud enough for the rest to hear though. 'I'm Callum Nixon. That's all you need to know.'

'Leave him alone, Callum,' Lee said, noticing the look of horror on Ryan's face.

'I'm just acclimatizing him to our little fun house. He needs to know who he's going to be living with for the next few years.'

'No, he doesn't. None of us need to know.'

'Look at him, Ryan, he hates horror films and practically shits himself whenever anyone talks about violence, yet he can happily kill his parents without giving it a second thought. Stick with me, Ryan. They're a bunch of nutters in here.'

Ryan broke free of Callum's hold and backed away. 'I need the toilet,' he said, barely above a whisper and ran out of the room.

'You can't leave it can you, Callum?' Lee said.

'What?' he asked as if he'd done nothing wrong. He looked around at the accusing faces staring at him. 'What?'

'You're a real dick, do you know that?'

Ryan entered the toilets. He didn't need the toilet, he just wanted a few minutes to himself. He felt overwhelmed.

Ryan looked at himself in the mirror. He looked grey and drawn. How had he ended up here like this?

He turned on the cold tap and splashed his face a few times but it didn't make him look any different. The main problem was how he felt on the inside. He felt sick, his stomach churning and performing somersaults. Ryan hadn't been here a day yet and he was already panicking about the rest of the week, let alone the next three years. After that was Wakefield. He knew about Wakefield. It was category A – where all the serious criminals went.

'I'm so sorry, Mum. Please come and visit me. I need you,' he said to his reflection.

CALLUM NIXON

Liverpool. March 2015

It was my first day back at school. I'd been suspended for five days after having a fight with Harinder Goswami in the chemistry lab. He started it but, just because he got burnt with some kind of acid, I ended up getting suspended. He wasn't even that badly burnt. Talk about an overreaction. All the teachers have it in for me, just because I won't take any of their crap. Teachers think they own the pupils and we'll do what they say. Well, they don't own me. My dad taught me from an early age that you have to stand up for yourself in this world and not take any shit from anyone – and I've got the belt buckle marks to remind me.

I was told to use my suspension to think about what I'd done, to think about what I wanted out of life and where I wanted to go. Mr Stockwell said I was on the road to failure. Mr Chandani said I was on a slippery slope. Who do they think they're talking to? Well, I knew where they were going to end up. In a shallow grave, that's where.

I spent my week off playing on my Xbox and planning how to get back at that fucker Harinder Goswami. I'd been banned from Facebook for racist abuse, which was a load of bollocks, and Twitter had closed my account. I wasn't bothered. Social media's for wankers anyway.

First day back and it was the only time I've ever looked forward to school.

I stood at the gates and watched everyone arriving. They didn't have a clue. I was going to own this school. I was going to be remembered. I walked up the drive and heads turned. Kevin Walsh looked shit scared; he's always looked like that since I threw that lit firework at him. Fiona Bishop smiled. She wanted me, but she's been with Harinder so I'm not going anywhere near her. Who knows what she's got! Barry Richardson saw me but quickly turned away. I smiled at my handiwork. His hair still hasn't grown back.

Mr Chandani said I had to go straight to his office before I started class. Fine by me. If he wanted to be my first victim, so be it. I went straight into his office. There he was, sitting behind his desk in his cheap suit. Fat bastard. God I hated him. Before he had the chance to look up I pulled the knife out from up my sleeve and slammed it into his neck. Piece of piss. I pulled it out and kept ramming it in and out until he fell off his chair. He was on the floor, his hands covered in blood as he tried to stop the bleeding. It didn't take him long to die. The blood soon stopped pumping out between his fingers and he closed his eyes. Bastard. I hacked up some phlegm and hit him right in the face.

I was surprised he didn't scream. I suppose it's difficult to scream when you've got a knife in your throat. I was really disappointed. I wanted to hear him begging and pleading as I took his life. Never mind. There's always next time. One down, one to go. Maybe two.

Mr Stockwell was in his chemistry lab getting ready for the class to begin. There were a couple of swots in there before the bell. I slashed at one girl, – never seen her before, and Kieran Ashley was there so I stabbed him in the shoulder. Prick. He sold me a dodgy iPhone last Christmas. Stockwell stood up. He looked like he was going to piss himself. He told me not to do anything stupid. I'm not stupid. He's stupid – three years at university, ten grand in debt – and working in a shitty school teaching a bunch of scallies. I stabbed him in the stomach; he bent forward so I got him in the neck. He fell to the floor so I got him twice more in the back.

That pervert who teaches us rugby, Mr Rushworth, charged into the classroom with that Irish teacher no one can understand, Mr Allen. They tackled me to the floor. I looked up at the clock on the wall. It had only taken ten minutes to off two teachers. I'd like to have got Mrs Pritchard who takes me for maths, snotty cow, but, never mind, I got the main two.

I looked over to Stockwell and saw the life in his eyes fade. That was cool – actually seeing someone die.

I was pinned to the floor for ages until the police arrived. Mr Rushworth was calling me all kinds of names. I just looked up at him and smiled. I'd never felt so alive. Best. Monday. Ever!

FOUR

The first day at Starling House for Ryan Asher had been daunting and frightening. After a mediocre lunch he had been to see the therapist, a Doctor Henrik Klein. He was a tall man who looked long past retirement age. He was completely bald with a bushy moustache that covered the whole of his mouth, muffling his words as he spoke. Originally from the Ukraine, he had lived in Britain long enough for his accent to morph into a broken attempt at English. He spent the first few minutes of the session leaning back in his armchair, arms folded, looking at the frightened teenager sitting opposite.

'So, how are you feeling?' His moustache bobbed up and down as he spoke.

'OK.'

'OK? You're only feeling OK? Anything else?'

'No. I don't think so.'

'You don't think so? How can you not think so? Surely you know how you feel.'

'I'm fine.'

'What are you fine about? You've been brought to Sheffield under the cover of darkness and find yourself living in a maximum security youth prison with seven other killers, and you're fine?

You're not scared, frightened, petrified? Shouldn't you be crying in agony? Or are you so hardened that nothing fazes you anymore? I need more from you than "fine".'

The forty-five minute session continued like that with Dr Henrik Klein learning absolutely nothing about Ryan Asher other than the fact that he was scared and wanted to see his mum, even though he knew it was never going to happen.

After therapy, Ryan needed a few minutes alone. The session had been heavy and demanding with Dr Klein throwing question after question at him as he tried to get him to admit his real feelings. He had no idea what his feelings were. He felt numb and wanted to go home, yet there was no longer a home for him to go to. Unfortunately, there was to be no respite. He was sent straight into the office of Mr 'Call Me Fred' Percival, as the other boys referred to him, for a basic English and maths test. He was an imposing man with a high forehead and fat stomach. With a thick Brummie accent he told Ryan that he lived on the premises during the week so would be around if he had any questions about absolutely anything.

'It's a tad overwhelming, all this, isn't it?' Fred said, looking at the wide-eyed teenager. 'You've nothing to worry about. It'll take you a few days to settle in, get to know your way around, and the other boys, but you'll soon find your feet.' He smiled.

'Thanks,' Ryan said, and smiled for the first time in months.

Fred climbed down from the desk he was perched on and went to sit next to Ryan, placing a large hand on the back of his shoulders, similar to what Callum had done, but Fred wasn't threatening at all, although he did seem to be standing a little too close.

He leaned in, merely inches from Ryan's face. 'If you ever want to talk about anything, not just maths and English, don't hesitate to ask, OK?'

'OK.'

'Good lad,' Fred said. 'Right, shall we get started?'

The tests were relatively easy. He struggled on a few of the maths questions but managed to answer them all within the time limit. He breezed through the English test. He remembered one of his teachers, Mrs Moore, had told his mum one parents' evenings that if he concentrated more in class instead of messing about he'd go far. She envisioned a bright future for him. Her powers of clairvoyance were obviously having a day off. He had no future of any colour.

With the tests finished, Ryan was shown into the recreation room where the other seven boys residing in Starling House were whiling away the dull afternoon.

He tried to sneak in undetected but the creaking hinges on the door betrayed him. The boys were scattered around the room – some were playing pool, others table football, and the rest were watching a DVD. He slinked over to the sofa and perched himself on the end. He looked uncomfortable as he leaned back and watched the TV. It was showing a *Star Wars* film but he had no idea which one.

He kept looking at the boys around him but didn't see their faces or their awkward smiles, just their crimes. Lewis Chapman murdered his younger brother. Mark Parker beat his father to death and strangled his mother. Lee Marriott killed his parents by setting them on fire, and Craig Hodge killed his aunt and uncle. Then there was Callum Nixon. Ryan had taken an instant dislike to the cocky show-off. He seemed to delight in people knowing he had killed two teachers. What the hell was he doing here living with these evil monsters? Then he remembered. Ryan was an evil monster himself. He wondered if the other seven felt the same regret and remorse as he did.

'You been to see Call Me Fred?' Lee Marriott was a thin boy with brilliant blond hair, piercing blue eyes, and skin so pale he was almost translucent.

Ryan smiled. 'Yeah. Just finished the tests.'

'Here's a tip: when he gets on a subject he really likes he spits when he talks; so always lean back when he comes near you.'

'Cheers.'

'You any good at pool?'

'Not really.'

'Table tennis?'

'A bit.'

'We'll have a game after tea if you want.'

'Yeah. Sure. Thanks.'

'No problem.' Lee moved up the sofa so he was next to Ryan. 'Look, don't worry about this place. It's scary at first but you'll soon settle in. Miss Moloney's all right as long as you're all right by her, and the other staff are pretty cool too. As for the rest of us lot, we all get along just fine – we have to really,' he sniggered.

'Thanks.'

'Let's have that game now. I fucking hate *Star Wars*.'

By the time the evening meal came around at 6 p.m, Ryan had spoken to all seven boys and was relatively relaxed in their company. There were a couple who seemed a bit distant but, when he factored in the reason why they were all here, he could perfectly understand that.

Ryan entered the dining room with Jacob, Mark, and Lewis. They were laughing and joking. To the outsider they looked like four school pals on their lunch break. Once they were seated the plastic cutlery gave away the seriousness of where they were.

Ryan had been too knotted up to eat at lunchtime. Now he had settled in and relaxed with his contemporaries for a few hours, he found he was hungry, and was the first to finish his bland chicken dinner. They all chatted between mouthfuls: safe subjects like football, TV, and the fact Mark Parker couldn't do more than ten press-ups in the gym.

Following dessert (soggy treacle sponge and lumpy custard), it was back into the recreation room for a few hours before they went to bed at nine o'clock.

Ryan beat Lee easily at table tennis but there was no malice, no arguments, no threats of reprisals – it was all good-natured fun.

Nine o'clock came far too quickly for Ryan's liking and he was soon locked up in his small room (not a cell). He was finally alone after a hectic first day at Starling House. He wasn't tired. It had been years since he had a bedtime. As he lay wide awake on the single bed, looking up at the ceiling with its cracked paint and damp patches, his mind drifted. How did he end up here? Where were his mum and dad? What were they calling themselves now?

The room was sparse. A single pine bed with matching bedside cabinet. A cheap veneer wardrobe secured to the wall and a plastic chair. There was one shelf which had a few dusty paperbacks. The room lacked atmosphere and there was a cold draft coming from somewhere. There was nothing personal or comforting about it. He wondered what the other boys' rooms were like. Had they brought items from home: posters, photographs, games? He wondered if he was allowed to visit the other boys in their rooms. Something else to ask Lee in the morning.

Ryan listened to the silence. He couldn't hear anything from the outside, no traffic on the roads, no people walking by. He wondered how far he was from civilisation. He'd never been to Sheffield before so had no idea of the layout. It was in Yorkshire, which had two shit football teams, was about all he knew. He remembered his uncle coming up to Sheffield for the snooker once when Ryan was a little boy but that was the only time the city was mentioned in his house.

There were no sounds coming from anywhere else in the building. He strained to hear any of the other boys talking, either to themselves or each other through the walls, or any of them crying, but he guessed the walls were too thick.

He took a deep breath and sighed. His first full night in Starling House. His first of many. Lee and Jacob had made the first day manageable but he would give anything to be back home with his mum and dad, to be hugged by them one more time.

A tear fell from his eye, down his face and onto his pillow.

'I'm so sorry, Mum. For everything I did. I'm really sorry,' he said, quietly, under his breath. 'Please find it in your heart to forgive me. I need to see you.'

Ryan turned over and hid his face into his pillow to muffle the sound of his sobbing. Just because he couldn't hear anyone else, it didn't mean they couldn't hear him.

He cried uncontrollably; cried himself to sleep. He was just nodding off when his door was unlocked from the outside.

LEE MARRIOTT

Blackpool. August 2013

I was born by accident. It's not that my parents didn't want me, they did, well, Mum did. It's just that I was a surprise for them both.

Mum and Dad had tried for years to have a baby. They married when Dad was twenty-five and Mum was twenty-one. They tried from the honeymoon onwards but nothing happened. Twenty years later, out I popped. I was their middle-age miracle.

I've heard that story so many times from Mum that I could give a lecture on it. I could go on that boring quiz show with the leather chair and have it as my specialist subject. At first it was a sweet story, as if I had waited more than twenty years for the right time to be born, or the angels were preparing my mum and dad to be the best parents ever (that's a direct quote from Mum's story, by the way – pathetic, isn't it?). After hearing it more than ten million times it starts to get annoying; more than annoying, it's irritating. It's a fucking pointless story, and I hate it.

Mum took her role of mother far too seriously. She refused to let me out of her sight. I wasn't allowed to play out, in case I fell and hurt myself. I wasn't allowed to climb trees, in case I fell out and cracked my skull open. I wasn't allowed to the shops on my own, in case I was knocked down by a car and killed. Dad wasn't allowed to take me to a football match, in case I was kidnapped. I lived in a bubble.

Every summer we went on holiday for two weeks to the same place – Blackpool. Have you ever spent two full weeks in Blackpool? Fuck me, it's boring! Have you ever spent two full weeks in Blackpool living in a tin-can caravan with your parents every single year since you were born? It's torture! I'm fifteen – why do I want to go to Blackpool? Why do I want to go on holiday with my mum and dad? Why do I want to spend two weeks in a shitty caravan the size of a public toilet? I tell you, torture.

This year was different. Actually, no, it wasn't. It was exactly the same, only this time I met someone, someone fun. Liam.

Mum and Dad allowed me some freedom for the first time. I was allowed in the arcade in the caravan park but I couldn't go off-site without their permission. I looked up from the slots to see this guy looking at me. That was Liam, and he looked just as bored as I was. I smiled. He smiled. I went for a drink, so did he. We got chatting. He was on holiday too, with his nan and granddad, but they spent all day playing bingo so he was allowed to do whatever he wanted – lucky sod.

Liam asked if I wanted to go down to the beach. I didn't even think of asking Mum and Dad. I just went. We had some chips and swapped stories. He was from Carlisle. His Mum and Dad were working all summer so his grandparents were looking after him. As a special treat, they'd brought him to Blackpool for the week – some treat!

We went to the top of the Tower and spent a good half hour looking at the view. Then Liam invited me back to his caravan and we drank a few cans of lager. Can you believe that was my first taste of alcohol? I tried vodka too but I didn't like it, and I wouldn't even try the whisky – the smell alone was too much. I decided to stick to lager and I had a few cans, followed by a few more. It wasn't long until we were both seriously pissed. I'll always remember that day as being one of the best ever. Liam was everything I wanted to be – fun, free, happy, good-looking.

It was after midnight when I got back to my caravan. It was a cool night and the breeze seemed to sober me up a little. Mum and Dad were still up, obviously, and they were both angry. At first Mum was thrilled I was safe, until she smelled the lager on my breath. They both kicked off, saying how I'd disappointed them and let them down. I heard the story of how I was a miracle birth again. I always had that thrown in my face. Dad sat calmly while Mum ranted. She said we were going back home first thing in the morning. I said no as I'd arranged to go out with Liam. I refused to leave. I was having fun for the first time in my life. Dad told me off for cheeking my mum, and he sent me to bed. Well, it was the table turned into a bed. Not the same thing.

I can't actually remember what happened next. One minute I was lying in bed, the next I was turning on the gas canisters for the stove. I didn't think of the consequences until afterwards but I'm not sorry. They were suffocating me. For how long did they think I was going to put up with being their prisoner?

I stood well back from the caravan as I struck the match. The wind blew out the first few; the fifth one went straight through the window. The curtains caught fire so I ran, knowing this would be it. I hid behind another caravan a few rows back and watched as the flames took hold. Suddenly, bang, the caravan was torn apart and a massive fire ball flew into the air. It was well impressive. The baked-bean-tin caravan just disintegrated.

Now I'm free of them. I can do whatever I want without having to answer to anyone. I'm so relieved, like a weight has been lifted from me. I'm free. I'm finally free.

FIVE

Prompt as always, Adele Kean knocked on Matilda's door at seven o'clock sharp. She opened it to find her best friend standing on the doorstep with a bottle of wine in one hand and a takeaway curry in the other.

It was a special day for Adele. Nothing to celebrate, there would be no cards or presents, it was something to reflect upon. Twenty years ago today, Adele's then boyfriend had gone off with another woman leaving her in a bedsit in Manchester to look after a two-year-old baby alone. It had been a nightmare time for Adele and thanks to the intervention of her parents, and meeting Matilda, she had been able to pull herself out of her quagmire, qualify as a pathologist and regain control of her life.

They sat at the kitchen table, curry laid out before them, wine poured, and raised their glasses to a toast.

'To proving that fresh starts are achievable,' Matilda said, surprisingly optimistic for her.

'To hoping that bastard suffered a painful death from some flesh-eating virus,' Adele offered.

'I don't think I want to eat this now,' Matilda said, looking down at her curry.

'OK, we'll be sensible and toast achievements,' she said, rolling her eyes. They clinked glasses and began to eat.

'Do you ever hear from Robson?'

'Any chance we can refer to him as The Bastard, please?'

Matilda sniggered. There was definitely no love lost between Adele and Robson. She had called him The Bastard for as long as Matilda had known her. It was a stark contrast to the relationship Matilda had enjoyed with her late husband. He had been dead almost two years, and she would give every single possession she owned to have him back.

'Do you ever hear from him?' Matilda asked, unable to refer to him as a bastard.

'No, thank God.'

'What about Chris?'

'Not since he was ten. A couple of years ago, when I'd had a few to drink, I tried looking him up on Facebook.'

'And?'

'He wasn't there. I thought he'd have gone in for the whole social media thing – an entire world of women at his fingertips. He's either changed and is now a one-woman man, or he's dead. I like to think it's option two. More wine?'

'Better not,' Matilda said, placing her hand over the glass. When James died, Matilda had turned to drink to cope with the loss and it had got out of hand. Like she had saved Adele when she moved to Sheffield, Adele had returned the favour and helped her through the torture of losing the man she loved. Now, Matilda didn't trust herself around alcohol. She never drunk when she was alone and only dared to have a glass or two with friends. Just to be on the safe side.

The conversation over dinner moved on to safer territory like Matilda's visit to her parents earlier in the day and the prospect of Adele's son, Chris, starting a new job, hopefully, as a teacher. However, during the quieter periods, Matilda could see the loneliness in Adele's eyes. She always said she didn't need, or want, a man in her life to be happy, but now that Chris was out of university and would be leaving home soon, the prospect of living alone and surrounded by silence was beginning to dawn. They would have to do more things together; Matilda would make sure of that.

Adele stuck to the wine while Matilda made herself a coffee, and they went into the living room.

'Oh, I didn't know this was out,' Adele said, picking up the hardback copy of *Carl* from the side table.

'It's not. It comes out this Thursday. Sally Meagan left it on my doorstep this morning.'

Adele opened the cover and looked at the inscription. 'Bloody hell, she's not going to let you forget, is she?'

'As if I could anyway. I think about him every day. I drove past Graves Park yesterday and I almost had to pull over I teared up so much.'

'Is there no news?'

'There's no one looking for him. The case is shelved. There have been no sightings for months.'

'It'll get reviewed at some point though, won't it?'

'Oh yes, but not by me, and not for long either. I honestly don't think we'll know anything until a body turns up.'

'You think he's dead?'

'As much as I hope he's still alive, yes, I think he's dead.'

'Oh God, the poor mite,' Adele said, looking at the front cover and the smiling little boy looking up at her. 'God only knows what his mother's going through. Are you going to read this?'

'I read the introduction. I've looked in the index and I'm mentioned all the time, and it's not going to be complimentary, is it? I don't think I'm ready for that kind of character assassination just yet.'

'Why don't you put it away, then, instead of leaving it around tormenting yourself? You've got a library now, haven't you? Oh, I thought you were going to show me around.'

Matilda had inherited thousands of books from a young man she befriended during a murder case she'd worked on the previous year. Jonathan Harkness had lived in self-induced isolation, surrounding himself with crime fiction novels to escape the reality of the outside world. When he died, he left his entire collection to Matilda. She wasn't sure whether he was gifting them to her because she had shown an interest or it was his final act of sticking two fingers up to the police.

At first, Matilda had been so angry she had wanted to dump them all. On closer inspection she saw some were first editions and some were signed copies. They might even be worth quite a bit of money one day. She had read a few and become hooked and promised herself she would look after the collection and even add to it when new books were released.

Since James's death, Matilda now lived alone in a four-bedroom house. She had ample space to turn one of the rooms into a library. She'd had floor to ceiling shelves fitted, a new carpet, and had replaced the glass in the window with an expensive tinted glass so the sunlight wouldn't bleach the pages and spines of the books. Matilda had even treated herself to a comfortable Eames chair with matching footstool so she could sit in here of an evening and read whenever she wanted to escape from a difficult murder case for an hour or two. The irony of reading crime fiction while investigating real life crimes was not lost on her.

'I'm impressed. It looks functional yet cosy,' Adele said, standing in the doorway (shoes off, of course).

'You don't like it, do you?'

'No. I do. I just think it's a waste of a perfectly good bedroom.'

'It was you who said I should keep them. What else was I supposed to do with them?'

'No. You've done the right thing. I like it. I really do. Wow, this chair is very comfortable,' Adele exclaimed, sitting back and putting her feet up.

'It should be for the money it cost.'

'I can imagine myself sitting here, glass of wine, maybe some sushi. I could actually fall asleep in this chair.'

Matilda smiled. 'You could book a weekend break here if you like?'

Adele picked up the nearest novel. 'So how is the humble pathologist represented in crime fiction then? Am I a maverick who works outside the rules to nail the killer at any cost?'

'No. You're either grumpy, moody or an alcoholic.'

'Oh, not like me at all then,' she smiled.

By the time the evening was at an end, Adele was in no fit state to drive so Matilda said she could stay over. Adele went up to one of the spare rooms while Matilda went around the ground floor to make sure all the windows and doors were locked. As she whispered goodnight to James in their wedding photograph on the mantelpiece, she shed a tear. Every night, she cried for the man she loved who had been taken from her far too soon.

The following morning, Matilda was woken to the unfamiliar sound of life going on in another part of the house. It had taken her a long time to adjust to living on her own after James's death, especially as James had been a noisy bugger. She had discovered new sounds – the clocks ticking, the fridge humming, and the house settling. At first, they scared her: they were the sounds of loneliness. Now, she was used to them.

As Matilda descended the stairs she recognized the noise straight away – Adele was on her treadmill. She went into the conservatory to see Adele running at speed; yet she didn't have a hair out of place and there was just a hint of sweat on her forehead.

'This is actually quite a good treadmill. I might have to get one myself.'

'I thought you enjoyed going to the gym?'

'I do. Especially when that Scottish bloke is working there. I love a man with a Scottish accent.'

'You're a tart, Adele. Are you nearly finished? I'd like to get 5k in before work.'

'Almost.'

Matilda stood back and watched while Adele slowed down to a trot. She turned the machine off.

'I just did 5k,' she said, barely out of breath.

'How long did it take you?'

'Twenty-two minutes,' she said, reading the display. 'What are you on?'

'I can't remember off the top of my head,' Matilda replied, trying hard not to be jealous that Adele was ten minutes faster.

The phone started ringing just as Matilda stretched her limbs.

'Would you like me to get it?' Adele asked.

'Please.'

By the time Adele returned, Matilda was trotting on the treadmill to give her legs the chance to wake up properly. Her left leg felt a bit stiff this morning.

'Matilda, you're not going to believe this … ' Adele began. The look on her face said it all.

Matilda turned off the treadmill. 'What's happened?'

'There's been a murder.'

'Someone I know?'

'What? No, nothing like that. An inmate at Starling House has been killed.'

There was nothing Matilda could say. Starling House was a bone of contention for Sheffield. Everyone would prefer that it was closed down. They hated the fact their city was synonymous with a home for evil young boys. This could be the answer to their prayers.

SIX

'How long has Starling House been open, now?' Adele asked from the front passenger seat of Matilda's silver Ford Focus.

'I've no idea. Mid '90s wasn't it?'

'Something like that. Have you ever been inside?'

'No. I know people aren't too happy about it being used as a prison. However, there's never been any trouble – no riots, no break-outs, no deliberate fires or anything.'

'Until now.'

Matilda looked across at Adele. 'The press are going to have a field day, aren't they?'

'They certainly are. If this isn't a hot topic I don't know what is.'

Matilda turned down Limb Lane. With drystone walls and tall trees on each side, they were plunged into darkness as the thick branches blocked out the autumn sun. On the right was farmland, on the left was an open playing field. Matilda indicated left and they turned onto a dirt track. The car struggled over the cavernous potholes and breaks in the single lane road. They pulled up at the security gates, and Matilda leaned out of the window to press the intercom.

'Yes?' asked a tired voice.

'DCI Matilda Darke from South Yorkshire Police and Doctor Adele Kean.'

There was no reply, just a long wait while the gates slowly opened. The second set of gates were already wide open to avoid any delay to the emergency vehicles.

At the end of the long drive, a fleet of marked and unmarked police cars, along with a Crime Scene Investigation van were parked haphazardly. All vehicles were empty. As Matilda pulled up, DC Rory Fleming stepped out of the building as if he had been waiting just inside the door. Always the gentleman, Rory opened the door for her.

'Good morning, Rory.'

'Morning, boss. Nice day off yesterday?'

'Fine, thanks.'

'You know, I've never taken much notice of this building before. It's gorgeous. Have you seen those gargoyles?' He looked up at the imposing building and marvelled at the intricate architecture. 'According to one of the staff, this place was built in—'

'Perhaps we can save the history lesson for another time, Rory. I've been told there's a little matter of a dead body?'

'Yes, sorry. He's through here. Follow me.'

Rory led the way with a scowling Matilda and a smiling Adele following.

This was the closest Matilda had ever been to Starling House. Up close it was an ugly, dark, crumbling building. The brickwork was gnarled from centuries of harsh Yorkshire weather battering it. The features on the gargoyles had almost been rubbed away; yet their unwelcoming stare and toothy grins were frighteningly detailed. Matilda turned to look at an upstairs room and saw a curtain twitch. *Alfred Hitchcock would have loved this place.*

'Where are all the inmates?' she asked as she looked around the large open foyer, finding nobody.

'There are currently only eight boys staying here – well, seven now – and they're all in the dining room.'

'Staff?'

'The manager is Kate Moloney. She was down at the recreation room when I left. She's milling around trying to show her authority but she's just getting in everyone's way. A couple of the guards are in the dining room with the inmates along with a few PCs. I think the remainder of the staff are in the staffroom. Aaron's told them all to stay there until you decided what you want to do.'

'Good. So what—?'

'Speaking of Aaron – Katrina's pregnant. Can you believe that? I didn't think he had it in him.'

'That's brilliant news,' Adele chimed in. 'I know they've been trying for ages. Aaron said Katrina's had a few miscarriages in the past. How far gone is she?'

'About three months I think he said.'

'Oh I am pleased. Do they know what they're having yet? I'll have to—'

'Any chance of getting back on topic here?' Matilda interrupted. 'Rory, what do we know so far?'

They turned down corridor after corridor. Rory stopped suddenly at one point to get his bearings.

'Well, the young lad is Ryan Asher. He arrived on Sunday night under the cover of darkness by all accounts. Very military. He was locked in his room at nine o'clock last night, which is normal, and this morning he was found dead on the pool table in the rec. room.'

'Who found him?'

Rory looked at his notebook. 'One of the senior officers, an Oliver Byron. Apparently, when Ryan didn't turn up to breakfast Mr Byron went looking for him and discovered him in the recreation room.'

They arrived at the room which had been sealed off by tape. Inside, a team of forensic officers was examining the scene. Floodlights had been erected and white suited CSIs were busy looking for evidence. Adele slipped into a blue forensic suit and

47

went to join her assistant, Victoria Pinder, who had arrived shortly beforehand and was busy laying foot plates on the floor.

'Rory,' Matilda took the young DC to one side and lowered her voice. 'The press is going to be all over this but I don't want anything getting out until it's absolutely necessary. Get uniform to give you a hand and move all the vehicles at the front to the back of the building. I don't want photographers taking snapshots and making up their own stories.'

'Will do. Oh, by the way, the ACC is on her way over.'

'I thought she would be. Thanks for the heads-up.'

The Assistant Chief Constable rarely attended a crime scene. The fact she was on her way was testament to how serious this case was going to be. Obviously, every murder was serious, but this was Starling House. The place was already swarming with killers. This is the kind of case tabloids have wet dreams about.

DS Sian Mills handed Matilda a forensic suit and waited while the senior officer struggled to get into it. Once inside the recreation room, Matilda stood in silence and surveyed the scene. She wanted to take it all in: the dimensions, the furniture, the layout. This room was going to be vital in solving this case, she could feel it.

It was a large room at the back of Starling House and looked out onto a wide open space of well-kept garden. The room was decorated in magnolia and the carpet was hard-wearing, but looked tired. There were scuff marks on the walls, and the carpet was stained. In the corner of the high ceiling, a few dark cobwebs hung down, evidence of a lack of regular cleaning.

'Right, Sian, talk me through it.'

'Well, I'm sure you know who Ryan Asher is.'

'Is there anyone in this country who doesn't?'

'Sadly, I did have to explain him to Rory. Anyway, Ryan Asher arrived on Sunday night. He spent the whole day yesterday being shown around, introduced to the various members of staff and the other boys. In the evening he and the others spent a few hours in here playing pool, watching TV or what have you, and then they were tucked up in bed by nine o'clock.'

'Fast forward to this morning.'

'The doors are unlocked and the boys make their way to the dining room for breakfast. However, one of them is missing. Off goes an officer to find him, and there he is.' Sian pointed to the pool table.

Lying on his back in the centre of the pool table was the cold, lifeless body of fifteen-year-old Ryan Asher. He had been posed: legs straight and arms by his sides. His body was saturated in his blood, which had run into the pockets of the pool table and dripped onto the floor.

Matilda slowly approached the table. It was never easy attending a crime scene. It didn't matter who the victim was: a person; a former human being with feelings and emotions who had been subjected to the most heinous crime imaginable. Their life had been tragically stolen from them and their body just dumped. The fact the body, in this instance, was that of a convicted killer made no difference. He was still someone's son.

Matilda looked down at the pale face of Ryan Asher. He looked much younger than his fifteen years. His eyes were closed. He looked at peace, as if he were in a deep sleep. The splashes and flecks of blood on his face told her he would never be waking up.

'I've counted twelve stab wounds,' Adele said, breaking the silence.

'Jesus.'

'I know. A frenzied attack.'

'Was he killed here?'

'Yes. There's far too much blood around to suggest otherwise. A lot has been soaked up in the – what is this, felt?' she asked stroking the pool table.

'Baize,' Victoria Pinder replied.

'What is baize?'

'It's a felt-like woollen material.'

'What's the difference between felt and baize?'

'Can we do this another time?' Matilda interrupted.

'Sorry. Anyway, best guess is he was laid out on the pool table and stabbed to death.'

'Surely he didn't voluntarily lie down on the table while someone stabbed him.'

'I don't know about that. He may have been drugged. We'll have to wait for toxicology before we find out.'

'Any sign of a murder weapon?'

'Not so far. The stabs are large and appear to be very deep. I'd say you're looking for a seven-inch blade, smooth edges. A kitchen carving knife, perhaps.'

'There are no splatter marks,' Matilda said, looking down at the pool of blood on the floor. 'It's not been smudged in any way. It's like he just bled out while lying on the table.'

'It does look like it's been staged, doesn't it?'

'I don't like the feel of this at all.' Matilda shuddered. 'Sian, were those doors locked?' she asked, moving away from the table and indicating the patio doors.

'Yes. They're double-bolted and there's an alarm too. If they're tampered with in any way, it'll go off.'

'And did it?'

'No.'

'Is it working?'

'Apparently, yes.'

'I want it tested.'

'Will do.'

'I see there are cameras in here too,' Matilda said. She pointed to a couple of outdated CCTV cameras in the corners of the room. 'I want the recordings. Not just from the ones in here but from everywhere else in the building.'

'OK.'

'Sian, I'm going to want to talk to the bloke who found him, and the woman in charge. Get a room set up for us to use too. All the staff and the inmates will need interviewing. I want you and Aaron to lead the interviews. Get all the files pulled on all the inmates. I want us to know everything about them, and their crimes, before we interview them. I don't want anyone going in blind.'

'No problem.'

'DCI Darke?' Matilda turned at the mention of her name to see ACC Valerie Masterson standing in the doorway of the recreation room.

'Shit,' Matilda said under her breath. 'I'll be back in a bit, Sian. Oh, find out if there are any knives missing from the kitchen.'

Matilda headed for the exit, ducked under the crime scene tape and followed the ACC down the corridor to a quiet corner.

'It's definitely Ryan Asher?' Masterson asked.

'Yes, ma'am.'

'Bloody hell. I always knew something like this would happen here. I've never liked this place. I want this solved quickly, Matilda. No pissing about.'

Matilda had to bite her tongue. A few months before she'd led a very prestigious Murder Investigation Team dedicated to hunting killers within South Yorkshire. Budget cuts, apparently, had called time on the MIT and Matilda, and her team, were transported back to CID. Suddenly, a major case occurs and she is expected to move heaven and earth without the necessary resources.

'Ma'am, I never piss about on a murder case. This will get the full attention of my officers, and we will work to the best of our ability.'

'You're not giving a press statement, Matilda. Now, is there anything you need?'

'I'm going to need the case files of all the inmates. These are dangerous boys here; I need to know who I'm dealing with.'

'I'll get them sent to you. Anything else?'

'Just a full team at my disposal.'

'You're in charge of CID now, Matilda, use whoever you need on this. Just get it solved and get it solved quickly. Oh, and not one word to the media.'

With that, the five-foot-nothing ACC stormed past Matilda and disappeared around the corner.

It was no exaggeration to say that ACC Valerie Masterson had been under a cloud in the last year or so. She was criticized by the media for allowing Matilda to return to work following the collapse of the Carl Meagan case. Add to the mix the lengthy Hillsborough enquiry, the unprecedented levels of sexual abuse in Rotherham and the constant unrest at Page Hall, and the media was endlessly on Masterson's case demanding answers. A murder in the most secure and controversial place in South Yorkshire could be the final nail in the coffin of her career if it wasn't successfully solved. Matilda could understand her brusque behaviour.

Matilda walked back to look at the crime scene. With hushed tones everyone seemed to be engrossed in their task. Matilda went over to the pool table and looked down at the dead teenager. Ryan Asher, fifteen years old: face of an angel; soul of the devil, if the press were to be believed.

'Why here?' Matilda asked whoever was in earshot.

'Sorry?' Sian asked.

'He was locked in his room at nine o'clock last night. If anyone was going to murder him surely the best time to do it would be while he was in bed. Why risk being seen bringing him down to the recreation room to kill him?'

'I've no idea.'

'Look at him, he's been posed. This is a stage. This is drawing attention to his killing.'

'What does that tell us?'

'It tells us that this is a killer with a message. And if we don't understand the message straightaway, there'll be another body.'

SEVEN

The staffroom was usually a quiet, lifeless room. As their breaks were staggered there were rarely more than two or three people there at any one time. It was a case of make a coffee, drink your coffee, rinse your cup, then leave. The room wasn't enticing either. Painted in drab creams and browns almost a decade before, it was dirty and there was a smell of rubbish coming from an overflowing bin. The painted door was covered in handprints, the mis-matched chairs were rickety and the table wonky. Even the microwave was ancient and when in use loud enough to shake the foundations.

Now, it was a buzz of conversation and gossip as officers, cleaners, and cooks gathered to talk about what had occurred overnight.

'You know what he did, that Ryan Asher, don't you? He killed his grandparents. I remember reading about it in *The Sun* – he beat them to a pulp, the bastard.'

'He got what he deserved then, didn't he? Some of the lads in here – locking up's too good for them. They ought to bring back hanging for some of these killers,' one of the cleaners, Roberta Del Mar said. 'I hate having to go in that recreation room, especially when they're in there. I just give it a quick flick then come straight out.' She shuddered at the memory.

The door opened and a slim, short officer in her mid-twenties entered the room, closing the door behind her.

'Rebecca, I didn't know you were back,' Doris Walker said, cheering up at the sight of one of her favourite co-workers.

'I came back yesterday.' She smiled.

'You picked a great time, didn't you? What's going on out there?'

'The police have arrived and they've sealed off the room. The inmates are all in the dining room.'

'I hope they're not making a mess,' Roberta said. 'I only polished that floor last night.'

'Is it true he was stabbed twenty times?' Doris asked.

'I've no idea. Nobody's saying anything. The police are all talking in hushed tones.'

'They would do,' Roberta said, taking another biscuit from the tin and dipping it in her tea. 'When we were burgled a few years ago and the coppers came out, I heard a few of them whispering. They were only criticizing my carpet, cheeky buggers.'

'I hope you put a complaint in,' Doris said.

'I bloody did. I got a half-hearted apology from some short woman in a hat about three sizes too big.'

'They'll have a lot to criticize about this place. It's a dump,' Rebecca said.

'Don't go looking at me. I work my fingers to the bone here,' Roberta defended herself. 'I can only work with the equipment I'm given. I've been asking for a new mop for three months.'

'Did you see the body?' Doris asked Rebecca eagerly, wanting to get back onto the more exciting topic.

'No. You should have seen Oliver's face though; he was so white, bless him. He could have had a heart attack.'

'Who do they think's done it?'

'I've no idea. It's got to be one of the other inmates though, hasn't it? They've all got form,' Rebecca added.

'I wouldn't be surprised if it wasn't that lad with the Liverpool accent,' Roberta said.

'What makes you think it's him?'

'Well, you've only got to look at him. He's a cocky little shit in my book.'

'To be honest,' Doris began, 'I blame the parents, these days. They don't correct their kids. If they gave them a slap from time to time instead of pandering to them the country wouldn't be in the state it's in. My dad hit me when I was a lass. I knew never to step out of line. It didn't do me any harm.'

'Parents don't hit their children anymore,' Rebecca said, looking shocked. She was a generation younger than the cook and the cleaner and, with a new-born, the thought of raising a hand to her child sent a shiver down her spine.

'And that's why some of them grow up to be killers, like that Callum Nixon,' Roberta said. 'I've seen those profiling programmes on Sky.'

'So, tell me about that new baby of yours, Rebecca,' Doris said. She saw how Rebecca was getting uncomfortable about the topic of children becoming killers and decided to give the new mum a break. 'Keeping you awake at night?'

Kate Moloney was stood at the window in her office looking out at the lawn. Her face was its usual stony expression, giving nothing away. She knew the people of Sheffield didn't want a youth prison in their city.

Over the years there had been a number of campaigns to have Starling House closed down. When a high-profile murder case hit the headlines, and the perpetrator was under the age of eighteen, it was obvious he would end up here. Ryan Asher was such a child. He had been snuck in under cover of night like a secret SAS mission, and, up to now, his presence had gone undetected. Now he was dead, the entire country would know where he had been sent following his very public trial.

The firm knock on the door brought Kate out of her thoughts. She sat down behind her desk and tried to look busy. She had a difficult job and could never allow her emotions to show through – something she perceived as a weakness. She presented herself to the world as cold and hard-hearted. It wasn't easy to keep up but it worked.

'Come in.'

The door opened and Oliver Byron poked his head through the small gap. 'Have you got a minute?'

'Yes. Come on in. How are you feeling now?'

Oliver was a tall and wiry man in his late-forties. He was dedicated and efficient. As head of officers, it was his duty to sort out any disputes before Kate became involved. Oliver was the man for the job. He didn't stand for any nonsense and soon ironed out any issues the officers had. It wasn't easy to pacify the staff as well as keep the inmates in line but Oliver was more than capable.

'I'm OK,' he said, though his colour hadn't come back. He sat down with a heavy sigh and took a deep breath. 'I think the main detective in charge has arrived.'

'Oh.'

'They've sent DCI Matilda Darke. You've heard of her, I'm guessing.'

'Isn't she the one who couldn't find Carl Meagan?'

'That's the one.'

'Oh, bloody hell.' Kate rolled her eyes.

'Don't worry, I'm sure she knows what she's doing.'

'It's not that. I think the press like to follow DCI Darke around just to see if she'll slip-up again. I don't want them sniffing around here,' she said, lowering her voice.

'I think it's safe to say the press are going to be crawling over each other to get here. What are we going to do, Kate?'

'About what?'

Oliver looked at her with a furrowed brow. Was she in denial about what had happened in the past few hours? 'Ryan Asher has been murdered. We've got seven obvious suspects. Police and press are going to be swarming for days, weeks, months even. We're going to be under some intense scrutiny.'

Kate took a deep breath while she took his words on board. 'Starling House has been open for almost twenty years. In that time, we have not had a single issue to bring this place into disrepute. Yes, we have a high turnover of staff, and, yes, there have been some problems, but we have always managed to sort them out internally and with the highest professional standards.'

Kate's voice crackled with tension and nerves. She may have said the words but did she believe them herself?

'Kate, I don't want to speak out of line here, but you're going to need to practise that speech a few more times before the detectives turn up.'

'I'm sorry?'

'You sound like you're giving a statement you don't believe. You sound like you're hiding something.'

Kate's eyes widened. 'I have nothing to hide,' she said with severe conviction.

'What about Elly Caine?'

'Elly Caine has no bearing on what has happened.'

'If the police don't dig her up then the press will. You know they'll go over everything with a fine-tooth comb. They'll want to tear this place apart.'

'Oliver—'

A knock on the door silenced Kate. The manager and head of officers looked at each other. They both recognized the heavy knock of an official. There was a detective behind the door. The nightmare was about to begin.

'Come in,' Kate managed to force out despite her rapidly drying throat.

The door opened and a dishevelled-looking woman entered followed by what seemed to be a male model.

'I'm DCI Darke and this is DC Fleming from South Yorkshire Police. Kate Moloney?'

'That's right. Please, come on in. Can I get you a drink of tea or something?'

'Tea would be nice, thank you.'

While Matilda and Rory took their seats, Kate got on the phone and ordered drinks from her secretary.

'I'd just like to say,' Kate began, fiddling with the items of stationery on her desk. 'What happened here is completely out of the blue. We operate a zero tolerance policy, and my staff and myself will offer you our total cooperation.'

'Thank you. That's good to know,' Matilda responded, slightly perplexed by Kate's nervous demeanour. 'I'm going to need to see the files on all the inmates.'

'They are confidential.'

So much for total cooperation.

'Ms Moloney—'

'Kate, please.'

'Kate. This is a murder investigation and you have seven convicted murderers living on-site. I need to know who I'm dealing with before I interview them. Obviously, we will have our own files on the boys, but they'll be coming from different police forces around the country and could take some time. Besides, we know all about confidentiality. My team is hand-picked and know how to deal with sensitive information.'

'I understand all that … '

'I could obtain a warrant from the magistrate's court, but I really don't want to go down that route.' Matilda added, her voice growing louder and sterner with every sentence.

'Of course. I'll get whatever you need,' Kate relented with a painful smile.

'I'll need the files on your staff too.'

'Now steady on—' Oliver Byron chimed in.

'And you are?' Matilda asked, looking across at the grey-haired man with the shocked expression on his face.

'Oliver Byron. I'm head of officers here. Why do you want to see the staff files?'

'Mr Byron, my job is to interview everyone involved, and eliminate where possible. My team will be interviewing everybody on-site. That includes all staff, all officers, yourself, and even Ms Moloney.'

Kate stood up. 'Oliver, it's fine. DCI Darke, I'm sorry. As I'm sure you can guess, emotions are running high at present. Don't worry, we will all cooperate with your investigations.'

'I appreciate that. I'll need our forensics team to go through the CCTV footage from all the cameras throughout the building.'

Matilda noticed Kate and Oliver exchange glances briefly. For a single moment, they looked worried.

'Is that a problem?'

'No.' Kate smiled nervously. 'Not a problem at all.'

'Thank you. I'll need a room for my officers to work in while we're here. Would that be possible?'

'That's not a problem. We have a boardroom we use for staff meetings. Oliver, can you make sure it's suitable for DCI Darke and her team?'

'Of course,' he said reluctantly.

'Thank you. Now, what can you tell me about Ryan Asher?' Matilda leaned back in her seat and crossed her legs. She was going to be here for a while so she may as well make herself comfortable.

'There's not much I can tell you. He only arrived on Sunday night. I met with him on Monday morning. Told him about the place, what would be expected of him; showed him around and that was it.'

'How did he seem?'

'Like all the other boys who arrive here, he was nervous. He didn't speak much, but he looked like he was paying attention.'

'You know of his crime?'

'Of course. I was sent his file before he arrived.'

'What did you think of him?'

'From my point of view he was another inmate. His crime has nothing to do with me. Like all the boys.'

'You could get past what he had been convicted of?'

'Yes. I look at it this way: without these boys being here I would be out of a job. They're here, so am I. It's that simple.'

A tiny knock and the door opened to reveal an elderly woman struggling under the weight of a tea tray. Rory jumped up to take it from her. She thanked him and left, closing the door behind her.

'Shall I be mother?' Rory asked.

Matilda tried to hide her smile. Kate's face remained solid stone.

'Did he speak to any of the other boys while he was here?'

'Yes. I believe he spoke to all of them at some point.'

'Any in particular?'

'I saw him deep in conversation with Lee Marriott in the dining room last night.'

'Lee?'

'Yes. He was—'

'I know of Lee Marriott, thank you.' Matilda said, making a note of his name.

'DCI Darke, the boys are currently all locked in the dining room. How long will it be before they're allowed out?'

'Until we've interviewed and been able to eliminate them from our enquiries. Of course the recreation room is going to be out of bounds for the foreseeable future.'

'Of course.'

'Is there anything you think we should know about any of the boys or the staff before we get started?'

Silence. There was a look on Kate's face that Matilda couldn't quite make out. An expression flitted across it and disappeared just as quickly. Her stoical persona, for a split second, had dropped. Why? Had Matilda's question conjured up something she wanted to keep private? Matilda decided not to push it – not yet. Whatever secrets were buried within these thick stone walls, Matilda would uncover.

MARK PARKER

There was a story in the newspaper the other day about a woman in Leeds who had stabbed her husband 119 times. That was in the headline. I wouldn't normally have read a story like that but it caught my attention. How could you stab someone that many times? It turns out she was being mentally and physically abused by her husband for the whole of their married life, and they'd been married for over thirty years. I kept thinking: why didn't she just leave him? It's not as simple as that, though, is it? I can't just leave my dad.

Mum was lucky, she got out before she snapped and stabbed dad over a hundred times. She's now living in a woman's refuge on the other side of town. I go to see her sometimes. I want to ask her why she didn't take me with her but it never comes up. I could bring it up, I suppose, but I think I'm scared of the answer. Did Mum honestly think Dad wouldn't start hitting me once she had left?

I first noticed Dad hitting Mum when I was five years old. I was in the living room playing and went into the kitchen for a drink. Dad was sitting at the table and he had a face like thunder.

Mum was at the sink; her face was red and she'd been crying. She looked in pain too. I remember asking her why she was crying, and she said it was because she was peeling onions. I don't know why but that scene always stuck in my mind, and I kept looking back on it. It was a few years before I realized there were no onions. Dad's face was like thunder because he was angry, and Mum looked like she was in pain because he'd hit her. I never found out why though.

I often saw my mum crying. I thought she was an emotional person. I mean, she used to cry at soap operas all the time, but it wasn't that – she cried for a reason.

I don't blame Mum for leaving. I don't blame her for not taking me with her. I blame her for leaving me behind to take her place. I blame her for me being covered with burn marks and bruises. I blame her for me snapping and killing dad.

I remembered the story of the woman in Leeds, and when I first started stabbing Dad I began to count the stab wounds. I lost count after thirty. I don't think I made it to 119. It's tiring stabbing someone over and over again.

I left Dad in his bedroom. Someone will find him. I needed to see my mum, tell her what I'd done. She needed to know it was OK to come back home now.

I got off the bus and she was waiting for me at the bus stop. I wanted her to hug me but she didn't. She didn't like any physical contact anymore; she told me that on my last birthday. She didn't even kiss me hello or goodbye anymore. She was empty of all emotion. That's what dad had done to her.

We went for a walk in the park. It was quiet. In the middle of a weekday there were very few people around. We walked past the playground area, by the abandoned tennis courts to the woodland area. Mum always enjoyed walking among the trees; she found it relaxing. There was an awkward silence between us as if we were two strangers. We were mother and son for Christ's sake. Eventually, I started the conversation. One of us had to.

'Mum, would you ever come back home?'

'No. I couldn't,' she said quickly, shaking her head.

'What if Dad wasn't there?'

'He'll always be there.'

'What if we moved somewhere, just you and me?'

'I don't think so. It wouldn't work.'

'Why not?'

'It just wouldn't.'

'But you're my mum. We should be living together.'

'Don't start this again, Mark. Just leave it for now.'

I took my coat off and started taking off my jumper and T-shirt too. Mum asked me what I was doing. It was October, and I'd catch a chill.

I showed her the cigarette burns; the scald marks; the bruises from his shoes with the steel toecaps that wouldn't fade; the bite marks on my arms. I turned around to look back at Mum; her face was blank. Didn't she care? Wasn't she interested in what was happening to her only son?

'Did you honestly think he wouldn't start on me if you left me alone with him?'

A tear fell down her face but I think it was a habit; there was no emotion on her face at all.

I told Mum everything. It wasn't just the beatings; Dad used to swear at me and call me names. I'd be sat eating my tea and he'd walk past and spit in it and still make me eat it. There are refuges for Mum to go to, but where do I go? I get put into care. I get sent God knows where to another family and live with complete strangers. I should be living with my mum.

'Mark, I'm sorry, I can't deal with any of this right now. I'm not strong enough.'

She wouldn't even look at me.

'So what am I supposed to do?'

She didn't answer. She shrugged. Thirteen years old and my mum was leaving me to suffer at the hands of an evil bastard.

Mum started to walk away. I asked her where she was going and she said back to the refuge. I told her we'd only just met up; she'd promised me a panini in Costa. She said she couldn't handle it and she wanted to go back.

For the second time that day I saw red. I snapped. I had an evil father and a pathetic mother. I know it wasn't Mum's fault she was pathetic; Dad had turned her that way, but I was her son. She should have helped me. She should have saved me, and she was turning her back on me. I called her a selfish bitch.

That stopped her. She turned back to look at me. She was about to say something when I grabbed her by the throat and started squeezing.

'I've killed Dad, you know,' I told her as the life drained from her. 'About an hour ago I went into his bedroom with the carving knife and I stabbed him repeatedly, over and over and over again. It felt good. You should have done that years ago. You should have stopped him instead of leaving him to turn on me. I hate you. I'll never forgive you for what you've done, what you've forced me to do.'

I removed my hands and she dropped to the cold, wet ground.

I looked at my watch. The bus to take me back home wasn't due for another thirty-five minutes. I took the change out of my pocket and counted it – there wasn't enough for a panini.

EIGHT

The boardroom on the top floor of Starling House was large and dark. It was rarely used, and there was an underlying smell of dust and damp. The decoration was simple and neutral: light cream walls, dark cream carpet, pastel-coloured Roman blinds, and reproduction prints on the walls. In the corner was a fake potted palm with a thick layer of dust on each leaf.

Richard Grover, a heavyset guard with a dour expression and sad eyes led the way into the room and turned on the lights. His breathing was laboured after walking up four flights of stairs without stopping. He went to the back of the long room to pull up the blinds and open a few of the windows.

'As you can tell, we don't use this room too often. Only for the larger, more formal staff meetings, and we don't have many of them.' His voice was monotone and lacked an accent.

'This will be perfect. Thank you,' DS Sian Mills said.

'The large table is detachable if you want to have smaller working areas. I can show you how if you like?'

'Thanks,' Sian placed her laptop and folders down on one of the hardback chairs. 'So, what's it like working here?' she asked, helping Richard pull the table apart.

'It's interesting.'

'Have you been here long?'

'Three or four years, give or take.'

'You must have met some dangerous boys over the years.'

'They're all dangerous. They wouldn't be here otherwise.'

'How do you feel when you see another fresh-faced inmate arrive?'

'Trust me, they're anything but fresh-faced. By the time they get here they're hardened. They may have the face of an angel, but I can see right through them. There's evil in their eyes.'

Sian stopped what she was doing and looked at Richard's cruel expression. She felt a chill run through her. 'How does that make you feel?' she repeated, slower and quieter this time. She wasn't sure if she wanted to know the answer.

'Part of me feels sad that they've ruined their lives. Part of me feels sick to my stomach. Part of me feels hatred.'

'Hatred?'

'Of course. These boys are killers. Why would I feel anything else?'

The boardroom door was kicked open by Aaron Connolly. Sian was relieved. For some reason, she didn't like the thought of being alone with Richard Grover.

It didn't take long for Sian, with the hindrance of Rory, to fill the boardroom full of detectives and computers from HQ. The usual suspects from the old Murder Investigation Team were there: Aaron Connolly, Scott Andrews, along with Sian and Rory. DI Christian Brady was also in attendance, and he had brought some of his more dedicated detectives with him, like DC Faith Easter.

Matilda Darke made her way up to the boardroom. She took long strides and her facial expression was tense with determination. She had received a warning from the ACC and already a wall of silence was in place among the staff of Starling House. On the one hand, this could be a difficult case to crack; on the other, this was the kind of case Matilda loved. It would be all-consuming and require a great deal of her time. This was going to be a distraction she needed right now as the book about Carl Meagan was hitting the shelves and once again her competence would be called into question.

At the top of the room, standing next to her was her second in command – DI Christian Brady. He was a natural-born copper who always stood tall and erect. With the firm jawline of an Action Man (and matching crew cut) he was an imposing figure. When riled, his deep, terrifying baritone could strike the fear of God into God himself.

Sian had made a good attempt at turning the boardroom into a makeshift briefing room. The wall behind Matilda had a police mugshot of Ryan Asher Blu-Tacked to it and his basic information underneath.

'We all know why we're here,' Matilda began. She spoke louder than usual to reach the back of the room. 'Fifteen-year-old Ryan Asher was found stabbed to death this morning in the recreation room on the ground floor,' she paused while all this was taken in. She half-expected someone (possibly Rory) to have muttered 'good riddance' but nothing was said. 'Sian, would you like to tell everyone what led Ryan to being at Starling House?'

Sian struggled with the files on her desk. She eventually found the one she wanted and joined Matilda at the top of the room. She cleared her throat several times before beginning.

'Ryan Asher was born and raised in Norwich to Paul and Belinda Asher, who have since left the area and changed their names. At the age of fourteen, Ryan burgled his grandparents' house while they were sleeping. During the event, his grandfather woke and decided to fight back. According to his statement, Ryan was masked but his grandfather pulled it off during the fight. His grandmother started to scream when she saw it was their only grandchild who was robbing them. Ryan said he panicked. He hit his grandfather, knocking him to the ground. This made his grandmother screamed louder so he hit her too.'

The silence around the room was heavy as shocked and appalled officers looked at the floor. They often questioned how anyone could attack a vulnerable and innocent elderly person, but when the attacker was a relation it made the crime more difficult to come to terms with.

'Ryan was obviously aware the bedroom would be covered in his fingerprints and DNA so he set fire to the duvet. He waited until the room was ablaze before fleeing. The post-mortem examination on his grandmother showed smoke in her lungs. She was still alive when he started the fire.'

'Bastard,' someone muttered.

Sian closed the file but remained standing. It was difficult to listen to but it was just as difficult to describe.

'Thank you, Sian,' Matilda said after a short silence. 'Now, I'm sure the majority of you are thinking Ryan Asher got what he deserved and that his killer deserves an OBE. However, we are police officers and our task is to find the perpetrator of this crime and prosecute him to the full extent of the law. We cannot allow our feelings to cloud our judgement on this. If you think you're unable to detach yourself enough to find Ryan's killer, you need to speak up now.' She paused and looked around the room at a sea of blank, expressionless faces. She continued: 'good. Now, any questions?'

'Yes,' DC Scott Andrews raised his hand. 'Why was Ryan burgling his grandparents' house?'

'They were due to go on holiday the following morning,' Sian said. 'Ryan had overheard his parents talking about how his grandmother had drawn all their holiday money out of the bank in cash – five thousand pounds.'

'Did he get the money?' Rory asked.

'No. It went up in smoke with everything else in the room.'

Silence gripped the room once again. Two elderly people were murdered in a senseless act by their grandchild. The fact his crime had failed too made their deaths even more pointless.

'Moving on,' Matilda said, bringing the room back to life. 'What do we know so far? Who found Ryan Asher?'

'Oliver Byron,' Sian said. 'He's the head of the officers. When Ryan didn't turn up for breakfast he went looking for him. His room was empty so he looked in the recreation room, where he found him on the pool table.'

'Was the recreation room the first place he looked?'

'I've no idea. I only had a brief chat with him. He hasn't been formally interviewed yet.'

'Right. Who knew Ryan was at Starling House?'

Aaron flicked through his notebook. 'I was chatting to one of the security blokes and he said it wasn't mentioned in any of the newspapers Ryan was being transferred up to Sheffield. The only people who should have known are Norwich police, the staff at Starling House and Ryan's solicitor.'

'To be honest though,' Scott Andrews chimed up, 'anybody who knows about Starling House will have realized Ryan would have ended up here.'

'Is Starling House well known to people outside of the police force?' Faith Easter asked.

'Well, the entire population of Sheffield know about it. As do the press. As does anyone who reads the newspapers. As does anyone who can use the internet … '

'Thank you for that, Scott,' Matilda said. 'Sian, I know you said Ryan's parents have moved away. Do we know where?'

'I'll look into it.'

'Try and find out if he has any family still left in Norwich. They'll need to be interviewed too.'

DC Faith Easter raised her hand. 'Ma'am, I was looking online and there are plenty of websites and forums about Ryan Asher. People were calling for the death penalty to be brought back. There were campaigns at the time of his trial, and plenty of online posts where his parents were blamed.'

Matilda blew out her cheeks. She hated the internet for things like this: people used it as a mouthpiece for their most disturbing and violent thoughts and expected to get away with it. The majority of the time these people didn't act on the threats. They just wanted to voice their opinion. However, every angle had to be covered.

'Faith, have a good look on the Net, see if there have been any direct threats against Ryan or his parents. They'll need contacting too and eliminating from our inquiries. Anything else we should know about before we begin?'

'What about the other inmates?' DI Brady asked. He'd perched himself on the edge of the desk and folded his arms.

'Sian, do you have all their files yet?'

'More or less. Rory's been having a read.' She looked across at Rory, who was engrossed in a file. He didn't look up at the mention of his name.

'Rory!' Sian called.

He looked up. His usual cheerful face looked blank. 'What?'

'Who are we dealing with here?'

'Well, I've … I … ' he stumbled, obviously disturbed. 'I've been reading up on Callum Nixon.' He filled the group in on Nixon's murder of two teachers in Liverpool. His voice was shaking as he ran his eyes over the file. He then went on to discuss Mark Parker, who had stabbed his violent father and strangled his mother. He was about to start on Lee Marriott when he looked up and made eye contact with Matilda. His look was almost pleading with her to intervene and tell him to stop.

'OK, let's leave it there for now. We'll have another briefing towards the end of the day. Sian can fill us all in then on the rest of the inmates. In the meantime, let's hope one of them confesses to it and we can wrap this up by tea time.'

Famous last words.

NINE

The remaining seven inmates of Starling House were becoming restless as their incarceration in the dining room entered its third hour. They were being watched by two of the guards, who, despite the inmates' pleas for information, remained silent, leaving the boys to concoct their own theories.

'Well, it's obvious something's happened to Ryan, otherwise he'd be here,' Lewis said. 'You think he's dead?'

'Of course he's dead, you nob,' Callum replied. 'I saw the cop cars come down the drive. They wouldn't send all them out if he'd fallen downstairs or something. I reckon he's been murdered.'

'What makes you say that?' Thomas asked, looking up from the book he was reading. 'He could have died in his sleep, had one of those underlying heart conditions.'

'Yeah, and I've got Scarlett Johansson coming over tonight to tuck me in.'

'Why would anyone want to kill Ryan?' Lee asked. 'He's only been here a day.'

'Because he's murdering scum,' Callum answered.

'We're all murdering scum if you read the papers.'

'You know what I think?' Lewis asked, leaning back in his seat with his arms folded. 'I think there's a serial killer on the loose and he's stalking Starling House. One by one we'll all get bumped off until only the killer is remaining.'

'You've seen too many horror films,' Mark said.

'Of course he has. That's why he killed his brother,' Callum said. 'You can't believe anything he says. His mind's fucked. He'd love it if there was a serial killer loose.' He chuckled to himself. 'He's probably the one doing it.'

'Fuck off, Callum. I slept right through last night.'

'We've only your word for that.'

'Why would someone want to kill us all anyway, Lewis?' Mark asked.

'Don't encourage him.'

'I'm just saying,' he continued, 'people don't bother with us; we're just left here. What would be the point?'

Lewis leaned forward. The twinkle in his eye was evidence he was enjoying this conversation. 'It could be motiveless. That's the scariest crime of all. When the murderer has no reason for killing and does it out of pleasure.'

'There speaks a man of experience,' Callum said. 'Fuck off to another part of the room, Lewis, you creep me out.'

The key turned in the door to the dining room and all the inmates stopped in their tracks and wondered who was coming in. Kate Moloney entered, flanked by DCI Matilda Darke, DI Christian Brady, DS Sian Mills and several tall and well-built uniformed officers.

As they saw Kate enter, the inmates all talked over each other, demanding answers. Matilda hoped nobody saw her roll her eyes when she heard one of the inmates say they 'had no right to be locked up in here like this'. Had they forgotten their reason for being here in the first place?

Kate, hands up to silence the boys, said: 'Please, calm down and I shall inform you of what has occurred here this morning.' It didn't take long for the inmates to be quiet. Kate clearly commanded a great deal of respect among them. 'You'll obviously know that Ryan Asher is not among you. He was discovered in the recreation room this morning. He died during the night.'

Matilda looked quickly at each of the seven blank faces to see if she could recognize any hint of a guilty expression. There wasn't any. She didn't expect there to be. After all, these were convicted murderers. They knew all about hiding their emotions and the tell-tale signs of their guilt.

'This is Detective Chief Inspector Matilda Darke from South Yorkshire Police,' Kate said, stepping to one side to allow the spotlight to fall on Matilda. 'She is leading the investigation into finding out what happened to Ryan, and all of us, not just you, but myself, and all the staff, will need to be interviewed and give a statement as to our whereabouts—'

'So he was murdered then?' One of the boys interrupted.

'At the moment, Callum, we don't know what happened to him.'

'Of course he was. You wouldn't have a DCI here if he'd hung himself or he'd choked on his Weetabix.'

'What was he doing in the rec. room when we were all locked up by nine o'clock last night?' another boy asked.

Matilda raised an eyebrow at a very good question. She wondered if any of the boys knew the answer.

Kate ignored the question. 'It's still early days in the investigation but I've no doubt in my mind that DCI Darke here, and her team, will soon get to the bottom of it. As I said, you'll all need to be interviewed, and, unfortunately, you'll need to remain here in the dining room until you're called. Obviously, the recreation room is going to be out of bounds for the foreseeable future. We shall be adapting the library to accommodate you all.'

'There are going to be three uniformed officers staying with you until you've been interviewed,' Matilda began after clearing her throat. She spoke louder than she intended and her voice bounced off the walls. She suddenly felt very self-conscious about her appearance. Next to the neatly turned out Kate Moloney she looked like DCI Vera Stanhope from the Ann Cleeves novels. 'If there is anything you need, or if you need to go to the toilet, let them know and someone will accompany you. We will be calling you in very soon.'

Matilda gave them a small smile before turning and leaving the room. She nodded at the three uniformed officers (she had purposely chosen the three tallest and fittest ones she could find) as she left the room.

Just before the door closed, the chattering among the inmates started up again. Maybe she was mistaken but she was sure she heard one of them mention Carl Meagan's name.

TEN

Oliver Byron was sitting in an uncomfortable wooden chair, gripping the arms firmly, his knuckles almost white. His unruly mound of salt-and-pepper hair seemed to have greyed more in the few hours Matilda and her team had been at Starling House.

'Mr Byron, I know you've had a shock this morning, but I'd like you to talk me through everything that happened,' Matilda began.

DC Scott Andrews was sitting next to her, pen poised and hovering over his notepad. Kate Moloney had asked if they wanted to be alone, but Oliver had requested she stay.

'I'm sorry,' he said, shaking his head, 'it really has been a massive shock. I've never seen anything so … '

'It's OK, Oliver. Do we have to do this now?' Kate asked Matilda.

'It would be best if it was sooner rather than later.'

'It's OK, Kate.' Oliver took a deep breath. 'Well, as usual the doors were unlocked at seven o'clock, and the boys were to get ready and come down for breakfast. Ryan Asher didn't so I went to look for him.'

'Why you?'

'Sorry?'

'Why did you go and look for him? You're head of the other officers, aren't you? Surely you'd have sent one of them.'

Oliver looked to Kate then back at Matilda. 'I don't know. I didn't really think. I noticed Ryan wasn't there so thought I'd go and find him.'

'OK. So you went straight to his room?'

'I did. It was unlocked and I went inside. His bed hadn't been made but the room was empty.'

'Who unlocked the room?'

'The locks are on a timer. They're automatically unlocked at seven o'clock.'

'OK. What did you think when you saw his room empty?'

'Nothing. I thought maybe he'd taken a wrong turn on his way to the dining room or decided to have a shower first.'

'So where did you go first to look for him?'

'The bathroom.'

'Then?'

'Then the recreation room.'

Matilda looked down at the plan of Starling House she had on her lap. The bedrooms of the inmates were on the first floor; the recreation room was on the ground floor. There were other places upstairs he could have looked before going down. So why didn't he? 'Why there?'

'Sorry?'

'After the bathroom, why did you go to the recreation room?'

'I don't know. I just did,' he replied.

'What did you find?'

'Well, the door was locked so I unlocked it and went inside. Ryan was ... ' He choked on his words and had to swallow hard. 'He was ... '

'In your own time, Mr Byron.'

'You know what I'm going to say. You saw it yourself. He was on the pool table. Dead,' he snapped.

'Did you know he was dead?'

'Yes.'

'How?'

'He wasn't breathing.'

'How far into the room did you go?'

'Not far. Just a few steps.'

'The pool table is right at the other end of the room from the door. How could you tell he was dead from just inside the doorway?'

'Judging by how much blood there was. It was obvious he was dead.'

'So you didn't interfere with the crime scene or try to administer first aid?'

'No. I didn't do anything like that. I know I probably should have. We're taught first aid, but I panicked. I've never seen anything like it before. I didn't know what to do. I closed the door behind me and went to fetch Kate.'

'Who else has a key to that room?'

'We all do,' Kate said. 'All the staff have keys to the communal rooms. There's no reason for them not to.'

'The only other way into the recreation room is from the patio doors. Is that correct?'

'That's right,' Kate said. 'They're double-locked, and there is an alarm on the doors which will sound if they are interfered with in any way.'

'Is the alarm working?'

'It is tested every two days. Yes, it's working.'

'What about the windows?'

'They are all locked and on separate alarms to the door. And before you ask, they are also tested every two days and are working perfectly.'

'So we have a murdered young man in a sealed room and the only people who have a key are members of your staff, Ms Moloney.'

'If you think one of my staff is capable of that then you're very much mistaken. All the staff are vetted many times before being employed here. I know all of their employment and personal history. None of them have a history of violence and all are capable and credible,' she said with strong determination.

'It would appear, on the face of it, one of them has slipped through the cracks. The only person who could have committed the crime had to have a key to the recreation room. Have any been lost or stolen recently?'

'Not that I have been made aware of,' she looked over to Oliver who quickly shook his head.

'Then it would appear you have a killer on the loose here, Mrs Moloney.'

'The whole place is full of bloody killers. Take your pick, Inspector.'

ELEVEN

A couple of small offices had been taken over by South Yorkshire Police to use as makeshift interview rooms. Ideally, Matilda would have liked to take all the inmates to the station where their interviews could be recorded and videoed in specially equipped rooms. Matilda could monitor them from her office and potentially feed the detectives with questions through their ear pieces. However, logic, and ACC Masterson, dictated that the interviews take place on-site. It would cost money and resources to securely transfer each inmate individually to HQ and back. It was not feasible.

The rooms themselves did not have the grandeur of high ceilings and cornicing of the original building. It was obvious these had been adapted from a once larger room. The small, soulless boxes were all plasterboard, faux sash window frames and watered-down magnolia paint. The smell was of stale air. These rooms were rarely used. It wasn't difficult to understand why.

Sian and Aaron were to each lead separate interview teams and report back to Matilda.

'Are we all set up?' Matilda asked.

'Yes. Aaron and Scott are at one side of the room, myself and Rory at the other. Some of the officers are acting as appropriate adults as everyone here is under eighteen.'

'Aaron, I hear congratulations are in order,' Matilda said on seeing the sprightly detective bounce into the room.

'Sorry? Oh, Katrina, yes. Thank you.' Aaron's face lit up. He was beaming and delighted at the thought of impending fatherhood. 'It's still early days but we're both very happy.'

'I'm pleased. Send my love to Katrina, won't you?'

'Of course. Thank you.'

Matilda and Aaron stood smiling at each other. Neither of them knew which way to progress this conversation. When it came to small talk, they weren't in the same league as mothers at a school gate. The awkward silence grew. It was getting embarrassing.

'Right, shall we get on then?' Matilda asked.

Aaron and Scott sat close together at one side of a small table. Opposite was fifteen-year-old Callum Nixon. He was slouched in his seat. Sitting next to him, but at a safe distance, was one of the officers, bolt upright in clean, crisp uniform.

It was no exaggeration to say Aaron and Scott felt slightly uneasy in Starling House. They were away from their home ground so didn't feel in complete control. Although they had quickly glanced at Callum's file, they had no idea who the boy sitting across from them was and how he was going to react to their questions.

Aaron cleared his throat. 'Callum Nixon, yes?'

'That's what it says on my birth certificate.' His accent was thick Scouse.

'How long have you been at Starling House?'

'Since February.'

'How are you finding it?'

'It's a palace. I'm loving every minute of it. Could do with having room service though.' His replied dripped with sarcasm.

'Do you get on with the other lads?'

He shrugged. 'They're all right.'

'What do you talk about?'

'The pros and cons of Brexit—'

'That'll do, Callum,' the officer chimed up.

'Did you meet Ryan Asher yesterday?' Aaron asked.

'Yes. He seemed like a sound lad. We played a bit of table tennis.'

'What did you think of him?'

'Like I said, he seemed sound.'

'Do you know why he was here?'

'On a £9.50 holiday from the *Sun*?'

'I won't tell you again, Callum,' the officer scorned.

'No. I don't know why he was here. He didn't say.'

'And you didn't ask?'

'It's nothing to do with me.'

'Did you notice Ryan talking to anyone else yesterday?'

'Just the other lads?'

'Which ones?'

'I don't know. He spoke to Lee and Craig a bit, I suppose.'

'Did any of the other lads say anything to you about Ryan?'

'Like what?'

'I don't know. That they didn't like him, maybe?'

'He was only here five minutes. We didn't get chance to like him.'

'What did you do last night?'

'The usual: dinner, theatre, then off to the club for a nightcap.'

'Final warning, Callum,' the officer raised his voice this time.

'We had tea. We went into the rec. room from six till nine then we were locked up in our cells until this morning.'

'Did you hear anything during the night? Anything wake you up?'

'Well, Scarlett Johan—' he looked at the officer who raised an eyebrow. 'No. Nothing. I sleep like the dead.'

'What did you think when you found out Ryan had been killed?'

'Nothing. Jammy bastard doesn't have to serve his sentence though now, does he?'

Aaron and Scott exchanged glances.

'Who do you think could have done it?'

'No idea. Have you asked Officer Phipps here what he was doing last night?' He leaned back in his seat and let out a loud throaty laugh.

On the other side of the thin partition wall, Sian and Rory made themselves as comfortable as they could on hard chairs. They waited patiently while an officer brought an inmate for them to interview.

'Do you ever wonder why kids kill?' Rory asked.

'I try not to, seeing as I've got four of my own.'

'That's what I mean. You've got kids; all of them are decent, law-abiding and do well at school. What turns a child from that into a killer?'

'I've no idea, Rory,' she answered quickly, not wanting to dwell on the subject.

'I mean, when I was fourteen I didn't think about setting fire to my grandparents. I was always out on my mountain bike and trying to get Rosie McLean to go out with me.'

Sian looked over at Rory and noticed the intense look of sadness on his young face. 'Background, upbringing, I honestly don't know, Rory. You'd need to ask a psychologist that one.'

The door opened and a female officer brought in a fifteen-year-old taller than she was. Sian wondered whether she should really be left alone with someone who could so obviously over-power her.

'Name?' Sian asked.

'Craig Hodge.'

'Where are you from, Craig?'

'Hull.'

'And how long have you been in Starling House?'

'About a year.'

'What did you do?' Rory asked.

'That's not important, Rory,' Sian said as an aside. 'Craig, did you speak much to Ryan Asher yesterday?' she asked quickly. She knew of Craig's crime and didn't want to hear him describe his actions in glorious technicolour to a captive audience.

'A bit. Me and Mark Parker were having a pool tournament so we kept to ourselves yesterday.'

'But you did speak to him?'

'Kate asked me to show him around but, as usual, Callum Nixon stepped in and took over.'

'Why did he do that?' Rory asked.

'Because he's a tosser,' Craig said, spitting his words out with venom. He clearly didn't like Callum.

'Did you overhear anyone talking about Ryan?' Sian wanted to keep the interview on topic.

'Nope.'

'Did anyone say if they liked him or not?'

'Nope.'

'Do you know why Ryan Asher had been sent here?'

'Not a clue,' he replied nonchalantly.

'What did you do last night after your evening meal?'

'Nothing.'

'When did you find out about Ryan being killed?'

'Just after breakfast when we all tried to leave the dining room.'

'Were you surprised?'

He shrugged. 'Dunno. Didn't know the lad.'

Sian rolled her eyes. He may as well be answering 'no comment' to every question. Was he doing this on purpose, she wondered. 'Do you have any idea who could have killed him?'

'I'm not answering that. Why should I help out the pigs when you got me locked up in here?'

'That Callum's a right little bastard,' Aaron said to Matilda.

'They're all right little bastards, Aaron, that's why they're here in the first place.'

There was an empty office Matilda had managed to secure for them all to use when they wanted to have a cup of coffee and a break from interviewing. It was cramped and cold, but it would do.

'He's a sarky shit as well.'

'Did you get anywhere?'

'No. He was locked in his room from nine o'clock until seven this morning. They all were.'

'And even if one of them had got out of his room he's hardly likely to admit it,' Scott said. 'We have to remember these boys are killers. Even if they made a full confession and begged for mercy, they're killers and they've lied to and manipulated their victims.'

'Scott's right,' Matilda said. 'We can't treat these boys in the same way as we do regular witnesses. They could be covering up for each other.'

'This is going to be fun,' Aaron began but stopped when his mobile phone started ringing. 'It's Katrina,' he said, moving away from the group for a bit of privacy.

'Are you all right, Scott?' Matilda asked, offering him a biscuit from a battered tin.

'Yes. I'm just a bit uncomfortable around all these killers. First time I went into a prison I didn't sleep for a week afterwards. My mum always said I'm too sensitive to be a copper. I'm starting to think she might be right.'

'You're not thinking of leaving the force, are you?'

'No. I've always wanted to be a detective, even when I was a child. I just need to toughen up a bit, I suppose, not be so—'

'Sorry, boss, I'm going to have to go. Katrina's bleeding.' Aaron burst in on the conversation, grabbed his coat from the back of the chair and charged out of the room before Matilda could say anything.

CRAIG HODGE

Two years ago I was in a car crash that killed my parents. I was in the back seat, safely strapped in. I was stuck in that car for nearly an hour before someone came along to help. I couldn't move. I was trapped against a wall. Dad smashed his head on the steering wheel, and Mum had taken her seatbelt off, I'm not sure why, and went straight through the windscreen. They were both dead by the time help came. I knocked my head and had to have a few scans but I'm OK.

I went to live with my aunt and uncle. I don't think they wanted me living there. They didn't want kids, and, all of a sudden, they end up with me on the doorstep. But I'm family, so they had no option but to take me in. Aunt Susan always said that Mum was her sister and she was doing it for her.

I don't know when they noticed a change in my behaviour. Uncle Pete said it was probably to do with the car crash and watching my parents die. Aunt Susan said I should have come out of it by now because kids are resilient. She wanted me to go to see someone. Uncle Pete was against it. So was I. I didn't need to see anyone.

One night, Aunt Susan sat me down and asked if I was OK. She asked if I was being bullied at school, if I was taking drugs, if I was in trouble, if I was gay. I answered no to all her questions. There was nothing wrong with me.

The thing that changed it all was during the October half-term holiday. Uncle Pete was at work, and Aunt Susan was doing the washing. I was in the kitchen having breakfast. The washer finished and Aunt Susan was unloading my football shirt when it got caught on the catch on the door and it ripped. She held it up.

'Oh Craig, I'm so sorry,' she said. She didn't sound sorry.

'What have you done?' I said, shocked.

'It was an accident, Craig. I got it caught, I'm sorry.'

'You've torn my shirt.'

'I didn't mean to.'

'That's my best shirt. That's my football shirt and you've fucking torn it,' I screamed at her.

'Craig, watch your language. It was an accident. I'll replace it.'

'Damn right you'll fucking replace it.'

'Craig, I won't tell you again. Don't speak to me like that.'

'You can't do anything right, can you?' I shouted at her. 'All you do is cook, clean, and wash and you balls that up too.' I snatched the torn shirt from her and looked at it.

'Calm down, Craig, it's only a football—'

She didn't finish as I threw my arm out and slapped her hard across the face with the back of my hand. She fell against the fridge, held a hand to her face and ran out of the room crying.

She must have called Uncle Pete as he came straight home from work and had a go at me for hitting Aunt Susan. I just sat there and let him rant.

Aunt Susan didn't speak to me much after that. It was like she was scared of me.

I lost it again with my aunt over Christmas. I can't remember what happened. I've tried but I just remember shouting at her and her cowering when she thought I was going to hit her again. Uncle Pete said he wasn't going to put up with my outbursts anymore. He didn't care if I was grieving or suffering from a head injury, I couldn't keep getting away with it. They were going to see someone about me.

At the end of January, Aunt Susan said they'd got an appointment with a specialist at the hospital. I was going to have a brain scan and see a therapist. It was a day off school so I wasn't bothered.

I've no idea of the results of the scan, even to this day, and I don't know what the therapist thought about our session as we didn't have a second appointment.

Everything was quiet on the way home in the car. Uncle Pete was driving, and keeping an eye on the road; Aunt Susan was looking out of the window, chewing on her fingernail.

'What did you talk about?' Aunt Susan eventually asked me.

'Not much,' I replied.

'What did she ask you?'

'Just about school and stuff.'

'Did you talk about us?'

'A bit.'

I could see Uncle Pete shaking his head at my answers. He looked across at Aunt Susan and she nodded once. He nodded back. Something was going on. They'd planned something while I'd been having tests and talking to that therapist woman with one blue eye and one brown. I bet they were going to send me away, get me locked up or something. Talk about déjà vu. This is exactly what Mum and Dad had done, and here we were again on the same stretch of road. Talk about history repeating itself. I wondered if I could get away with it a second time. I took off my seatbelt and leaned forward. I grabbed the handbrake and pulled it up.

I leaned back in my seat, quickly put my seatbelt back on and bent forward into the crash position. I closed my eyes as the car swerved, hit an embankment and ploughed straight into a tree.

I opened my eyes and saw Uncle Pete with his head bloodied and slumped over the steering wheel. Aunt Susan was breathing heavily. Her head had smashed against the window. She turned around to look at me. Her face was covered in cuts where shards of glass had hit her. I looked at her and saw the large piece of glass sticking out of her throat, blood was pouring out and down the front of her white shirt. She tried to say something but she couldn't speak. Eventually the blood stopped flowing and she died. I'd banged my head and was slightly dazed, but I'd be all right. I was trapped in the back of the car though. It took over half an hour for another car to come along and find us. Just like last time.

TWELVE

With DS Aaron Connolly out of action, Matilda sat in for him during the next interview alongside DC Scott Andrews. The door to the poky room opened and in walked Thomas Hartley. The timid sixteen-year-old had his head down and he took small steps to the table. He perched on the edge of the seat and nervously adjusted himself until he was comfortable. The female officer who accompanied him plonked her ample frame down on the seat next to him.

Matilda waited and studied the young man in front of her. He had shorn mousy hair, and his grey sweater was a size too big for him. He had a slight frame and the large wide eyes of a rabbit caught in the headlights.

'Good morning,' he said to them both. The first one of the inmates to make a polite gesture.

He made eye contact with Matilda, and the DCI stared back, mouth open. Matilda had sat opposite many killers during her time in the force. She had looked into their eyes and seen the violence and horror they inflicted on their victims and the lack of remorse. She knew evil and hatred when she saw it. When she looked across the Formica table at Thomas Hartley, she saw someone who did not belong in Starling House.

'Ma'am,' Scott urged when Matilda didn't begin the proceedings. 'Ma'am,' he repeated.

'Yes?'

'Shall we start?'

'Oh. Sorry. Right. You're Thomas Hartley, yes?'

'That's right.' Thomas was holding himself rigid: hands clasped between his legs, arms held taut. His shoulders were hunched.

'Did you … did you speak to Ryan Asher yesterday?' Matilda was distracted. Thomas's name was familiar but she couldn't quite remember the crime he was guilty of. She tried searching her memory but nothing came up. She really should have read Thomas's file before the interview. She'd glanced at a couple but wanted to get them over with.

'No. Well, only briefly in the dining room.'

'What did you say?'

'I asked him to pass the water jug.'

'That's it?'

'Yes.'

'Did you know Ryan Asher before you saw him yesterday?'

'No.'

'Do you know what crime he had committed?'

'No.'

'What did you do in the evening after your tea?'

Matilda, pen poised over an A4 writing pad, looked down. She wasn't writing a single thing. Her knuckles were white as she gripped the biro firmly in her shaking fingers.

'We all went to the rec. room.'

'But what did you do?'

'I usually just sit and watch television.'

'Usually? Did you do that last night?'

'Yes. We were watching all the *Star Wars* films on DVD.'

'Are you a *Star Wars* fan?'

'No.' He gave a nervous smile, quickly looked up to Matilda then put his head down again.

'Do you play pool or table tennis with the other boys?'

'Not really. I'd rather just watch television. Or read.'

'So at nine o'clock you all go to your rooms?'

'Yes. We're locked in from nine until seven the next morning.'

'Do you sleep well?'

'I do now.'

'Have you had problems sleeping?'

'I did when I first got here. I'm OK now.'

'Did you wake up at all last night?'

'No.'

'Did you hear anything unusual?'

'No.'

'When did you first hear about Ryan being killed?'

'Just as I was finishing breakfast. I overheard a couple of the officers talking. One of them mentioned something. I don't know.'

Thomas's replies were baseless. There was no emotion to his voice: he spoke in a flat drone. He looked downtrodden, as if every ounce of fight and drive had been drained out of him. This was not a sixteen-year-old boy who revelled in the glory of his crime, or a boy who felt remorse for his victims; this was an empty shell of a boy who had no idea what had happened to bring him to the dark world of Starling House.

'Who do you think might have killed Ryan Asher?'

'I've no idea.'

'One of the other boys?'

'I don't know.'

'Thomas, is there anything you would like to tell me?'

Thomas made eye contact with Matilda again and neither of them wanted to be the first to look away. The silence was palpable.

'Like what?' Thomas eventually asked.

'Anything at all.'

He looked over to the officer whose stare was like acid burning into him. He turned back to Matilda. 'No. Nothing.'

'What was that all about?' Scott asked Matilda when the door closed and Thomas was being taken back to the dining room.

'What?'

'Asking him if he had anything to tell you. Do you think he knows something?'

'No. I don't think he does. I'm going to give DI Brady a call. He can conduct the rest of the interviews with you.'

Matilda stood up and left the room with a perplexed look on her face. She had just interviewed a young man who did not belong here. Which begged the question: what the hell was he doing in Starling House?

THIRTEEN

Matilda went back to HQ alone. It was a good twenty-minute drive from Starling House on the outskirts of Sheffield to the city centre; longer, if traffic was bad. Fortunately, luck was on Matilda's side (for once) and she managed to sail through. Her mind was on Thomas Hartley. She knew the name, and vaguely remembered the case, but she would have to look him up.

Matilda's office was smaller than the one she was used to in the Murder Investigation Team, and she had only one window. The view wasn't inspiring as it overlooked the back of the station and the large car park. She kicked the door closed and sat behind her desk.

Thomas Hartley was the first inmate of Starling House she had spoken to on their own. She had no idea if all the other inmates gave off the air of nervousness and appeared terrified of their own shadow. From what Aaron had said about Callum Nixon she didn't think so. She had, however, spoken to many criminals in prison and not one of them had an ounce of innocence about them. Many claimed to be innocent; for some, it was a coping mechanism. Most were lying.

Matilda booted up her computer and brought up Thomas's

file. She was taken back to Manchester in January 2014 in the grip of a bitter cold snap for the north of England.

WITNESS STATEMENT

Name: Thomas Hartley
Date: 7 January 2014

My name is Thomas Hartley. I am the son of Daniel and Laura Hartley. My sister is Ruby Hartley.

I wasn't feeling well. I'd eaten some left-over curry for my tea and I don't think I'd heated it up enough because it made me sick. I couldn't sleep and it was gone one o'clock by the time I was actually sick. It woke my sister up. During the Christmas holidays she'd promised us that she would try and sleep in her room all night without going to mum and dad's room. She used to have nightmares quite a lot. Anyway, whenever she woke up she'd just go along to our parents' room and they'd let her in. That's what she must have done when I woke her up. If I hadn't been sick she would have probably slept through the night and wouldn't have gone to their room. She would still be alive now.

I took something to settle my stomach and I let the dog out because he was fussing. Then I went into the living room to lay down on the sofa. Max, he's our dog, he woke me up by barking and nudging me, and I heard dripping. I thought we had a leak or something. I turned on the light and there was blood all over the coffee table. It was dripping onto the carpet. It was coming through the light fitting. I had no idea what was happening. I ran upstairs to get mum and dad and when I opened their bedroom door I saw that … oh my God. All I saw was red. The walls, the floor, the ceiling, the bed, it was all just red. It took me a while to work out what I was seeing. I didn't think my parents and sister were there at first. It didn't seem possible but when I looked closer I could see them. I recognized the watch on my mum's arm and Ruby's pyjamas and then I saw my dad's face.

I didn't know what to do. Usually if anything happens my mum or dad take control but they couldn't so I called my Auntie Debbie. She's my dad's sister. She doesn't live far away. I can't remember what I said but she said she would come straight round. I sat at the bottom of the stairs waiting for her and saw her coming up the road. I opened the door and she came straight in and went upstairs.

I don't know how long she was up there for. She came down and went into the kitchen to phone for the police. Then she came and sat with me until they arrived. I don't think we spoke to each other. I can't remember. I can't remember much of anything.

WITNESS STATEMENT

Name: Debbie Hartley
Date: 7 January 2014

My name is Debbie Hartley. I am the sister to Daniel Hartley, sister-in-law to Laura Hartley, and aunt to Thomas and Ruby Hartley.

I was asleep when the phone rang. It woke me up, and I didn't answer it at first as it scared me but it kept on ringing so I answered. I remember looking at the clock on my bedside table. It was almost eight o'clock. It was Thomas. It didn't sound like him because he was talking fast and loud, and I think he was crying. He said everyone was dead and there was blood everywhere and he didn't know what to do. Then he hung up.

I got dressed, and I went straight round. There are three different buses to get to Daniel's house so I didn't have too long to wait. It's only a ten-minute journey. Thomas opened the front door as soon as I got onto the street. I think he'd been waiting for me to arrive. He was literally covered in blood. I pushed past him and went straight upstairs to the bedroom.

It looked like a horror film: one of those slasher films that's all blood and gore. It was horrible and smelled really bad as well. I saw Daniel straightaway on the bed. I saw his head. It didn't look as if it was attached to his body. Then I saw Ruby. She's only eight years old, bless her. My legs felt wobbly and I had to lean against the wall. I didn't know it was covered in blood, and I got it all over me too. I felt sick. They're my family. I don't have anyone else.

I went downstairs, and Thomas was sitting at the bottom. I went into the kitchen and dialled 999. Then I went back to Thomas and put my arm around him. We waited until the police arrived.

The case appeared to be open and shut. There was no evidence of a break-in. None of the windows had been tampered with. Thomas's fingerprints were all over his parents' bedroom. There were no other foreign prints anywhere else in the house. However, there was one very important aspect missing from the case – a confession. Thomas vehemently denied killing his family. He stuck to his story, and it never varied no matter how many times he said it. Throughout the trial he maintained his innocence. There was absolutely no evidence to prove Thomas Hartley didn't kill his family. A negative could not be proven.

What was Thomas's motive for killing his family in such a disturbing and shocking way? Nobody knew. Almost three years later and still nobody knew.

Matilda turned away from the computer and looked out of the window. The clouds were gathering over the Steel City. She had heard on the radio that a storm was due later in the week. By the thickness and colour of the clouds it looked as if it had arrived. It was only early afternoon yet appeared to be late evening.

Matilda's mind was full of questions. The case against Thomas Hartley was flimsy at best. There was no sign of a disturbance or break-in, but that didn't mean Daniel Hartley hadn't let his killer into the house; a killer who then let himself out afterwards. That was never followed up. And what about the sister? Debbie Hartley was home alone and didn't have an alibi. Again, it seemed the police took her word for it. There was no mention of a murder weapon either. Had one been found? As far as Matilda was concerned the Senior Investigating Officer liked Thomas Hartley for the killings, and as there was no evidence to the contrary he didn't bother looking too deeply.

Maybe that was true but all Matilda could think was that Thomas Hartley was innocent.

This had nothing to do with Matilda or South Yorkshire Police. The murders were committed in Manchester. She had no reason to investigate, no reason to stick her nose into a closed case apart from a gut feeling. She leaned back in her chair, a pensive look etched on her face. She picked up her phone and dialled.

'Rory, have you been sent all the case files for the inmates?'

'Yes. I'm going through them now.'

'All of them?'

'Yes.'

'Good. Are you OK?' she asked, noticing his less than cheerful voice.

'Yes, fine. It's just, well, it's not exactly light reading, is it?'

'No. I suppose not.'

'Ma'am, about these boys, I was wondering … '

'I'll talk to you about it later, Rory.'

She ended the called without saying goodbye. None of it was light reading. These boys were murderers; their crimes were shocking and deplorable. They were in Starling House until they were old enough to be moved to an adult prison. They had accepted their fate. Yet Thomas Hartley didn't seem to be coping very well living among killers. Why was that?

FOURTEEN

Matilda was glad of the phone call from Adele Kean and a reminder that the post-mortem on Ryan Asher was due to take place. She had tried to concentrate on the case but the thought of an innocent young man being held at Starling House and the difficulty of trying to prove it kept distracting her. She closed down her computer and grabbed her coat. She couldn't leave the station fast enough, even if it was to attend an autopsy.

'I didn't think you'd be doing the PM this quickly,' Matilda said.

'I've been asked very kindly by your ACC to bump him up to the front of the queue,' Adele said. She did not look happy about having received a phone call from Valerie Masterson, who had obviously thrown her weight around. However, for a quiet life, Adele had acquiesced.

The door to the autopsy suite opened and in walked Claire Alexander, a small woman with a neat hair style cut into a short bob.

Adele immediately dropped her voice. 'Whatever you do, don't tell Claire about Valerie getting on the phone. She doesn't like being told how to do her job.'

'Matilda, nice to see you again,' Claire Alexander said, a wide smile on her blemish-free face.

Claire Alexander was the senior radiologist at the Medico Legal Centre. Claire had been instrumental in bringing Digital Autopsy to Sheffield and was proud to be a trailblazer in her field. At first, Claire thought the police were sceptical of Digital Autopsy as it wasn't something they readily accepted. It was only after a quiet word with Matilda that she realized it was all down to budget.

'And you, Claire. I like your new haircut.' Matilda smiled.

'Thank you,' she said, running her fingers through it. Claire looked at Matilda, clearly trying to return the compliment, but nothing had changed in the month or so since they'd last met. 'So, shall we begin?' was all she said.

Ryan Asher, still in a sealed and padlocked body bag, was lying on the bed of the scanner in the main section of the Digital Autopsy Suite. As a sign of respect, and the unspoken knowledge that a teenage boy was inside that bag, the atmosphere upon entering the room changed immediately. Yes, he was a two-time killer, but he was still just a teenager.

As Matilda, Adele, and Claire made their way to the control room, the two uniform police officers standing guard over the body followed them, making the cramped office seem even smaller.

'At least you've got the air con on this time,' Matilda said as an aside to Adele.

'It can get very warm in here,' she agreed.

'Tell me about it. Last time I was in here I'm sure I lost five pounds through sweating alone.'

'It doesn't help when you have such burly coppers.' Adele nodded to the two large uniform officers standing at the back of the narrow room.

'I'm just waiting for us all to be ready before I begin,' Claire said loudly.

Matilda and Adele exchanged glances.

Claire Alexander was an acutely professional woman. She was all for office banter and gossip but her body language told Matilda she thought there was a time and a place for that, and it was not in the Digital Autopsy Suite. She pressed a few keys on the keyboard and the scanning of Ryan Asher began. It took minutes. Eventually, an X-ray image of the fifteen-year-old killer came up on the large computer screen. Claire looked at it briefly before selecting the trunk of the body and rescanned it to get a closer look at the areas where he was stabbed.

'As I'm sure you know, Matilda, skin is the most resistant soft tissue to stab wounds in the body. It takes effort to penetrate it. Once you're through very little force is needed to penetrate what lies beneath.'

'So you'll be able to see exactly what damage each stab wound did?'

'Absolutely. Look at the heart—'

'Can you point it out for me?' Matilda said trying to make sense of the black-and-white X-ray.

Claire circled the heart with her index finger. 'See that black blob? In layman's terms, that is air. The edge of the heart, here … you can see a disruption. That is where the knife stabbed the heart.'

'So he stabbed the heart, letting air in?'

'That's right. Obviously, you don't want air in your heart. This darker shade of grey outside of the heart is blood. The heart is still pumping and blood is rapidly seeping out of the organ and into the chest cavity.'

'Is that what killed him? A stab wound to the heart?'

'There are twelve penetrating injuries on the body. I've no idea what order they came in. This one would definitely have done it but so would the ones to his lungs too. Look here.' Again Claire pointed out the lungs for Matilda's benefit and showed how the punctured lung had let in air and deflated. 'This would have caused a pneumothorax and would almost certainly have killed him too.'

'He could have been killed twelve times over,' Adele said, leaning in to the screen.

'If we look at the 3D image.' Claire clicked with the mouse and a brilliantly clear image of Ryan Asher came up on-screen. It showed the ribs and organs perfectly. Matilda didn't need anything pointed out this time. 'You can see the deflation of the organs more clearly.'

'What's that there?' Matilda asked, pointing to a very large balloon-like object towards the bottom of the screen.

'That would be his bladder. It's quite full and probably the only thing that wasn't stabbed.'

'And what about this ribbing here?'

Adele suppressed a laugh and turned away.

'What? Have I said something I shouldn't have?'

'The ribbing is the elastic from his underwear,' Claire said with a small smile on her lips.

'Oh.' Matilda turned red with embarrassment. 'Well, it's incredibly detailed, isn't it?'

'So what happens now?' Matilda asked once she and Adele were back in the pathologist's office.

Even with the air conditioning on in the Digital Autopsy Suite, the closed space and the number of people had made it warmer. When they left, Matilda had felt damp. She wiped her forehead and ran her fingers through her hair. Her hand came away wet. Maybe she was warm. Maybe it was the sweat from an impending anxiety attack. Either way, a bottle of water from Adele's table-top fridge was enough to cool her down.

'Ryan will be brought in for a full invasive post-mortem.'

'I didn't think you'd need to do one.'

'In a forensics case, such as this, we always need to do an invasive post-mortem. It's just that, now I've seen the scans and X-rays, I know the areas to concentrate on. When your lovely ACC rang and so pleasantly asked for Ryan to be bumped up the queue I thought she'd want the very best treatment so I took it upon myself to book in a digital autopsy.'

Matilda smiled and felt herself relax.

'Tell her from me she can expect a bill for five hundred pounds coming her way very soon.'

'Are you doing more of these digital autopsies?'

'We would do if you lot would put your hands in your pockets. You've no idea how effective they are in a forensic case. Ryan Asher is still in the body bag, yet we've been able to see how he died, what happened to him internally, without losing a shred of evidence. Once I've cut him open it's not like I can put him back together as he was before. Now, I can go into the invasive PM knowing exactly what to look for.'

'Well, from now on, I want a digital autopsy done on all my cases that come through here. Screw the cost. I'll sneak it through somehow.'

Adele smiled. 'You'll have made Claire's day with that remark.'

'She seemed a bit feistier than usual today.'

'You don't mess around in Claire's autopsy suite.'

'When will you be doing the full PM?'

'You sound like Valerie Masterson.'

'Sorry.'

'I'll do him next. From the X-rays and 3D imaging I counted the stab wounds – eight in the stomach, three in the chest, and one in the shoulder. I can tell you in what order to stab a person to make the death linger but I have no idea in which order Ryan was stabbed. Only the killer can tell you that.'

'It seems like he knew what he was doing. By the look of things, he punctured all the major organs,' Matilda said, taking another sip of cold water. 'Is that why there was so much blood at the scene?'

'Yes.'

'Will you be able to check for a needle mark or something? I find it very difficult to believe Ryan just hopped onto the pool table and allowed himself to be stabbed to death.'

'Don't worry. If he was drugged, I'll find it. I'll send samples of his blood and stomach contents off to be analysed. Fancy coming over for dinner tonight?'

'How you can ask that question in the same sentence as stomach contents and not want to vomit is beyond me.' Matilda half-smiled.

'I can do a vegetable lasagne.'

'No, thanks, Adele. I think I'm going to have an early night with Tony Hill.'

'Oh yes?' Adele's eyes lit up. 'You never mentioned this.'

Matilda smiled. 'He's a character in a book I'm reading.'

'Oh. Well if you prefer a book to my burnt offerings ... '

'To be honest, Adele, I just fancy an early night.'

'Everything OK?'

'Yes. Everything's fine.'

Matilda had been saying everything was fine since James died almost eighteen months before. She had taken his death very hard, even though they both knew it was coming. She had received great support from Adele, her son Chris, Sian at work, and even the ACC had visited her a few times while she was on compassionate leave, and the first question asked was 'how are you feeling?' to which Matilda had always answered 'I'm fine.' It was the standard, staple reply. They all knew she wasn't fine; Matilda knew she wasn't fine, but it was understood by everyone that they shouldn't dwell any further on the subject.

One day, Matilda suspected, she would genuinely be fine. When? She had absolutely no idea.

LEWIS CHAPMAN

Nottingham. October 2012

I know I shouldn't have watched it. I know it was wrong, but everyone said it was the film that reignited the horror genre.

I first watched *Scream* at the age of eight, and I loved every minute of it. That opening with Drew Barrymore getting terrified by a psycho-stalker was perfect. I've lost count of the number of times I've seen that part – definitely a few thousand. I've seen it on DVD, on YouTube, on my phone on the bus to school. I know it word for word. It's brilliant. The second and third films were good but there weren't any stand out scary moments like the opening to the first film, and don't get me started on *Scream 4*, or *Scre4m* as it's known.

I've been obsessed with horror films ever since I first saw *Scream*. Not obsessed, that's the wrong word, I'm just a big fan, that's all. I've seen them all, from the classics like *Psycho* and *Misery*, *Silence of the Lambs*, *The Exorcist*, *Night of the Living Dead*, and *Rosemary's Baby* to the modern ones like *Scre4m*, *Saw*, *Cabin in the Woods*, *Insidious*, *Let Me In* and *Fright Night*. I've got hundreds on DVD.

Funnily enough, I don't like Halloween. Not the film, I love that, I mean the event. I've never seen the point in dressing up and knocking on people's doors. However, last Halloween, I was looking out of my window at the kids going around in masks and costumes and I thought that 31st October would be the best time of year to commit a murder.

I had a whole year to plan my crime and choose my victims. It didn't take long to come up with my younger brother, Jason. I've never liked him. It's always been obvious my parents preferred him to me – he always got bigger presents at Christmas, extra pocket money, and he didn't have to do any chores to earn it. He always got more ice cream than I did too. He was nothing special. He was shorter than me, fatter, and he had a lisp. Why did they like him more than me?

The year seemed to drag on, and the longer I waited, the more anxious I was. I couldn't bear it. I was genuinely excited.

When the summer holiday came around I took that as my opportunity to put my final plan into action. I knew that once we returned to school in September it wouldn't be long before Halloween.

I didn't write anything down. I didn't want to leave any evidence. So I sat on my bed and pictured everything in my head. I went over it again and again and again. It was like watching a horror film on a loop. It was brilliant. I was the writer, director, and star of my own slasher movie.

Halloween fell on a Wednesday, and Mum and Dad always work late on Wednesdays. It was meant to be. Jason was two years younger than me, and I always waited for him after school so we could walk home together. I asked him how his day had been and if he'd done well in his English test – everything had to be normal. He didn't suspect a thing. I asked if he wanted to go out trick-or-treating, he said no. Thank God.

I waited until seven o'clock. It was dark and the streets were filling up nicely with kids in badly home-made costumes. It was time to act. I called the landline from my mobile, putting 141 in front of the number so it would come up as withheld on the display. Jason didn't answer at first. He probably thought I was going to answer it. Eventually, he picked up.

'Hello.'

'Hello.'

'Who's this?'

'Who's this?'

'It's Jason.'

'Hi Jason. What's your favourite scary movie?'

'What?'

'Scary night tonight, isn't it? Ghosts and demons running around screaming. It's like something from a horror film.'

'Who is this?'

'Are you scared?'

'Hardly, Lewis. I can hear you in your bedroom. Nice try though.'

Shit! I saw red. I couldn't believe he'd guessed it was me. I'd been practising that American accent since the summer. I threw my mobile on the floor and ran into his bedroom. He was still holding the phone in his hand. He jumped as I kicked the door open, but when he saw me in my Ghostface costume he started laughing.

He didn't laugh when the knife tore into his throat. He gasped for breath and grabbed his neck as if he could keep the blood from flowing out. I stabbed him twice in the stomach and he dropped to the floor. He looked up at me, his eyes wide, tears rolling down his face. He was desperate to speak, but the words wouldn't come out.

I leaned over him, knife dripping blood, raised high above my head.

'"It was a simple game, Cotton, you have told me where Sidney was. Now, you lose!"'

I brought the knife down into his chest and watched as his eyes closed for the last time.

End of Act One.

FIFTEEN

Sian and Rory were alone in the boardroom of Starling House. The files of staff and inmates were all mingled together in a disorganized heap in front of them. Matilda had set them the difficult task of getting to know the people living and working at Starling House in order to brief everyone else later. Nobody wanted this task and nobody had volunteered.

Rory had taken off his jacket and rolled up the sleeves of his shirt. His tie was loosened and the top button undone. His hair was ruffled too. The usually pristine and well-kept Rory looked more like the dishevelled and downtrodden Matilda.

'I think I need a cigarette,' Rory said, shattering the heavy silence.

'I didn't think you smoked.'

'I don't. Bloody hell, this is depressing stuff. On the drive over here I actually wanted to know what all these boys had done. Now I'm not so sure. Have you read about that Lewis Chapman?'

'No.'

'He killed his little brother like he was a character in a horror film. Can you believe that? There was no motive at all, other than because he wanted to. I mean … why?'

'I've no idea, Rory.' Sian looked down at the desk. She was

struggling with this case. Two of her four children were teenagers like the inmates of Starling House, and she couldn't help but make comparisons. Would any of her kids turn out the way Lewis Chapman or Lee Marriott?

'And look at that Callum Nixon? He purposely went into school with a knife to kill two teachers. I never … '

Rory kicked his chair back and walked over to the window. It was open slightly to let in the autumnal breeze but he pushed it fully open. He leaned on the frame and stuck his head out, taking deep breaths. Sian went up behind him and put a protective arm around his shoulders.

'Rory, you can't let these lads get to you. Yes, they've committed the worst crimes imaginable but they're paying for them. That, at least, should give you some comfort.'

'It's the fact they committed them in the first place. I've got a brother and cousins who are the age of some of these lads. What if they turn into killers?'

'I don't think it works like that, Rory. You don't just turn into a killer. It's background, circumstance, upbringing. So many factors go into creating who we are. Your brother, and your cousins, will be well-loved, looked after, brought up in a stable environment. I bet the majority of the boys in here didn't have any of that?'

'And what about the minority?'

'Sorry?'

'You said the majority of the boys in here won't have had a stable environment, but not all of them. So there will be a couple who did have a stable background. Why did they turn to murder?'

'Oh Rory, I wish I could answer your questions but I can't. I'm not a psychologist. I have no idea what makes the mind of a murderer tick.'

Rory took a deep breath. 'I think I need to know.'

'Really? Are you sure you want to do that?'

'Yes,' he said with conviction. 'If I'm going to be a good

detective, if I want to get promotion, I'm going to have to understand the killers, find out why they do what they do. Surely there's a recognized sign or brain patterns or something that can identify a killer.'

'Rory, before you even look into doing this kind of research talk it over with Matilda and Amelia first because it's really going to screw with your mind. I know you, you'll let this consume you, and you'll start looking for killers everywhere. That will have an impact on your relationship with Amelia and your role within the force.'

'I don't need to talk it over with anyone,' Rory said. He moved away from the window and picked up his jacket from the back of his chair. 'Read what Craig Hodge did, what Lee Marriott did, what Jacob Brown did – we need to understand why they killed and look at ways to prevent it happening again, not just shutting them away in a building in the middle of nowhere and pretending they don't exist. Besides, what relationship with Amelia? I moved out last week.'

Leaving Sian open-mouthed, he took large determined strides to the door and left, slamming it shut behind him.

Sian sat back down and blew out her cheeks. She knew this was going to be no ordinary case, but she had no idea it was going to be such a game changer among the team.

SIXTEEN

'Who is your head of security here?'

'Gavin Ryecroft. He's on holiday in Norfolk. I've contacted him and he's on his way back.'

'Who is in charge when he's not here?'

'That would Charles Dillane. He's on long-term sick at present.'

Matilda was back in Kate Moloney's office going through the day-to-day running of Starling House. She was trying to get a feel for the place, the outline of an ordinary day. Although, was there such as thing as an ordinary day in a building full of multiple murderers?

'So who takes care of the alarms and CCTV when Gavin is away?'

'The staff have been sharing the duties. They're all very capable.' She couldn't make eye contact with Matilda.

'I'm sure they are but they won't be as qualified as Gavin Ryecroft, will they?'

'Well, no.'

'So mistakes could have been made.'

'Such as?'

'Such as the alarms on the patio doors in the recreation room. Are you sure they were switched on last night?'

'Of course I'm sure.' Kate went on the defensive straight away. 'DCI Darke, I don't know what you're implying here, but none of my staff will have knowingly left this building in a compromising position. Besides, there is no need for the patio doors to be opened at this time of year. It's cold and damp. They're only open during the summer months, and only then during hot weather.'

'Kate, I'm merely trying to find out how the killer gained access to the building. I'm not accusing anyone at this stage.'

'I'm sorry but I think you are.' She folded her arms in defiance. 'I think you're purposely trying to find something so you can accuse one of my staff. I am aware the people of Sheffield don't approve of Starling House but I thought the police would at least be on our side.'

'Kate, we have interviewed all of the boys and they have all said the same thing. By nine o'clock last night they were all locked in their rooms and didn't leave until they were unlocked this morning. If one of them was the killer, then someone with a key had to have let them out. That would be one of your staff.'

'You seem to be looking at the inmates like they're boys at a camp. They're killers. They're manipulators. How do you know one of them didn't have a key hidden somewhere?'

'If one of them did have a key then where did he get it from?' Matilda asked, raising an accusatory eyebrow.

'I will not stand for any of my staff accused without evidence. Now, if you don't mind, I have a lot of work to do.'

Matilda stood up slowly to leave. 'We're still waiting for that CCTV footage.'

'I'll get onto it.'

'Thank you. I'll be upstairs in the boardroom.'

The inmates of Starling House had been transferred to the library. The tables had been pushed back to create more space but it lacked the relaxed atmosphere of the recreation room. There was no pool table, no table tennis, and no football tables. There was no television and no drinks. It was wall-to-wall books.

Thomas Hartley was in his element. He took a Paul Torday from the shelf and tried to make himself comfortable in a lumpy armchair. A few of the other boys helped themselves to graphic novels. Nobody could concentrate on reading. Speculation was rife.

'Come on then; now we're all alone, who did it?' Callum said, breaking the heavy silence with his gruff accent.

Eye contact was avoided wherever possible. Nobody dared look at anyone else, in case they were accused of pointing the finger at a fellow inmate.

'Well, I didn't do it,' Jacob Brown said. 'Them tablets I had for that eye infection make me drowsy. I'm asleep as soon as my head hits the pillow,' he chuckled to himself.

'It can't be any of us, can it?' Lewis Chapman asked. 'We're all locked in. The locks are on a timer. There's no way we can get out of our rooms until morning.'

'So, one of the guards wants to see what life is like on the other side of the bars, does he?' Callum said, relishing the situation. 'Hartley, you've always got your head in a mystery, put your Poirot hat on and tell us who did it.'

Thomas didn't say anything. He looked up then back down at his book.

'Suit yourself. It's a frightening thought though, isn't it? Say one of the guards is the killer, well, they've got keys to every room in this place. They could creep up in the middle of the night, unlock the door to one of our rooms and strike while we're asleep.' He leaned over the edge of the sofa and lowered his voice. 'We'd all better start sleeping with one eye open. Who knows which one of us could be next.'

'Oh piss off, Callum.' Jacob jumped up.

'Have I scared you?' He smiled.

'No.'

'I bet I've scared Lee though, haven't I? You're frightened of your own shadow.' He went over to the skinny blond boy sitting at one of the tables. He looked as if he was concentrating on his magazine but he hadn't turned the page once. He had been listening the whole time. 'How you managed to set fire to your parents' caravan is beyond me. Are you sure you're guilty? Would you like me to keep you company tonight?' Callum said, whispering in Lee's ear, trying to sound threatening and seductive at the same time. 'You'd like that, wouldn't you? Fucking gay boy.' He pushed him in the head, almost knocking him off his chair. The rest turned away. They would only intervene if it turned violent.

'My money's on Grover,' Jacob said, trying to move the subject away from Lee. He felt sorry for him – always the butt of Callum's cruel jibes. 'It's always the quiet ones.'

'That puts Hartley to the top of the suspect list then,' Craig grinned. 'He's very quiet. I bet he's not reading at all. He just sits there, listening, plotting, choosing his next victim.'

Thomas looked up and saw Craig leering at him. He decided not to answer back and returned to his book.

'Of course.' Callum smiled. 'Thomas Hartley, the machete man of Manchester. You're very handy with a blade, aren't you? According to Grover, Ryan Asher was stabbed twelve times. How many whacks did you give your family?'

Thomas remained silent.

'He's not biting, Callum. You may as well leave him alone,' Jacob said.

'Fair dos. So who else is handy with a knife? Apart from my good self, obviously.' He bowed to the room. 'Lewis Chapman.' His eyes fell on the dark-haired teenager in the corner of the room. 'What was it you did again: dressed up as Ghostface and stabbed your little brother? Ryan Asher's killing is like something out of a horror film. Come on then, Lewis, how did you get out of your cell?'

'Fuck off, Callum.'

'Jacob, I've got one who's bitten.' He smiled. 'I bet you think you're a killer in a horror film, don't you? What's the guy in the white mask? He kept coming back from the dead, didn't he? Do you want a high body count? Is that why you killed Ryan Asher? Do you plan on killing others?'

'Leave me alone, Callum,' Lewis said, barging past him and moving out of the corner of the room where he was feeling trapped.

'You've hit a nerve there, Callum,' Jacob said, egging him on.

'It would seem so. Are you writing *Scream 5*? I suppose this is the quiet bit after the first killing as the investigation begins. It won't be long before the next victim turns up. So who will it be? Lee's expendable. He can be the next victim nobody remembers. Then Hartley. Save me and Jacob for the final showdown.'

'I don't want to be killed in the final act,' Jacob chided.

'No, we'll survive. We're the tough guys. We're like that Neve Campbell chick. We'll be in the sequel.'

With the main focus in the room on Callum and Jacob discussing how the other inmates would die, Craig was still occupied with Thomas. His stare was burning through the book he was holding. Thomas could feel the glare. Eventually, slowly, Craig stood up and slunk over to where Thomas was sitting. He crouched down next to him and whispered in his ear.

'I saw how your expression changed when Callum said you were the killer. He hit a nerve, didn't he? It always is the quiet ones. I tell you something, you even try anything with me and I'll cut your fucking heart out, understand?'

He didn't wait for a reply. He stood up and returned to his seat, completely unnoticed by the other inmates.

Thomas tried not to react but it wasn't easy. His bottom lip began to quiver. He couldn't allow himself to cry, not in front of the others. He needed to save it up until he was locked in his room tonight and soak his pillow with tears like he had done every night since he arrived.

The door to the library opened and in walked one of the guards, Rebecca Childs. 'Sorry to have left you alone for so long, call of nature. Now, what's everyone talking about?'

SEVENTEEN

'Any news from Aaron?' Matilda whispered to Sian on her way to the front of the room to begin the final briefing of the day.

'Not yet. I've sent him a couple of texts but he hasn't replied. By the way,' Sian grabbed Matilda's sleeve as she moved away. Sian indicated she wanted to whisper so Matilda lowered her head. 'You might want to have a word with Rory.'

'Why? What's he done?'

'He hasn't done anything. He's taking this case rather personally. He wants to look into the psychology of why these boys have killed. I think he's using it as some kind of a distraction: he and Amelia have split up.'

'Really? When?'

'He said he moved out last week.'

'Poor bugger. I'll have a word. Thanks Sian.'

Matilda looked out on the sea of detectives. They were smaller in number than this morning; many had been sent back to HQ as they had other duties to attend to. It felt strange to be standing in front of a room full of detectives after five years of addressing the elite few of the Murder Room. She still directed most of her comments and remarks to her own small team – something which she knew rankled the other officers. It was a bad habit she would have to kick into touch.

'Have all the inmates been interviewed?'

'Yes,' Sian began, 'all of their stories seem to be the same. The ones that did talk to Ryan Asher said he seemed like a nice lad: quiet and a bit nervous. They all said they went into the recreation room at around six o'clock before being locked in their rooms at nine, and not hearing or seeing anything until they were woken at seven the next morning.'

'What about staff?'

'We haven't interviewed any of them yet,' Christian Brady said. 'They've been helping us out with the inmates – either accompanying them to and from their rooms or acting as appropriate adult.'

'Has anyone left or entered Starling House?'

'The shifts work four days on and three days off. The current staff are on day two. They've had no reason to leave yet.'

'Christian, do me a favour: tomorrow, I want you to tear this place apart. The head of security is coming back from his holiday in Norfolk. When he gets here I want him shadowed. Also, I've asked for all CCTV footage to be made available to us. I want to know their entire security procedure.'

'Not a problem. I'll handle it.'

'Now, are we all up to speed on who Ryan Asher is?' There were nods around the room. 'Who would want to kill him? Rory?'

'Well, I'm guessing Jane Asher's cookbook sales will have dropped – she could be a suspect.'

A ripple of laughter echoed off the walls. If Matilda hadn't been told about Rory's current personal status she wouldn't have known anything was amiss. He was his usual jokey self. Normally she discouraged it, but on a case as difficult as this the odd joke was good for morale – even a bad joke.

'Have we located his parents yet?'

'Not yet,' Scott said. 'I've been looking through the file, and during Ryan's trial his parents attended the court every day and so did his auntie, his mother's sister. She has stayed in Norwich and, get this, moved into Ryan's old house when his parents left.'

'Really? That's a bit bizarre, isn't it?' Sian asked.

'That's what I thought.'

'OK, Scott. First thing tomorrow, I want you and Faith to go to Norwich and interview the aunt. Find out if she knows where her sister is, how she feels about Ryan, and why she's decided to move into his home.'

'Do I tell her about Ryan being killed?'

'No. Tell her he's been attacked and we need to get in touch with his parents. However, if it's leaked out by the time you get there then you may as well tell her.'

'Yes, boss.' Scott turned and made eye contact with Faith Easter, who smiled at him.

'Faith, you were looking into web forums. Have you discovered anything?'

'I have, actually. There's a woman in Bristol who was arrested for issuing death threats to the judge. She was given a caution. I've called Bristol police and they're going to send someone out to have a discreet word with her – make sure she was actually in Bristol last night. I think the rest are all talk but I'll keep at it.'

'Thanks, Faith.'

'However,' she continued, 'there was a man who attended the trial every day and sat in the public gallery next to Ryan's parents. At one point he was removed by court staff for turning on the parents and blaming them for bringing a monster into the world.'

'Do we know who he is?'

'No. I suppose we could ask the court staff if they remember him, or if he's been hanging around before or since.'

'Good thinking. Scott, while you're in Norwich tomorrow, pop along to the courts and have a word.'

'Will do,' he said, making a note.

'What about Ryan's Facebook page? I'm assuming he had one.'

Faith quickly flicked through her notebook. 'He did. It doesn't exist anymore. However, I've been trawling the internet and found a news story from around the time his trial started. His Facebook page was bombarded with death threats from all over the world: not just to him but to his family too. In the end Facebook closed the page at the request of the police.'

'Great work, Faith, thank you. Rory, you seem to have had your nose stuck in Ryan's file for most of the day. Is there anything else Scott and Faith can look into while they're in Norwich tomorrow?'

'I don't think so,' Rory replied, looking up from the file. 'There are statements from a few of the neighbours saying he was a quiet lad, but that's about it. I've found a newspaper cutting about him being involved in an attack on a teenager called Malcolm Preston, but I was thinking … ' he sat back and folded his arms. He had a worried look on his face. 'Ryan was an only child. His parents worked hard, and he was quiet. Maybe he was acting out of neglect, trying to seek some form of attention. He may not be the monster he's being painted by the media. Couldn't we run all this by a psychologist?'

'Rory, whether he was trying to get his parents' attention or not, he killed his grandparents. He's still a murderer,' Sian said. 'When my kids want mine or Stuart's attention they stop tidying their room or turn their music up loud. They don't go around killing people.'

'Sian's right,' Matilda said. 'Don't read too much into these inmates, Rory. The killer is in this building and we need to find him. That's all you need to know. Now, Christian, how did the search of the grounds go? Any sign of the murder weapon?'

'I'm afraid not. As you know the grounds are surrounded by high fencing, topped with razor wire. Nothing has been cut, and there is no evidence of footprints around the fence. We've found no weapon or anything.'

'So the weapon is still in Starling House then?'

'The kitchen isn't missing any knives, and they've all been taken away for analysis.'

'Thanks, Christian. Any suspects so far?' There was no reply. 'OK, tomorrow we move on to the staff. You may as well go home and get an early night. Don't talk about this to anyone. We can't afford to have this leaking out. The people of Sheffield already have a bee in their bonnet about Starling House, we don't want to have a mob descending.'

As the room began to empty, Matilda called for Sian to stay behind.

'Sian, do you know anyone in Manchester?' she asked once the room was empty.

'Yes, I know loads of people from Manchester. Stuart's got family there.'

'No, I mean in Manchester police.'

'A few. Why?'

'Anyone discreet?' Matilda asked, ignoring Sian's question.

'That depends,' she shrugged, looking perplexed. 'Actually, remember DI Pat Campbell? I think her son is high up in Manchester police.'

'Really? I didn't know she had a son in the force.'

'Yes. He moved away from Sheffield after university; trained in Manchester and decided to stay there. Any particular reason?'

'No. Just being nosey. You have a good evening, Sian.'

Still with a face of confusion, Sian turned and left the small office, closing the door slowly behind her.

Matilda made a note on a Post-It pad to remind her to pay a visit to Pat Campbell tomorrow morning before work. She had been retired for more than ten years. Matilda hoped the passion for crime solving was still burning within. She needed the help of someone she could trust.

EIGHTEEN

Matilda arrived home to a cold and empty house. She threw her bag on the floor in the living room. It landed on the carpet with a heavy thud. The book about Carl Meagan was weighing it down. She had no idea why she'd felt the need to take it to work with her.

Most evenings when Matilda arrived home she wasn't in the mood to exercise. She often looked at the treadmill and wondered if she could manage another five kilometre run, or maybe even a brisk walk. Her heart wasn't in it. The weight of the day felt heavy on her shoulders; the stress and tension made her sluggish and lethargic. A run would help. She knew that. She just couldn't find the motivation.

She had a quick meal of scrambled eggs on toast, which she didn't enjoy, then went into the living room and lolloped onto the sofa with a heavy sigh. She looked across at the wedding photograph: James looking handsome and gorgeous with his beaming smile and his ice-blue eyes. Their arms were linked and they both looked happy. For the majority of the time Matilda was sad he had gone. There were times she was angry he had left her alone. She didn't just want him here with her, she needed him. Right now she needed him to walk into the living room, put his arms around her and hold her tight. She needed to smell him, to feel him, to taste him.

Her eyes fell on her bag on the floor. Sticking out of the top the smiling face of Carl Meagan was looking at her with his innocent eyes. He was a beautiful little boy. She picked up the book and held it firmly in her hands. She looked deep into the photograph and wondered what had happened to him. Where was he right now? Was he still alive and living a good life with a couple who couldn't have kids of their own? Had he been sold to paedophiles and was currently being handed around for sordid pleasure? Or had he been sold so his organs could be used on the black market for transplants?

A tear fell from Matilda's eye and dropped onto Carl's.

'I'm so sorry I failed you,' she said.

While the kettle boiled in the kitchen Matilda looked in the cupboard for a snack. Like Sian at work, Matilda had created a snack drawer at home for when she felt the need to comfort eat, which was most evenings. It was full of multipack bars of chocolate, packets of biscuits, and bags of crisps. She chose the largest bar of Cadbury Whole Nut she could find, made her tea and headed upstairs.

She stood in the doorway of her library and surveyed what was laid out before her. She really did love this room. She inhaled the smell of new carpet and old books and it brought a smile to her lips. She could understand why Jonathan Harkness had lost himself in the world of fiction. It was an aid to forget life and the horrors of reality for a few hours, to sit back and escape what happened in the real world. Within the pages of these books she could ignore whatever was going on in Starling House and the politics of South Yorkshire Police.

Matilda made herself comfortable in her Eames chair and picked up the Val McDermid hardback. She was over halfway through and loving the highly disturbed Tony Hill and his complex relationship with Carol Jordan. The story was dark and intriguing. She put her feet up, snapped off a few squares of Whole Nut and settled in for a few chapters.

Stuart Mills was a burly man of six foot one. Built like a rugby player he gave the impression of a man to be feared, a man not to be messed with. Beneath the façade he was a gentle giant who would lay down his life for his wife and four kids.

He was sitting on the sofa in the living room of their four-bedroom house in Shiregreen, watching the local news with his youngest son, Gregory, aged eleven. The presenters were talking about the threat of a storm forecast for later in the week.

'Apparently, they've had a month's worth of rain in twelve hours in Bristol,' Stuart called out to Sian who was making a cup of tea in the kitchen.

'Are we going to get a lot of rain, Dad?' Gregory asked.

'It looks like it,'

Sian walked into the living room. She cast a glance at Danny studying at the dining table. She had a mug of tea in each had and handed one over to Stuart.

'Is it going to be as bad as 2007?' Sian asked remembering the night in June nine years before when she was stranded at work because she couldn't get home. Meadowhall had been flooded and closed for days. Sian's sister, Ruth, who lived in Brightside at the time, had to be airlifted from her home. Looking back, it was the best night of Ruth's life, she'd told Sian. At the time she was petrified.

'They don't know yet,' he replied. 'Do you think I should get some sandbags for those patio doors? That garden's on a slant as it is. If it is going to be bad we don't want water coming in. The carpet's only been down a few months.'

'You don't need sandbags. It's a storm door.'

'Is it?'

'Yes.' She rolled her eyes. 'I knew you weren't listening to the bloke. Why do you think it cost so much?'

'There you go, Gregory, it can rain all it wants, we're going to be safe in here. We might even get airlifted out.'

'Ah, cool.' He boy beamed.

'I'd stay off the KitKats then, Stuart,' Sian said, nodding at his full stomach. 'It's a helicopter they'd be coming in, not a crane.'

Sian turned and went to sit next to Danny at the dining table. He hadn't taken part in the conversation. His head was down and the pained expression on his face showed he was concentrating hard.

'What are you doing?' she asked, swiping away some of his long hair that had draped over his face.

'Maths. I've got a mock exam next Wednesday.'

'How's it going?'

'All right.'

'Is it difficult?'

'Of course it's difficult. It's maths.'

'Do you need any help?'

'Nah.'

'You sure?'

'Yeah.'

He didn't look up once from his studies and just answered his mother's questions as simply as he could.

'Danny, I know we've always told you school work is important and you need to do well in your exams in order to get a good career, but, if you don't, it's not the end of the world, you know.'

'I know.'

'I don't want you to think you're under a lot of pressure to get a good grade. You're studying hard, that's the main thing. Whatever mark you get I'll be proud of you.'

This made Danny look up. 'You've changed your tune. At the beginning of the year you were telling me how important this year is for me and not to mess around.'

'I know I did and it is an important year. It's just … ' she struggled to find the words. 'It's not … if you don't pass or you don't get the grades you want I don't want you to get too down-hearted. There are more important things in life, OK?'

Danny looked on with a perplexed expression. 'OK' he replied, confused.

'Good. I'm here for you too if you ever need to talk. About anything. We both are. Me and your dad,' she looked over at Stuart, who was having a competition with Gregory to see if they could fit a KitKat vertically into their mouths without it breaking. 'Well, maybe just me.' She smiled.

Since breaking up with Amelia, Rory Fleming had moved back in with his parents. It wasn't ideal and it certainly wasn't going to be permanent, but it was the only option.

If he was honest, he would say the break-up had been a long time coming. They hardly spoke to each other; they never had sex anymore, and Amelia was constantly studying to become a solicitor. When she eventually succeeded, there would be a conflict of interest if their professional lives crossed, which they were bound to do. The death of their relationship was inevitable.

Sitting in the living room, lit only by the dull light of a standard lamp, Rory balanced a laptop on his knee and tucked into a bland takeaway he'd picked up on the way home. His parents had long since gone to bed, leaving him with the house to himself.

His mind was full of the seven boys in Starling House. Not just their crimes, the horrors they inflicted on others, but the need they felt to commit the crime in the first place. What could possibly be so bad in a teenager's life that the only solution was murder? Rory remembered what it was like to be a teenager. He was all mood swings and raging testosterone. Did hormones play a part in why a child went on to kill? Was there some chemical imbalance in their brain that changed them from a rational individual to a cold-blooded killer?

Rory searched Google. He couldn't find the right answers because he didn't know the right questions. There were essays written by psychologists on the behaviour of young people and whether they were influenced by films and computer games, but a lot seemed to be playing it safe. Nobody wanted to stick their neck out and give a firm answer.

He scrolled through his phone and sent a text to Scott:

Did you ever think about killing your parents as a child?

The reply came back almost straightaway:

What? No I didn't. What kind of a question is that?

I'm trying to understand why the boys in Starling House killed in the first place.

Not this again!! Rory, it doesn't matter. They've killed. They're in there. Surely it's good 2 know they've been caught and no longer a threat to society.

Aren't u curious as 2 y people kill?

Not at this time of night. See you in the morning.

Rory threw the phone down onto the sofa and sighed. He seemed to be the only person interested in what made these boys tick. He placed the laptop on the seat next to him and went into the dining room where he'd put his bag when he arrived home from work. He listened carefully to check for any sounds from upstairs; it was all quiet. From his bag he pulled out a thick brown file. He took it back into the living room and began reading.

Before coming home, Rory had gone back to South Yorkshire Police HQ and photocopied all the case files of the inmates of Starling House. He had managed to sneak them into his car without anyone noticing.

Now, sitting in the dull living room, Rory started to read and re-read about the murders committed by Jacob Brown, Ryan Asher, Craig Hodge, Callum Nixon, Mark Parker, Lewis Chapman, Thomas Hartley, and Lee Marriott. There had to be something in their pasts, some trigger that made them kill, but what?

Rory reached for the laptop and went to the Google home page – 'why do children kill their parents?' he typed. He looked at the results and rolled his eyes. It was going to be a very long night.

NINETEEN

Kate Moloney walked the dark corridors of Starling House on the way to her room. It was approaching midnight and the house was silent. Usually, it didn't bother her to be alone in the dark, but tonight was different. Try as she might, she couldn't stop thinking that there was a killer on the loose.

This morning all the doors had been locked, apart from Ryan Asher's. Who had opened it? The only people who had a key were the staff. So did one of them open it? If so, why? Who, among them, was capable of stabbing a fifteen-year-old boy twelve times? She shook the thought from her mind. She didn't want to start questioning her staff as that would lead to her questioning her own judgement – she hired them after all.

Elly Caine. The least said about her the better. She was the one blot on Kate Moloney's perfect record. Fortunately, Elly didn't work at Starling House anymore. Although, she was related to Richard Grover and he still worked here.

'No!' Kate chastised herself. Her cry echoed around the silent corridors. It was not possible one of her staff was a killer. It had to be one of the other boys. They had all killed before, it was obviously part of their make-up. As much as Kate wanted to believe the inmates had accepted their punishment and were atoning for their sins, not all of them were sorry. One of them still had the capacity to take another life.

Kate's bedroom was at the top of the building, in the eaves. She locked the door behind her and pushed a heavy wooden trunk in front of it. Never before had she been frightened of sleeping in Starling House.

A very quick shower, during which she strained to listen for the sound of her door opening over the hot water raining down on her, a quick brush of her teeth and then she went straight to bed. She picked up an Anne Tyler paperback and put it straight back down again. She wouldn't be able to concentrate tonight.

She turned out the light and snuggled deep under the duvet but sleep wouldn't come. Her mind was busy with dark thoughts. After half an hour, she was still tossing and turning. The fitted sheet had come off the mattress at one corner and she was tangled up in the duvet. She climbed out and made the bed. Getting back in, she turned on the television. There was already a DVD in the player for when she felt like a bit of light relief before going to sleep. She switched it on and made herself comfortable once again. By the time the theme tune had finished on her fourth episode of *Friends*, she was fast asleep.

TWENTY

'Bollocks!'

Matilda looked down at the stopwatch on the treadmill: 31:22. She'd hoped to run under thirty minutes this morning. When she woke up she felt refreshed after a good night's sleep. She'd kicked back the duvet and hopped out of bed, changed into her running gear and headed straight for the conservatory. She was adamant she would break the thirty-minute mark.

An angry shower under blistering hot water and a slice of burnt toast later and she was ready for work. She blew a kiss to James on the mantelpiece, gave the treadmill a dirty look and left the house with a travel mug of coffee in hand.

Instead of turning left out of the drive she turned right and headed towards the outskirts of the Steel City.

'I wasn't expecting to see you on my doorstep this morning.'

Pat Campbell was still in her dressing gown. Her bed-hair was an unruly grey mop and in need of a trim. She was tall and slightly chubby since her days on the police force but she looked better for it. She had taken early retirement due to ill health but there didn't appear to be anything ailing her on first sight. She stood up straight, moved about easily enough and didn't have problems breathing.

She ushered Matilda into the living room and told her to make herself comfortable while she made coffee. Despite having drained most of her travel mug in the car, Matilda thought it would be rude to refuse, especially as she had a massive favour to ask.

The large living room was tastefully decorated in neutral colours and all the furniture was very modern. It was simple and minimalistic with everything neat and tidy. An unread newspaper was perfectly positioned on the coffee table. It was this morning's *Daily Mail*. She flicked through the newspaper and glanced at the headlines but didn't take in any of the stories. An advert stopped her dead. There was that smiling face of the blond-haired, blue-eyed boy again glaring up at her. *Carl* by Sally Meagan was out tomorrow in hardback.

Matilda could feel her blood beginning to boil; the prickly sensation of a panic attack crawling up her neck. Her throat dried, she had difficulty breathing and her vision began to blur. She staggered back and slumped into the sofa.

It had been over two months since her last panic attack. She thought she was over them and was finally getting to grips with whatever life threw at her. Her mind began to run away with itself: thousands of people would read this newspaper, buy the book, discuss it with others in the street, in coffee shops and online, and spread the word of Matilda's apparent incompetence. Would she ever be free of it?

'Would you like any breakf—?' Pat walked into the living room carrying two mugs of coffee. She saw Matilda on sprawled on the sofa. 'Jesus, Mat, what's happened? What's the matter?'

'Nothing. I'm all right.'

'You're not. You're as white as a ghost.' She moved to put the coffees down on the table and saw the newspaper. 'Ah, I forgot it was there. I'm sorry. I'd have moved it had I known you were coming.'

'It's all right, honestly. It's me. I'm taking all this too person-ally. Give me a minute.'

Pat opened a window and let in a stiff cool breeze. She went over to her usual armchair and sat patiently until Matilda was ready to talk.

'How long have you had panic attacks?' Pat eventually asked.

'How did you know?'

'My husband, Anton, had them when he first retired. He got it into his head that retiring meant he didn't have long left. It scared the shit out of him. At times he thought he was having a heart attack. I recognize the signs.'

'Ever since James died my confidence has been shot. This hasn't helped either,' she pointed at the newspaper. 'I've tried to move on, but I'm reminded of Carl all over the place.'

'I honestly don't know what to say to you, Matilda. Sally Meagan is going to keep doing things like this to keep everyone aware that her son is missing and to keep looking out for him. From her point of view it's all she's got.'

'She sent me the book. She hand delivered it and left it on my doorstep. She personally signed it saying she would never let me forget. It's things like that I have a problem with.' Matilda wiped her eyes. She suddenly noticed she had been crying. How long had that been going on?

'You can't report her either, can you?'

'Not really. How bad would that look to the media?'

'Does Valerie know about your panic attacks?'

'She did when I first came back. I've hidden them though. I think she thinks I'm over it all now.'

'You can't carry on like this, Mat. Have you considered seeing someone?'

Matilda smiled. 'I already do. I'll be fine, honest. Once it's out the adverts will stop.'

Pat wasn't convinced. The terse look on her face said it all. However, she let it slide. 'Are you sure you wouldn't like any breakfast?'

'No, I'm fine, thank you.'

'So, what is it you want from me then?'

'How do you know I've not popped round to say hello?'

'The last time you paid me a visit you had reopened the Harkness case and asked for my opinion. Good work by the way.'

'Thanks. Not the result I was expecting.'

'Me neither. However, case closed. That's the main thing.'

'Exactly.'

'So, have you reopened another case I worked on?'

'No. MIT doesn't exist anymore. We're just one big CID with many branches forking off into different teams.'

Pat looked deeply at Matilda. 'I'm guessing your reaction to that was akin to forking off too.'

Matilda smiled. 'Something like that. Look, Pat, I want to ask a favour but it really is in the strictest confidence.'

'I like the sound of that.'

Matilda told the former detective inspector all about Ryan Asher's murder at Starling House and the interviews with the inmates the previous day. Then she got to the business of her visit.

'Thomas Hartley was convicted for murdering his parents and his young sister. Trust me, Pat, one look at him and you'd know he didn't do it. Do you remember the case?'

'I do. It's not often a teenager slaughters their entire family. As I'm sure you know, my son's on the force in Manchester. He worked on the case. He's often said it's the most disturbing crime scene he's ever seen.'

Matilda looked to the floor. 'I'm not saying your son got it wrong or anything like that. I don't know how the case was investigated. Something is telling me Thomas Hartley didn't kill his family, and I can't shake that thought at all. If I'm right, he should not be in Starling House.'

'Why are you tell me all this? There's nothing I can do about it, surely. Unless you're asking me to have a word with my son.'

'Well, I was actually wondering if you'd do a bit of digging around for me. In Manchester.'

'What? You've got to be joking! Imaging if Valerie found out. She'd roast you alive. Not to mention how it would look from my son's point of view. I'm sorry, Mat, I can't put his job at risk.'

'I'm not asking you to put anything at risk,' Matilda quickly interjected. 'All I want is to make sure the case was investigated to its fullest, that's all.'

'I'm not sure,'

'Pat, you know me. You know I wouldn't ask if I didn't think there was a possibility of Thomas Hartley being innocent.' Pat was silent, as if she was mulling over the proposition. The look of angst on her face told Matilda she wasn't happy about this. 'Remember the Williamson killings? I was only a DC then but it's not something I'm going to forget. You had me and DC MacBride turn away while you spoke to Paul Williamson in the back of the squad car. He was underage, too, remember?'

'I hope you're not blackmailing me, Matilda,'

'Of course not. You did say at that time that you owed us one, me and DC MacBride.'

'I did, didn't I? I reckon I owe you two, especially after what happened to poor MacBride.' Pat took a deep breath. 'OK, leave it with me. I'm not promising anything, mind.'

'That's fine. I really do appreciate it.'

'I should hope so. Is there any chance I could get a copy of this Thomas Hartley's file?'

Innocently, Matilda bent down to retrieve her bag from the side of the armchair and pulled out a thick brown envelope. She handed it to Pat.

'You've certainly come prepared.'

'You know I wouldn't ask on a whim.'

'True. I'll get Anton to drive me over to Manchester and I'll test the water.'

'Pat, you're a star,' Matilda said, standing up.

'I'm aware.' She smiled, holding the file firmly to her chest.

TWENTY-ONE

Kate Moloney was sitting at her desk with her head in her hands. She was shattered. She woke several times throughout the night with bizarre dreams. Eventually, at six o'clock, she decided to get up. The birds outside her window were making it difficult for her to get any more rest.

A knock came on her office door. It opened and Oliver Byron walked in.

'Morning Kate. You OK?'

'Yes. Why?'

'You look tired.'

'Bad night.'

'I didn't sleep much either. I see we've managed to keep the press at bay so far,' he said, looking out of the window at the main entrance to the house.

'Yes. I was just looking on the news. I'm surprised they haven't sniffed it out yet. With all the traffic coming and going yesterday you would have thought someone would have alerted them.'

'It goes to show how much people ignore us.'

'True. Oliver, do you have any idea what could have gone wrong the other night?'

Oliver came away from the window and sat down in front of

Kate's desk. 'I've no idea. I've been through it all in my head from the second Ryan Asher arrived and there's nothing. We didn't do a thing differently that we normally do with a new arrival.'

They both fell silent while contemplating the worst. Kate continued. 'DCI Darke wants all the CCTV footage from Monday night. Can you get it sorted for her?'

'Ah,' he uttered.

'Ah?'

'The camera in corridor A isn't working?'

'What? Since when?'

'I've no idea.'

'Why isn't it working? Has it been broken or what?'

'I don't know?'

'Was it logged?'

'There's nothing written down anywhere. We'll have to ask Gavin when he comes back.'

'He's on his way. He said he was driving through the night. Jesus. DCI Darke already suspects one of the staff; the camera on the accommodation block being down is not going to help at all.'

'She thinks one of us killed Ryan Asher?'

'She doesn't have any evidence as such. She's basing it on the principle that all the boys were locked in their rooms so it has to be one of the staff who are free to roam the building as they please and have a key to the rooms.'

'But why would one of us kill him?'

Kate shook her head in defeat. 'I've no idea, Oliver.'

'They'll almost be there, now,' Rory said looking at his watch.

'Do you know what you sound like?'

'What?'

'A child who's not been allowed to go on a school trip,' Matilda said. 'They've only gone to Norwich. It's not like they're crossing the channel to France.'

138

'It would have been nice to get out of Sheffield for a day,' he said, yawning and rubbing at his eyes – evidence of a poor night's sleep.

'You had two weeks off in July. Didn't you go away then?'

'I wish. Amelia had exams all summer.'

Matilda turned her silver Ford Focus onto Limb Lane, and the tall trees lining both sides of the road cast a shadow over the car. Rory turned to look out of the window. As it was relatively dull outside, Matilda could see his face reflected back through the glass – he looked maudlin, dejected, and unloved. She felt sorry for him. Despite his bravado all he wanted out of life was a good career and a woman to love.

'Look, Rory, Sian told me you and Amelia have split up.'

'I thought she would have.'

'You know Sian, we're her extended family. She's worried about you. So am I.'

'I'm fine.'

That's exactly what I say so I know you're not.

'What happened between you and Amelia?'

'We had a massive row. She's studying to become a solicitor and I want a social life. It was our anniversary a couple of weeks ago. We'd been going out for four years. It was on the calendar and everything so there was no reason for her to forget. I certainly didn't. I bought her some flowers and a necklace. Do you know what she said to me?'

'What?'

'She said, "What are these for?" She'd completely forgotten. We started arguing and it just escalated. She said I resented her for wanting to achieve something. I said I wanted a girlfriend who liked going out for a Chinese once in a while. By the time the row ended I just packed a bag and walked out.'

'Any chance of a reconciliation?'

'No,' he said firmly. 'Do you know, when I left and was in the car, I felt lighter, like a weight had been lifted from my shoulders. I think the break-up had been a long time coming.'

'Where are you living now?'

'I'm back at my parents until I can sort something out. It's not ideal but I've nowhere else to go.'

'Rory, Sian also mentioned about you getting all psychological on our little house of killers.'

'I just want to understand why they did what they did.'

'Are you sure? You seemed to drift off at the briefing last night.'

'Of course I'm sure,' he almost snapped. 'Is Sian worried I'm going to turn into Hannibal Lector and become a serial killer myself?'

'I don't want you letting this case get to you. If you're looking for something to take your mind off Amelia, then I've got a dead tree that needs digging up.'

Rory laughed. It was a genuine belly laugh. He threw his head back and looked at Matilda. The sparkle was back in his eyes.

The second set of gates to Starling House were open. After announcing their arrival over the intercom they drove straight up to the front door. The forensic team were still there, combing through the recreation room for a second day. Fortunately, they had parked out of sight.

Entering Starling House was like entering the House of Horrors. There was a chilling atmosphere that consumed you. It had only been a prison for twenty years yet it felt like its entire history was shrouded in murder, rape, and arson. The souls of the most violent boys in history were imbedded in the walls and it seeped out to cast an eerie shadow over everyone who entered.

Matilda took the stairs two at a time to the boardroom on the top floor. She didn't like the atmosphere in here and longed to be back at HQ. However, it was sensible for the detectives to be based here while the interviewing process was underway. She opened the door and was surprised to find Aaron Connolly waiting for her.

'Aaron, what are you doing back? How's Katrina?'

'She's stable. They're keeping her in hospital for a few days. She has pre-eclampsia. She also has endometriosis which is why she had problems getting pregnant in the first place. They want to make sure she's OK before they let her home.'

'You shouldn't have come back.'

'I'd have only been sat at home worrying. I'm better off at work.'

'If you're sure.'

'I am.'

'Good. Look, if you need to rush off or anything, don't hesitate. Just let me know, OK?'

'Will do. Thanks, boss.'

'Right, everyone,' she said, clapping her hands together and bringing everyone to order. 'Day two of this investigation and we still have no idea who the killer of Ryan Asher is. Now, all of the inmates have been interviewed, and Sian and Rory have been going through the files on everyone here. Has it thrown anything up?'

'Chillingly, a majority of them are here for killing their parents,' Sian began.

'That's comforting,' Aaron said which led to a smatter of laughter.

'The question is: why would they want to kill a fellow inmate? What would they possibly gain by turning on one of their own?' Matilda asked.

'Do any of these boys know each other from before they came here?' DI Brady asked.

'Sian?' Matilda nodded.

'I doubt it. They're from all over the country. We've got Norwich, Liverpool, Southampton, Bristol, Worthing, Nottingham. It's highly unlikely their paths would have crossed.'

'So we can rule out some kind of feud then?'

'It would appear so.'

'And Ryan Asher was only here a day before he was murdered. He wasn't here long enough to gain an enemy,' Rory said.

'OK. Well, Scott and Faith are on their way to Norwich to talk to Ryan's aunt. Fingers crossed that gives us something to work on. Until we hear back, we need to interview the staff. So, like yesterday, I want two teams. Christian, can you sort that out?'

'Sure.'

'Thank you. I want you to press them hard. Don't forget, Ryan's door was opened from the outside and only they have keys. If they all admit they were asleep at the time, at least one of them will be lying.'

Sian's mobile rang. She mouthed an apology to Matilda and went to the back of the room to answer it.

'I was thinking,' Rory said. 'Whoever killed Ryan must surely have been covered in blood. It was a brutal stabbing. Where was the trail of blood from the pool table to the exit? If the killer got blood on him, where are his clothes? They're either very well hidden so we haven't found them yet or there's more than one person involved and they've managed to cover up for each other.'

There was a silence as they all thought about what Rory had said.

'That's what I can't get out of my mind,' Matilda said. 'The crime scene is too perfect. It was deliberately staged to tell us something.'

'Tell us what?'

'If we knew that, Rory, we wouldn't be asking the question.'

'Ma'am,' Sian said. 'That was forensics. They've got the results back from the knives they took from the kitchen. One of the carving knives had traces of blood in the gap between the handle and the blade. It matches Ryan Asher's blood.'

'So the killer thought he'd washed the knife thoroughly before putting it back,' Matilda said. 'At least we now have our murder weapon. Something else to ask the staff – who has access to the kitchen?'

TWENTY-TWO

Ryan Asher's former home was in a quiet leafy street just outside the centre of Norwich. Semi-detached houses lined both sides of the road. They all had neatly tended front gardens, driveways, and garages. It was an archetypal English suburb.

Scott pulled up outside number forty-two and turned off the engine. Both he and Faith looked up at the nondescript home.

'Nice house,' he commented.

'Yes. It looks like a nice area to grow up in, doesn't it? Quiet, private. I wonder what happened here to make Ryan commit such an evil crime?'

'You sound like Rory. I had him on the phone last night quizzing me about what makes a child kill.'

'What did you say?'

'I told him I've no idea. My degree is in English, not psychology.'

'Come on then, we've got a busy day ahead.'

Scott rang the doorbell and stood back. Looking around, the majority of the houses seemed empty, as were the driveways. Most of the residents would probably be at work and school. A burglar's paradise.

The front door was opened by a small woman in her mid-forties. Her hair was dull and lifeless which matched her skin and her dress sense. She had the expression of a woman who had given up on life and had nobody to neaten herself up for.

'Julia Palmer?' Scott asked.

'It depends who wants to know. If you're press, you can piss off.'

Scott and Faith both showed their ID. 'I'm DC Andrews and this is DC Easter. We're from South Yorkshire Police. Would it be possible for us to have a word?'

Julia folded her arms and leaned against the doorframe. 'South Yorkshire? Look, if this is about Brian I'm not interested. We're divorced. Whatever he's done it's nothing to do with me.'

'It's about your nephew.'

Her eyes widened briefly. 'I don't have a nephew.' She began to close the door.

'Ryan Asher.' Scott held his hand firm against the door to stop Julia from closing it.

The silence grew. Scott and Faith had all the time in the world. They could stay here forever.

'I'll give you ten minutes,' she said, opening the door wider and standing back to let them in.

There was no offer of tea or coffee. Julia led them into an old fashioned living room, told them to sit on a threadbare sofa and waited for them to get to the point. She had no intention of prolonging their stay.

'Mrs Palmer, we're trying to get in contact with Ryan's parents but nobody seems to know where they are,' Faith said.

Julia leaned back in her chair and once again folded her arms. There was a slight smile on her cracked lips. She had the upper hand here.

'That's how they want it.'

'Ryan has been involved in an incident and we need to inform his parents,' Scott said, slightly disgruntled by Julia's behaviour.

'What's that got to do with South Yorkshire Police?'

'Ryan is at Starling House. It's a … '

'I know exactly what Starling House is. His solicitor said he'd end up there. Look, whatever's happened to him, if someone's beaten him up or he's got himself into even more trouble then that's his problem. Lynne made it perfectly clear she wants nothing more to do with him.'

'Who's Lynne?'

Julia crossed her legs and began playing with her knotted hair. 'Sorry, I meant Belinda. Ryan's mum. I've just been chatting to Lynne on the phone. I work with her. That's probably why I said Lynne,' she stumbled, lying unconvincingly.

'Where were you on Monday night?' Scott asked.

'Monday night? Why?'

'Just wondering.'

'I was at work.'

'What do you do?'

'Monday, Wednesday and Thursday night I'm a bingo caller.'

'Can anyone verify that?'

'No. I was calling out numbers to an empty hall,' she said, relishing her sarcastic reply. 'What does it matter where I was on Monday night?' Her patience was wearing thin.

'It must be difficult for you living here with everyone knowing all about you,' Faith said, changing the subject.

'Not really. I've lived around here all my life. Everyone knows who I am.'

'There haven't been any reprisals or anything?'

'Why should there be?'

'During the trial your address was a two-bedroom apartment in the city centre. How come you've moved in here?'

'I wanted a house. St— Ryan's parents wanted to sell quickly and move so I bought it off them. I know you probably think it's weird but it's got nothing to do with you, or anyone else for that matter. It's not like this is where Ryan … ' Julia swallowed her words. It was obviously still very raw to talk about. Ryan's grandparents were her parents too.

'Do you have much contact with Belinda and Paul?'

'No.' She looked down at her feet.

'That must be very hard for you.'

'It is. I love my sister. I can understand them wanting a fresh start though. I would too if I was in their position.'

'Why didn't you go with them?' Scott asked.

The look on Julia's face was one of sadness. She opened and closed her mouth a few times but no words came out. She had obviously wanted to go with them – a fresh start together – but maybe the topic of Julia going never came up. Or maybe Paul had put his foot down.

'Do you have kids?' Faith asked. She raised her voice and smiled as if trying to lighten the atmosphere.

'No. I found out I was pregnant about a month before Ryan killed my parents. I had a miscarriage.'

'I'm sorry. Did your husband mind moving here?'

'Brian divorced me. Who wants to be married to the aunt of Ryan Asher? Look.' Julia stood up and wiped away a tear before it formed. 'I'm not going to tell you where my sister is, and I don't care what kind of trouble Ryan has got himself involved in so you've had a wasted journey.'

Scott fished a card out of his inside pocket. 'Would you please pass on my details to your sister? Tell her there has been an incident involving Ryan and to get in contact with us.'

He held the card out but Julia didn't take it. He placed it carefully on the coffee table.

'I'll think about it,' she said eventually.

'Thank you. We'll see ourselves out.'

'Bloody hell, she's full of anger, isn't she?' Faith said once they were back in the car.

Scott looked out of the driver's side window at the house and saw Julia Palmer looking back at him through the grimy living room window.

'I can understand why.'

'She's not going to be able to move on while she's still living here. Did you see the furniture? It's so old. I bet it's the same furniture Ryan's parents had. I'd love to have seen upstairs – I bet Ryan's room is exactly how he left it. Creepy.'

'So, Belinda Asher has changed her name to Lynne. What did she call the husband before she called him Paul?'

'Oh … It began with an S.'

'St … Stephen, Stan, Stefan … '

'Stewart, Stafford … '

'Stafford? Who the hell calls themselves Stafford?' Scott said.

'I've got an Uncle Stafford, thank you very much.'

'Oh. Sorry. OK, Stafford then. Maybe even Stanislav.'

'OK, say, for example, they've changed their names to Lynne and Stanislav, how are we going to track them down with no surname and no idea where they are?'

'I don't know,' Scott sighed. 'They need informing of their son's death before the press end up printing it.'

'You heard Julia, they want nothing more to do with Ryan. You can't blame them either after what he did. They obviously don't care. Look, you've given her your details. I think she'll ring her sister and pass on the information. She's probably on the phone to them right now. If we don't hear anything then we leave it at that, and they'll find out when it's in the papers. We've done all we can.'

'Hmm.'

'And what does "hmm" mean?'

'Nothing. Just hmm.'

Scott started the engine and drove away. On closer inspection there was something strange about number forty-two. There was a sense of sadness emanating from the brickwork. Maybe the dark aura of grief, loss, betrayal, anger and disbelief had remained in the house following the Asher's departure.

Rory was in the boardroom at Starling House on his own. Before him on the table were the case files of all the inmates, which he kept adding to. On his laptop the night before he had found more and more cases from all over the world of children committing murder. He made notes and printed off potentially useful information that could help him understand why a child would kill. The only common link he could find so far, especially among children who killed their parents, was that they were abused, either physically, sexually, or mentally, by the very people they should have been able to trust.

One case he found online stood out more than the others. Thirteen-year-old Kyle Fisher from Scranton, Pennsylvania had been abused by his father for three years after his mother died in a car accident. The day before his fourteenth birthday, his sister, Tiffany, confided in him that she was pregnant and their father was the father of her baby. Kyle had no idea his sister was being abused too. The next morning, when Kyle should have been excited about opening birthday gifts, he sneaked into his father's bedroom and shot him point-blank in the face, killing him instantly. During the trial, fifteen-year-old Tiffany stood in the dock, and, with her pregnancy showing, told the packed court room everything her father had done to her. Although Kyle admitted his crime, he walked away from court a free boy.

According to Callum Nixon's file, he had been beaten by his father on a regular basis throughout his life. During a physical examination upon him entering Starling House, evidence of old injuries had been noted. His father must have hit him hard and often to sustain such signs of abuse.

Mark Parker had witnessed years of his father physically and mentally abusing his mother. When she left for sanctuary, he turned on Mark. His medical records showed signs of historic beatings, and his back was covered in burn scars.

So Sian appeared to be right. Upbringing was a definite factor in why these boys went on to kill. Lee Marriott's parents had been overprotective. They refused him a life of his own and

148

smothered him with their rules. He had rebelled against them in the only way he knew how. It was either kill them or, probably, take his own life.

Craig Hodge had killed his parents and his aunt and uncle. A psychiatric report dated before his crimes took place showed he had disturbed views on the world and was often paranoid his family were acting against him. A brain scan showed shadowing on his brain. Again, this was before the car crash which killed his parents. Was he led to kill because of his upbringing or from the way his brain was wired?

Then there was Lewis Chapman. Why had he decided to kill his little brother? Had he simply been watching too many horror films and become blurred with reality? Was he really just evil or was there something inside him which connected with killing? Maybe there was a chemical imbalance in his brain. Something else for him to Google when he got home.

TWENTY-THREE

'Would you like an apricot Danish?'

Matilda was taken aback. ACC Valerie Masterson often offered a coffee whenever Matilda entered her office but this was the first time she had a plate of pastries presented to her. Had Sian been baking again?

'Erm ... thank you,' Matilda replied, gingerly taking one.

'We can all do with a sugar rush from time to time.'

Matilda took a small bite. It tasted nice: moist and fluffy. But Matilda was suspicious and that tasted foul.

'I'm sure you already know about Sally Meagan's book being released tomorrow. Have you seen the adverts and interviews in the newspapers?' Valerie began, settling herself in behind her oversized desk.

So it's a 'sorry to hear your reputation is being dragged through the press' Danish.

'I've seen the adverts, yes,' was all Matilda could say with a mouthful.

'I want you to know that you have my full support on this. I've had a journalist from the *Daily Mail* phone – they're running a feature tomorrow. He wanted to know if we want to reply. I said no. Once the book is finally out it will all die down. By next

150

week the world will have moved on. You can cope with that, can't you?'

Matilda swallowed but the pastry stuck in her throat. 'I have to.'

'The feature seems to focus on you and the investigation. I suppose from the press point of view you're a more interesting aspect of the story. I'm sure the book will focus more on Carl.'

Don't you believe it. I'm mentioned on pages 3,4,7,12,28,35,55,61 …

'Now,' Valerie clapped her hands together, 'how's everything going with Starling House? Have you identified a suspect yet?'

'Not yet. Do you know anything about the woman who runs it? Kate Moloney?'

'Not a thing. I know she's been there since it opened but it's a building shrouded in mystery.'

'You can say that again. I think she's hiding something, but I don't know what. I get the feeling Ryan Asher's death could have been avoided if it wasn't for a lack of something.'

'A lack of what?'

'I don't know. Maybe a security issue. I've got Christian out there now going over the whole place.'

'It's got to be one of the other boys, surely.'

'I'm not ruling anything out.'

'We've managed to keep the press at bay so far but, once they find out, I'm going to have the council, the government, the Home Office, victim support groups, you name it, calling me and demanding answers. This cannot run and run.' The sheen of sweat on her forehead and the dark circles under her eyes were evident this case was causing Valerie a great deal of distress.

Matilda frowned. It was unusual for the unflappable ACC to allow a case to get to her. If there were any failings at Starling House then it would be Kate Moloney and her staff who were to blame.

'How are your team dealing with it?' Val asked, taking a long drink of coffee with a shaking hand.

'They're fine. Professional, as always.'

'There's no resentment, no feelings of animosity towards the inmates?'

'No. Should there be?'

'Starling House has seven violent young men living there. It can have a serious effect on people when they're dealing with child killers, especially when they have children of their own. Is Sian coping?'

Matilda almost sniggered. 'Sian is one of the most capable people I know. If she—'

'If she what?' Val asked.

'No. It's nothing.' A thought had struck Matilda. If Val is worried about the effects of being surrounded by killers on her officers, what about the staff at Starling House? It would affect them in the same way too. Maybe one of them has finally snapped. Kate Moloney had been there from the beginning. In twenty years, what had being surrounded by murderers done to her state of mind?

Thomas Hartley enjoyed being in the library. He preferred being here to the recreation room with its loud voices, clacking of pool balls, banging of the table football, and the television at high volume. He liked the peace and quiet the library offered. However, that peace was shattered now it was being used as a free-for-all. A battered table tennis table had been dragged out of storage and set up in the centre of the room.

'Thomas,' Callum Nixon called out, 'we want a fourth for table tennis doubles. Get your arse over here.'

Thomas looked up over the book he was reading and shook his head.

'Come on, don't be a tosser. What about you, Jacob?' he asked the sixteen-year-old in the corner of the room flicking through a magazine.

'No, thanks. I smashed my wrist on the table last time. It still hurts.'

''Course you did. Too much wanking you mean. Come on, one of you poofs had better come and play. Lee, get up here and play, and I'll let you blow me off later.'

'Fuck off, Callum.' Any comment on being gay was always thrown at Lee Marriott. It was completely unnecessary, but his very smooth complexion and long blond hair gave him a feminine look which made him the target for homophobic jibes, and Callum used it as another way to get under Lee's skin.

'Come on, lads. If you don't play, I'll do to you what I did to Ryan Asher.'

A heavy silence fell on the room and everyone turned to look at Callum. He had a cruel smile but his eyes were cold and staring. Was he serious? The boys looked at each other and put their heads down. They didn't want to be a part of this. If Callum really had killed Ryan then they would rather not know any other details so they wouldn't have to lie when questioned further.

'I'll play, Callum, if it'll shut you up,' Jacob said, throwing his magazine down.

'Good lad.'

The foursome began playing table tennis but nobody's mind was on the game. Callum was enjoying himself, but the others kept exchanging steely glances.

Thomas continued to read, but he wasn't taking in the plot. Lewis tried to concentrate on some maths Call Me Fred had given him but he was making simple errors. The atmosphere was dark and heavy. They all wanted to leave, go to a different part of the building, but none of them were allowed. Thomas looked up through the toughened glass in the door. There was a uniformed police officer standing guard outside the room. He hoped he could hear what was being said in here.

They all knew the reason why they were here – they were murderers – but in the relaxed environment of the recreation room, the gym, and the library, they were teenage lads messing around. Suddenly, the thought that one of them wanted to be the last man standing was too terrifying to contemplate. Suddenly, they all knew how their victims felt.

JACOB BROWN

Bristol. April 2014

There was a gang of four of us – me, Darryl Price, Steven Richards, and Pablo Romero. We all fancied Natalie Barker. It wasn't difficult to see why; she was fit as fuck. She'd moved to Bristol from London during the Christmas holiday and when we went back to school in January she was sitting opposite me in English. It was love at first sight. Well, it was for me, anyway.

She was so hot. She was tall, fit, had light brown wavy hair which went just past her shoulders and bounced when she walked. Her eyes were light blue and hypnotic. She had full red lips and a natural pout; none of this fake Victoria Beckham shit some of the girls tried to do. No, Natalie was naturally hot. She had great legs too, and her white shirt was always tight. I used to watch her playing netball when I should have been playing basketball.

I often watched her. It was difficult not to. She was hypnotic. I eventually learned her timetable by heart. When I hadscience, she had English. When I was skipping maths, she was doing art. Our lunchtimes were the same, and I'd always make sure she was ahead of me in the queue. She always sat with Ramona Park, and I'd sit a few rows away watching her eat. I've never been jealous of a salad sandwich before but I'd give anything for her to put me in her mouth like that.

At the end of January, we had a big snowstorm. I was late leaving school because that prick Mr Hutchinson had made me stay behind for fighting with James Baxter at lunch. He didn't have to stay behind, though, just because his mother was on the board of governors. Anyway, by the time I left school the snow was coming down really heavy. Just across the road was Natalie Barker. This was my perfect opportunity to talk to her – finally.

As I passed the bus stop there was an old woman. She had an umbrella poking out of one of those annoying trolley things. I swiped it and ran to catch Natalie up. I asked if I could walk her home. She looked up at me and smiled. It was a great smile. She thanked me and I put the umbrella over her.

The journey should have only taken five minutes but the snow slowed us down. At one point she slipped and grabbed on to my arm to stop herself from falling. She flashed me that smile again. Blimey, she could stop traffic with that smile.

We reached her front door, and she thanked me. I loved her accent. It was so soft, so posh. She lived in a better part of Bristol than I did. I lived in a maisonette on a shitty council estate with burnt-out cars and a drug addict on every landing. Natalie lived on a tree-lined street with driveways; people looked after their gardens.

Natalie leaned up and kissed me on the cheek. Her lips were so warm on my cold face. I almost melted. Before I could think, I asked her out on Saturday. She said yes. She said fucking yes. I couldn't believe it. Me and Natalie Barker – get in!

On my way home I texted Darryl, Steven, and Pablo. *I've got a date with Natalie Barker. Jealous?* Of course they were jealous. They all wanted her, and I'd got her, me.

Saturday went well. We had a walk around town, went for a burger, then to the cinema. On the back seat of the bus on the way home we snogged. She pulled my hand away when I tried to put it up her skirt. Apart from that, it was a good date and we arranged to go out again the following Saturday.

From then on, I walked her home on the nights I didn't have detention, and we went out every Saturday too. We were very different people but it worked. Her dad was high up in banking; my dad ran out on my mum almost as soon as she told him she was pregnant. Natalie's mum was a GP; mine worked cash-in-hand at the local corner shop. Natalie was academic, always getting As and read for pleasure. I couldn't give a toss about anything like that. I've had four copies of *Frankenstein* off Mr Hall, and they've all been used for blocking the bogs in the bus station.

We'd been going out for just over a month when the subject of sex came up. I was gagging for it. I thought of shagging Natalie every night. I asked her if she wanted to do it, and she said she did. It would be her first time (mine too, but I didn't tell her that) and she wanted it to be special. She wanted it to be in a bed, not in a bus shelter or in the park at night. I kept trying to find somewhere for us to go but couldn't come up with anything, and I couldn't afford a hotel.

Then Mum said she was going away for the weekend with her new boyfriend. That was a shock in itself; she never usually told me anything, just took herself off and left a twenty pound note under the kettle with a note telling me to feed myself. I told Natalie my house would be free, and she was up for it. I couldn't believe it.

I had Pablo drooling. Darryl asked me to take photos, and that pervert Steven asked me to set up a webcam. I did like the idea of filming it to re-watch, but I doubted Natalie would be up for that. Not yet, anyway.

That Saturday, we went to the cinema and watched *Pompeii*. It was a shit film, but the effects were good. After, we went back to mine. I ordered us a pizza and we got comfortable on the sofa.

We kissed and it started to get heavy. I unbuttoned her top and lifted up her skirt. She had an amazing arse: small, firm, I wanted to bite it. She jumped up when I tried to put my finger inside her. She didn't like that. I'd seen it in a porno and it looked hot, but, each to their own. After a while, I took her hand and led her upstairs.

I'd spent all morning cleaning my room – something I hadn't done for years. I took down the footy posters and hid all my magazines in Mum's room. It looked nice. It looked grown-up.

We were on my bed. Natalie's top was undone, her skirt was off, and I was just in my boxers when she jumped up and said she couldn't do this. She said she thought she was ready but she obviously wasn't. She started getting dressed. She started talking about wanting her first time to be special again. I told her it was; we were in a bed for fuck's sake. I begged her not to leave and told her that I really fancied her. She had to stay. Then I accidently let slip that I'd told the lads we were doing it that night. She was well pissed about that.

Natalie Barker was hot. Everyone knew that. I wasn't keeping it to myself that we were going all the way. She went downstairs saying all kinds of things under her breath. She was fuming. She was at the bottom putting on her coat, while I was still struggling into my jeans.

She ran out of the house, and I eventually caught up with her at the bottom of the road at the bus stop. It was gone eleven so the buses had stopped running. I invited her to come back with me. I'd let her sleep in my mum's room and I'd stay in mine. We didn't have to do anything if she didn't want to.

She started calling me all sorts then, a pervert, a deviant – other words I'd never even heard before. She said I was only after one thing. I knew the score. She was a posh tart from London and I was her bit of rough. I bet her and her snobby friends were laughing at me behind my back. When we got to bed she realized she'd gone too far and tried to back out. Well, you know something, you can't treat people like that.

She stormed off and headed for the park to go home. I followed her. I kept calling her name, telling her to come back, to not turn away from me while I was talking, but she ignored me. I caught up with her, grabbed her arm and dragged her into the woods. What did she expect from me? I was a bit of rough; after all, I was just acting how she expected.

She kicked me on the shin. I pulled her again, and she tried to kick me in the balls but I jumped back. I slapped her with the back of my hand. She looked shocked. She tried to run but I grabbed her again and slammed her hard against a tree. She banged her head and was a bit dazed. I threw her down onto the ground and climbed on top of her. She struggled but I was stronger. I pulled her skirt up and tore her pants off. She started yelling but it was obvious she wanted it. I know she did.

I pulled my jeans down and realized my mobile was in my pocket. She couldn't tease me like this and expect me to just let her go. The whole school were going to know she liked it rough in the woods. She screamed so I put my hand over her mouth to shut up her. It was actually quite difficult concentrating on filming her and shagging her at the same time. It didn't take long, and she soon relaxed into it as she stopped moving. It was only when I'd come inside her that I noticed how hard I'd had my hand over her mouth and nose. She'd stopped breathing. Shit! She lay there; her angelic face was cut and bruised. Shit! Shit! FUCK!

I was hoping the scabs on my hands would have gone by the time the police came round, but they hadn't. If that old bloke hadn't been walking his Alsatian through the woods she wouldn't have been found straightaway. I had to confess. I had no choice. My DNA would be all over her. I genuinely loved Natalie but she really shouldn't have teased me like that. No girl should ever tease like that.

TWENTY-FOUR

'Mr Percival?'

'Call me Fred.'

Sian Mills and Rory Fleming sat down opposite the six foot three tutor in the staffroom of Starling House. He had a permanent smile on his face that was halfway between a grin and a smirk. Sian took an instant dislike to him, which was unusual for her.

Fred Percival was in his mid-fifties. He was rapidly balding and his thinning dark hair was greased to his scalp. His face was as shiny as his polyester suit.

'What's your role here at Starling House?'

'I'm the tutor. I'm no professor, obviously, but I teach basic literacy and numeracy skills.'

'Do you live on the premises?'

'Monday to Thursday. I go home on Friday afternoon and come back again on Monday morning.'

'Where is home for you?' Rory asked, looking up from his notepad.

'Birmingham,' he said, purposely thickening his Brummie accent.

'It's a long way to come for work.'

'That's why I live in.'

'How long have you worked here?'

'About three years.'

'So why Starling House?'

'There was a job vacancy and I needed one. Simple.'

'What did you do before coming here?' Rory asked.

'Quantity surveyor.'

'Bit of a difference.'

'I went on a course after I was made redundant. If you've got a degree you're halfway to being a tutor. It's not rocket science.'

'How do you get on with the boys here?' Sian asked.

Call Me Fred crossed and uncrossed his legs and adjusted himself to be more comfortable. He was too tall for the plastic seat he was perched on. 'I teach them. That's it. I don't have to get on with them.'

'Are they well behaved?'

'Some of them.'

'But not all?'

'Well, of course not. You know what boys are like.'

'I don't, actually,' Rory said. 'What are boys like?'

'Well, some of them want to learn; some of them don't.'

'So they misbehave?'

'Some of them do.'

'Are you strict?'

'You have to be, don't you? If they see you as weak they'll take the piss and walk all over you.'

'Is there any inmate in particular who has taken the piss lately?' Rory asked.

Sian noticed Fred's hands were twitching.

'Not to my knowledge. They all try it on at least once.'

'Did you speak to Ryan Asher on Monday?'

'Yes.'

'What about?'

'We talked about how academic he was, what lessons he enjoyed, what books he liked to read.'

'What did you think of him?'

'He was quiet, nervous. They all are when they first arrive. He seemed like a bright kid. He took a numeracy test which he passed with flying colours.'

'Are they usually so bright?' Rory asked.

'Who?'

'Killers?'

'I can't speak for all of them, obviously, but the ones I've taught have limited brain power.'

'So you're saying they have below-average intelligence?'

'Yes.'

'Interesting.'

Sian could see what Rory was doing: compiling more data for his personal investigation. 'Were you shocked to hear he'd been killed?' she quickly asked, regaining control of the interview.

'Of course I was. We don't have any trouble here which is surprising when you think about it.'

'Where were you on Monday night?'

'I was in bed. I had a bit of a headache so I went to bed early and watched a few episodes of *Frasier*.'

'No one can verify that I take it.'

'Nope,' he smiled, or grinned.

'OK. Thank you for your time,' Sian said with a forced smile.

'What's it like to work here?' Rory asked as Fred stood up to leave the room.

'I like it. The staff are pleasant, and the majority of the boys I've taught over the years have been a pleasure to teach.'

They waited until he had left the room and his giant footsteps could no longer be heard before they spoke.

'The staff aren't pleasant at all,' Rory said once he knew Call Me Fred was out of earshot. 'Have you seen them? They're all miserable buggers. I don't think I've seen one of them smile yet. Apart from him. I wonder if he's had that smile stapled on.'

'What was that all about?' Sian said quietly.

162

'What?'

'Questioning about the intelligence levels of killers.'

'I was interested,' he shrugged.

'We're not here to look into brain patterns of killers, Rory. You need to focus on these interviews, understand?' she said, raising her voice slightly.

'Sorry,' he said, head down. 'So what did you think of Fred?'

'I didn't like him. There's something oily about him.'

'Probably the stuff he puts on what's left of his hair,' Rory sniggered.

'No it's not that. He comes across as a touchy-feely kind of bloke.'

'You think he's messing with some of the boys?'

'He probably isn't, but I wouldn't be surprised if he was.'

'It's not like you to make snap judgements, Sian. You're spending too much time with Aaron.'

'Hmm,' she replied, deep in thought. 'Make a note to run a check on him, Rory. There's something there and I can't put my finger on it.'

Richard Grover was next to be interviewed after Call Me Fred. He slumped down in the plastic chair in the staffroom. It creaked under his heavy frame. His breathing was laboured as if he had walked up several flights of stairs, even though they were on the ground floor. In his forties, Richard Grover was grossly overweight. His eyes were almost lost in the rolls of fat on his face, and he didn't so much as sit on the chair than perch. His pea green uniform strained at the seams.

'How long have you worked here, Richard?' Sian asked.

'Let's see. I was at Greggs from 2000 until 2003,' he said to himself, looking up at the ceiling as if the answer was written there. 'Then I was at Gunstones for a while until my operation. I was off for a while with that. I'd say about four years maybe.'

'OK. Do you live on the premises?'

'We all do. I only live in Derby. It's not far away but I don't like driving at night – with my eyes – so I stay here on shift days.'

'What's your relationship like with the other staff?'

He looked taken aback by that question. 'It's fine. We get along OK. Have a chat and a laugh.'

'Have there ever been any problems with staff?'

'In what way?'

'Any disciplinary matters, maybe?'

'Who's been talking?' he asked defensively.

'Nobody. Why do you ask?' Sian asked, sitting forward on her chair, suddenly interested.

'It's just … no … nothing.'

'Go on,' prompted Rory.

'Look, just because she's my cousin it doesn't mean I'm responsible for her, does it?'

'Sorry, because who's your cousin?'

'Elly Caine.'

'Who's Elly Caine?' Sian looked down at her list of all the staff members. There was no mention of an Elly Caine there.

'She used to work here.'

'When?'

'About a year or so ago. She wasn't here long.'

'And what happened to her?'

'She was … told to leave,' he replied, choosing his words carefully.

'Why?'

'Look, it's got nothing to do with me. I wasn't even on shift. You should speak to Mrs Moloney.'

'I'm asking you, Richard,' Sian raised her voice. 'You've just said you're family. I'm guessing you discussed it at some point.'

Richard's eyes travelled around the room. The expression on his face showed he was debating whether to reveal all or act dumb. A sheen of sweat appeared on his forehead and a bead slid down the side of his face.

'She hit an inmate,' he blurted out.

Sian and Rory exchanged glances.

'She was provoked. I believe her. Look, you don't know what it's like working in here. It's like a pressure cooker. They may be young lads but they're vicious bastards. They've got tempers. They've vindictive. Once they find your weak spot they'll press it and press it until you explode. That's what Elly did.'

'Who did she hit?' Rory asked.

'Jacob Brown.'

'So, on one hand we've got some members of staff saying everyone gets on and everything is happy and normal. Then on the other hand it's a pressure cooker and people are on the verge of snapping on a daily basis.'

Matilda was sitting in the boardroom of Starling House listening to the report from Sian and Rory about the staff they interviewed.

'It sounds to me like the staff are as unreliable as the inmates,' Rory said.

'I think you might be right there. I've thought Kate Moloney was hiding something from the moment I saw her. She's obviously keeping this Elly Caine woman to herself. I'm guessing Kate didn't give you her file?'

'No,' Sian replied. 'She only gave me the files on the current staff. None for the ones who no longer work here.'

'Right, go back to her and ask for all the files. Every single one of them. And find out where this Elly Caine is.'

'Will do.'

'Bloody hell, Sian,' Matilda sat back in her chair, exasperated. 'I'm really missing your chocolate drawer.'

TWENTY-FIVE

Pat Campbell was in her element. She rarely got the chance to drive these days. Anton said he didn't trust her behind the wheel as she was too impatient with other road users. However, on this occasion, Pat was driving while Anton studied the copy of Thomas Hartley's file that Matilda had given her. They were on their way to Manchester, ostensibly to do a bit of shopping and have a bite to eat (that's what they'd told their son), but really to track down some people Thomas Hartley knew and find out if he really was capable of butchering his entire family.

'It says here that Daniel Hartley was very vociferous about migrants coming to live in Manchester ... '

'Does it actually say vociferous?' Pat interrupted.

'No it says vocal.'

'Then say vocal then. Don't be so bloody pretentious.'

'Either way he was very outspoken when it came to foreigners entering the country. He attended rallies and protests and was arrested twice. Maybe that got him killed.'

Anton Campbell was a retired university lecturer. He had spent the majority of his career teaching physics at the University of Sheffield. As much as he enjoyed his job, the constant budget cuts, red tape, and bureaucracy sucked out all his love for the profession, and he took early retirement when Pat did. He was a tall man in his mid-sixties with a full head of brown wavy hair with just a hint of silver. He was active and went swimming most days. He loved a puzzle and was often engrossed in a crossword. When Pat had told him about the Thomas Hartley mystery, he jumped at the chance to become an amateur sleuth.

'Was he a racist?'

'I don't think so,' Anton said, scanning the various statements in the folder. 'He's quoted in the *Manchester Evening News* as saying he doesn't mind foreigners coming into England, providing they come here to work, speak English, and not sponge off our NHS and benefits. Is that racist?'

'Who knows today? It sounds like he's standing up for his beliefs.'

'People do get killed for their beliefs.'

'Yes, but they're usually political leaders and heads of state – not … what was it Daniel did for a living?'

'He was a rep for a confectionery company.'

'There you are then.'

'We all have to start somewhere. Do you think Saddam Hussein left college and applied for a job as a dictator?'

'So what are you saying: Daniel Hartley sold fun-size bags of Maltesers by day and was a Nazi sympathizer by night?'

Anton thought for a second. 'It's possible.'

'No. If someone killed him because of his beliefs he would have been shot in his car or beaten to death on his way home at night. He, his wife, and his eight-year-old daughter were literally hacked to death. The killer knew them and wanted them all to suffer. He, for arguments sake let's call the killer a he, hated the Hartleys so much that he wanted to obliterate them.'

'So it's a personal crime then?'

'Exactly.'

'So why not kill Thomas too?'

'I'm not sure. Hang on, doesn't it say in the file that Ruby used to go to her parents' bed when she couldn't sleep?'

'Yes.'

'Maybe the parents were just the target. The killer got into the house, went to kill Daniel and Laura, found Ruby in bed with them and killed her too.'

'Again, why not Thomas?'

'Because their argument wasn't with the children.'

'But if you've just killed an eight-year-old girl you're not going to have any qualms over killing a fourteen-year-old boy.'

'Anton, look … oh we're here.' Pat was pleased they had arrived at their destination as she had no idea how she was going to finish that sentence.

Anton had raised an interesting question: when you're killing an entire family, why leave one person behind? If the killer was known to the Hartleys then he would have known how many people were in the house. It wouldn't have taken long to find Thomas and kill him like he just killed his father, mother, and sister. Another question: how had Thomas managed to sleep through an entire massacre? She knew teenagers enjoyed their sleep, but a mass murder would wake them up, surely.

Pat was beginning to have doubts about Matilda's theory. Yes, she saw a timid and frightened young boy in Starling House, but maybe he was finally sorry for what he had done. Or, maybe he was a very talented actor.

TWENTY-SIX

Faith and Scott were sitting in a coffee shop close to Norwich Crown Court at Bishopgate. As usual, Scott was hungry. The large latte, panini, and double chocolate chip muffin would keep him going until lunchtime – and that was only two hours away.

'How do you manage to stay so slim when you're eating all that?' Faith said as she gave her green tea and mini biscotti a pathetic glance.

'I have a high metabolism,' he said, tearing a huge chunk off his tomato and mozzarella panini. 'Also, I go to the gym with Rory four times a week and I go running at the weekends.'

'I should hate you. You're so bloody perfect. You've even got great skin.'

'Yeah, I'm a real catch,' he said with a mouthful.

'You are. Look at you, tall, good-looking, great hair – why aren't the girls flocking around you?'

Scott blushed slightly. 'If you didn't have a boyfriend, I'd think you were flirting with me, Miss Easter.' He gave a nervous smile. He hated personal conversations. Fortunately, a barista dropped a tray full of mugs and their attention was drawn in his direction. Once the laughter and applause had died down, the subject changed to safer territory – like a killer on the loose in Starling House.

'There are some court cases that stay with you. The Ryan Asher case is one of them.'

The court usher, Gerald McCarthy, was getting ready to attend another case that had been delayed due to the judge being stuck in traffic. He was in his black gown but had not yet put on his wig, which was sitting next to him like a faithful cat. He was a tall man with bug-like eyes and a prominent Adam's apple. The broken capillaries on his face were evidence he enjoyed a liquid lunch. His shaking hands were a clear sign he lived on his nerves.

'It was standing room only most of the time,' he continued. 'We had to turn people away.'

'Was that just because it was a high profile case, or supporters of Ryan Asher and his family?' Scott asked.

'If memory serves me correctly, there weren't many of his family there. His mum and dad and maybe one or two others. It's usually old women and gawkers.'

'We read online that there was an incident. One guy had to be removed from the public gallery or something?' Scott asked, not wanting to prompt Gerald, or lead him into giving a false statement.

'That's right, I forgot about him,' Gerald replied, pausing while tying his shoelaces to look up. 'Funny looking guy. Big moustache. Tall and thin. He turned up every day in the beginning. Then he just suddenly burst into this tirade about how it was all the parent's fault, that they didn't bring him up properly. He really laid into them.'

'Who was he?' Faith asked.

'I've no idea. It took three security personnel to drag him out of the court room. We called the police and they took him away – probably just gave him a caution because we didn't see him again after that.'

'Did the Asher family know who he was?'

'No. I asked – can't remember her name – a woman; she was always comforting Mrs Asher. I took her to be her sister or something. Anyway, I apologized for the disturbance, like you do, and asked her if she knew who he was. I mean, it was a family case, wasn't it? He killed his grandparents. The only people who should be baying for blood should be the family. But she said she'd never seen him before in her life.'

Scott and Faith exchanged a frowned expression.

'And you've never seen him since?'

'Nope. And I'm good with faces. Names I forget as soon as I've heard them. But I never forget a face.'

'Would there be CCTV footage of him being escorted out of court?'

'Not after all this time.'

The door opened and a small woman popped her head through. 'Gerald, the judge has arrived.' She disappeared just as quickly.

'Right, that's me. Time to wig up and get to it.'

'What's the case today?' Scott asked as all three of them left the room.

'Start of a new trial. A teenage boy killed his twin sister,' he shook his head. 'It makes you wonder what this world's coming to doesn't it?'

'What's he pleading?'

'Not guilty. He'll probably end up at your Starling House.' He let out a huge belly laugh that ricocheted around the open reception then he disappeared among the throng of visitors in the direction of the courts. With his maniacal laugh and flowing black cape he looked like a superhero heading into battle.

'A tall man with a big moustache. It doesn't give us much to go on, does it?' Faith sighed.

'No. It doesn't,' Scott said, not paying any attention to Faith.

171

'Come on, we'd better go and book into the hotel before they give our reservation away.'

Faith stood up to leave but noticed Scott sitting on the bench. He looked pensive.

'What's wrong?' She asked.

'Nothing. I just had a thought: why would you attend a trial if you had nothing to do with the case?'

'To be nosey I suppose.'

'Or maybe you're planning something depending on the outcome.'

'You think Ryan's murder was planned long before he ended up at Starling House?'

'I don't know,' Scott mused with a heavy frown. 'It was a quick flash of something that stayed in my head for seconds then just flew out. Ryan was killed after only a day in Starling House. It's like he was killed at the first opportunity to get him alone.'

'But if that's the case then the killer is someone connected to the family, and also to Starling House.'

'So either the family is hiding something,' Scott continued Faith's thought, 'or someone at Starling House is.'

TWENTY-SEVEN

Matilda looked out of a top floor window at Starling House overlooking the driveway. It was a cloudy day and a fine mist covered the landscape. The view was limited but there was a good angle of the entrance gates and winding drive. She watched as a dark red Audi crawled gently over the gravel. It didn't stop at the main doors but turned left into the staff car park and parked in the bay for visitors. After a short while, the driver's door opened and an elderly man struggled to climb out. The low autumnal sun bounced off his bald head. He took a tweed fedora from the passenger seat and placed it carefully on his head. From the boot he took a heavy-looking briefcase, then locked the car. He took long strides to the main entrance. Matilda hoped the uniformed officers would stop him entering.

Matilda reached the foyer just as the smart looking man with the bushy moustache was talking to the uniformed officers.

'Can I help you, at all?' Matilda asked.

'Ma'am, this man says he works here,' one of the officers said.

'Really?'

'Yes. I'm Dr Henrik Klein. I'm a therapist. Has something happened?'

Matilda baulked at the word therapist, remembering an

appointment was due with her own in a few days' time. It seemed she couldn't get away from them at work or in her private life.

'There has been an incident. Would it be possible to have a word—?'

An alarm sounded, interrupting the conversation between Matilda and Dr Klein. A troop of officers came out of different doors and flew down the corridor behind the stairs. Kate Moloney stepped out of her office.

'Matilda, Henrik, come in here. Now,' she shouted abruptly.

'What's going on?' Matilda asked, following Kate inside.

'A fight has broken out in the library. The alarm is just a precaution until it's under control,' Kate said as she closed the door and locked it behind her.

'Is that necessary?'

'A fight can lead to other things.'

Matilda pulled her mobile phone out of her pocket and dialled Sian's number.

'What's going on?' Sian shouted down the phone. An alarm speaker in the boardroom was drowning out what she was saying.

'There's been a fight in the library. Get everyone into the boardroom and lock yourselves in until you hear from me.'

'What? I can't hear what you're saying.'

Matilda repeated her warning, screaming down the phone.

'Shouldn't we help?'

'Not until we're asked to do so. It could be a storm in a teacup, in which case our presence would only escalate the situation. Just lock the doors.'

'Oh, right. OK. Will do.'

Matilda hung up. 'How often do these kinds of things happen?'

'Surprisingly, not as often as you'd think,' Kate said, returning to her desk. 'However, you get a bunch of boys together, tempers can flare up over the slightest of things. And remember, these are not ordinary boys, are they? So, I see you've met Dr Klein. Henrik, this is DCI Matilda Darke. She's investigating the murder of Ryan Asher.'

'Nice to meet you,' Henrik said, holding out a hand for Matilda to shake.

'Likewise,' she shook his hand, a firm grip for someone on the wrong side of seventy.

'I'm sorry … murder?' he asked, as if only just hearing Kate.

'Yes, Dr Klein. Ryan was found stabbed to death in the recreation room on Tuesday morning.'

'But he only arrived on Sunday. What happened? Was there a fight?'

'No. No, there wasn't a fight,' Kate said quietly. 'Nobody seems to know what happened,' she added, giving Matilda an icy look.

'How's the investigation going?' Henrik asked, fighting against the noise of the alarm.

'We're making progress.' The standard reply. 'I've got officers down in Norwich talking to Ryan's family. Don't you think we should help out?' Matilda asked, pointing at the door.

'Trust me, we're in the safest place.' Kate said.

'I don't like this,' Rory said, pacing the boardroom. 'I mean, what if there's a fire or something? We could be trapped up here.'

'Rory, come and sit down.'

There were five detectives in the room. While the alarm was sounding there was obviously nothing they could concentrate on, so they downed tools and waited for the situation to end. Rory was the only one fretting.

'What if they're rioting?'

'I think we'd have heard,' Sian smiled.

'You can't hear anything over that bloody thing,' he pointed to the alarm. 'They could have set fire to the furniture; they could have made weapons; taken hostages, anything.'

'Rory, calm down for crying out loud. Nothing like that is happening.'

He loosened the collar on his shirt. 'I don't like being locked in.'

Sian went over to him and guided him to the window. She opened it wide and allowed in the stiff breeze. Despite it being cold there was a sheen of sweat on Rory's forehead.

'Now, take deep breaths and try to relax.'

The fresh air took a while to calm Rory down. The screaming of the alarm did nothing to help him at all. Eventually, he felt relaxed enough to pull himself back into the room. He slumped down into a seat.

'I'm sorry. I don't usually panic like that.'

'That's all right.'

'I don't like not being able to get out. It frightens me. The first time I went into a prison was a nightmare. I was supposed to be interviewing this guy who'd admitted more crimes once he'd been sentenced. I was useless. It's lucky I recorded the interview as I had no idea what he said. I just kept thinking about what would happen if there was a fire or an explosion or something. I couldn't get out of the place quick enough.'

'You need to think rationally, Rory. Take lifts, for example. A lift in a busy hospital goes up and down several hundred times a day, thousands of times a week. If the cable snapped and it plunged to the ground don't you think something like that would be on the news? Now when was the last time you heard of that happening?'

'Never,' he replied.

'Exactly. Your thinking is irrational.'

'But, in this job, situations like this are heightened.'

'Yes, they are but none of us in this room have ever been caught up in a riot. Despite what the films tell us, being a copper is incredibly boring.'

'You can say that again,' said one of the DCs whose primary job seemed to be inputting data into the HOLMES system.

Rory looked up at Sian. 'I miss your snack drawer,' he said.

This triggered a laugh from around the room.

'So do I,' she said. 'I bet the rest of CID have cleaned it out by now. Greedy buggers.'

The alarm continued for fifteen minutes. As soon as a heavy silence fell, Kate opened the door to her office. All three of them stepped out into the corridor in time to see Oliver Byron walking a handcuffed and bloody Jacob Brown to the medical room.

'What's happened?'

'The usual. Callum Nixon was up to his old tricks again and Jacob snapped.'

'Wasn't there a guard in there with them?'

'No. The police keep pulling them off their duties for interviewing. I don't know where half of them are. We can't keep working like this, Kate,' Oliver said, looking at Matilda with scorn.

Kate was looking at Jacob's face. He had a bloody nose, and a black eye was already forming but he'd live. 'How's Callum?'

On mentioning his name, Callum was brought around the corner flanked by two officers either side. His face was a mess, but it probably looked worse due to the amount of blood that was covering him.

'A few cuts—'

'I'm the innocent party, Mrs Moloney,' Callum shouted, his voice muffled by the blood in his throat and his thick lips. 'I was minding my own business when Jacob here just jumped on me.'

'You fucking liar, Callum. He's been pissing me off all day. I'm not just going to sit there while he says crap like that.'

'I was just telling him about this thing I'd read online about blokes who are violent to women because they can't form proper relationships with them, maybe because they've got a small dick.' He smiled but the pain in doing so caused him to flinch.

'You're a twat, Callum. You should be put down.'

'That'll do, both of you,' Kate shouted above them. 'Oliver, take them both to the medical room and get them patched up. We'll talk about this later.'

Oliver was leading them both away when Callum looked at Matilda.

'Hel-lo, how are you doing, love? Fancy kissing my lips better? I've got some swelling down here you can help with too,' he said, grabbing his crotch.

'Piss off!' Matilda exclaimed.

Callum was dragged away down the corridor. He glanced over his shoulders and blew kisses towards Matilda.

'Is he always like that?'

'A complete shit? Absolutely,' Kate said, disappearing back into her office.

'Am I still needed here today?' Dr Henrik Klein asked.

'Now more than ever, Dr Klein,' Kate replied over her shoulder.

'Am I able to use my usual room?'

'Of course.'

Dr Klein nodded and headed off down the corridor.

Matilda followed Kate back into the office and closed the door behind her. She sat down in front of Kate's desk and crossed her legs. She intended being here for a while, much to Kate's obvious discomfort if her bemused facial expression was anything to go by.

'Kate, I wanted to ask you about visiting. Do the inmates get regular visitors?'

Kate scoffed. 'Visiting hours are once a fortnight on a Tuesday afternoon. However, nobody has visited for months.'

'Really? The boys don't have any family come to see them?'

'They're killers, Inspector. If a child or yours had killed someone would you want to visit them?'

Matilda pondered the question but found she knew the answer almost straightaway. No she would not.

'Kate, who owns Starling House?'

'Since it opened it's been owned by many companies. It's

currently owned by BB Security. They're based in Northern Ireland.'

'So why buy a place in Sheffield?'

'They own several sites all over the country. Starling House was simply an addition to their portfolio.'

'Do you ever see anyone from BB Security?'

'I'm in regular contact with the management over there, and every six months we get a visit to make sure everything is running smoothly.'

'Have you contacted them yet about Ryan Asher's murder?'

A guilty look swept over Kate's face. 'No. Not yet. I'd like to give them some information as to how the case is going. I was hoping an arrest would have been made by now.'

Was that a dig?

'This is a highly unusual case. Forensics have finished work in Ryan's room. There is no sign of a disturbance; the door wasn't forced, and the only fingerprints belong to Ryan. It would appear he left his room voluntarily. Now, the only people who have a key are your staff.'

Kate shook her head. 'Do you genuinely believe one of my staff killed Ryan Asher?'

'I don't know your staff, Kate, you do. Do you think one of them could have killed him?'

Kate took a while to reply. She looked as if she was mulling over the question, thinking of every single member of staff and trying to decide if one of them could stab a fifteen-year-old boy twelve times. Which one of them was capable of that? 'To be perfectly honest, I've no idea.'

'Have you ever had any problems with your staff? Any complaints?'

'No,' she answered; too quickly for Matilda's liking.

'What's the turnover here like?'

'We have a high turnover of staff,' she admitted. 'Some people have difficulty coming to terms with the boys and their crimes.

Some of the inmates look younger than they are. They're fresh-faced, almost childlike. It's difficult to get your head around the fact they're violent individuals.'

'So people tend to leave after a while?'

'Yes. I'm not surprised when I get a knock on my door and a resignation handed to me.'

'Is there anyone here currently serving out their notice?'

'No.'

'Is it true you don't have anyone from Sheffield working here?'

'Unfortunately, yes, it is. When a vacancy becomes available I do still advertise in the local job centre but I never get any response.'

'Do you sleep here?'

'Yes, I do. The majority of the staff do. The very top floor in the eaves is divided into twelve separate rooms we use as bedrooms. Some have en suites. There's a large communal bathroom though.'

'Do the inmates have access to the top floor?'

'What are you implying?'

'I'm not implying anything. They seem to be able to move around quite freely. I've seen them walking unaccompanied from the library to the gym. I wondered where else they were allowed to go.'

'DCI Darke, this may be an extraordinary set-up here – a secure unit for teenage killers – and yes, they are prisoners, but that doesn't mean we have to keep them in cages. We have an excellent security system here and state of the art CCTV. The inmates are allowed to access limited parts of the building as and when they see fit.'

'I wouldn't call your security system excellent or state of the art. You can hear the cameras whirring away from right down the corridor. I also noticed the cameras in the recreation room are dummies. Why is that?'

Kate looked down. She was biting her bottom lip. 'The cameras were outdated and needed replacing. Unfortunately, we didn't have enough money in the budget for new ones. Gavin said he would install fake cameras until the next financial year.'

'And do BB Security know about this?' Matilda frowned at Kate's lack of emotion. Everything she said was spoken like an automated machine.

'I am not required to inform BB Security on every tiny detail of the day-to-day running of Starling House. They have every faith in my management skills.'

'I wouldn't call a lack of funding for security equipment a tiny detail.'

'I have been here for almost twenty years. I've been in charge almost eight. I am more than capable of running this place without outside interference.'

'Until now,' Matilda said with a sly smile.

'Are you questioning my leadership?'

'I am.'

'You have absolutely no right—'

Finally, a raised voice, a display of emotion.

'Mrs Moloney,' Matilda interrupted. 'You have been able to run this place without any form of supervision. You're hiding something from me, I know you are, and I intend to find out.'

'I am hiding nothing.'

'Really? Tell me about Elly Caine.'

Kate's eyes widened at the mention of the name and her lips pursed. She stopped breathing. 'Elly Caine?'

'Yes.'

'How do you know about her?'

'I just do.'

'Elly Caine,' Kate began, choking back the words, 'Elly Caine was a member of staff here. She only stayed a few months. She had trouble with the boys.'

'What kind of trouble?'

Kate closed her eyes. It was as if thinking about the woman

and what she had done caused her great physical pain. She unlocked a drawer in her desk and took out a thin brown file. She handed it across to Matilda.

'This is Elly's file. Obviously, I'd like it back. What Elly did was an incredibly dark day for Starling House. However, I sorted it out. I don't want to be reminded of it again.'

Gingerly, Matilda took the file and placed it on her lap. Kate's eyes would not leave it.

'You should have given me this earlier,' Matilda said. The terse look on her face showed she was fuming with Kate.

'I know. I'm sorry.'

'There better not be anything else you're hiding from me.'

The walls of the room felt as if they were closing in on them both. The tension had ratcheted up several degrees. 'Tell me about the inmates. I'm guessing once they reach eighteen they're moved on,' Matilda said eventually.

Kate took a slow deep breath. 'Once a place becomes available. We've had some inmates here until they're twenty. As you know the prisons are awfully overcrowded.'

'Have you had any inmates who have given you cause for concern?'

'They all give me cause for concern. When you take away someone's freedom and force them to be with people they wouldn't normally associate with on the outside, tempers can become frayed. Sometimes this place is like a volcano just waiting to erupt. It is the duty of my staff to help calm matters before they explode.'

'But that's not always possible – like we've just seen.'

'That's right. Obviously, I don't know the circumstances over this current upset, but I'm guessing it will be something incredibly simple. Maybe one of the boys was reading someone else's magazine or something petty like that.'

'After Monday night I would have thought you'd be more concerned than you seem to be.'

'DCI Darke, if I took every little outburst to heart then I'd be a nervous wreck by now and probably not in a fit state to work here.'

'So it's a stressful job.'

'Highly.'

'For you and your staff.'

'Yes.'

'Someone could just snap at any moment.'

'Ye—' Kate stopped herself. 'I suppose it's possible,' she admitted finally.

'So one of your staff could have snapped on Monday night and killed Ryan Asher?'

'Although I agree that that it is possible, Ryan was only here for a day. What could possibly have happened in that short time for one of my staff to snap – as you call it?'

'I've no idea,' Matilda said, stressing the 'I'. 'You were here. What did happen on Monday?'

'Nothing.'

'Well, something must have. Who knew Ryan was coming on Sunday night?'

'Just the staff working here at the time. We don't get a lot of notice when a new inmate is arriving, for obvious reasons.'

'You must have all suspected Ryan was going to end up here during his trial. It was well publicised. The odds were in favour of a guilty verdict.'

'Yes,' Kate nodded. 'We did talk about him coming here.'

'So, in actual fact, everyone who works here assumed Ryan Asher would end up here.'

'Yes.'

'What were people's feelings towards Ryan and his crime?'

'The same as everyone else's in the country. We're not robots, DCI Darke. At the end of the day we're people and we have families. We all knew what Ryan did and we all had our opinion. However, we're all professional and able to put our feelings to one side.'

'Well, someone obviously wasn't able to because they took Ryan from his room, laid him out on a pool table and stabbed him twelve times. Who do you think could have done that Mrs Moloney?' Matilda was getting riled. Kate's stony façade and reluctance to name any member of staff with a short fuse or a quick temper was starting to get on her nerves.

'I don't know. I genuinely, honestly, hand-on-heart, do not know,' she said, raising her voice for the first time. 'I personally hired and vetted all staff working here. Obviously, if one of them turns out to be a killer I will feel betrayed.

Kate stood up and went over to the small window in the corner of the room which looked over the rear of Starling House and the well-kept sprawling grounds. The window had bars on the outside and Matilda noticed several locks on the inside.

'DCI Darke, I'm sorry. I'm not being very helpful at all, am I? But you must see this from my point of view. I appointed the staff here so if I hired a murderer then I will feel just as guilty. My position will be untenable and I do not want to have to give this job up.'

'Kate, you have no reason to blame yourself. You said that staff often have trouble seeing a young, fresh-faced teenager as a killer. The same thing happens with an adult too.' Jonathan Harkness came into her mind. She had no idea he was a murderer when she first met the young man who was frightened of his own shadow and lived in self-induced isolation. Admitting it to herself was incredibly difficult and it took a while to come to terms with. Matilda had liked Jonathan. She had a great deal of sympathy for him. She often wondered, had she met him twenty years earlier, would she have been able to save him, prevent him from committing his crimes? Maybe. But that brings up the question of whether killers are born or created.

TWENTY-EIGHT

There was a knock on the door. Dr Henrik Klein was preparing himself for anyone who might want to come for a chat. He imagined, after the murder, several of the inmates would want to talk. He didn't expect to be troubled so soon after arriving.

'Come in,' he called.

The door opened and a young man popped his head into the room.

'Would it be possible to have a quick word?'

'Of course. Come on in.' He had never seen this man before. He was tall and good-looking with a dishevelled hairstyle which probably took a while to perfect every morning. This was not an inmate of Starling House.

'I'm DC Rory Fleming from South Yorkshire Police. I'd like to ask your advice, if I may?'

'Is this to do with the murder?'

'No. This is purely me wanting to ask a question. It's totally off the record.'

'I see.' Henrik looked bewildered. 'Well, come on in. Sit down.'

Rory did as he was told. He seemed nervous as he unbuttoned his suit jacket, smoothed out his tie, adjusted his collar, swept away imaginable dust from his trousers and tucked his hair behind his ears.

'What is it you wanted to ask me?' Henrik prompted.

'Well,' Rory cleared his throat, 'can you tell me ... how a murderer becomes a murderer?'

'What do you mean?'

'These boys in here ... I keep remembering what I was like at the age of fourteen and fifteen. I was out on my bike all the time, and I played a lot of football. It never occurred to me to kill someone.'

'Is this your first murder investigation?'

'No.'

'Why are you questioning this now?'

'I don't know what you mean.'

'You'll have met a number of killers in your career. Did you often wonder what made them become a killer?'

Rory frowned while he thought. 'No.'

'So why now?'

'Because a fourteen-year-old boy shouldn't be a killer,' Rory almost snapped.

'You're right. He shouldn't. From my point of view, you were the ideal teenager: you rode your bike and played sports – that's what a fourteen-year-old should be doing.'

'So why did these boys become killers?'

'Every case is different. However, it depends on your own theory of whether you believe a killer is born or created.'

Rory leaned on the arm rest, his head being supported by his left arm. This subject was obviously weighing heavily on his mind and it was having a deep effect on him. 'I don't believe a child is born evil.'

Henrik smiled, although it was difficult to see under his moustache. 'Neither do I. Young people who kill tend to fit into one of three categories: the large majority of them will have been abused or witnessed abuse. Maybe their father abused them or

186

their mother and they were protecting the mother from the father. Things escalated and the father ended up dead. It is this situation, where the young person is subjected to abuse, that is the most common. They're fighting back.

'The second category is if the young person is mentally ill and they haven't received any or sufficient treatment for their illness. Detecting a mental illness in a child is difficult as, more often than not, a parent will put their child's behaviour down to hormones and the perils of being a teenager.

'The third category is where the young person has a long history of severe antisocial behaviour. They will be difficult for the parent to control at home and for teachers at school. They will be emotionally detached, cruel to others, insensitive and incredibly thick-skinned.'

Henrik paused and watched Rory's expression while he took in what he said. He seemed an intelligent and capable young man. It was clear he was listening.

'Most of the boys here seem to have killed their parents. Is that normal? Well, I know it's not normal, obviously, what I mean is … is it …?'

Henrik smiled again. 'I know what you mean. Like I said, the majority of children who kill will kill a parent or relative because they're being abused or witnessing abuse. If a child is mentally ill, they will see their parents as being in the way. There was a case in France last year. A sixteen-year-old boy asked his parents for some money so he could meet a girl he had been chatting to online. They refused so he shot them. He also killed his two younger brothers and the family pets too. He then stole money from his father's bank account and caught a train to meet the girl. He was arrested when he returned home as if nothing had happened. When the police interviewed the girl he'd gone to meet she said he was charming, sweet, funny, the perfect gentleman. He displayed absolutely no signs that he'd just killed his entire family.'

'Bloody hell,' Rory uttered. 'So, the boys in here—'

'I can't comment on their mental health conditions, obviously. However, I will tell you that many of them are on medication to control or subdue their behaviour, and all of them are required to attend regular therapy sessions as part of their sentence.'

'Can a child be cured?'

'You've said yourself you don't believe a child is born evil so you must believe circumstance has led them to commit their crime. Therefore, if it is a mental illness then it can be controlled with medication and therapy.'

'It's a lot to take in,' Rory said, blowing out his cheeks.

'It is, but don't allow yourself to be consumed by it.'

'That's what my boss always says.' He smiled.

'Your boss is correct. You seem like a capable detective. You're looking at these boys wondering what you personally can do to help them, aren't you?'

'Yes.' He nodded.

'By the time you meet people like the inmates in here they've already committed their crimes. What you can do is make sure they're heard when it comes to their defence. Treat each one differently, and with respect. It's rare for people to kill just for the fun of it. Take Ryan Asher, for example; someone had a reason to kill him. They didn't do it because of what he'd done to bring him here. They did it because they felt it made sense to them. That's what you need to find out.'

'So the killer is someone who knows Ryan.'

'As Ryan wasn't here for very long, I'd say it's almost a certainty he was killed by someone who knew him.'

'So we're not looking at a fellow inmate as his killer then?'

'No,' Henrik replied firmly. 'I would stake my career on it not being a fellow inmate.'

TWENTY-NINE

Pat and Anton Campbell were sitting in Costa in the centre of Manchester. It could have been any Costa in any city in the country as they all looked alike. Pat had even chosen a two-seat table by the window like she did her favourite coffee shop in Sheffield. While Anton fetched the coffee and muffins, Pat sent a text to her son asking if he had time to meet them.

'Has he got back to you yet?' Anton asked.

'What's that?' Pat asked looking at the heavy tray Anton was carrying.

'Carrot cake.'

'You're on a diet.'

'Only in Sheffield.'

Pat struggled to hide her laughter. 'That's a cop-out if ever I heard one.'

'Today is a break from the norm so I'm having a treat. If you don't want your blueberry muffin I can take it back and buy you a packet of raisins or something.'

'Don't you bloody dare.'

Anton sat opposite his wife and greedily tucked into his large slice of carrot cake. He looked content. Pat wondered if she should slacken the reins at home and allow a packet of chocolate biscuits into the cupboard occasionally. What was the point in living a long life if you were miserable because you ate nothing but Ryvita?

Pat's phone beeped an incoming text message. 'He's on lunch in half an hour. He says he'll come and say hello.' She relayed the message to Anton.

'You're not just going to jump straight in, are you? We don't see him that often. I don't want him to think we've only come over because we want a favour.'

'I'm not totally insensitive, you know.'

Anton rolled his eyes.

Detective Sergeant John Campbell met his parents within ten minutes of receiving his mother's text. It was rare for them to come to Manchester, and he had a feeling they hadn't come to do some shopping. His father hated shopping, and his mother preferred to do it online as she always said she had more important things to do with the time she had left than trying on clothes in a fitting room cubicle the size of a public toilet.

He found them in the corner of Costa and greeted them both with a hug, then sat on the seat next to his father.

'There seems to be something growing out of your upper lip,' his mother said.

'It's called stubble, mother. I can't be bothered to shave every day.'

'Appearances are very important, John. I don't want people thinking you were dragged up to go to work looking like a vagrant.'

'Are you going to check behind my ears while you're here and ask if I'm eating enough fruit and vegetables?'

'No,' Pat replied, giving him a scornful look she only half meant. 'I will enquire as to how you and Diane are getting on.'

'Diane's fine, thanks. She's in Glasgow this week on a training course.'

'Lovely. She still doesn't want kids I take it?'

'No, she doesn't and neither do I, Mum. Don't you think you've got enough grandchildren with our Cheryl popping one out every five minutes?'

'Your father wants you to have a child so you can carry on the family name.'

'No, I don't,' Anton chimed in. 'Don't let her pressure you, John. I think it's admirable you don't want kids. It's a rotten world to bring children into. Fingers crossed Cheryl stops at five.'

'So.' John exclaimed loudly before Pat could continue. 'What's your real reason for coming over the Snake Pass?'

'I told you – shopping.'

'Where are your bags?'

'We haven't started yet.'

'It's almost two o'clock. Don't you think you should have started by now? I know how you hate driving in rush hour traffic.'

'Oh, just tell him Pat, for crying out loud,' Anton moaned, his mouth full of carrot cake.

'Tell me what?'

'I want to ask a favour,' Pat began. 'Do you remember the Hartley murders from a couple of years ago?'

'Of course I remember. I'm hardly likely to forget am I? It's the worst crime scene I've ever come across.'

'Well, Thomas Hartley is in Starling House in Sheffield.'

'I'm aware.'

'Are you aware that he's innocent.'

'You don't know that,' Anton injected.

'DCI Matilda Darke believes he shouldn't be in Starling House. She's asked me if I'll look into it.'

'DCI Darke? There's a story in the paper today about the book of the Meagan kidnapping.'

'Yes, well, don't believe everything you read, John. DCI Darke is an exemplary detective. If she believes someone to be innocent then I'm inclined to trust her. Look, I know you were only a DC at the time of the Hartley killings and won't have had much input on the case but surely you must remember something from the

191

investigation; there must have been some other angle that wasn't pursued or a suspect not chased up. Anything.'

John leaned back in his chair. He had been pleased to see his parents though he knew there was an underlying reason for their visit. He had thought they were going to spring some devastating health news on him, or maybe they were planning on emigrating to a hotter country. He could have thought all day and not come up with the Hartley case for their reason for driving over to Manchester.

His expression had softened and he looked into the middle distance as he pictured the crime scene all over again. The large main bedroom in the semi-detached house was a shock of red. Sprays of blood on the walls and ceiling – a horror against the neutral creams of the décor. The bare floorboards were a pool of blood of the three victims. Blood had seeped in between the floorboards and was coming through the ceiling into the living room below.

One of the first detectives on the scene, John made his way around the bed and tried to identify the victims. It took him almost half an hour to realize there were three bodies on the bed. Limbs were entwined and broken and everything was covered in blood. There wasn't an inch of flesh that didn't have a speck of blood on it. It was everywhere. Saturated was the only word he could use, and even then it didn't seem strong enough to describe the amount of blood.

'I remember when Thomas Hartley was brought into the nick,' John began. 'He looked lost. His expression was blank. He was in total shock. His life had been torn apart in the space of a few minutes, and he had no idea what was going on around him.

'I sat with him in the interview room while DI Spicer was called. I tried talking to him. I asked if he wanted a drink or something to eat but he didn't reply. He was physically there, but his mind was elsewhere.'

'What was his alibi for the time of the murders?'

'Time of death was put down at between two and four o'clock in the morning. Thomas was asleep at that time.'

'Whereabouts in the house was his bedroom? Next to the room the bodies were in?'

'No. He wasn't sleeping in his bedroom. He woke up in the early hours and was sick. He went downstairs to take something to settle his stomach and decided to sleep on the sofa.'

'Why?'

'I don't know. He just did.'

'Surely when you're feeling ill you want to be in the comfort of your own bed.'

'Sometimes when you've just vomited up your internal organs the last thing you want to do is climb a flight of stairs,' said Anton. 'Remember how I was after that quiche at your sister's? Nothing could have moved me off that sofa.'

Pat nodded her agreement. 'So he didn't have much of an alibi then?'

'Not as such.'

'What did your DI Spicer think?'

'DI Spicer took it very hard. He has a son the same age and name as Thomas. It got to him. He wanted Thomas to be innocent.'

'Was he innocent?'

'Thomas said he was.'

'What were the other lines of investigation?'

John looked down at the floor. 'There weren't any. There was no sign of a break-in, no forced entry, nothing. If it wasn't someone already in the house – Thomas – then it was someone who had a key and made sure they didn't leave a single trace of themselves.'

'Is there any chance I could speak to DI Spicer?'

'I very much doubt it. Last week he became Superintendent Spicer. He's very busy learning his new role. Besides, I don't think he would be too happy to find out you're meddling in one of his cases.'

'I'm not meddling,' Pat protested. 'I'm … concerned,' she said, choosing her words carefully.

'Why does DCI Darke think Thomas Hartley is innocent? What's she got to do with this?'

Pat leaned forward and lowered her voice. 'There's been an incident at Starling House. She met Thomas Hartley and believes him to be innocent.'

John thought for a while. 'There is someone you can talk to.'
'Who?'

'Thomas's father, Daniel, had a sister, Debbie. I think she still lives in Manchester.'

'Could you get me her address?'

'Mum, I don't want you stirring anything up here.'

'I'm not going to stir anything up. I just want to satisfy my own mind. I don't like the thought of an innocent man – or in this case, boy – imprisoned for something he didn't do. If he is innocent then the killer is still out there. And judging by how disturbing that crime was, who knows if the killer will strike again knowing he got away with it the first time.'

THIRTY

As she made her way to leave Starling House for the day something caught Matilda's eye. She looked into the room through the small glass window in the door and saw one of the inmates sitting alone at a table. His head bowed over a book. Matilda moved closer to the door and looked through the glass. It was Thomas Hartley.

She opened the door to the library and stepped inside. The door closed behind her with a bang but didn't seem to register with Thomas, so engrossed was he in whatever he was reading. Looking around her, Matilda saw the library was empty apart from Thomas. She wondered where the other inmates were until she heard laughter coming from the small gymnasium.

It wasn't a large room and there couldn't have been more than a few hundred books to choose from. Since she had inherited the collection from Jonathan Harkness, there were probably more books in her home than in this so-called library. Her eyes fell on similar editions to the ones she had, though hers were in much better condition. Books by Simon Kernick, Tom Rob Smith and Peter Robinson stood out and made her smile. She felt comfortable and at home among books, just like Jonathan Harkness had.

She coughed to make her presence felt. Thomas jumped and placed a hand to his chest.

'Sorry, I didn't mean to disturb you.'

'That's OK.' Thomas closed his book and stood up. To Matilda it looked like he was standing out of respect for a woman entering the room, or was it to attention?

'Is it a good book?'

'Yes.'

'What is it?'

He lifted up the book and showed Matilda the cover: *The Legacy of Hartlepool Hall* by Paul Torday.

Matilda smiled. 'I've only read *Salmon Fishing in the Yemen.*'

'I read that last week.'

'Do you spend a lot of time in here?'

'Yes. I think I'm the only one here at the moment who reads for pleasure.'

'Do you mind if I sit down?'

'No. Go ahead.'

Matilda sat on the opposite side of the table to Thomas. He waited until she was settled before he pulled out his chair and sat back down. He played with the dog-eared book in front of him. His fingers were thin and shaking. Matilda looked at his stiff frame. She tried to read the expression on his face but there was nothing there. His eyes darted rapidly from left to right. It was as if he wanted to make eye contact with Matilda but couldn't.

'Is Paul Torday your favourite author?' Matilda asked, not really knowing what to talk about.

'I don't have a favourite. I read a couple of Agatha Christie books a few weeks back. They were good.'

'Poirot?'

'Yes. *Death on the Nile* and, I can't remember the other. A young man was on death row and Poirot helped to get him off.'

'*Mrs McGinty's Dead.*'

Blimey, how did I know that?

'That's the one. I liked that one.' He smiled which seemed to light up his face, briefly.

'I have quite a collection myself. Mostly crime fiction.'

Thomas sniggered. 'As a detective you'd think you'd want something else to relax with at the end of the day.'

'Well, I inherited the collection.'

'That was very generous. Handed down through generations.'

'No. It was from a fr—' Jonathan Harkness could hardly be called a friend, though she did like him. What was he? An acquaintance?

'Do you want to question me about Ryan Asher again?' he asked.

'No. I was passing and thought you could do with some company for a few minutes.'

'Company?'

'Yes. A chat maybe.'

'About what?'

'I don't know. Is there anything you'd like to talk about?'

'I don't think so.' Thomas frowned.

'Have you seen the film of *Salmon Fishing in the Yemen*?' Matilda asked after an awkward silence.

'Yes. I didn't like it.'

'Neither did I. Thomas, can I ask you a personal question?'

This time he did make eye contact with Matilda. She was taken aback. She saw straight through his stare and into an empty and broken soul.

'OK.'

'Why are you here?'

'Because they think I killed my mum and dad and my sister,' he replied, his voice breaking slightly.

'And did you?'

It was a while before Thomas could speak. He swallowed and opened and closed his mouth a few times as if trying to get the words out before the tears came.

197

'No,' he croaked.

Matilda could feel her heart beating rapidly inside her chest. 'So who did?'

'I don't know. All I know is that it wasn't me.'

It would be wrong of Matilda to say she would help him get released. It would be wrong for her to go around to his side of the table, hold him and tell him everything was going to be all right. However, that's what she wanted to do. She knew the second she laid eyes on him that he didn't belong in Starling House, and she now had confirmation, of sorts.

She sat back in her chair and looked intently at the young man in front of her. What was going on behind those wide, dull eyes? He obviously spent his days reading to try to block out the nightmare he was living, but what about at night when he was locked in his room? His mind was probably torturing him, trying to make sense of the cruel hand life had dealt him. He looked sad and resigned to the fact he would be spending the rest of his life behind bars. Had he given up? Had he accepted his fate? It would appear so.

'Are you OK here? Any trouble?'

'No, to both questions.' He gave an awkward smile. 'Well, there wasn't any trouble until Ryan was killed.'

'I meant are you having any trouble? Some of the inmates seem a bit ... well, full of themselves.'

'Callum Nixon? I've learned to ignore him.'

'Good.'

'I read about you?'

'Sorry?'

'On the internet. The Carl Meagan case.'

'Oh that. Yes. Not my finest hour.' She gave a nervous smile.

'You're a good copper though. I was reading about the Jonathan Harkness case. You got him after twenty years. That's something to be proud of, surely?'

Except I thought he was innocent.

'I should be going,' Matilda said, scraping back her chair. She wanted to question him further about his family, their background and what led to their deaths, but the mention of Carl and Jonathan made her want to flee.

'Sorry. Have I said something I shouldn't?'

'No. I just need to get back to work.'

Matilda stood at the door, her hand gripping the brass handle. She turned back to see Thomas engrossed once again in his book. She opened her mouth to say something but nothing came out. What could she say?

Matilda left the building quickly. There was a stiff breeze blowing as she made her way over to her battered Ford Focus. Before she drove away she looked back at the threatening building. Behind those thick walls were murderers, arsonists, and rapists. There was also one innocent and petrified young man.

THIRTY-ONE

Matilda wasn't hungry when she arrived home. She couldn't remember the last time she had eaten, and, despite her stomach rumbling, she didn't feel like eating. That was the problem of living alone – what was the point in getting all the pots and pans out, all the ingredients, and making a meal from scratch just for one? If she sat at the dinner table on her own she'd feel sadder than she already did.

The cupboard contained tins of beans, soup, and rice pudding. She could heat one of those up and sit on the sofa in front of the television, but that was one step away from eating it cold straight from the tin. In the end, she decided on a cup of a tea and a packet of Bourbon biscuits. Not very nutritious, not filling, but it was something at least. She took the tea and the biscuits upstairs to her library.

There were two hardback books on the table next to the reclining chair. One was the Val McDermid novel she was thoroughly enjoying, the other was *Carl* by Sally Meagan. She picked up the book with the blond-haired, smiling, blue-eyed boy on the cover. He had the face of an angel; his entire life ahead of him. What horrors had he seen out of those innocent eyes?

Matilda placed it back on the table beside her. Why was she torturing herself like this? Just because Sally had hand delivered the book with a threatening inscription didn't mean she had to continue the agony by reading it. Would reading it bring Carl back? No, it wouldn't. Would going over every single moment suddenly release some hidden clue leading to where Carl was being kept? No, it wouldn't.

She knew what James would say if he were still here. He'd take the book from her and throw it out and tell her to get on with her life. Yes, it was fine to think about Carl, to cry for him even, but not to give up your life. You had to move on.

'You're right,' Matilda said out loud. She picked up her Val McDermid hardback and went into her bedroom. She wouldn't allow Carl in there.

Before getting into bed she looked out of the window. The sky was cloudless, and the moon was full and bright. She had so many questions running around her mind but no energy to answer them. She should concentrate on finding Ryan's killer, on trying to prove Thomas Hartley's innocence, but there was nothing left of her tonight. She was spent. Her grief for James and Carl saw to that. She left the curtains open just enough so she could see the moon from her bed. It was comforting.

Matilda had read three chapters when the phone started to ring. She looked at the alarm clock: 23:47.

'Hello?' she answered cautiously. An anonymous call at this time of night would never be good news.

'Detective Chief Inspector Matilda Darke?' the caller asked.

'Speaking.'

'I'm Danny Hanson. I'm a crime reporter on *The Star*. Is it true an inmate of Starling House has been murdered?

Matilda knew she wouldn't get much sleep following the call from the crime reporter. She rummaged around in the bathroom cabinet for her sleeping tablets, took two and went back to bed. However, sleep did not come. Still awake at 2 a.m. she kicked back the duvet and went downstairs.

The rain had started and was coming down in stair rods, as her father said. She stood at the living room window looking out onto the dark street ahead watching the rain pouring down. She missed the moon. Another thing her father said was that a good storm washed away all the detritus of the city. Once the storm passed the air would smell fresh and clean, and so would the mind.

Matilda moved into the conservatory. Was it too early to go on the treadmill? Probably. Maybe she should join a twenty-four-hour gym. At this time of the morning there definitely wouldn't be anybody there for her to feel self-conscious around. She could use the weight machines or go for a swim.

The rain was bouncing hard on the conservatory roof. Against the backdrop of the night's silence it sounded loud and each drop echoed. Matilda sat on one of the easy chairs and listened, trying to focus on every single drop. It was calming, relaxing. It was pleasant hearing noise in an ordinarily silent house. She leaned back and closed her eyes while the rain washed away her dark thoughts.

Twelve stab wounds.

Ryan Asher's body on the pool table came to mind, and Matilda's eyes shot open. He had been laid out perfectly. Posed. Why? It was obviously a message but to whom and what was the message? Ryan was laid out on his back, his legs straight and his arms by his side like he was in a coffin. Was that the message? A way of saying he deserved to die; a nod to bringing back the death penalty for killers like Ryan Asher. If that was the case then why Ryan? He had only arrived at Starling House the night before his death so why had he been chosen?

Twelve stab wounds.

Why did that keep coming back to haunt her? What was the

significance of twelve stab wounds? If Ryan had been drugged and incapacitated then the killer could have struck many more blows: twenty, forty, a hundred. So why only twelve?

Twelve disciples.

Twelve signs of the zodiac.

Twelve months in a year.

Twelve days of Christmas.

Twelve Labours of Hercules.

Twelve inches in a foot.

Twelve members of a jury.

Matilda shot up out of her chair. That was it. Twelve members of a jury. That was the significance of Ryan being stabbed twelve times. The killer was the judge, jury, and executioner sentencing Ryan Asher to death.

Twelve stab wounds. Twelve members of a jury. Murder on the Orient Express. Agatha Christie. Thomas Hartley was reading Agatha Christie last week.

She shook the thought from her head and turned her attention to the victim. Ryan Asher. Maybe Ryan was the first because his surname began with 'A' and the killer was working in alphabetical order. The other boys at Starling House were also potential victims, and as there was no evidence of a break-in the only possible killer had to be a member of staff.

Matilda ran into the hall and searched through her bag. She pulled a dog-eared notepad and quickly flicked through the pages until she found what she was looking for:

Ryan Asher.

Jacob Brown.

Lewis Chapman.

Thomas Hartley.

Craig Hodge.

Lee Marriott.

Callum Nixon.

Mark Parker.

They were the boys currently residing at Starling House. Eight inmates. Eight killers. One was already dead, and Thomas Hartley was in the top half of the list.

THIRTY-TWO

Matilda had briefly nodded off around four o'clock. Two hours later and a passer-by with a barking dog woke her up. She had fallen asleep on the sofa in an uncomfortable position. Now her neck ached; her legs were cold; her back was stiff and her eyes were heavy. She'd taken two sleeping tablets the night before and only managed two hours' sleep. Her body was screaming to return to the comfort of her double bed and spend the rest of the day catching up on much needed sleep. However, her mind wasn't prepared to listen to her body. It was chock-full of theories about a potential serial killer bumping off convicted killers in a secure unit for young offenders. Sleep would have to wait. So would the treadmill.

A quick shower while the coffee was brewing and bread was toasting. She ran downstairs and ate the toast at speed, tearing off large bites while she poured the strongest black coffee she could stomach into a travel thermos. She grabbed her bag, coat, and a couple of pieces of fruit from the bowl and left the house, slamming the door behind her. The rain had eased slightly, but she still dashed to the car.

Today was the first day since her return to work in almost a year that she had not said goodbye to her husband. Every day she looked at his handsome smiling face, those piercing, ice-blue eyes, and that heart-melting smile and told him she loved him and asked him to give her the strength to make it through another day without him. Today she didn't do that. Why? Had she simply forgotten or didn't she need James anymore?

Matilda bounded into the briefing room at South Yorkshire Police HQ to find the room already full. She looked at her watch: 8:20. What time did she have to get here to be the first one in? Now that the majority of the crime scene work and interviews had finished at Starling House, there was no need for the detectives to work permanently from there. She signalled to DI Christian Brady that she was ready to begin and had a quick word with Aaron Connolly and asked how his wife was doing.

'She's back home now and resting. She's going to need regular check-ups at the hospital to make sure she isn't bleeding internally, but she's fine. She just needs to take it easy. The next six months are going to be a nightmare.'

He had been all smiles on Tuesday. The first time any of them had seen him smile in all the years they had known him. Now, the smile was a distant memory, confined to the pages of history. His face was a map of worry and angst.

'Good morning, everyone,' Matilda began from the top of the room. 'I had a phone call last night from Danny Hanson, a reporter on *The Star*, asking me if an inmate of Starling House had been murdered. I put him off as much as I could but I don't think he believed me. Did anyone here talk to the press yesterday?'

Everyone looked at each other and shook their heads.

'I'm guessing some of you will have spoken to your partners, relatives, friends, et cetera. Could any of them have contacted the press? Have a think. I'm not asking you to tell me but you need to know for yourself. This kind of news cannot be allowed to leak out. It has to come from us in an official statement. If any of you do get a call from the press, act dumb and end the conversation as quickly as possible. Is that clear?'

There were nods and quiet assents from around the room.

'Now, what's been niggling me about this crime is the way Ryan Asher was placed on the pool table as if he was posed.' She pointed to the blown-up photograph of the crime scene on the whiteboard behind her. 'This position he was laid in is significant. As was the number of times he was stabbed. So, any suggestions?'

Matilda already had her own ideas, but she wanted to know what her team were thinking. Since the Murder Investigation Team had been disbanded and everyone was now one big CID she had more detectives under her, more to choose from. The ones who thought like her were obviously the ones who were going to be picked first.

'He looks like he's laid out on a mortuary slab,' DC Kesinka Rani said.

'Or in a coffin,' Rory Fleming added.

'My thinking exactly,' Matilda said with a smile. 'According to the toxicology report he wasn't drugged; there was no sign of a struggle. He was placed on the pool table and stabbed twelve times. Why?'

'Because somebody wanted him dead,' offered one of the DCs Matilda didn't know.

'I'm tempted to say "no shit, Sherlock", but I won't,' Matilda said, which garnered a ripple of laughter from around the room.

'You want to know the significance of twelve, don't you?' Sian asked with a sly grin on her face. 'The first thought that comes to mind is that there are twelve members on a jury. You think someone laid Ryan Asher out on the pool table and stabbed him twelve times as if it's the jury sentencing him to death.'

Matilda smiled. 'Usually, I'd say help yourself to a snack from Sian's snack drawer but it seems like hollow praise.'

'Thanks. I don't mind if I do,' Sian opened her drawer and

took out a fun-size Twix. She quickly replaced it for a full-size Twix.

'In Agatha Christie's *Murder on the Orient Express*,' Kesinka began, 'a man is murdered on a train. He's stabbed twelve times, and the killer is twelve different people who all take it in turns to stab him. They all want their revenge on him. They all stab him but nobody knows who actually strikes the fateful wound.'

Not another crime fiction fan.

'So what are you saying then, Kes?' Aaron asked. 'Twelve people from Starling House took Ryan Asher to the recreation room and took their vengeance out on him?'

'No. I'm saying maybe someone doesn't agree with his sentence and believes he should have been sentenced to death.'

Thomas Hartley was reading Agatha Christie.

'But we don't have the death sentence in this country. We haven't done for years. And, no offence to Ryan's victims, but there have been far more disturbing killers to kill if someone wants to make a case for the death penalty to be restored,' Christian Brady said.

Was Thomas Hartley being manipulative? He brought up Agatha Christie. Was he saying he knew more of Ryan Asher's death than he was letting on?

'I'm not suggesting it's someone wanting to bring back the death penalty,' Kesinka said. 'Maybe the killer thinks Ryan Asher should pay for his crimes with his own life. The killer is acting as the jury. Twelve stab wounds. One each.'

Matilda forced herself back to reality. 'So, is this a one-off crime by someone closely affected by Ryan's crime or is this the beginning of a lengthy campaign targeting killers?'

The room fell silent. While serial killer cases were considered great stories from a press point of view, and the public loved reading about them, the police did not enjoy investigating them. The fear, the horror, the disturbing scenes they had to endure at the hands of a sadistic killer was not one they relished.

'Personally, I think it's a one-off,' Rory said with confidence. 'If it was a serial, why start with Ryan when he's only just arrived at Starling House? Why not kill one of the others weeks ago and start there?'

'I agree with Rory, and I never thought I'd hear myself say that,' said Sian.

'Christian, you spent the afternoon with the security guy, didn't you?'

'Gavin Ryecroft? Yes, I did. He's a nice bloke. Knows his stuff. He took me through the entire system and spoke very passionately about it. There are locks and alarms on all external doors, which all have backups should they fail, not that they ever do. The codes to the keypads are changed on a two-weekly basis on different days, and all staff and inmates are searched on a regular basis at random intervals. All new staff are vetted many times before they even reach the interview stage.'

'So what happened with the CCTV on Monday night?'

'Gavin Ryecroft was on annual leave. There is a deputy but he's off on long-term sick. The other staff know the basics about the cameras and all have the codes for alarms but, as nothing major has happened since Starling House opened in '97, nobody was expecting anything to go wrong.'

'What does Gavin think went wrong on Monday night?'

'He has no idea. He's checked and double-checked the CCTV camera in question and can't find a fault. He didn't want to admit it but he seems to think it may have been deliberately tampered with.'

'And as the boys were all safely locked up in their rooms logic would suggest a member of staff tampered with the camera,' Matilda said.

'Gavin didn't want to admit as much but, reading between the lines, he seems to think so. Also, while Gavin was showing me around, there were a couple of staff members talking in one of the rooms. When we entered, they stopped and quickly left. It could be something and nothing but I just get the feeling they're not telling us everything.'

'I've had that feeling too, Christian. Have all the staff been interviewed?'

'Yes,' said Sian. She dug around on her desk for her file. 'The ones on duty have been at Starling House for at least three years, the longest for five. They all have a clean record, haven't taken advantage of sick days, never been late, or had a mark against them.'

'Nobody is squeaky clean. There has to be something.'

'Say this is personal,' Rory began. 'Say a member of staff is the killer and had a personal reason for killing Ryan. There wouldn't necessarily be a black mark against their employment record. We need to look at where Ryan came from to find the killer.'

'Well, you've been reading into the pasts of the killers, Rory, haven't you dug something up?' Aaron sniggered.

'But none of the staff at Starling House come from Norwich. None of them have a personal connection to Ryan Asher. We would have noticed it yesterday,' Sian said.

'What if the killer paid a member of staff at Starling House to let them in to kill Ryan,' Kesinka said, almost thinking out loud.

'Blackmail?'

'It's possible.'

'It's too risky,' Matilda injected. 'The killer has staged this to tell us Ryan Asher should have been put to death for his crimes. The less people involved the better. The killer wouldn't have wanted to involve anyone else.'

'So then it has to be a member of staff,' Christian added.

'Does anyone get the feeling we're going around in circles here?' Rory said. 'Sian, throw us a KitKat, will you?'

'Aaron, yesterday Scott called me and said when he first knocked on Julia Palmer's door and told her he and Faith were from South Yorkshire Police she thought it was something to do with her ex-husband, Brian Palmer. Apparently, he's now living in Barnsley. Track him down and get an alibi from him for Monday night.'

'Will do.'

'Sian, you and Rory go back to Starling House and quiz the staff more. Start off with a friendly chat, then try and get under their skin if you can. If there's anything about any of them you don't like the sound of let me know, and we'll interview them formally.'

As the CID room began to empty Matilda picked up her mobile and made a call. Scott Andrews answered straightaway as if he had been waiting for her to ring.

'Yes, boss?'

'Where are you?'

'We're just about to head back home.'

'Don't bother. I need you to go and see Julia Palmer again. It's leaked out about Ryan being murdered. Tell her the story is going to break later today and it'll be all over the TV news channels. She needs to tell us where Ryan's parents are.'

'I doubt she will.'

'Don't give her the option, Scott.'

Matilda hung up and suddenly wished she had sent Rory Fleming to Norwich instead. He had a much more forceful temperament about him than Scott. Fingers crossed he would find his inner Rory.

THIRTY-THREE

Matilda didn't bother knocking on the door to the ACC's office. She pushed down the handle and flung the door open. Valerie sat up, startled.

'Matilda! What's going on?'

'The press know there's been a murder at Starling House?'

'What? How?'

'I've no idea.' Matilda stormed to the desk and stood in front, hands on hips. She didn't bother taking a seat. She didn't plan on staying. 'I got a call from a crime reporter on *The Star* asking about it.'

'What did you say?' Valerie asked looking nervous, probably remembering the last time Matilda had spoken to the press and landed herself, and the force, in a heap of trouble.

'Nothing. I didn't say anything,' Matilda replied firmly. 'You'll need to give a statement though. They're bound to print something in today's paper. Once it's out we'll have press from all over the country descending. And not just the newspapers either.'

'Yes, Matilda, I know,' Valerie said, gripping the bridge of her nose. The tension and agony of worry was etched on her face. 'We don't need this right now. South Yorkshire Police has been in the news enough to last us a lifetime.'

Matilda's eyes fell on a book hidden beneath a file on Valerie's desk. When she entered the room, the ACC had quickly moved things around. She squinted and angled her head to get a look at the spine. She was reading *Carl*.

Shit, it's out today.

'How's the investigation going?' Valerie asked, following Matilda's gaze, and clearly wanting to distract her.

'What? Oh. Well, all the inmates and staff have been interviewed but there are some I want to talk to again.'

'Any in particular stand out?'

'Not at the moment.'

'How's DC Andrews doing in Norwich?'

'He's going back to speak to Julia Palmer. She knows where Ryan's parents are but she's not telling us.'

'Right.' Valerie's face was almost red. She looked tired, stressed, and like her blood pressure was off the scale. 'I'll give *The Star* a call and go from there; maybe a full statement later if a fleet of media turn up. In the meantime, I want you to make some headway on this case today. I want either an arrest or an arrest imminent by the end of the day.'

Matilda could understand Valerie's angst but it was hard not to take her tirade personally. Yes, the case needed to be solved quickly, but she could only go where the evidence took her.

'Keep me informed, Matilda,' Valerie called out as the DCI made her way out of the office. 'I want to know everything that is going on. And I mean, everything.'

In the corridor, Matilda could feel the tell-tale signs of a panic attack coming on. Why was Valerie reading the book about Carl Meagan? What was the purpose of knowing what a grieving mother thought of South Yorkshire Police, and Matilda Darke as a detective? She wondered how many other officers in the station would be reading it. She had noticed people giving her lingering glances as she passed them in corridors, hushed tones from uniformed officers in the canteen.

This wasn't going to go away. With the release of the book there were interviews and recaps on the case in the media. When the paperback came out there would be additional material and an update, so more interviews would appear in newspapers and on TV. If the book led to more sightings there would be pressure on South Yorkshire to reopen the case and act on information received.

There was no escaping the fact that Carl Meagan was to be a permanent resident in her head and would forever be reminding her of her failings. With nobody actively looking for him it was highly unlikely he would be found. The seven-year-old would be a fixture alongside her husband.

Carl, meet my husband, James. James, please take care of Carl.

THIRTY-FOUR

Pat Campbell had stayed the night in Manchester, inviting herself back to her son's flat. She sent Anton back to Sheffield. He hadn't brought his medication with him, and the fish needed feeding anyway. Pat had spent the evening trying to get John to reveal more information about the Hartley case, but he made it obvious he didn't want to talk about it. Every time she brought up the subject he had a look of faraway sadness, as if he was reliving the horror all over again. Eventually, she took the hint and probed him further about his relationship with Diane.

The next morning, she cooked John a fry-up for breakfast, which brought back the smile she missed seeing on a regular basis. As they parted, she gave him a tight hug and told him to take care of himself. Pat had been in the police force her whole working life; she knew of the dangers her son faced on a daily basis. John told her he would be fine, then warned her not to go kicking the hornet's nest while she played at being Jessica Fletcher.

The taxi turned slowly onto a narrow road with cars lined on both sides. The road was built up of two rows of terrace proper-ties – no front gardens, one window up and one window down. Pat looked closely at the dull front doors, once bright, vibrant colours, now faded from the years' worth of pollution and car fumes. She spotted the green door of number twenty-seven and asked the driver to stop. He couldn't pull over as there were no spaces left, so he stopped in the middle of the street. She paid, told him to keep the change, and stepped out into the cool Manchester air.

A stiff breeze blew around her. She pulled up the collar on her coat and gave a little shiver. She looked up at the dark sky; heavy clouds were looming and there was a rumble of thunder in the distance. Pat looked at her surroundings. There was nobody about. There were no lights on behind the grimy windows and dirty net curtains. The whole road seemed abandoned. She almost expected a bale of tumbleweed to pass by on the pavement.

She knocked quietly on the door and waited. Eventually, it was opened by a frail-looking woman in her late forties. She didn't open the door fully, just wide enough to test the tension on the security chain. She poked her head through the small gap but didn't say anything.

'Debbie Hartley?'

'Yes.'

'My name is Pat Campbell. I'm a retired detective inspector with South Yorkshire Police. I'm currently back working on cold cases—'

'Like *New Tricks*?'

Pat smiled. 'Exactly, like *New Tricks*.' She hated that programme, but was thankful to it for allowing her gain Debbie Hartley's trust. 'Would I be able to come in for a while, have a chat?'

'I'm guessing this is about Thomas.'

'That's right.'

Debbie seemed to think for a while before closing the door. There was rattling of the chain before the door opened fully.

Pat stepped inside the dark hallway. There was a fusty smell of damp and dust. The inside of the house looked just as uncared for as the outside.

Pat was shown into a small living room. The thick, yellowed net curtains up at the window cast a gloomy shadow over the room. The carpet had once been an amalgam of vibrant colours but had dulled over time. The sofa, a throwback to a time when wooden frames and green leather were in fashion, looked ready to be taken to the skip. There was nothing cheerful about this front room, nothing inviting. Pat guessed Debbie didn't have many guests.

The lack of life in the room was mirrored in Debbie. Tall and painfully thin, she had shoulder-length dirty blonde hair which hung lifeless around her frame. Her clothes were tatty and would have been rejected by a charity shop. Her face was gaunt with prominent cheek bones and jawline. Her bulging eyes gave her a frightened and frightening appearance.

'Would you like me to make you a cup of tea or coffee? I've got some hot chocolate if you'd prefer. I love a hot chocolate. Don't you?'

'I'm fine, actually. Thank you.'

'OK. Well, if you change your mind, just say. Sometimes I must drink about a dozen cups of tea a day. I love it. It's so refreshing. Even on a hot day.'

'Do you mind if I sit down?'

'Oh, God, I'm sorry. I should have said, shouldn't I? Please do. Sit down. Make yourself comfortable.'

'Do you mind answering a few questions about your nephew?'

Was she mistaken or did Pat see Debbie flinch at the mention of her nephew?

'No. What do you want to know?'

'What did you think when you first heard your nephew had killed his parents and sister?'

Debbie's bottom lip began to wobble. Her eyes darted around the room. 'I couldn't believe it. Thomas was a good boy. Daniel and Laura loved him. And Ruby too. They loved them both. Equally. They gave Thomas a lot of freedom. He was never in any trouble.'

'Did you see much of your brother and his family?'

'Yes. I saw them all the time. Their house wasn't far from here. I used to go over most days, or Daniel would come and visit me here after work. It's been sold now, obviously. A Chinese family live there.'

'Did Laura not mind you going round so often?'

'No. She said I could. She worked funny hours so I sometimes looked after Ruby. Thomas didn't need looking after but Laura liked me being there when she wasn't. Just in case.'

'Just in case?'

'Well, if they needed anything. It was nice to be wanted,' she said with a proud smile.

'Do you work?'

'No.' She looked at the floor. 'I'd like to, but I don't have … what is it when you're not clever enough?'

'Qualifications?'

'That's it. I don't have any of those and bosses like you to have them. I've been on some courses, literacy and numeracy, but I found them quite hard. I do three days a week in the Age UK shop in town, and sometimes they ask me to go in on Saturday too when they're busy. I like that.'

Pat smiled. Daniel, Laura, Thomas, and Ruby were obviously the centre of Debbie's world. She literally had nothing else in her life. The box television in the corner of the room was off when Pat entered, and there were no books or magazines lying around so what had Debbie been doing before Pat knocked on the door? She imagined her sitting in the armchair staring through the window into another world, reliving her memories of her brother, sister-in-law, nephew, and niece – trying to make sense of what had happened and what had gone so horribly wrong.

'Debbie, have you ever been to see Thomas?'

'No.'

'Do you know where he is?'

'Yes. He's in Startling House in Sheffield.'

Pat didn't correct her. 'If you don't mind me asking, why haven't you been to see him?'

She opened and closed her mouth a few times as if trying to find the correct words. 'I … it's … he killed my family,' she practically spat out the words. She bit her bottom lip hard, holding back the tears. 'He's written to me a few times though.'

'Has he? Did you write back?'

'No.'

'Do you still have the letters?'

'Yes.' She smiled. 'I don't get many letters so I like to keep the ones I do get. Would you like to see them?'

'Yes, please.'

'OK. They're upstairs. You'll wait here, won't you?'

'Of course.'

Debbie shot out of the room and bounded up the stairs like an excited puppy. While she was gone, Pat took the opportunity to have a snoop around. There was an old veneer wall unit in the corner of the room. She opened one of the drawers which was chock-full of paperwork, bills mostly, by the look of them. The next one down was an odds-and-ends drawer. The third one held more paperwork – this time more interesting. The headings on the letters were of a firm of solicitors based in Cornwall. Underneath them was an old passport. Pat looked inside at the photograph of a young girl. Her face was round and her eyes were bright and sparkling. The passport had expired years ago and was in the name of Catherine Downy.

The sound of Debbie charging down the stairs made Pat cease her search and quickly return to the sofa. Debbie entered, red-faced and flustered.

'Sorry I was a while; I couldn't remember where I put them.' She held aloft a battered cardboard shoe box. 'I keep everything in here. It's my treasure box. I've got postcards from Daniel and Laura when they went on holiday without me and pebbles and shells from the beach and tickets from the cinema when I was first allowed to take Thomas and Ruby on my own. I love the *Toy Story* films, don't you?' she asked, looking at the ticket stubs with wide eyes.

'Yes, I do,' Pat replied. Or, she used to before she had to endure them over and over again with her grandchildren.

'I've had four letters from Thomas. Here you go.' She handed them over carefully as if they were fragile objects.

'Thank you. Would it be possible to have that hot chocolate now?' Pat asked.

Debbie's eyes lit up. 'Oh, yes, of course you can. I'll join you if you don't mind.'

'No, I don't mind.'

'That's great.' Debbie jumped up from the sofa. 'I'll go and make them then.'

Pat waited until Debbie was out of the room before she opened the envelopes and took out the letters. Each one was only a single page long. She lined them up neatly on the coffee table and took out her iPhone. She selected the camera, turned on the flash as it was so gloomy in the living room, and began taking photos of each of the letters. Front and back. She had taken shots of the first two when the door to the living room was thrown open.

'Would you like little marshmallows in your hot chocolate?'

'Yes, please,' Pat said, frozen to the spot. Had she been caught?

'OK. I've got pink ones and white ones.' She left the room in the same whirlwind she entered.

Pat blew out her cheeks and quickly took photos of the remaining letters before turning her phone to silent and placing it back in her inside jacket pocket.

The letters were written simply. Thomas had received a good education and had excelled at English. He had purposely written in a childlike language for the benefit of his aunt.

Dear Auntie Debbie,

I hoped you would have come to see me while I waited to find out how long I have to go to prison for. I really want to see you and tell you face to face what happened. They said I was guilty. They said I killed mum and dad and Ruby but I didn't. I couldn't have. You know how much I loved them all, how much I still love them. I haven't done anything wrong yet I'm going to be locked up in prison for a very long time. I want you to come and visit me, Auntie Debbie. I need someone to talk to, someone who knows me, and you're the only person left who really knows me.

My solicitor says that when I am sentenced I will most likely be going to a place called Starling House in Sheffield. Sheffield isn't far from Manchester. It's only about an hour or so on the train. You could come and visit me there.

I'm sorry you've been left on your own but if we see each other, send letters, talk on the phone, then we won't be alone, will we?

I hope you come and see me soon.

Love,

Thomas.

THIRTY-FIVE

Matilda was alone in the boardroom of Starling House. Most of the work to be done by the detectives could be done back at HQ, and Sian and Rory were around somewhere having a more informal chat with the staff. Matilda was left with her thoughts – never a good idea for Matilda.

She looked out of the window at the grey sky. Both sets of security gates were closed and there was no one around. News of Ryan Asher's death had obviously not been revealed yet or the press would have arrived by now. Matilda was grateful for that, although slightly suspicious at their absence.

Her mind kept returning to Thomas Hartley. She had sent a text message to Pat Campbell to see how she was getting on in Manchester but hadn't received a reply. She knew she should be concentrating on the Asher case, but she couldn't. An innocent boy was living in this prison and that was causing her great distress. She wondered where he was right now: the library, the gym, the dining room? Wherever he was, he was with six other boys who had either admitted their violent crimes or accepted their fate. Thomas didn't fit into either of those categories. He was trapped in a building full of killers and nobody seemed to care. Nobody except Matilda.

'Snap out of it,' she told herself.

She turned away from the window and went back to the desk she was working at. The file Kate Moloney had given her on Elly Caine was open and the woman in question was staring up at her with a blank expression. She was a strange-looking woman. Her features seemed out of proportion to her small face. Her eyes were too close together, her nose was bulbous, and the tops of her ears poked out of her thick wavy hair, giving her the look of an extra from *Lord of the Rings*. According to her age and height she was short and looked older than the twenty-eight years her date of birth suggested.

The date of her leaving day was just sixteen months after she started. When Matilda turned the page she saw why Elly had left so abruptly. A photograph of a badly beaten and bruised Jacob Brown was shocking. One eye was swollen shut; there was a thick padded bandage on his forehead; he had a split lip and bruises on his cheeks.

'Bloody hell, she really laid into him,' Matilda said to herself.

Putting the file to one side she reached for her laptop and spent the next ten minutes trying to find any record of the assault being reported to South Yorkshire Police. There was none. A minor had been assaulted by an adult. The police should have been called in to investigate. Kate had obviously dealt with it in-house and dismissed Elly Caine as part of a cover-up. It seemed Kate would do anything to stop Starling House falling into disrepute including ignoring serious crimes. If she could gloss over an assault, what else had been swept under the carpet over the years?

'Kate, we need to talk,' Matilda said when she found her in the middle of the corridor.

'Of course,' Kate said, leading the way to her office. 'Take a seat.'

'I won't say you've been lying to me but you've certainly been holding things back.'

'What are you talking about?'

'The extremely high staff turnover; Elly Caine and the reason she left.'

Kate swallowed hard. Despite being questioned about her staff and her running of the place, her iron-maiden façade refused to drop. 'Do you have any idea what it is like running this place? Nobody wants to work here. Not just people from Sheffield, but anywhere. You should see the dregs I get applying for jobs, and I have no option but to hire them because they're the best I can get. When they start and they see the boys staying here, the crimes they've committed, the way they're nonchalantly getting on with their lives, well, it's not easy to see, and some of the staff can't cope with it.'

For the first time since she'd met her, Matilda started to have empathy with Kate. She may seem cold and hard, but she had to be. The people of Sheffield were against her, the media were itching for her to fail so they could write a scathing exposé, and her staff were woefully underqualified. She was one woman fighting a bitter battle.

'Tell me about Elly Caine,' Matilda said.

'You've read the file. You know.'

Matilda sat in silence, arms folded. She had no intention of leaving this office without the full details.

Kate took a deep breath. 'Elly didn't interview for the job. Her cousin works here, Richard Grover. He mentioned that she was looking for work so I told him to get her to come in for a chat. We're always looking for staff here.'

'Did she have the experience and qualifications to work here?'

'Of course she didn't,' Kate admitted. 'Not many of them do. I try my best with them. I give them training. Oliver Byron gives them training.'

'So what happened?' Matilda asked.

'I think it was a clash of personalities between Elly and Jacob Brown. Elly wasn't a strong person and Jacob found that out quite quickly. He often played up when she was on duty. When she wasn't he was a model inmate. They didn't get on. It really was that simple.'

'I've seen the photograph of what she did to Jacob. That was a very brutal beating.'

Kate took a deep breath and swallowed hard as she conjured up the memory. 'There was a football match on. Now, we have rules that all inmates should be in bed for nine o'clock but they're not set in stone. During the Olympics and the Euros this year, for example, we allowed the inmates to stay up late. However, Elly took the rules too far and demanded the television be turned off at nine o'clock while the match was still going on.

'Jacob stood up to her. She wouldn't back down. An argument between the two broke out and it ended up getting personal. Elly just snapped.'

'Was she in the room on her own with the boys?'

'Yes.'

'Was that normal?'

'Yes it was. It still is. The recreation room is their room to relax in.'

'What happened when she snapped?'

'She slapped him with the back of her hand. The other boys said she just lost it. It was a massive slap and it almost knocked Jacob off his feet. Then he retaliated. He went for her, but he's only fifteen. Elly is older, taller, and since working at Starling House she had enlisted in a self-defence course, in case she ever needed to stand up for herself. She laid into him.'

'Didn't the other inmates try to intervene?'

'No. I believe they were taking bets. Fortunately, one of the other guards was walking past and heard the commotion.'

'What injuries did Jacob have?'

'It was mostly bruising and a few cuts. He had a bruised rib and a fractured wrist. He didn't need external hospitalization though. We have adequate medical care here.'

'Why didn't you call the police?'

Once again, Kate looked down. She knew she was in the wrong for keeping this incident private. 'I didn't want the negative attention.'

'Elly Caine committed a serious assault on a minor. She should have been charged.'

'She lost her job. Surely that was enough.'

'Do you honestly believe that?'

After a beat Kate said: 'Yes. I do.' The lie was obvious.

'What else have you been hiding from us?'

'Nothing,' Kate replied firmly.

'In the twenty years Starling House has been open you're telling me there have been no serious incidents you've covered up?'

'I haven't covered anything up, and I resent the accusation. I've dealt with everything internally.'

'You're not answering my question.'

'No. There have not been any other incidents here that I haven't told you about.'

'I'm sorry, Kate, but I don't believe you at all.'

Kate shrugged. 'That's not my problem.'

'It most certainly is,' Matilda replied.

THIRTY-SIX

Scott Andrews reversed carefully into a tight spot on Julia Palmer's road. Lined with cars on both sides it wasn't easy to find a space for the pool car and they almost had to drive into the next street to find one. He turned off the radio, which had just broken the news of a dead body being found at Starling House in Sheffield.

'We couldn't have timed this better,' Scott said.

'How do you want to play this, good cop, bad cop?' Faith asked as they walked the several hundred yards to Julia's home.

'No. I was thinking more bad cop, bad cop.'

'You can't bully her.'

'I've no intention of bullying her. It's time we stopped pissing about though and she told us where Ryan's parents are living. The news is out. It's only a matter of time before they discover their son is dead from the six o'clock news. That's not how it should be.'

'Maybe we should have come first thing instead of going back to the court to ask about that CCTV footage again. I knew it was going to be a waste of time.'

'We have to check these things for ourselves, Faith. We can't just take one man's word for it that there won't be any saved footage.'

Faith sighed. 'Fine. But if Julia won't help us then I can't see any other way. Besides, if they do hear it on the news, maybe they'll get in touch themselves.'

'Would you?'

Faith stopped as she thought for a moment. 'To be honest, no, I wouldn't. If I had a son and he murdered my parents I'd wash my hands of him.'

'There you go then. If Ryan's parents feel the same way, finding out he's dead is only going to make them even more invisible. We need to know where they are before they turn on the news.'

They reached the garden path leading to Julia's home just as the front door was opening. Cynical as ever, Scott wondered whether Julia had seen them arrive and beaten them to the door to pretend she was on her way out. She was wearing a long thick overcoat that was in great need of dry cleaning.

'You again! Look, I told you I'd pass on your details the next time they ring. If you keep badgering me I won't bother.'

'Julia,' Scott began. 'Ryan's dead.' He tried to speak quietly but the sound of passing traffic threatened to swallow his words.

Julia stopped in her tracks. She was midway through locking the front door. Her back was to the waiting detectives and they couldn't see her facial expression but they saw her bow her head. Sadness? Regret? Shame?

'Dead?'

'Perhaps we could go inside,' Faith said.

'I have things to do.' Julia buttoned up her coat and walked down the cracked path, head bowed. She passed the detectives and didn't make eye contact.

'Julia—'

'No!' she snapped, turning to face them. 'Don't say anything. I don't want to know and neither do Ryan's parents. He destroyed this family.'

'Don't you want to know how he died?'

'No, but I hope it was painful.'

Julia turned on her heel and was about to walk away when Scott called her back.

'You don't have kids, Julia, so you won't know how it feels, but put yourself in Belinda's position. She may not want anything to do with Ryan – at the end of the day he is still her son. She gave birth to him. She will still have feelings for him. She needs to know he's dead, but not from hearing it on the news.'

An elderly woman passed by. She slowed as she approached them; obviously eavesdropping on a personal, and interesting, conversation.

'Julia, I really think we should talk inside,' Faith said.

'Why? So one of you can pretend to need the toilet and rummage through my drawers to find out where Belinda's living? I don't think so. Look, I'm not going to tell you where they're living and you can't force me. I will pass on the news of Ryan's death. Now, please, leave me alone.'

Once again she turned and headed off down the pavement, taking large and determined strides.

'She is one screwed-up woman,' Scott commented.

'Can you blame her? Look at the lives Ryan has ruined. No one is mourning his death. Nobody cares he's dead. So why are we sodding bothering with all this?' Faith turned in the opposite direction of Julia and headed back to the car.

THIRTY-SEVEN

By early evening the press had descended on Starling House. At first it was only the local media. Danny Hanson was first at the gates from the *Sheffield Star*. He had tried to get buzzed in but his pleas fell on deaf ears. There was no way he was getting past security. He had taken a few photographs of the building and grabbed his binoculars from the glove box of his car to get a closer look, but it was futile.

A BBC Radio Sheffield van pulled up close to the gates and a young man and woman stepped out.

'Anything?'

'Nothing so far. I can't see any movement at all,' Danny said. He held out his hand to introduce himself.

'Glenis Bishop and Leroy Price.'

'Nice to meet you.'

'What do you know about Starling House?'

'Absolutely nothing,' Danny replied. 'I'd never heard about it until this afternoon.'

'I had, but I'm Sheffield born and bred. I had to give Leroy here a quick history lesson on the way over.'

'I had a look on the Net while I was waiting but there's not much information.'

'There won't be. That building is the original mystery house. Frankenstein could be creating monsters in there and we wouldn't know about it,' Glenis smiled.

After an hour of waiting for something to happen, and watching a building shrouded in silence and mystery, another news van pulled up. This time, a man climbed out and unloaded his camera equipment from the back. A reporter from *BBC Look North* smartened herself up, and prepared her piece to camera. By dusk news vehicles from BBC national news, ITN, and Sky had pulled up, blocking the entrance to Starling House.

There was nothing more from the police, no statement from Starling House, and no sign of anything going on behind those thick stone walls.

'How long do you plan on staying?' Glenis asked Danny.

'Not much longer. It's going to piss it down tonight by all accounts, and I've no intention of catching pneumonia. You?'

'We're heading off in a bit. I think if Starling House was going to give a statement they'd have done it by now. Maybe they're waiting until the next of kin have been informed. It'll probably be tomorrow before we hear anything.'

'I think I'll have a chat with a few of the television boys then head back myself. I might give them my CV.' He smiled.

Inside, Kate Moloney was looking out of one of the barred windows in her office. She couldn't move from watching the country's press gather at the gates. She bit her bottom lip furiously, a nervous habit. There was a knock on the office door and she almost screamed out as she jumped.

'Come in,' she called.

Oliver Byron entered. He looked tired. His collar was unbuttoned and his tie askew. 'You've seen the press then?'

'Yes. I've had several emails and phone calls too. Not that I've answered any.'

'Are you going to give a statement?'

'I've had a word with DCI Darke. They still haven't been able to locate Ryan Asher's parents. Until they do she recommends we keep this to ourselves.'

'But our shifts finish tomorrow afternoon. There will be new staff arriving and us leaving. We'll have to pass the press. They'll ask questions.'

'And you'll ignore them, Oliver,' Kate raised her voice. 'Look, I don't have time for this right now.' The phone started ringing. Kate had to shout to drown out the sound. 'I have no intention of talking to the press yet, and I don't want anyone from here doing so either. Now you go and tell the rest of the staff to keep their mouths shut.'

'Is everything OK, Kate?' he asked, a worried frown etched on his face.

'Oliver, concentrate on your own work. Now get out. Go on.'

The phone stopped ringing, and Kate turned back to look out of the window, just in time to see yet another news van pull up.

'Shit,' she said under her breath.

She turned her back to the window and saw Oliver still standing in the doorway. 'What are you still doing here? I told you to leave,' she shouted.

Reluctantly, he left, closing the door firmly behind him. Kate returned to her desk and slumped into the chair. For years she had told herself she was calm, cool, and composed during a crisis. Now one had actually happened and she couldn't cope. She was clueless. The phone started ringing again. Kate jumped, picked it up and threw it to the other side of the room with as much force as she could muster. It smashed against the wall and stopped ringing.

She sat down in the leather seat and looked ahead. On the far wall was a framed photograph: an aerial shot of Starling House. She had always liked the picture, taken on a sunny day in mid-summer. Now, she looked at it with scorn. The realization dawned. She hated Starling House and every single person in it.

THIRTY-EIGHT

'Welcome back. Did you buy me a present?' Rory asked when he saw Scott and Faith slink into CID.

The drive back from Norwich had been a long and painfully slow one as the motorway was reduced to just two lanes of traffic for several miles due to road works. Scott had tried to engage Faith in conversation and deliberate on whether Julia Palmer would contact Ryan's parents about his death but Faith's replies were mere grunts, and she spent the majority of the journey rapidly texting on her phone.

'A present? From Norwich? Hardly,' Scott said, slumping down in his seat.

'Was it a productive visit?' Sian asked.

'Not really. We don't know where Ryan's parents are and the mysterious bloke at his trial is still a mystery. We've basically just had a night away in a dull hotel room with a flavourless curry and worn down four perfectly good tyres.'

'You wouldn't recommend Norwich as a holiday destination then?'

'There were some lovely open areas to go walking but we weren't there for that.'

'Faith,' Rory began with a twinkle in his eye that suggested he was about to be embarrassing. 'Was there a mix-up with the hotel rooms and you had to spend the night with Scott?'

'No.'

'Did he "accidentally" open your door in the middle of the night thinking it was the bathroom and climb into bed with you?'

'No, Rory, he didn't.'

'Did he knock on your door and ask if you were lonely?' He grinned.

'Oh for goodness' sake. Not every bloke is a chancer like you, Rory.'

'Bloody hell, Scott, do you put bromide in your tea? What's wrong with you, man?'

'Drop it, Rory,' Sian spoke up as Matilda entered the room.

The room fell silent while Matilda brought them all up to speed on the events of the day. The investigation was still no further forward but Matilda believed Kate Moloney's recent outburst was a sign that all was not well at Starling House. It had convinced her that a member of staff was the killer of Ryan Asher rather than a fellow inmate.

'Aaron, tomorrow morning I want you to track down Elly Caine. Bring her in and formally interview her. I want to know where she was on Monday night. Run her through the computer too. I want to know if she's been in trouble in the past. Does she still keep in touch with any of the staff working at Starling House?'

'Will do,' he said, making a note in his pad. 'By the way, Julia Palmer's ex, Brian, has an alibi for Monday night. He's currently in Malta with his new wife.'

'I'm beginning to wish I was in Malta,' Matilda said. 'Scott, Faith, thank you for your efforts in Norwich, and I'm sorry they didn't amount to much. You never know though, Ryan's parents may call in. Faith, take over from Rory and keep looking into the family's past. I still think there is something lurking in there that's led to him being killed. Maybe check in with his schoolteachers. I doubt we can afford to send you back to Norwich but give them a call and send a local uniform round if you need to.'

'OK.'

'Sian, how did you get on talking to the other staff at Starling House this afternoon?'

'They are a real mixed bunch. None of them seem to get on with each other. The atmosphere in the staffroom was practically arctic. They don't mingle; they don't chat; they don't joke. It's a very dark place to work.'

'In what way "dark"?'

'There's no interaction. The officers just work there. They do their shifts, take their breaks, eat their lunch, then go to their rooms. Everything is so structured and orderly. They're a group of people thrown together and they've no idea how to get on with each other. It's like *Big Brother* but without the laughs. Not that I watch it,' she quickly added.

'Did any of them say anything about another member of staff to give you cause for concern?'

'Not really. There are a couple who think capital punishment should be brought back for the serious criminals but nothing militant about them.'

'No racism or bullying among the staff?'

'No. Nothing. All very dull and boring, I'm afraid. I've got the sneaky feeling I've missed something though and it's annoying me. It could be the atmosphere or me reading too much into it but I get the impression someone is hiding something they don't want getting out.'

'They could all be worried about the Elly Caine story.'

'It's possible, I suppose. Maybe it's just Rory's deep thinking that's rubbing off on me,' Sian said, which raised a laugh from around the room. 'Let me have a think tonight and I'll get back to you in the morning.'

Matilda's phone burst into life with the sound of a breaking news alert. She fished it out of her pocket and looked at the lit-up screen. 'Fuck!'

The entire room stopped. The look of horror on her face told them everything they needed to know.

BBC BREAKING NEWS

Ryan Asher, 15-year-old killer, has been murdered at Starling House, the maximum security youth prison in Sheffield, South Yorkshire. More to follow.

THIRTY-NINE

The breaking news had sent Matilda charging up to the ACC's office to tell Valerie of the leak before she found out from another source. However, as soon as Matilda saw the pale look on her boss's face, she knew she had been beaten.

'I've already heard,' Valerie raised a hand to stop Matilda in her tracks. 'I just want to know how it was leaked and who leaked it?'

'I've no idea,' Matilda replied, breathless. She thought her daily jogs on the treadmill were benefiting her legs but taking the stairs two at a time wasn't the same thing. Her thighs ached. 'I can say, hand on heart, that it was not one of my team.'

Valerie nodded. 'I believe you. It must have been someone from Starling House.'

'The longer we spend there the weirder the place becomes. I had a very succinct chat with Kate Moloney today. I'm surprised she hasn't had a stroke with the amount of pressure she puts herself under.'

'You don't think she's fit to run the place?' Valerie asked, eyebrows raised.

'I'm not saying that.' *Yes I am.* 'I'm just surprised that it's not inspected regularly. I know people don't want Starling House on their doorstep but do Sheffield City Council actually monitor the place? Does anyone?'

'It's a private company who runs it.'

'But it's housing convicted killers. Surely the Home Office should have some involvement.'

'I'm sure it does. However, the day-to-day running of the place is down to Kate Moloney.'

'So who monitors her?'

The question went unanswered. As Matilda drove slowly through the congested streets of Sheffield, she went over the same question again and again.

Starling House was owned by a private security company based in Northern Ireland. They were, in effect, Kate's bosses. How much of an input did they have in what went on behind those thick walls? Did they just hand over a budget every month and allow Kate to do with it whatever she liked? If so, should one person really have that much power and influence over convicted killers? It was a scary thought. Something else to check out tomorrow.

Matilda had hoped to get home before her guests arrived so she could have a quick shower and change her clothes. The two cars in her driveway told a different story. She unlocked the front door, and the sound of laughter coming from the living room was evidence she was late to her own party.

'We let ourselves in. I hope you don't mind?' Adele said.

'No, not at all. That's what your key's for.'

Adele Kean and Pat Campbell were sitting on the sofa with a glass of wine each. The log fire had been lit and there was a cosy feeling about the place. Matilda couldn't remember the last time she had lit the fire. There didn't seem much point in lighting a fire just for one. Whenever she was cold she either put on one of James's big sweaters or went to bed early.

'Adele gave me the guided tour. It's a gorgeous house, Matilda,' Pat said, looking around the living room.

'Thanks. I like it,' she said, her smile wistful as she thought of the man who had built it.

'Great library too.'

'You want it?'

'Anton would kill me. Thanks for the offer though.'

'So, Mat, are you cooking up something wonderful or are we having a takeaway?' Adele asked.

'After the day I've had I'm thinking of pizzas all round and a bottle of wine each.'

'Sounds like my kind of evening. I'll get the menus,' Adele said, heading out into the kitchen.

'I saw the breaking news on the way over. I'm guessing Ryan's name was leaked.'

'Yes. I wouldn't like to be at Starling House right now. The press will be all over the place.'

'Shouldn't you have someone guarding—'

'Uniform are already there,' Matilda said with a smile, guessing Pat's question.

'Sorry. Habit.'

'Do you miss the force?' Matilda asked, sitting down on the sofa next to her. She kicked off her shoes and settled back. She was beginning to relax in the warmth of the room and the friendliness of the company.

'I didn't think I did but I've really enjoyed these last couple of days.'

'Have you dug anything up?'

'I may just have.'

Pat lifted her bag up off the floor and began rifling through it for her notebook. Adele returned with the pizza menus, another bottle of wine and a spare glass for Matilda. She poured half a glass and handed it to her. Only Adele knew of Matilda's drinking problem, and how she never drank alone as it made her maudlin. A maudlin Matilda was a self-destructive Matilda.

'Choose your pizza and I'll order online.'

They decided to hold off until the pizzas arrived before they began talking shop. While waiting the twenty minutes for them to turn up they made small talk and caught up on each other's lives.

Adele and Pat had crossed during the line of duty and they knew the basics about each other. Pat was shocked to find Adele's son all grown-up and on the cusp of a teaching career. In her mind he was still a five-year-old giving Adele a headache while she juggled her work and tried to find a babysitter.

Pat filled Adele in on what life was like for the retired. Random days away in the countryside and at the coast were wonderful, longer holidays, lie-ins during the week – all were bliss. Anton constantly in her way wasn't as fun. She wished he'd take up golf or bowls or something to get him out of the house without her once in a while. Still, she shouldn't complain. Without Anton she would be incredibly lonely, she didn't mind admitting.

'What's Debbie Hartley like?' Matilda asked.

The pizza boxes were open on the coffee table. Pat and Adele were on the sofa, a plate on each lap, while Matilda was cross-legged on the floor. They'd spread out to make room for the food and their paperwork.

'Well, in my day I would have called her simple. I don't know what you'd call her now.'

'Learning difficulties?' Adele suggested.

'I don't know. She's certainly lacking in something. Daniel, Laura, and the kids were her life. Now they've gone she really has nothing else left. She lives in a grotty terraced house and works voluntarily in a charity shop.'

'How old is she?'

'I'm not sure. Mid-forties I'd say. I didn't think to ask. I managed to take some photographs on my phone of the letters Thomas sent her. He's written to her four times. The first was while he was on remand waiting for trial. The second was after he was found guilty but waiting for sentencing. The third was just after he arrived at Starling House, and the fourth was on her last birthday.' Pat wiped her hands on a napkin and found the photographs on her phone. 'Do you want me to email them to you?' she asked Matilda.

'Please Pat. That's brilliant, thank you.'

She handed Matilda her phone. 'Can you email them as I've no idea how to do it from a phone.'

'Where was Debbie at the time of the murders?' Adele asked.

'Home alone. She spends every night at home on her own. No visitors, no friends.'

'No alibi either.'

'Exactly.'

'Could she have killed them?' Matilda asked.

'I doubt it. I personally believe anyone has the capability to kill – it's all down to circumstance. What I don't believe is that Debbie Hartley has the mental capacity to frame Thomas and keep it to herself all these years. She's an incredibly lonely woman. She was thrilled when I arrived as it meant she finally had someone to talk to. She made me a hot chocolate and we spent over an hour talking. Well, she did most of the talking, I just sat there listening. I couldn't shut her up.'

'What was she talking about?'

'Nothing. It was about her colleagues at the charity shop, walks she goes on, her favourite ice cream flavour. It was just jibber-jabber. I felt sorry for her.'

'Did she see Daniel often?' Matilda asked.

'All the time.'

'Didn't Laura mind?'

'She said not.'

'Hmm,' Matilda thought aloud.

'What is it?' Adele asked.

'Put yourself in Laura's shoes. You're married. You have two kids. You and your husband both work so your time in the evening as a family is precious. Do you really want your sister-in-law coming round every night?'

'Well, I know I wouldn't,' Pat said. 'Anton's sister gets right on my nerves. If she's not trying to flog her Avon she's showing me her bunions.'

'Exactly.'

'So you think maybe Laura put her foot down and said Debbie shouldn't go round as often.'

'It's a possibility.'

'But would Debbie resort to murder?' Adele asked.

'Like I said, she's certainly lacking in something. Maybe she saw Laura as a threat to her happiness and decided to get rid of her,' Pat mused.

'But then why kill her brother and niece?' Adele asked, reaching across for another slice of pizza.

'I've no idea. If she is, for want of a better word, simple, maybe her reality became blurred. Maybe she thought if Laura didn't want her around after all these years of welcoming her into their home, then Daniel and the kids felt the same way too.'

'Then why leave Thomas alive?' Adele asked.

'That's what I have a problem with,' Matilda said. 'Whenever I think of who could have killed the Hartleys, I always ask why Thomas was left alive.'

'No. I'm sorry,' Pat came back from her reverie. 'I don't see Debbie as the killer. It doesn't fit.'

'Would you say she had the mind of a child?' Matilda asked.

'Yes, I would. Why?'

'Like an inmate of Starling House.'

'Only this particular inmate is still free,' Adele finished Matilda's thought.

'Cup of coffee and chocolate, ice cream and crushed-up cookies, or continue with the wine?'

Pat and Adele pondered for a brief second before answering in unison. 'Ice cream and crushed-up cookies.'

A few minutes later Matilda returned with a tray carrying three bowls and spoons, a large tub of vanilla ice cream and a packet of chocolate chip and hazelnut cookies.

'Tell me about this passport you found,' Matilda asked as they all helped themselves to dessert.

'I should have taken a photograph of it but I didn't think at the time. It was out of date and the photo showed a chubby girl. For the life of me I can't remember the surname, but she was called Catherine.'

'Could it have belonged to Debbie and Daniel's mother?'

'No. The dates didn't match. The date of birth was March 1977.'

'Making her thirty-nine,' said Adele as she shovelled ice cream into her already full bowl.

'Could Debbie and Daniel have had another sister?'

'Surname wasn't Hartley,' Pat added, taking the ice cream from Adele.

'It'll probably be something simple like it was left behind by whoever had the house before Debbie,' Matilda laughed.

'No. I've got the feeling it's relevant. The chubby girl looked familiar. I just can't place her. It'll come to me, I know it will.'

'Adele, did you get the post-mortem and crime scene report I called you about earlier?'

'No. I've just come for the free food and wine.'

'I genuinely believe that,' Matilda smirked.

'Cheeky cow. Yes, I have your reports. I was reading them when I was stood up at lunchtime,' she said, a slight dig at Matilda having to cancel their lunch meet at the last minute.

'You can read a PM report while eating your lunch?' Pat asked.

'Yes. Why?'

'I could never do anything like that. One mention of an enlarged liver and my stomach would turn right over.'

243

'You don't seem to do too badly now,' Adele remarked as Pat opened her mouth wide for a spoon laden with ice cream and chunks of cookie.

'I'm retired. It's different now.'

'Well, seeing as Pat is no longer squeamish I shall keep in the gory details,' Adele took the file from her bag and opened it on her lap. 'I've got the PM report and a lovely Crime Scene Manager in Manchester who I flirted with emailed me a CSI report on the Hartley house. It's not known how the killer gained access to the Hartley home as all entrances and exits were locked from the inside. However, none of the ground-floor windows had locks. They were of a design that was recalled because of their lack of safety features. There's a diagram in the crime scene file that shows how easy it is to pop the frames open from the outside.'

'Had any of the windows been tampered with?'

'There's no evidence of that but there wouldn't have been anyway.'

'So the killer could have gained entry from any window on the ground floor, escaped through the same route, and the police wouldn't have been able to tell?'

'That's about the size of it, yes.'

'Bloody hell. The killer could be anyone then,' Matilda groaned.

'What type of weapon was used?' Pat asked.

'Something resembling a meat cleaver.'

'You're joking!'

'Bloody hell!'

Adele leaned over the side of the sofa and pulled an iPad out of her bag. She turned it on and tapped on it a few times. 'The lovely crime scene manager I spoke to emailed me over a few crime scene photos. As you're retired, Pat, you can have first look.'

Pat placed her bowl of ice cream on the coffee table and took the iPad from Adele. 'Oh my God, Adele,' she placed a hand to her mouth. 'This is just … oh God.' She handed the iPad to Matilda.

'According to the PM report Laura Hartley received eighteen blows to her head, chest and neck. Her head was almost severed from her body. Daniel received twelve blows. They were mainly to the arms, which suggests he was awake and trying to protect himself. The blow that killed him was the one to his face. It split his skull wide open.'

'Jesus Christ,' Pat said. 'What about Ruby?'

Matilda was flicking through the photographs on the iPad. Her screwed-up face evidence of how disturbing the images were.

'Ruby received more nicks from the blade than actual blows, which suggests she was caught in the crossfire when her mother and father were attacked. There were ten marks on her body, mostly to her arms and body, which were either deflected off her parents or where the killer missed. She received two direct blows with the cleaver, either of which could have killed her.'

'Eighteen blows for Laura, twelve each for both Daniel and Ruby,' Pat said. 'That's forty-two swings with a meat cleaver. How the hell did Thomas Hartley manage to sleep through all that?'

'According to Thomas's statement,' Matilda said, glad of an excuse to turn away from the crime scene photos and pick up her own notes. 'Once he was comfortable on the sofa he fell asleep and didn't wake up until the dog started fussing around him.'

'Wouldn't the dog have woken and barked when the killer broke in?' Pat asked.

'If the dog knew the killer he wouldn't have made such a fuss though, would he?' Matilda suggested.

'What happened to the dog?' Adele asked, digging around in her bowl of ice cream to find more cookie pieces.

Matilda flicked through the file. 'I've seen it here somewhere. Here it is. Debbie Hartley said she took the dog back to her place but he missed the others so much. He was pining all the time and stopped eating. He went to sleep one night and just didn't wake up again.'

Pat placed a hand on her heart. 'Oh the poor thing.'

'Going back to the murders,' Adele said with a mouthful of ice cream. 'Wouldn't the Hartleys have screamed when they were being attacked? If someone's going at you with an axe you're going to scream loud enough to wake the dead.'

'That depends,' Matilda said, going back to the crime scene photos. 'Look at the position Laura is lying.' She held up the iPad showing three mangled bodies saturated in blood on a double bed. Pat winced. 'She looks like she's sleeping. Maybe she was attacked first. When Daniel and Ruby woke up the blows could have been coming thick and fast. They didn't have time to register what was happening before they were silenced. When you're woken so suddenly, you're dazed and confused as it is without being faced with the horror of a killer wielding a meat cleaver. It's just possible they didn't have time to scream.'

'OK. I'll agree with you there,' Pat said. 'But what about the lack of forensics? The killer left nothing of themselves behind.'

'That I can't explain,' Matilda said honestly.

'So, the questions we're left with are why did the killer leave no trace, why not kill Thomas, and, more importantly, why kill them in the first place?' Pat said, counting the questions on her fingers.

'Back to square one,' Adele added.

'I'm so pleased you two came over here tonight,' Matilda smiled.

'How far back into Daniel and Laura Hartley's past did the original investigation go?' Adele asked.

Matilda frowned and all eyes turned to Pat.

'Not very. There seems to be a wall of silence around it. John said there was no evidence of an intruder so the only logical explanation was that someone already in the house had to be the killer. As there was only one person remaining, he was the only suspect. I could give John another call tomorrow if you think it will help.'

'If you wouldn't mind, Pat.' Matilda smiled. 'Any chance of speaking with the original SIO?'

'I doubt it. DI Spicer is now Superintendent Spicer.'

'Really? He's made Superintendent from a DI in just over two years?'

'I think I need more wine,' Adele said, pushing aside the PM reports and turning off her iPad.

The conversation soon moved away from the Hartleys, and Pat Campbell started talking about her husband wanting to go on a cruise around the Greek islands in the spring. Adele joined in as it had always been her dream holiday. Matilda found herself drifting. She hadn't thought about holidays since James died. Together they had enjoyed several trips abroad, and in the UK. Now he was gone, a holiday was never on the agenda. A holiday was something couples and families did together. Matilda wasn't part of a family and she wasn't half of a couple either. She was a widow.

What a horrible word. Widow.

Did Matilda feel like a widow? Yes, she did. She was alone in the world. No husband, no children, no future. She had friends but they had their own lives and families. They wouldn't want Matilda tagging along all the time. The thought struck her that she would end up like Debbie Hartley; sad, lonely, and alone.

Conversation continued in the background but Matilda wasn't listening.

'So, Adele, do you think you'll find someone else and get married?' Pat asked.

'No, I don't think so. Chris has been on at me for ages to get out there and meet a bloke. He's enrolled me on a dating website. I've chatted to a couple of men who seem nice enough to meet for a drink, but I'm not sure.'

'You should give it a go. What have you got to lose?'

'Knowing my luck I'd meet some psycho and I'd end up losing my organs.'

Matilda blinked away a tear before it had the chance to form and looked up at the wedding photograph on the mantel. James looking stunning as always, his beaming smile, his eyes twinkling. Whenever she conjured up a happy memory of their time together, it was always tinged with tragedy, and she measured the amount of time between the memory and his death.

Matilda thought back to Debbie Hartley. *Maybe I should pay Debbie a visit, myself. Look my future in the face and see what's in store.*

FORTY

Nine p.m.

It was unusual for Kate Moloney to be walking the corridors of Starling House at this time of night. From six o'clock onwards she was typically found in her office answering emails and reading reports. Beneath her desk she would kick off her heavy shoes with the pointed toes and thick heels that resounded around the high corridors of the building, announcing her presence before she arrived. The top button of her shirt, usually done up tightly around her neck, was undone to allow her to relax and breathe a bit more freely.

Tonight she had abandoned her routine and joined Oliver Byron in taking the inmates from their makeshift recreation room, the library, to be locked up in their rooms for the night.

Books and magazines were left on the tables as the boys silently made their way out of the room. There was no fuss, no moans, no pleas for just one more game of table tennis. The boys simply downed tools and followed the guards out of the room, along the corridor, and up the stairs to A corridor.

Kate followed several steps behind. She walked slowly. The boys shuffled along, dragging their feet, the soles of their trainers barely making a sound. Kate's shoes were clack, clack, clacking from behind – a sinister metronome.

Oliver Byron, Richard Grover, and Rebecca Childs led the boys to their rooms, locking them in one by one.

'Goodnight, Kate,' Callum Nixon called out, giving her a flash of his cheeky smile.

'Goodnight Callum,' she replied.

'Goodnight everyone. I hope you all make it to the morning,' he said.

Everyone froze at Callum's crass joke, if that's what it was, and turned to look at him. His grin was more of a sneer. What secret was lurking behind his deep eyes? Did he know more than he told the police about Ryan Asher's death or was he playing with them all, drawing attention to himself?

'That'll do, Callum. In you go,' Rebecca said. She was small compared to the inmates. At only five foot four, everyone else towered over her. However, she was strong and fit and made up for her lack of height with her no-nonsense attitude.

'Sweet dreams, Rebecca,' he said, lowering his voice. There was a flirtatious, yet sinister edge to his voice.

Kate kept her eyes on Callum until his door was closed and securely locked. She watched Rebecca turn the key and try the handle to make sure it was completely locked. It was. She watched carefully while all the doors were locked by either Richard or Rebecca and then double-checked by Oliver. Satisfied, they all left the corridor, locking the gate behind them.

Oliver and Richard were finished for the night and were to retire to their bedrooms. Rebecca, along with junior guard, Peter McFly, was to remain on duty throughout the night should anything happen they may be needed for.

Kate followed Rebecca back to the staffroom where Peter was waiting for the kettle to boil. At twenty-three, he was the youngest guard at Starling House. He was well over six foot and beanpole thin. An unruly mound of fiery ginger hair and pale skin gave him a fragile, almost petrified look. However, he had already wrestled Jacob Brown from Callum Nixon and jumped in without a second thought. Looks, in his case, were very deceiving. A new recruit of only two months, he seemed unfazed by the inmates and their crimes and didn't shy away from the night shifts. Kate believed him to be an ideal candidate for the job. But since Ryan's death and Matilda planting the seed of suspicion in her mind, she was looking at everyone with an unnerving frown. Was one of her staff a killer?

Oliver? No. He was good at his job and had a great deal of respect for her.

Richard? No. He walked around Starling House as if in a daze. He didn't have the energy to commit murder.

Rebecca? No. For one thing she was a new mother. She had more things on her mind than planning a murder.

Peter? He was very useful in a ruckus but was he capable of starting one? Maybe.

Gavin? As head of security he knew where the black spots in Starling House were. He knew the weaknesses in the security system. Maybe.

Kate shook the thoughts from her head. This was insane. She didn't care what Matilda said, none of her staff were murderers. There were seven killers living here who had admitted their crimes, of course it was one of them.

'Are you two all right?' Kate asked Rebecca and Peter as they sat down with a cup of tea and a sandwich.

'Yes. Fine thanks,' Rebecca answered for them both.

'Good.' Kate's smile was forced and fake. 'I doubt there'll be any problems tonight. I've just looked and all the press have gone. I never thought I'd be so happy to see a torrential downpour,' she laughed; again it was forced. 'However, if the phone does ring, and it is someone from the newspapers, be polite and end the call as quickly as possible without giving anything away.'

'Will do,'

'How are you settling in, Peter?' Kate seemed reluctant to leave.

He quickly chewed and swallowed his bite of sandwich. 'Fine. Yes, it's OK. Good group of people to work with.'

'Good. Rebecca, how's … ?'

'Lucy? She's fine. She stays with my mother while I'm here.'

'Oh, doesn't your husband look after her?'

'No. He works in the middle of the North Sea.'

'Oh, I see. Well, we all have to do whatever we can to earn the money these days, don't we? I'll leave you to it then. I hope you have a quiet evening.'

Kate left the room and headed back down the corridor. She walked slowly and tried to lessen the sound her heels made against a background of nothing, but it wasn't easy. She looked up at the high ceiling, at the intricate carvings in the corners, the ceiling roses, the cornicing, all covered with cobwebs. She really must find a feather duster with a long handle.

At the end of the corridor she turned around and looked back. The lighting was soft and muted. A faint glow came from the room at the end where Rebecca and Peter were currently enjoying their late-evening snack. She heard their distant chatting and giggling. From this angle, taking in the framed prints and the solid oak wooden doors, Kate wondered why such a beautiful old building was being used to house such violent and evil boys. It didn't seem right. She unlocked the door behind her, went through, and locked it.

Two floors up from A corridor, Kate sat at her dressing table looking at her reflection in the mirror. She looked tired and worried. For the first time in her twenty years of working here she questioned her role and her ability to carry it out. In the background, the theme tune to yet another episode of *Friends* began. It was really the only time she could relax at the moment, watching her favourite programme.

She leaned back on her bed and watched as, in a candlelit apartment in New York, Chandler romantically proposed to Monica. This episode never failed to bring a tear to her eye. She smiled as the audience whooped and the rest of the friends entered the apartment for a group hug. Kate really was relaxed. If only she knew what was about to happen two floors below.

FORTY-ONE

With the fire blazing in the living room for the first time since James's death, Matilda had decided to stay up beside the fire rather than go to bed early or sit in her library with a mug of tea and packet of biscuits.

She was glad she didn't have to go out anymore tonight. When she opened the door for Pat and Adele to leave, the rain had intensified. They didn't linger on the doorstep. A quick goodbye before they ran to their cars. Matilda waited in the shelter of the doorway before they drove away. She closed the door on the foul weather and shivered.

Adele and Pat had long since gone home leaving Matilda alone in the living room with her thoughts on Thomas Hartley and the riddle that was Debbie Hartley. Thomas was obviously anxious to see his aunt, so why hadn't she visited? If she believed him to be guilty then why not reply to his letters asking him not to write anymore? In fact, why had she kept the letters at all?

'I'm going to drive myself insane with all this, aren't I?' she said aloud to James's photo on the mantelpiece. 'What do you think? Is it Thomas or Debbie or someone else completely? I know what you'd tell me to do – concentrate on the Ryan Asher case and move on.'

Matilda sighed and hoisted herself up from the sofa. The living room was warm and comfortable. It was homely and felt lived in. The heat from the fire and the presence left by two good friends made the house feel like a home for the first time in more than eighteen months. She left the room and went into the kitchen to make herself a cup of tea.

The kitchen was large with more fitted cupboards than was necessary. A handmade oak breakfast table and chairs in the corner of the room had been a gift from one of James's friends when the house was complete. She flicked the kettle on and opened a cupboard for her mug. It wasn't technically her mug; it was James's but she used it all the time. While waiting for the kettle to boil she rested against the marble worktops – again this had been a dream of James's. She smiled at the memories. James may no longer be with her in person but he was still in this house, and in her head. He was still looking after her; she could feel it.

She was settled in the large sofa with her tea, a packet of biscuits and the last hundred pages of a Val McDermid novel when a loud knock on the front door frightened the life out of her. It was just after eleven o'clock. Who called at this time of night?

Quietly, she walked to the solid windowless door and looked through the spyhole and instantly relaxed when she saw her caller. She pulled back the bolts at the top and bottom of the door, took off the security chain and unlocked the Chubb.

'Dad, what the hell are you doing here at this time of night?'

'I've come to see you,' he smiled.

'You're soaked.'

'That'll be due to the rain. I'll probably dry off if you let me in.'

'Oh God, sorry.' She stepped to one side. 'Come on in. I'll get you a towel. Is Mum with you?'

'No. I dropped her off at her sister's this lunchtime in Kettering.

I thought I'd call in on my way home and see how my favourite daughter is doing.'

'Don't let Harriet hear you say that,' Matilda said, handing him a towel she'd fetched from the kitchen. 'Go through to the living room, the fire's on. I'll make you a cup of tea.'

Harriet? She hadn't thought of her sister in a while. She couldn't remember the last time she'd spoken to her. Didn't one of her nephews have a birthday coming up? At some point, she must pop over to Grimsby and visit them.

When Matilda returned her father had pulled an armchair close to the fire and had his legs raised, warming his cold, damp feet.

Frank Doyle was tall and looked after himself. He walked whenever possible and played tennis three times a week. He had a sensible diet and had given up alcohol since a close friend had died from liver cancer three years before, not that he was big drinker to begin with. He was sixty-eight and had only recently started losing his hair.

'Why has Mum gone to see Aunt Sophia in Kettering then?'

'Sophia has got to have an operation and, well, you know what she's like, bloody drama queen; she's asked your mother to go and stay with her for a few days.'

'What kind of operation?'

'I've no idea. I was sent out of the room so I'm guessing it's a woman problem.' He smiled.

'So you've got a few days of freedom?'

'I certainly have.' His smile grew. 'I'm not sure whether to invite some of the lads round for an all-night poker game or throw a house party.'

'You've not played poker for years and you hate parties.'

'Yes, those are the only drawbacks.'

'So I'm guessing you'll be letting the dirty laundry pile up while you eat takeaways until Mum comes back.'

'Very probably.'

'Dad, I'm not on your way home.'

'Sorry?' he asked, innocently looking over his mug of tea at his daughter.

'You have to pass the turning for Bakewell from Kettering to get to me. In fact, I'm quite a distance out of your way. And at this time of night, in these conditions, you've obviously come for a reason. Has Mum put you up to this?'

'You're a suspicious woman, Matilda Darke, do you know that?'

'It's my job.'

'Take a night off.'

'Come on, Dad, what's the reason for your visit?'

'Sophia asked how you were. We said you were fine. We know you don't like people prying. Anyway, she'd bought that book about the missing boy, and while your mother and Sophia were talking I started reading it. It made me feel sad for you; the things that are said about you. I wanted to come and see how you were coping.'

Matilda swallowed hard and broke eye contact with her dad. The last thing she wanted him to see were tears welling up in her eyes. 'Well, it's not going to be a happy story, is it? Carl's still missing. I failed to find him. It's only natural that the parents are going to blame me.'

'There were extenuating circumstances, Mat. James had just died.'

'They don't care about that. Besides, I should have handed the case over. I should have taken time off when James went into hospital that last time, but, as usual, I thought I could do a thousand things at once. It backfired and I lost the Meagan's their son,' her voice broke and she couldn't hold on to her emotions any longer.

Frank went over to the sofa and put his arm around his daughter. He pulled her into him. Matilda allowed herself to be comforted. The tears came and refused to stop. This wasn't just a short cry while she looked over her wedding photos, this was months of pent-up grief and anger finally flowing free.

'Oh God, Dad. I didn't get Carl back,' she was barely audible through the tears. 'He's dead. I know he's dead, and I let that happen.'

Frank didn't say anything. There was nothing he could say. He sat back with his daughter in his arms and allowed her to cry herself out. This is what she needed.

Matilda was shocked awake. She looked around wondering for a brief second where she was.

She had cried herself to sleep on her father's lap. He had obviously managed to wriggle himself free and place a blanket over her, not that she had noticed. There was a note on the coffee table written in her father's flowery handwriting:

I didn't want to wake you. I was going to go home but the rain is biblical out there. I thought I'd sleep in one of your spare rooms. I hope you don't mind. Dad, xx.

Matilda smiled. The relationship she had with her mother had always been fractious. It wasn't that they didn't like each other or get on, they did, they were just two very different people. It was the same with Harriet. They may be sisters but they weren't close at all. With her father, Matilda felt more relaxed. She could say anything to him without feeling like she was being judged. She could announce she was giving away all her money and possessions to charity and spend the rest of her life in a kibbutz in the third world and Frank wouldn't bat an eyelid. In fact, he'd probably ask if he could join her.

The fire was dying, just a few embers remained. It was cold. The wind was howling and the rain lashing against the windows sounded like someone was trying to break in. She felt safe knowing her father was asleep upstairs. Although how he could sleep through what seemed like the end of the world was beyond her.

She pulled the heavy curtains back and looked out. The road

was a torrent of fast-flowing water. There was bound to be flooding in some parts of the city. She cast her mind back to the floods in June 2007 and tried to remember which parts of Sheffield had succumbed to the elements of a freak summer storm. Meadowhall had been closed for days. The River Don burst its banks, Heeley and parts of Milhouses Park flooded too. Hadn't someone died at Milhouses?

Her mobile phone burst into life on the coffee table. She looked at her watch. It wasn't quite three o'clock yet. The screen informed her Rory Fleming was calling and she'd missed five calls from him already. So it wasn't the weather that had shocked her awake.

'Rory, what's wrong?'

'Ma'am, I'm on my way over to yours,' Rory was screaming down the phone over the sound of the weather that was obviously buffeting his car. Matilda could hear the windscreen wipers thrashing loudly in the background.

'Why? What's happened?'

'Jacob Brown has escaped from Starling House.'

FORTY-TWO

While waiting for Rory to arrive, Matilda scribbled a quick note to her father and ran upstairs to make herself look more presentable. A quick wash, a comb dragged through her hair to untangle the knots, and a pair of waterproof trousers and she was ready. She ran downstairs as the doorbell chimed.

'I think you're going to need something better than those,' a soaked Rory Fleming said looking down at Matilda's walking boots. 'Don't you have any wellies?' He was soaked despite only being in the elements from the top of the drive to the front door.

'I'm not sure. Come in. I'll have a look. What's happened anyway?'

'We had a call about half an hour ago. Kate Moloney was frantic. She said an alarm had gone off. At first, she thought it was the weather. She went around the building with the two night guards – Jacob Brown's door was wide open and a window in the recreation room had been smashed from the inside.'

'Shit.'

'That's what I thought.'

Matilda was in the cupboard under the stairs looking for something, anything, that would protect her in the harsh weather outside. 'Anyone on-site yet?'

'Apart from a couple of PCs parked outside, DI Brady is going to wake up a few DCs and meet us there. He's organizing a full search of the house and grounds and he's going to try and scramble SY99. Though in this weather I'm not sure it'll be safe enough to take off.'

'Probably not,' Matilda said from inside the cupboard. 'Jesus! How could the uniforms have missed this?'

'They were parked at the front. Everything happened around the back.'

'Matilda, what's going on down there?'

Frank Doyle stood at the top of the stairs wearing only the white towelled dressing gown that had been on the back of the door in the spare bedroom he had gone to sleep in.

'Oh, Jesus, sorry,' Rory said, turning away in embarrassment. 'I didn't realize you had … you know … that you were—'

Matilda scoffed. 'Oh for God's sake, Rory, he's my dad. Dad, this is DC Rory Fleming. Rory, my dad, Frank Doyle.'

Rory's red face turned almost purple as he flooded with embarrassment. 'Sorry, I didn't mean to … well … it's nice to meet you, sir.'

'You too. What's happening, Mat?'

'Long story, Dad. Go back to bed. I'm not sure when I'll be back but help yourself to anything in the fridge.' She had found some wellington boots and was quickly pulling them on. Time was of the essence.

'Drive carefully,' was the last thing she heard as she slammed the door shut behind them both.

'I'm really sorry, ma'am. I had no idea you had a dad,' Rory said, driving as fast as he was able through the treacherous conditions.

'Of course I have a dad. How did you think I got here? Trust me, my mother was no Virgin Mary.'

'No. I just meant, I'd never thought of your dad as—'

'What? Being still alive? How old do you think I am, Rory? Don't answer that.'

Matilda looked out of the window as Rory drove the police Land Rover towards the outskirts of Sheffield and Starling House. Drains at the edges of the road were already overflowing because the torrent of rain was too much for them to cope with. Abbeydale Road was, thankfully, empty of traffic as it was so early in the morning. However, it was flooded and impassable. Rory took the side roads, which were on a slight incline. In the distance, there were blue flashing lights from a fire engine heading in their direction.

'This is worse than 2007,' Matilda said to herself as she looked up at the dark sky.

The rain continued to fall, and the windscreen wipers were useless. Driving down Ecclesall Road South, once past the houses, Matilda looked at the fields submerged under water. Rory turned into Limb Lane and immediately slammed on the brakes. Up ahead was a similar police Land Rover. DI Christian Brady was outside talking loudly to another officer. Both were in thick waterproofs. Matilda jumped out.

'Christian, what's going on?' she had to shout over the noise of the rain.

'We can't get through. The road's flooded.'

Matilda looked round the front of the car. Water from the saturated farmland to the right of the lane was pouring through the gaps in the drystone wall. The whole of Limb Lane was cut off by a deep pool of dirty water.

'Is there another way to get to Starling House?' she shouted.

'No. This is the only road in.'

'Can't we risk driving through?'

'It'll flood the engine.'

'What about SY99? Can't they fly us closer to the building?'

'I've just got off the phone to HQ, ma'am,' Scott Andrews said, who had been talking to DI Brady when Matilda joined them. 'It's too windy for them to take off.'

'What are we going to do? We can't just stand here.'

'We can walk across the field, ma'am,' Rory said, pointing through the trees to Starling House in the distance.

'The fields are saturated. It's not safe,' Christian said.

'We don't have much choice. Jacob Brown is missing. He's an escaped killer. He could be anywhere.'

'In this?' Christian looked up at the sky. 'I doubt he'll be wearing waterproofs and wellies. If he has escaped, he'll be hiding somewhere waiting for all this to die down.'

'What do you mean by "if"?'

'We don't know he's escaped. We've only got Kate Moloney's word for it. He could still be in there somewhere. We need to search the house before we put any officers at risk searching in this weather.'

'All the more reason for us to get there as soon as possible. Christian, there's no alternative. We'll have to walk.'

Rory helped Matilda over the drystone wall. Together, the four of them set off through the squelching field to Starling House.

'Kate, it's DCI Darke,' Matilda shouted into her mobile phone. She was surprised it was still working as it had been floating around in a puddle of water in her pocket. 'We can't get to you by car; we're walking across the field. Can you make sure the gates are open for us?'

'Of course. Jacob's escaped. I don't know how or what or … this is a nightmare,' she broke down.

'Kate, I can't hear you very well because of the weather. Just have the gates open for us, and a few towels would be great too.' Matilda disconnected the call before Kate could reply.

'You should have asked her to put the kettle on,' Rory said.

After turning onto Limb Lane, the drive to Starling House should take less than three minutes. On foot it would probably take about seven. Crossing a flooded field in darkness in a gale-force wind took Matilda, Christian, Rory and Scott more than twenty minutes. By the time they arrived at the front door they were freezing cold and soaking wet.

They stood in the foyer and removed their wellington boots and waterproof coats. Kate handed them each a towel and told them Rebecca Childs was making tea and coffee for them all, which put a smile on Rory's face.

'Kate, what happened?' Matilda asked.

'I was in bed, asleep. I was woken by the sound of the alarm going off. By the time I was downstairs Peter and Rebecca were already at the recreation room. That's where the alarm was coming from. The windows in the patio doors had been smashed.'

'Smashed? I thought they had bars on them,' she said.

'It's supposed to be toughened glass. The security company who fitted the doors said we didn't need bars.'

Matilda rolled her eyes. 'What did you do then?'

'We all went up to A corridor to check on the inmates. As soon as we went onto the corridor we saw one of the doors was open.'

'Jacob Brown's?'

'That's right.'

'Had the door been forced?'

'No. It had been unlocked.'

'And they can't be unlocked from the inside, can they?' Matilda asked, double-checking what she already knew.

'No.' Kate shook her head and looked down. The weight of the situation was hanging around her shoulders. Matilda felt a great deal of sympathy for her. She was suffering from the collective guilt of everything that happened here, just like Matilda did with the collapse of the Carl Meagan case.

'Right. Who's on duty tonight?'

'Peter McFly and Rebecca Childs.'

Matilda turned to Rory. 'Were they interviewed?'

'Rebecca was but Peter wasn't. He'd worked a long night shift and was sleeping.'

Matilda gave him an annoyed look. They were investigating the murder of a convicted killer in a youth prison and Rory didn't want to interview one of the guards because he was sleeping. Typical. 'Get Rebecca and Peter isolated. I'll interview them myself. Christian, you and Scott give this entire building a going over – see if Jacob Brown is still on the premises. Kate, get all the other guards to join the search too.'

'What about the other inmates?'

'Keep them locked in their rooms. Nobody is to unlock those doors without my say-so.'

Everyone left to conduct their duties. Matilda went over to a window and looked out. Thankfully, the heavy rain had washed the press away. There were no cars, news van or waiting journalists. The two uniformed officers were standing at the gates with their torches aloft. She didn't blame them for not noticing the escape. She fished out her phone and searched for a number. It was several rings before it was answered by a groggy greeting.

'Ma'am, it's DCI Darke. We have a situation at Starling House,' Matilda said to ACC Valerie Masterson.

FORTY-THREE

It took over an hour for every single room, cupboard, nook and cranny in Starling House to be searched. There was no sign of Jacob Brown anywhere. The rain had stopped, and Matilda had called for a fire engine to pump out the water on Limb Lane so a search team could get through and begin a search of the grounds and surrounding fields at first light.

There was nothing the ACC could do. She told Matilda to keep her informed, and as soon as she was able, she wanted a meeting to be told 'what the fuck was going on at that bastard place' as she so beautifully put it.

Matilda had spoken separately with Rebecca Childs and Peter McFly. Their stories were identical. Kate had left them in the staffroom just before half-past nine last night. It was quiet from then until an alarm sounded over four hours later.

'I don't understand this,' Kate said for the hundredth time. 'I don't understand this at all. How can an inmate break out of his room and escape? It's not possible.'

Kate and Matilda were sitting in Kate's office. They were trapped by the localized flooding on Limb Lane. There was nothing they could do. Although Matilda felt a degree of sympathy towards Kate, she was beginning to tire with regards to how blind she was towards her own staff.

'Kate, I think it's time you realized that one of your staff is a killer and, for reasons unknown, helped Jacob Brown to escape.'

Kate shook her head. 'No. I'm sorry, no, that's not … no.'

'What do you know of your staff?'

'What do you mean?' she asked, fiddling with the collar on her shirt.

'We've searched their rooms as well, you know. Did you know Richard Grover has a stack of pornography magazines under his bed? Some of them you can't even buy in this country due to their content.'

The colour drained from Kate's face. 'Oh God. It's not kids, is it?'

'Let's just say if they're not kids they're extremely close to the legal age limit.'

'But that has no bearing on this case. Ryan Asher wasn't interfered with in that way, was he?'

'My God, you're still defending your staff,' Matilda yelled. 'Does one of them need to walk in here carrying a bloody knife and dragging a corpse behind them before you realize they're not saints?'

With shaking hands, Kate swept away a tear before it had time to fall down her face. 'I know they're not saints,' she said quietly. 'I also know they're not qualified. Not a single bloody one of them. Why would anyone want to work here? These inmates, these boys, these murdering scum,' she spat out her words. 'Nobody wants to be surrounded by the most evil children in Britain. I have to hire anyone who applies for the job whether they're capable or not. I have no choice.' Kate's entire body was shaking with anger. 'For all I know, any one of them could be a killer or a rapist or part of a paedophile ring. You want to arrest them, go ahead. Take them all. Close us down. I don't fucking care anymore.' Kate stormed out of the office and slammed the door firmly behind her leaving Matilda sitting in silence.

She was more shocked by the outburst than the language Kate used. She wasn't surprised Kate was beginning to unravel; it had been a long time coming by the look of it.

By the time it was light, a fire engine was parked at the gates of Starling House, draining away the water to allow access. It would be a long process. The field opposite was saturated and the water had to go somewhere. The water seeping through the cracks in the drystone wall onto the road was slowing down, but not by much.

Matilda looked out of the window watching the scene, wondering how far Jacob Brown had got during the storm overnight. He could be anywhere by now.

'I've got some news but you're not going to like it,' Rory said as he entered Kate's office.

'It's been so long since I've had some good news, Rory, that I don't think it exists anymore. Let's have it.'

'I've just got off the phone with Sian. By the way, her house flooded last night. She's fuming.'

'Oh God. I'll give her a call. There's no reason for her to be at work.'

'She said she'd rather be here than at home. Her husband's dealing with it all, apparently. Anyway, Sian's been doing some digging into the staff here, and the tutor, Fred Percival, has a record.'

'Of course he has,' Matilda said, not surprised anymore by anything that happened in Starling House. 'What's he done?'

'In 1999 he was questioned for sexually assaulting a boy in Leicester. It went to trial and he was found not guilty. In 2002 he was found guilty of sex with a minor and sentenced to two years. He was out in nine months. In 2006 he was questioned for having sex with a boy under the age of sixteen. It didn't get to court.'

'Didn't he say he was married with kids though?'

'Yes, he did. And he was. At the time. What he didn't tell us is that his kids are now over eighteen and have disowned him. His wife committed suicide in 2010.'

'Jesus. Surely Kate knew all about this when she hired him.'

'I've been looking through the files again while we've been trapped here. They're very meticulous until around 2005. Then she stopped requesting references and DBS checks.'

'What's DBS?'

'Disclosure and Barring Service. It's what we now call CRB.'

'Oh yes, of course. But Kate told us she vigorously checks all staff before they're given a job here. She told us that on our first meeting with her.'

'She was obviously telling porkies.'

'I'm beginning to think Starling House is built on lies.'

FORTY-FOUR

It was time to take off the kid gloves. She understood the ACC wanted a fast result on Ryan Asher's murder, and now she did too. She was tired with everyone holding something back. It seemed strange how the convicted killers seemed to be telling the truth while the supposed honest, law-abiding staff kept wrong-footing the investigation at every turn.

Still using Kate's office, Matilda gathered Christian, Rory and Scott. She kept looking out of the window to see how the fire crew were getting on with draining the water. They appeared to be standing around chatting and looking at the large pool of water like it contained all of life's secrets.

'It's started raining again.'

'Thanks, Rory.'

'I bet we're going to be stranded here all day,' he said, looking up at the heavy grey sky.

'I don't want to have to spend the night with a bunch of killers,' Scott said, a genuine look of horror on his face.

'The same thing will happen as when you spent the night in Norwich with Faith – absolutely nothing,' Rory said with a smirk.

'Just because you spend the night in a hotel doesn't mean you have to have sex.'

'Bloody hell, Scott, what generation are you from? Of course it does. If I'd been there and Faith wasn't having any of it, I'd have been straight on Tinder.'

'Remind me not to send you anywhere that requires an overnight stay then, Rory,' Matilda said. 'Now, can we get on?'

'Sorry boss.'

'Right, there's no sign of Jacob; we haven't caught Ryan's killer. I think it's safe to say that whoever killed Ryan has somehow managed to get Jacob out of Starling House.'

'You don't think he escaped then?' Christian asked, sitting in the far corner of the room picking his fingernails.

'No, I do not. Those cells cannot be opened from the inside, and Kate, Oliver, Rebecca, and Peter said they were all locked in at nine o'clock last night. Someone went back to A corridor and let Jacob out of his room.'

'I've had a word with Gavin Ryecroft about the CCTV camera and he hadn't turned it back on. He said until he knows exactly what happened to it on Monday night he couldn't trust it not to fail again.'

'Knobhead,' Rory said. 'It didn't fail; someone turned it off, it's obvious.'

'I said that,' Christian admitted. 'He seems to have got the Kate Moloney syndrome and doesn't want to think his colleagues would do anything underhand.'

'And we all know the CCTV cameras in the recreation room are dummies.'

'It looks like everyone else knows too.'

'If it was the same person who killed Ryan why not just kill Jacob in his room or somewhere else in the building? Why let him escape?' Rory asked.

'Maybe he hasn't escaped,' Scott pondered. 'Maybe we're meant to think he's escaped.

'We've had this entire building upside down,' Christian said. 'He's not here.'

'There are six rooms we haven't searched,' Matilda said, turning back from the window.

The three men looked at each other with heavy frowns.

'Six?'

'The rooms the inmates are currently locked up in.'

'You think Jacob is hiding in one of the other inmates' rooms? What would be the point of that?' Rory asked.

'To be honest, I don't think Jacob is hiding in this building at all. I also think it is highly likely he's dead. The question is, why has the killer's MO changed? Why not have Jacob spread-eagled on a pool table or a table tennis table with twelve stab wounds? Why smash a window and make it look like he's hopped it?'

'To make it look like Jacob's the killer,' Scott said.

'Well done, Mr Andrews. If we ever get back to HQ help yourself to two items from Sian's snack drawer.'

'So you think that whoever killed Ryan is setting up Jacob? Why? Why Jacob above all the other boys?' Christian asked.

'I've no idea.' Matilda scratched her forehead. This case was beginning to give her a headache. Every day something else occurred to add to the confusion. She wasn't helping herself either by throwing Thomas Hartley into the mix.

'Maybe Jacob was the easiest to bribe,' Scott said, breaking the silence.

'Sorry?'

'Let's say the killer is a member of staff but didn't want to get his hands dirty – or her hands dirty. He, or she—'

'Let's just go with "he" for the moment, Scott,' Matilda interrupted. 'It'll save a lot of confusion, and I can already see smoke coming out of Rory's ears.'

'OK. He obviously knows the inmates, they're all killers, they all have the potential to kill again, but how many are open to be bribed into killing again? He arranges for Jacob to lure Ryan to the recreation room and kill him with the promise that a few days later he'll help Jacob to escape. The member of staff isn't going to care if Jacob is out there or not. He's achieved his goal: Ryan is dead. And, if Jacob is eventually caught and tells the truth, who are the police going to believe? A convicted killer on the run or a member of staff at Starling House?'

'You could be onto something there, Scottmeister,' Rory grinned.

'But we've been through all the files of all the members of staff, past and present,' Christian said. 'None of them have any links with Ryan Asher before he arrived at Starling House. As he was only here for a day nobody could have taken against him enough to warrant killing him the way they did.'

'Yes, Scott, idiot. You should have thought of that,' Rory again, smiling.

'Scott has a point.' Matilda had sat down on Kate's comfortable chair and was resting her head on her hands. 'All the boys were locked in the rooms on Monday night. Someone had to unlock Ryan's room to get him out. They unlocked the recreation room and killed him in there. When Oliver Byron went the next morning, the recreation room was locked. Last night, Jacob's room was unlocked from the outside for him to escape. Someone with a key is doing this. The only people who have keys are the staff.'

'That we know of,' Christian added.

'We're going round in circles here.'

'So where do we go from here?' Rory asked.

'We get the inmates out of their rooms and into the dining room, and I want their rooms ripped apart. I don't care if Jacob isn't hiding under the bed, I want them searched. Christian, you and Scott lead the search and use some of the staff we know are sort of decent to give you a hand.'

'Will do.'

'What about me?' Rory asked.

'We're going to talk to Kate again.'

'She's not going to like this.'

'Not our problem, Rory. We're hunting for a killer among killers here. It's time to stop pissing about and get some answers.'

FORTY-FIVE

'Good morning. I'm Detective Constable Faith Easter from South
Yorkshire Police. I'd like to speak to someone who can tell me
about Ryan Asher.'

The open plan CID seemed quiet without Matilda, Christian,
Scott and Rory. Scott was always quiet, but the exuberant Rory
Fleming more than made up for it with his puppy-like demeanour.
Faith liked working with what used to be the Murder Squad again.
She enjoyed Scott's company; they seemed to have a similar work
ethic. Rory, she could tolerate. Yes, he was handsome, but he knew
it, and that overconfidence could sometimes get on her nerves.
Unfortunately for her, he was funny, and she couldn't help
laughing at his jokes which seemed to encourage him. He was
harmless enough, though. Sian, she loved. She respected Sian and
looked up to her. Although their careers were going on different
paths – Sian was a DS and was happy to stay that way until
retirement – Faith had ambition. She would like a family, maybe,
one day, but at the moment she was concentrating on her career.
She liked the idea of having DCI in front of her name at some
point.

It hadn't taken Faith long to discover which school Ryan Asher
went to in Norwich. Unfortunately, it took her longer to find a

member of staff willing to talk to her. Hellesdon High School predominantly served pupils in the north-west area of Norwich and currently held around 1,300 students. While Faith was waiting for someone to answer her call, she perused the school's website and found out more than she needed to know about the school and the extracurricular activities it offered. It seemed like a very impressive school. If she did ever marry and have a child, Norwich was a possibility as a place to raise a family.

'DC Easter?'

Faith jumped as a loud booming voice came through the phone. 'Yes.'

'I'm sorry to have kept you waiting. I'm Geoffrey Hillingdon. I'm the head teacher here. I believe you have some questions about Ryan Asher.'

'That's right. Thank you for taking my call. I was wondering if you could tell me something about him: what he was like as a student, his academic success, that sort of thing.'

'I shall certainly try. I'm afraid that it's a sad state of affairs that only the really disruptive students seem to register on my radar so I do recall Ryan Asher before, well, before what he did. Academically, he was an above average student. He wasn't going to be a straight-A student but with a little hard work he would have passed all his GCSEs with excellent pass grades.'

'Was he disruptive in his lessons?'

'No, well, not in the beginning. Most of his incidents came during breaks and at lunch. I heard of a few moments, shall we say, out of school hours and at weekends, but they were not the responsibility of the school to sort out.'

'What kinds of incidents?'

'Fights and scrapes. The usual things that happen among teenage boys.'

'So what led from him being a typical teenage boy to murdering his grandparents?'

There was silence on the other end of the phone. Faith knew

they hadn't lost connection as she could hear everyday life of a normal secondary school taking place in the background. She could also hear Mr Hillingdon's strenuous breathing.

Sian placed a mug of tea on Faith's desk and added a Tunnock's Teacake from her snack drawer. Faith mouthed 'thank you'.

'I'm not a psychologist, detective. I'm just an ordinary head teacher. I have no idea what went through his mind to make him commit the crime he did.'

'Were you surprised when you found out?'

'Absolutely. I was devastated. To be perfectly honest with you, there are some pupils here who, if I heard they had killed someone, I would not be surprised. Ryan wasn't one of them.'

Maybe Norwich wasn't such a decent place to raise a child after all, Faith thought. A head teacher has admitted to there being potential killers in his school and he didn't seem too bothered by it. And she thought being a detective was a difficult job – who'd be a teacher?

'So what happened at the school for Ryan to appear on your radar?'

'In the last few months of Ryan being here his behaviour was more disruptive than usual. The number of fights, and their severity, increased. I had two meetings with his parents, who expressed concern for Ryan. They had spoken with him on many occasions. They'd grounded him a few times, removed certain privileges, but it didn't seem to make any difference.'

'Was Ryan mixing with any different people around this time?'

'Not that I'm aware of.'

'But surely something must have switched in his life for his behaviour to have changed so much.'

'I'm sure it did, but that was not at this school,' he seemed quick to add that Hellesdon High School was not to blame for the making of a murderer.

'Is there anyone else I could speak to who you think could help me find out more about Ryan Asher.'

'Not that I can think of. Oh, wait, yes there is. Ryan was in the scouts for a while. You could speak to the scout leader. I believe there was an incident which led to Ryan being excluded from the group. He'd know all about it.'

Faith frantically searched her desk for a pen. 'Do you have his contact details?'

'I do, actually. He's helped out with our school fetes a number of times.'

Faith took down the details, thanked Geoffrey Hillingdon for his time and hung up the phone.

'Get anywhere?' Sian asked.

'I'm not sure. I've got another person to try. How's it going at home?' she asked, nodding at the mobile phone in Sian's hand.

'The carpet and sofas will have to be dumped but the rest of the furniture should be OK. There's nothing we can do until all the water has gone and it's dried out. Stuart's been taking photos and videos for the insurance people. That carpet's only been down a few months.'

'Oh, Sian, I'm sorry. If there's anything I can do.'

Before Sian could say anything her office phone began to ring. She smiled at Faith and was pleased the phone rang when it did as tears were welling up in her eyes.

'DS Mills, CID,' she said into the phone.

'Hello, yes, I believe you've been asking after me,' the voice was soft and shaking.

'I'm sorry?'

'I'm, well, I used to be Belinda Asher. I'm Ryan Asher's mum.'

RYAN ASHER

I was in the kitchen making a sandwich and I overheard Mum and Dad talking. I wasn't purposely listening, they never said anything worth listening to anyway, but one thing caught my interest. Dad had taken Gran to the bank that morning to get some money out for her holiday. She'd withdrawn five grand in cash. Dad was fuming. He said it wouldn't be safe for an elderly couple to have that much money on them. Mum defended them; they were her parents after all. She said they didn't believe in things like credit cards and traveller's cheques. They preferred to deal with cash wherever possible.

It must have been the mention of the cash that pricked my ears up. Five thousand pounds. My grandparents had five thousand pounds in cash in their house.

They'd been talking about this holiday for ever. It was to be their last holiday as they were getting really old now, and they wanted to make it a memorable one. On their honeymoon, fifty-odd years ago, they went to a small village in the south of France. They couldn't afford much back then but they wanted to go back, and now they were planning to stay in a swanky hotel.

I started properly listening to Mum and Dad talking about Gran and Grandad's holiday plans. The night before they were due to go they decided to go out for a meal rather than cook. The house would be empty. That was when I'd go and help myself. It was only five grand, my grandparents were loaded, and Mum and Dad wouldn't see them miss their holiday either. Besides, Grandad had been getting a bit forgetful lately; they'd probably put it down to him losing it. It was a victimless crime.

The table at the French restaurant was booked for eight. Just before nine I made some excuse about needing to go round to Jenson Bright's house to get my homework back. Gran and Grandad didn't live far away from us, only a few minutes' walk. I was at the back door bang on eight thirty. I'd nicked the spare key from the hook on my way out. It was all going smoothly.

I pulled the balaclava out of my back pocket and pulled it over my head. I wasn't going to bother wearing one but then wondered about someone seeing me run away. I had every angle covered. I unlocked the kitchen door and waited for the alarm to start beeping. It didn't. Typical. They hated the alarm and hardly ever set it. This was going to be so easy.

I went into the living room and looked in the sideboard, but didn't find anything. It wasn't in any of the kitchen drawers, or the hallway either. It had to be upstairs. I tiptoed up. I knew they weren't in, but that Mrs Cole next door was a nosey bugger. If she heard a noise she'd be straight on the phone to my mum.

I got the shock of my life when I opened their bedroom door and found them both in bed fast asleep. What the hell!? They must have changed their mind. I remember Mum talking to Gran on the phone earlier. Gran must have said she wasn't feeling too well but Mum said they should go out and enjoy themselves. They obviously decided to have an early night instead.

Grandad always takes sleeping tablets as he's a really light sleeper, so he wouldn't be a problem; Gran could be. She often complained about getting cramp during the night and waking her up. I'd have to be very careful.

I went into the bedroom and slowly opened the drawers. I couldn't see much as it was dark but I had a feel. There was nothing that felt like five grand. There was only one place left to try – the bedside cabinets. I'd come this far. It would be daft to leave now.

Grandad was snoring loudly; he was obviously in a deep sleep. I ducked down and crawled to the bedside cabinet. I eased the drawer open just wide enough to get my hand inside. I felt around and touched an envelope. It was full. It had to be the money. I was touching it. I was actually holding five thousand quid in my hand. I pulled but it wouldn't come. There was so much junk in the drawer that it must have been stuck on something. I pulled harder and the whole drawer came open. The cabinet wobbled and a pen fell off a puzzle book, rolled to the edge of the table and dropped onto the floor. Shit!

I closed my eyes. The pen landed on the carpet but it sounded loud as it was so quiet in the bedroom. I could hear the clock in the hallway ticking all the way up here. There was no movement in the bed so I opened my eyes and looked across at Grandad. His eyes were wide open and staring straight at me.

I remember him saying: 'Who the hell are you?'

Shit!

I didn't know what to do. If I spoke, he'd recognize my voice. The bedroom door was open. I was pretty sure I'd be able to outrun an old man. I stood up and headed for the door, but Grandad was on me before I could do anything. He grabbed my arm. His grip was tight for an old man. I tried to pull away but I couldn't. I just froze. I heard Grandma stirring. Grandad reached out with his other hand and yanked the balaclava off my head.

Grandma sat up and turned the light on. The orange glow from the bedside lamp filled the room and almost blinded me.

'Ryan!' Grandad shouted.

Grandma screamed. I tried not to look at them. I couldn't face them. I knew they'd be disappointed in me. I knew Mum and Dad would kill me. This was going to be a nightmare for our family. Nobody would ever trust me again. I tried to run but Grandad's grip was really tight on my arm. It was the first time I'd ever heard him swear.

'Oh no you don't; you're not going anywhere, you thieving bastard.' He told Gran to call my mum.

I reached out for something and swung it at Grandad. I looked at the bed and saw him laid out there with a massive gash on his head where I'd hit him with the green glass paperweight in my hand. Blood was pouring from his head. Grandma looked and started to scream. She had her mobile phone in her hand. I ran over to her and hit her too, not as hard, just hard enough to stop her from calling Mum, and screaming, and waking the whole neighbourhood.

The room was suddenly quiet again. Standing in the doorway I looked back. This wasn't how it was supposed to happen. They should have been out. I would have been back home by now, sitting on my bed with the door locked.

I was just about to leave when I realized my fingerprints would be all over the bedroom. I'd be caught in no time. If Mum and Dad found out what I'd done they'd disown me; I know they would.

I ran downstairs and out to the garage where Grandad kept a plastic can of petrol for the lawn mower. I went back into the kitchen, grabbed a box of matches from the side and took them up to the bedroom. I sloshed the petrol all over the bed and my grandparents. I tried not to think about it. I really did love my grandparents but there was no other way out of this mess. I lit a match and threw it onto the bed. The fire took hold straightaway. I stood back for a few seconds but the heat was intense, so I left.

I was halfway down the stairs when I remembered I'd left the money in the bedside cabinet. It had probably burnt to ashes by now. All this had been for nothing.

FORTY-SIX

'We've found these in two of the boys' rooms,' Christian Brady said upon entering Kate Moloney's office, holding up five pornography magazines.

'Which boys?'

'Craig Hodge and Lewis Chapman.'

'Oh my God.' Kate slumped into her chair. The gradual falling apart of Starling House was having an adverse effect on her. Her hair, usually tied back in a severe ponytail, was a tangled mess and she hadn't put any make-up on this morning.

Matilda had been in conversation with Kate when Christian interrupted. 'Where did they get them?'

'I asked them both separately and they said Richard Grover sold them to them.'

'He sold them?' Kate again. 'How was he paid?'

Christian looked down at his feet. The answer must be difficult if even Christian Brady struggled to find the words. 'Ma'am, do you think I could talk to you alone?' he asked Matilda.

Matilda nodded to Rory to remain in the room with Kate. She led Christian out of the room and into the small office next door. 'Come on then, out with it,' she said after taking a deep breath, preparing herself.

Christian was obviously uncomfortable. 'Richard has been supplying Craig and Lewis with pornography magazines and in return they've been allowing him to perform oral sex on them.'

'What?'

'He's really been abusing his position here, ma'am.'

'Jesus. And they let him?' The look on her face changed to one of disgust.

'At the end of the day they were getting something out of it too. They were getting porno mags and they were being ... you know ... sucked off.'

'I don't believe this. Why hasn't this come up before now? We've interviewed all the boys and not one of them mentioned it.'

'We didn't ask though, did we? You know what convicts are like; they'll only answer the questions they're asked. Why help the pigs?'

'True. Bloody hell. Kate is going to go through the roof. Right.' Matilda ran her fingers firmly through her hair, pulling hard at the brittle strands. She needed to feel some pain to focus her mind. 'The boys are going to have to be interviewed again, and I don't care what the ACC said, I want them at the station. I want them taped and filmed. I also want Richard Grover and Fred Percival formally questioned.'

'Until the water clears we're still trapped here.'

'Then isolate them,' she said, raising her voice. 'This place is bloody big enough to have everyone in a separate room. Lock them all in their rooms if you have to until we can organize transport back to HQ.'

As Christian left the room Matilda's mobile phone started ringing. It was Sian.

'I've got some sort of good news and some shit-hitting-the-fan news,' Sian said.

'Oh God, I'm not sure I want to hear this.'

'The sort of good news is that Ryan Asher's mother has called. She'd like to speak to you.'

Matilda visibly relaxed. 'That's not sort of good news, that's brilliant news. Thank you Sian. Text me her details and I'll give her—'

'You may want to hold off on that until you hear the bad news.'

'Oh.'

'The ACC is on the warpath. She's ready to explode. She wants to talk to you about why the Thomas Hartley case has seemingly been reopened.'

'Bugger!'

Matilda quickly ended the call to Sian. She had been dreading this happening and hoping she could look into the Thomas Hartley case without it registering with anyone in a position of power; obviously, that hadn't happened. It was all rapidly falling apart.

FORTY-SEVEN

It was time for Matilda to face the music. She needed to speak to the ACC, and this was a conversation she could not have over the phone. Her coat was still wet from trudging through the saturated field next to Starling House in the early hours of the morning. She put it on and immediately felt cold.

The rain was starting to fall again, but only lightly. With her hood up and head down, she took large strides down the long driveway to the security gates.

'Hello, who is in charge?' she called out through the iron bars to anyone who would listen.

'Boss!' shouted the nearest fire officer. 'You're wanted.'

Gerry Markham was in his fifties and, judging by the size of his waist, he did very little in the way of rescuing people by throwing them over his shoulders and carrying them from burning buildings.

'Yes?'

'I'm DCI Matilda Darke,' she flashed her ID. 'My car is somewhere on the other side of this pool, and I need to get back to HQ. I'm investigating a murder and something has come up. Is there any way you can get me to my car?'

'Oh my God, you have got to see this. Scott, pass my mobile,' Rory said.

'What's going on?' Scott asked, handing Rory his iPhone.

'Matilda is being given a piggyback through the water to her car,' he said, trying, but failing, to hide his laughter.

'You're joking!'

'Nope.'

Rory lifted his phone up and started filming through the window in Kate's office as his boss held on for dear life to a firefighter who waded, thigh deep, through the murky water.

'This is gold. This is pure gold.'

'Let me see,' Scott said as he tried to get a better view out of the window.

Rory zoomed in. Matilda's arms were wrapped firmly around the young fireman's neck. The rest of the crew watched on as he sunk lower into the water.

'Ten quid says she goes in,' Rory said.

'No. He'll get her to the other side.'

'Oh my God, it's up to his waist now. I'm so pleased I'm filming this.'

'If she finds out, she'll kill you.'

They watched in silence as the fireman slowed down. The water was gradually lowering. He was more than halfway.

'There you go.'

To a roar of cheering from the other firefighters, Billy Norris set Matilda down on dry ground. As embarrassed as she was it was difficult not to smile. She had never been rescued before and, despite being terrified of falling into the dirty, smelly water, it was fun being carried by a tall, hunky firefighter.

'Thank you,' she said, unable to think of anything else to say.

'You're welcome,' he said, miming doffing his cap. 'We have to stick together in the emergency services.'

'We certainly do. Thank you, again.'

She waved at Gerry Markham and the rest of the crew, who waved back, and made her way to the police Land Rover Rory had driven her here in the night before. She just hoped it would still be there after being abandoned in the small hours of the morning.

As she struggled to find her feet in the waterlogged field she looked over to Starling House and hoped Christian, Scott and Rory hadn't seen her being carried to safety.

On the drive back to HQ, Matilda wondered what kind of mood she would find the ACC in. She was known as a fair woman who always stood up for her staff whenever they needed it. However, get on the wrong side of her and one look from those tiny steely eyes was enough to stop time itself.

Parking in her usual space, Matilda entered the back of the building and tried her best to get to the ACC's office without being seen.

The ACC's secretary was on the phone when Matilda entered the small anteroom. She mouthed for her to go straight in and wished her luck. The expression of sympathy and fear on her face told Matilda everything she needed to know – she was in for a real bollocking.

'Do you want me to lose my job?'

There was no greeting, no offer of coffee, and no small talk. The second Matilda entered the office, the tirade began.

Matilda frowned. 'No, of course I don't.'

'Then what the hell are you trying to do to me?'

'I'm sorry?'

'Don't even try to pretend you have no idea what I'm talking about. I trust you, Matilda. I respect you. I stuck up for you when everyone else wanted me to give you the push over the Carl Meagan case. I put my neck on the line and this is how you repay me.'

Valerie was red with rage. There were veins bulging where veins shouldn't be bulging, and her knuckles were clenched so tight her fingers could snap at any moment. Matilda had never seen her look so angry.

'I've had the Chief Constable from Greater Manchester Police on the phone asking me why a senior officer on my force is looking into an open-and-shut case that was solved years ago.'

'Ah,' Matilda said, looking at the floor.

'Ah? Is that all you have to say? How would you like it if someone started investigating a case you'd solved?'

'Ma'am, I'm simply—'

'You know the scrutiny South Yorkshire Police is under right now,' Valerie interrupted. 'We've got the aftermath of the Hillsborough Inquiry. The magnitude of the sexual abuse scandal in Rotherham is still being felt. Add to the mix the racial unrest at Page Hall and the tabloid press writing features about there being no-go areas for white British members of the public; we're hardly presenting ourselves in a positive light, are we?'

'I was … '

'And this little nugget being released hasn't helped.' She picked up the copy of *Carl* and slammed it down on the desk. Its booming echo could be heard out in the corridor. 'Who do you think this all comes back to? Not you. Certainly not the Chief Constable. It's me that'll get the chop. I'll be the fall guy in all this.'

Matilda couldn't take her eyes off *Carl*. His smile was haunting – emblazoned on her memory. 'May I sit down?'

'Please do. I'm eager to hear your explanation.' Valerie sat back in her seat and tried to relax but it was impossible. The fury she felt was coursing through her veins like an out-of-control juggernaut on a motorway.

'I interviewed Thomas Hartley at Starling House. The second I saw him I knew he didn't belong there. You should have seen him, ma'am. He's empty, broken, there's nothing there at all.'

'Guilt,' Valerie offered in an off the cuff way.

'No. It went deeper than that. His entire life has been ruined. He has no idea who did it and he's petrified.'

'He's a good actor.'

'No. Nobody could fake that. I believe he's innocent. I honestly do.' Valerie remained silent. 'I've not reopened the case – it's not mine to reopen anyway – all I'm doing is looking at it. I may be wrong.' She shrugged. 'But I need to satisfy myself.'

'Is that why you've got Pat Campbell running between Sheffield and Manchester like she's Miss Marple?'

'Pat's son works in Manchester. He worked on the original investigation. I asked Pat to have a quiet word with her son. It's obviously got out. I'm sorry about that.'

'I can't condone this, Matilda. I cannot have you upsetting other forces and acting like a one-woman police force.'

Matilda took a deep breath. She needed her boss on her side. 'Give me a few days' grace. Let me and Pat look into it, informally, and see what we come up with. It could be nothing, but it could be something. There could be an innocent boy in Starling House. How good would that look for South Yorkshire Police if we were able to free an innocent teenager?' She looked at Valerie whose face was expressionless. 'One force sends an innocent boy to prison and we get him out.'

Valerie stood firm. 'No. I'm sorry, Matilda. No. I cannot have a member of my force trying to overturn a solid conviction on the grounds of a feeling.'

'It's not a feeling,' she protested.

'Do you have evidence of Thomas Hartley's innocence?'

As much as she wanted to lie, she couldn't. 'No,' she replied, barely a whisper.

'Then forget it. As far as Manchester are concerned they have their killer. That's the end of it.'

No it is not.

'Now, tell me what the hell is going on at Starling House.'

Matilda took a deep breath. The subject of Thomas Hartley

was obviously over as far as Valerie Masterson was concerned. However, Matilda was more convinced than ever to carry on and find evidence of his innocence. Inside, Matilda was seething. She could feel a rage bubbling up inside her. She needed to calm down.

'Jacob Brown disappeared last night. It seems he's escaped. Personally, I think he was helped.'

'Who by?'

'I've no idea. But whoever did it also killed Ryan Asher, I'm certain.'

'You're sure it wasn't a fellow inmate?'

'Positive. They were all locked up. The cell doors cannot be unlocked from the inside. Besides, the more we look into Starling House the more we realize what a complete shambles it is. Kate Moloney's falling apart before our eyes, and the staff should be locked up themselves.'

'So what's the next step?'

'As soon as the flood water recedes, I'm having a search team go in to find Jacob Brown. Christian, Rory, and Scott are already on-site and will begin as soon as possible. I'm also having all the inmates and staff brought here so they can be interviewed under formal conditions.'

'Logistically, that sounds like a massive task.'

'It is but it'll be worth it. We need to get the staff and the inmates out of their comfort zone.'

'I really hope you know what you're doing, Matilda.'

You're not the only one.

FORTY-EIGHT

Matilda needed to get out of the police station. She had been blasted for allowing an inmate to escape while officers from South Yorkshire Police were supposedly guarding Starling House, but managed to come out of it with very few bruises. However, when it came to the Thomas Hartley case, she was skating on thin ice with heated blades.

She could feel the walls closing in as she made her way down the stairs and towards the back of the building where she was parked. She hoped nobody would stop her and try to talk. The message from Sian that Belinda Asher had been in touch was racing around her head. She should really call her back, but she wasn't in the right frame of mind to do so. One hour. All she wanted was an hour to herself.

Turning left out of the car park, she passed the pack of rain-drenched journalists from all over the country who were eager to find out what was going on in Starling House.

Let someone else deal with it.

There were plenty of people within HQ who were more than capable of handling questions from the press: the ACC could release another statement, or DS Sian Mills could talk to the press.

She would hate it but if it was her job then she would bite the bullet and do it.

Matilda pressed her foot to the floor and headed, without realizing it, for home. She needed familiarity. She needed somewhere she could fully relax. She needed James.

Following James's death one of the things Matilda hated more than anything else was coming back to an empty house. As a freelance architect, James often worked from home, and whenever she stumbled in James was either working in the office with music blaring, or watching some ridiculous sport on television and shouting mercilessly at the officials.

Now when she entered the house she was presented with a heavy silence. The ticking clocks drove her mad, and was the fridge supposed to be that loud or was it on the verge of breaking down?

Leaving the Land Rover in the drive, she threw open the front door and slammed it behind her. She needed noise. She needed to hear activity. She felt James's presence everywhere in the house but couldn't hear him and she couldn't see him.

'Hello? Hello? James, it's me. I'm home,' she called out. Her voice, loud and maniacal, echoed around the large hallway. 'Is there anyone home?'

If I receive a reply, I'll probably wet myself.

She suddenly remembered that when she left the house in the early hours of the morning her father was there. If he was still here and heard her calling for James, he would think she had completely lost it.

Maybe she had.

There was a note held down by an ugly ornament on the hall table. Matilda picked it up and smiled at her father's handwriting:

Matilda,

Thank you for the chat and keeping me company last night. I didn't want to go home to an empty house. I suppose you're used to it by now.

I finished off the cheese in the fridge and I washed every-thing up and ran round the living room with the hoover. I'll give you a call later tonight. Don't work too hard.

Love, Dad. xx

She wiped a tear from her eye and walked into the large kitchen, which was showroom-clean. She hardly used it anymore. When she did decide to sit down for a bite to eat in the evening it was either scrambled egg on toast or beans on toast. Sometimes she would go crazy and mix things up and have scrambled egg with beans on toast.

Matilda pulled open the fridge door and saw the packets of ready-made salads and microwavable meals for one. Her whole life was pathetic. She was completely alone. Yes, she had a friend in Adele Kean, and Pat Campbell was starting to feature in her life more, but they had their own lives. Adele had her son, Chris, and Pat had Anton and her army of grandkids to contend with. They didn't want a manic depressive on their doorstep every night looking for company.

She took a bottle of water from the fridge and drank half of it in one gulp. Her mouth was dry. A drawer next to the sink contained her antidepressants. She didn't like taking them. The thought of pumping goodness knows what inside her on a daily basis filled her with horror. Nobody knew what prolonged prescription drug use did to inner organs. However, occasionally, help was needed in the form of medication.

She felt angry at being told to lay off the Thomas Hartley case despite the fact that an innocent young man could be languishing in prison while the real killer was still at large. Surely even the slightest hint of suspicion should be followed up, not ignored for fear of upsetting someone across the Pennines.

She popped three Venlafaxine from the blister pack and threw them to the back of her throat, followed by another large slug of water. Hopefully they would start to kick in soon. She needed to get back to work. The floodwater at Starling House should have been pumped out by now so a minibus could collect the inmates and take them back to HQ. Or should it wait until tomorrow? It was gone three o'clock now. There was no chance they would be able to question all six remaining inmates. And what about Richard Grover, Fred Percival and the other staff who would need interviewing?

'Fuck!' Matilda kicked the dustbin, sending it skidding across the kitchen floor. It hit the dishwasher and toppled over, spilling its load all over the clean floor.

Her head was heavy with thoughts, doubts, questions, and Carl bloody Meagan.

Somewhere in the distance, Matilda's mobile phone started to ring. She had no idea where it was. She didn't care. She had no intention of answering it. All she wanted was some time on her own, an hour, half an hour, even ten minutes would do, but it would appear nobody could think for themselves anymore. They had to run everything past Matilda. DI Brady should be taking on more of the hassle.

The phone stopped ringing and then started again almost immediately.

'Jesus Christ,' Matilda hissed. 'Can't you leave me alone for just five minutes?'

She headed for the hallway where she had thrown her bag. The screen on her mobile phone was lit up and told her Rory was calling. Of course it was going to be Rory. It couldn't have been anyone else, could it? DC Rory Fleming – all style and no substance.

'What?' she barked as she swiped a finger across the screen.

'Sorry, boss. Am I interrupting?'

'Not in the slightest, Rory. You know I'm always pleased to hear from you,' her reply was laced with sarcasm but the thick-skinned DC didn't acknowledge it.

'We've found Jacob Brown.'

So much for an hour or two on my own.

FORTY-NINE

Scoutmaster, Murray Beck, was a difficult man to get hold of. Since he retired six months earlier from being stock controller of The Norwich Packaging Company, he had been busier than ever. He was an organizer of clubs and social events for the neighbourhood he lived in, helped out at the church and drove the minibus to take the elderly on day trips. His long-suffering wife, Millie Beck, hardly ever saw him. Reluctantly, she gave Faith his mobile number.

When Murray finally answered and Faith told him she was a detective constable with South Yorkshire Police, he spent the next five minutes trying to find somewhere private they could hold their conversation. Faith could hear noises in the background: Murray apologizing, saying this call was 'incredibly urgent', the sound of shuffling footsteps, doors opening and closing. Eventually, he found somewhere to settle. Judging by the echo on the line, Faith guessed he was in an empty room.

'Mr Beck, thank you for answering my call. I promise I won't take up any more of your time than I have to. You were a scoutmaster briefly; is that correct?'

'That's right. I gave it up about three years ago. I'm not as young as I was and I can't keep up with the energetic pace some of these boys have. It's my nephew who has taken over. If it's a scout-related matter then I'm sure he'll be able to help you. He's a bit wet behind the ears but he's a willing lad.'

'No, Mr Beck, it's you I need to speak to. It's concerning Ryan Asher. I believe you knew him when he was in the scouts.'

'Ah.'

'Is there a problem, Mr Beck?'

'Call me Murray, please. There's not a problem as such, no. I just don't like to talk ill of people.'

Faith found that hard to believe. A man who spent so much of his time within the community and had rebuked his own nephew probably enjoyed a gossip more than most. He was relishing the attention of a detective needing information and wanted it coaxed out of him. Faith had no intention of stroking his ego.

'Mr Beck, I am investigating the murder of a teenager and I need to find out as much as I can about the victim so I can find his killer. Time really is of the essence here.'

'I understand,' he replied, swallowing loudly. 'Well, Ryan Asher wasn't with the scouts for long. When he started he was a very willing and capable lad but it wasn't long before his attitude changed.'

'Go on,' Faith had to prompt when he stopped talking.

'I remember speaking to his parents about it. They said he'd got some new friends, but they weren't part of our scout group so I wouldn't know who they were. Anyway, his whole personality seemed to change. He wasn't as helpful, he slouched, he became cheeky and lackadaisical. And then he became violent.'

'Violent?' Faith's eyes lit up. 'In what way?'

'He'd purposely pick fights with the other boys. He'd try and find their weaknesses and bully them into a reaction. I couldn't have that among the other scouts. I gave him a warning. I even told his parents I might have to exclude him. Eventually I had no choice.'

'How did he take it?'

'I don't think he was bothered. When I told him he was no longer welcome, he just shrugged. As he walked out of our meeting hall he kicked over a few things and smashed a window in the door, but, to be honest, I was just glad to be rid of him. He'd become … frightening.'

'Do you think he may have started taking drugs?'

'I did think that, yes. I even mentioned it to his father but he said Ryan wasn't involved in that sort of thing.'

'Did you hear of any other incidents Ryan may have been involved in?'

He scoffed. 'Plenty. I'm assuming you know all about the Malcolm Preston incident?'

Faith had a copy of Ryan's file from Norwich Police Force on her untidy desk. She quickly flicked through it. The name sounded familiar. 'No, I don't believe I do,' she said.

'Oh. Well you should look him up. I don't like to say this about another person, especially a boy, but Ryan Asher was no victim. He was an evil and sadistic child. When it came on the news about him killing his grandparents I told my Millie that I wasn't completely surprised. I had a feeling he'd commit murder one day. I just didn't expect it to be so soon.'

'You knew he'd commit murder?' Faith was shocked. A community man like Murray Beck, a churchgoer, a scoutmaster – should he really be seeing evil in others?

'Some people are rotten to the core. I'm not saying he was born evil. His parents tried their best for him, I know they did, but he got mixed up with some very dodgy young boys – boys who probably were born evil. Look up Malcolm Preston on that internet thing, there's bound to be plenty of information about him. That'll tell you what kind of a person Ryan Asher was.'

Faith thanked Murray Beck for taking the time to talk to her and hung up the phone. While he had given her more of an insight into what kind of a child Ryan was, Faith found she had more questions than answers. Clearing a space on her desk, she pulled her keyboard towards her and typed 'Malcolm Preston Norwich' into a search engine.

THREE YEARS IN LIMBO

John Preston spends every single day by his son's bed. He reads to him from books, newspapers, and magazines. His conversations are one-sided but he believes his son can hear every word he is saying.

It will be three years next Tuesday since Malcolm Preston, then aged 12, was attacked, robbed, and left for dead in woodland surrounding Eaton Park, Norwich.

'It was broad daylight and Malcolm was out riding his bike. It was something every normal twelve-year-old boy does. There was nothing for me or his mum to worry about. He was a sensible boy and we just assumed he would come home when he was ready for his tea.'

John continues, 'When he didn't come home his mother tried his mobile phone. It was answered but the person on the other end quickly hung up. She carried on trying but then whoever answered kept laughing at her down the phone. She knew something had happened. She knew there was something wrong. On the sixth call, she asked where Malcolm was and a young voice said that as far as he knew Malcolm was lying dead somewhere.'

'My Pauline was frantic. I couldn't calm her down. I had a neighbour come round and sit with her while I went to find Malcolm. I sort of knew where he liked to cycle so I went on his route. I found his bike before I found him. The front wheel had been badly damaged and when I saw Malcolm's leg sticking out from behind a tree I thought he'd had an accident.'

Doctors later described Malcolm's injuries to be the most severe they had ever seen on a person to have survived. He had been kicked, punched, stamped on, been run over with his own bike, spat and urinated on. His trainers and mobile phone had been stolen.

Malcolm underwent four operations to relieve the swelling on his brain and to stop internal bleeding. He was placed in an induced coma where he has remained ever since.

'Malcolm is breathing on his own.' John said tearfully from his only son's bedside. 'He has regular brain scans to check it is functioning correctly but he just won't wake up.'

At the time of the attack on Malcolm, rumours were rife over who the culprit was. However, with no witnesses and poorly stored forensic evidence, nobody was ever caught.

Malcolm is not the only victim in this senseless crime. A year after the attack, Malcolm's mother, Pauline, was diagnosed with breast cancer. Despite extensive chemo-therapy she lost her battle just three months later, never able to say goodbye to her son.

'I still have hope. I have to have hope otherwise there would be no point in me being here. Malcolm will wake up again one day and he will tell me who did this to him and then we will have the proof we need to get a conviction. I don't care how long that will take.'

Norwich Evening News – Friday 5 August 2016.

FIFTY

The water had been drained from Limb Lane and the fire crew had left, much to Matilda's disappointment. Being carried over the pool of dirty water had been the first contact she had had with a man since James had died. It helped that he was young and good-looking too.

Matilda cursed herself. How could she allow herself to think about being with another man? It had only been eighteen months since James's death. Maybe because she missed him so much, his touch, his body, his smell, his hands, his long fingers, that she just wanted to feel another body close to hers, even if it was a man young enough to be her son carrying her over dirty, smelly water.

She saw Starling House in the distance but didn't turn left down the dirt track. Instead, she followed Rory's directions and continued a mile up the road and turned right. The smooth tarmac gave way to a bumpy road of loose gravel. Matilda wished she'd returned in the Land Rover rather than her aged Ford Focus. Ahead, she saw Rory, still in his wet-weather gear. He flagged her down and directed her to a safe parking space.

He opened the car door for her. 'I'm absolutely pissing freezing,' he moaned.

302

'Well, that's not the worst greeting I've received today,' she said, remembering the tirade the ACC burst into when she'd first entered her office. *Don't people say hello anymore?*

'My coat's wet, my trousers are wet, my shoes are squelching. If I end up with pneumonia—'

'Rory, go back to the station,' she said calmly.

'What?'

'Go back to the station and get changed.'

'But—'

'Just go. Oh, there's a police Land Rover outside my house that needs picking up too.'

Rory stood, mouth agape, as Matilda made her way over to where Christian and Scott were talking in hushed tones.

'Give me the bad news.'

Christian smiled and led the way through a thicket of bare trees to a small opening. He didn't need to say anything. Hanging from the thick branch of a gnarled oak tree swung the lifeless body of Jacob Brown. He was several feet from the ground, and he swayed gently in the stiff autumnal breeze.

Matilda stepped forward and looked up at the teenager. She tilted her head as she queried what she was seeing. The rope was expertly tied around the bough of the tree in a knot that would never come loose. Around his purple neck, the noose was perfectly drawn.

'Why would he escape just to hang himself?' Scott asked.

'He didn't,' Matilda said.

'Sorry?'

'This is another staged death. Call a forensics team and get Adele Kean down here. Jacob Brown was murdered.'

It was early evening before the full forensic team was in place and floodlights had been drafted in. Heavy clouds were once again looming and, according to the BBC Weather app on Matilda's phone, it wouldn't be long before another downpour arrived. They needed to move fast before darkness fell, and Matilda wanted Jacob cut down as soon as possible.

A large plastic sheet was placed directly below Jacob in case any evidence came loose from the body. Matilda, Christian, Adele and scene of crime officers were dressed in white forensic suits. Scott had been sent back to HQ to change into warm, dry clothes, though he was reluctant to do so. Sian was on her way to relieve him.

A stepladder was placed next to Jacob's hanging body, and Adele made her way cautiously up the steel rungs. Christian held onto the ladder as it was on rough ground.

'What first made you think of murder, Mat?' Adele said, always keen to see how other people's minds worked.

'His fingernails. They're broken; there's either blood or mud or fibres beneath them. He was very clean when I saw him last at Starling House. He's obviously been in a struggle and it obviously happened outside.'

'Anything else?'

'His clothes are torn. Again, he was a neat and tidy lad while in Starling House. If he had escaped and climbed over the fence he might have got caught on barbed wire but that wouldn't have torn his clothes to this extent.'

'Anything else?' Adele asked, trying to suppress a smile.

Matilda looked to Christian and rolled her eyes. It was like being back in training. 'Well, I'm not an expert on tree climbing but looking at the trunk there's no way you could climb that without a ladder. As there isn't one around and Jacob is dangling several feet from the ground, I'm guessing someone killed him then strung him up.'

'Well done DCI Darke. You can join my department any day.'

'That's handy to know.'

Adele leaned in to Jacob Brown to have a closer look at the rope around his neck. 'There is bruising, but it's not sufficient with the type of rope used and with the drop. Judging by the size and shape of the marks I'd guess he was strangled and then strung up. It's not easy to tell from this angle, or this light. There doesn't seem to be any sign of a broken bone either,' she said, firmly holding Jacob's head with both hands.

Matilda shivered as a gust of wind tore through the woods. 'Do you think he was killed here and then hanged, or killed elsewhere?'

'It's difficult to tell,' Adele said looking down at the mud. 'The ground is very soft due to the amount of rain we've had. It's obviously disturbed because we've all been walking on it, and the fallen leaves and branches from the recent storm could have covered up a lot of evidence.'

'What about time of death?'

'Due to the weather conditions since the time he was reported missing I'd say he wasn't missing from Starling House for long before he died.'

'So he was lured from Starling House, for whatever reason, brought here and strangled,' Christian said. 'But the killer wanted to make it look like suicide.'

'It makes no sense,' Matilda said, shaking her head. 'We're within spitting distance of Starling House. Why stage an escape just to make it look like he committed suicide when he could easily have been hanged in his cell?'

'Do you think Jacob was silenced?'

'It's a possibility. Maybe Jacob saw who killed Ryan Asher and tried to blackmail them. If it was one of the guards, Jacob could have said he wanted out in exchange for his silence. However, Jacob would have been a loose cannon so the killer lured him here and strangled him.'

'And made a botched attempt to make it look like suicide,' Adele said as she cautiously made her way back down the step-ladder.

'Maybe not botched. Maybe it isn't supposed to look like a suicide at all. Ryan Asher was stabbed twelve times, which we've said is reminiscent of twelve members of a jury. Maybe Jacob is hanging as if he's been sentenced to death by hanging for his crime,' Matilda said.

'But, like you said, why break him out when he could easily have been killed in his cell?'

'Jacob Brown was sentenced for killing his girlfriend. She was found raped and murdered in woodland. Maybe the killer is copying his crime. A sort of quid pro quo.'

'In which case,' Christian said, 'there are six more victims waiting in Starling House for the killer to choose from next.'

FIFTY-ONE

By the time Matilda left the woods it was pitch-dark and a fine drizzle had begun. Between them, she and Christian had decided not to interview the inmates and staff of Starling House that night but to leave them until the morning. In the meantime, uniformed officers were posted inside the building overnight to make sure another inmate or member of staff didn't flee, or wasn't murdered.

Once Adele had finished examining Jacob Brown in the woods, he was carefully cut down and taken to the mortuary, where Adele would carry out a post-mortem first thing in the morning. That left Matilda with nothing to do but go home and lick her wounds.

She had only been home a few minutes when her phone beeped an incoming text message:

My son has just told me his bosses have found out about us looking into the Hartley case. He's been suspended. Not sure how it leaked out. I'll phone you tomorrow. Pat.

Matilda didn't bother replying. It hadn't been the best day in either investigation. Ideally, she would like an evening off and to think of nothing work related. She knew that wouldn't happen. Her mind wouldn't allow it.

She should have a bath. A long soothing soak in the tub. But the thought of lying in warm water with her own filth floating around her didn't sound too relaxing so she settled on a shower instead. She turned the temperature up to as hot as she could stand it and stood under the cascade of scolding needles. When she stepped out her face was bright red from the heat, but she felt cleansed. She needed to feel the pain in order to begin to relax.

With James's dressing gown almost burying her, she slipped her feet into novelty slippers, made herself a mug of tea and went into the living room.

Starling House had been allowed to operate almost behind closed doors for twenty years. Kate had covered up every incident from minor ones to the biggies like Elly Caine assaulting Jacob Brown. She hadn't wanted the adverse publicity, that was understandable, but she must have realized one day it would all disintegrate around her ears. That day had arrived and Kate had to be held accountable.

She was struggling with these cases. Whatever was going on at Starling House was frightening, and Matilda was starting to worry she was in over her head. Kate Moloney was obviously a loose cannon. It was shocking to see how such a together, stern person when she first met her was now beginning to fall apart. Kate reminded her of herself. Matilda presented herself as a ball-buster at work who stood for no nonsense. Would she eventually implode and allow her emotions to get the better of her?

Then there was Thomas Hartley. Matilda couldn't help but feel sympathy for the teenager trapped in Starling House with those murderers, the abusive staff, and goodness knows what else went on that was being kept hidden from Matilda and her team. The evidence that had led him to being locked up was purely circumstantial so why had he been jailed for life? What had been uncovered, or not uncovered, during the investigation that had implicated Thomas Hartley as the most likely suspect? Did nobody think to question his motive? If Thomas was innocent, there must have been a massive cover-up at Greater Manchester Police. But who was involved, how high did this go, and what the hell was Matilda getting herself into?

FIFTY-TWO

Kate Moloney had hardly slept. She had still been awake at two o'clock. Her mind a whirl with everything that had occurred over the past few days – Ryan Asher's murder, now Jacob Brown being killed. Her staff all seemed to be hiding something dark in their past, and she was dreading what tomorrow would bring.

Tomorrow was now here. Kate was back in her office, hair uncombed, no make-up, no bright red lipstick, no killer heels. There was a large and very strong black coffee on her desk in front of her but it hadn't been touched. She had no drive or motivation to do anything.

An image out of the window caught her attention and she looked up to see a fleet of cars and police vans heading down the drive. What fresh hell was about to descend upon Starling House?

She opened the cupboard in the corner of the room and took out a black jacket. She pulled her hair back into a tight ponytail and looked at her reflection in the full-length mirror on the back of the door. She looked a mess. She looked tired. She looked as if she had given up. However, she would have to do for now.

'DCI Darke, how can I help you?' she asked as she exited her office and saw Matilda lead the way with a troop of uniformed and plain-clothed officers behind her.

'We're here to take all of the inmates back to South Yorkshire Police and formally interview them.'

'What? You can't do that?'

'I think you'll find I can. I'll also be doing the same with your staff, including you.'

'This is outrageous.'

'What's outrageous is the fact Starling House has been allowed to operate without being supervised for so long.'

Kate tried to say something but was too taken aback to speak. There was nothing she could do as a team of officers filed into the building and headed for the stairs to collect the inmates. This would definitely mark the final nail in the coffin for Starling House.

Within half an hour of them arriving, Matilda and her team had secured all six remaining inmates in marked police vehicles and were heading to HQ. There, they would be held in separate cells and interviewed individually. By the end of the day, hopefully, they would have a clear picture of just what had been going on in Starling House.

Kate stood in the doorway and watched as the fleet of police cars disappeared through the iron gates, turned left and headed for Sheffield city centre. When she turned around she saw Matilda in the foyer talking to some of the staff.

'Richard Grover, I am arresting you for causing a child to engage in sexual activity and aggravated assault by abusing a position of trust. You do not have to say anything; but it may harm your defence if you do not mention when questioned something which you later rely on in court. Anything you do say may be given in evidence. Do you understand?'

'What the hell—?' Kate almost screamed. 'This is too much. Abusing a position of trust? Richard is one of the most dedicated and hard-working members of staff I've ever employed.'

Matilda ignored Kate and moved on to Fred Percival. 'Mr

Percival, I'd like you to go with my officers to be formally interviewed back at the station. I believe you know what this is about.'

Fred didn't reply. His face said it all. Gone was the annoying smile and the air of superiority, replaced by a hangdog look of regret. Sian Mills led him out of the building by the elbow to a waiting unmarked car.

'Are you going to tell me what is going on?' Kate said, blocking Matilda from leaving.

'Fred Percival has a record of underage sex among young boys. Richard Grover has been engaging in sexual activity with some of the inmates here. God only knows what the others have been up to,' she said, looking at the remaining staff over her shoulder. 'I have put steps in place to have Starling House temporarily closed down while you can be replaced and a new team of staff can be employed. I'm waiting to hear from BB Security, Sheffield City Council, and the Home Office.'

'You're closing us down?'

'Temporarily.'

'No,' Kate said. Despite the fact she knew it was all over for her she couldn't quite let go. 'No, I won't have it. I'm not leaving. I've been here for twenty years. You know … You know what it's like … I've told you … You've seen.' She started panicking. A rage had taken over her and her entire body was shaking with adrenaline as she started to lose grip on her emotions and reality. 'I want you to leave. Until I'm told otherwise, I am still in charge of Starling House. I want you out. I want you and your team out of this building right now,' she screamed in Matilda's face.

'We will leave, but we will be back. And if you attempt to stop us gaining access I will have you arrested for obstructing a murder investigation. I'm going to be leaving police officers here too. I'm sorry Kate, but I can't trust you or your staff anymore.'

With the last word, Matilda turned and left the building with her team following. Kate and the remaining staff looked on with horror-struck expressions. Everything was falling apart.

FIFTY-THREE

DC Faith Easter was late arriving to work. The clear-up from the storm had caused delays on the roads as felled trees had blocked roads and the heavy rain had caused such damage to the tarmac that driving was no longer safe. Faith wasn't surprised. Sheffield City Council was famous for patching up when it should be fully repairing damaged roads.

The open-plan office of the CID was virtually empty. The odd plain-clothed detective here and there but the main players in the Ryan Asher case were absent. Late the previous night, Faith had been speaking to a DI from Norwich police about Malcolm Preston. Ryan's name was mentioned as the suspect the press had hinted at but there were no witnesses. Social media had, at the time, thrown Ryan's name around as the perpetrator and there were rumours he had admitted it in private circles. However, without evidence, and without a witness statement from Malcolm Preston, it would be a crime that Ryan would go unpunished for.

Faith was itching to talk to Matilda. DCI Darke had asked her to look into Ryan's past and find if there was anything there that would link to his murder. Surely this was worth following up. Malcolm's family hadn't received justice for what had happened to the twelve-year-old. Or maybe they had, if they were behind his killing.

Faith took a packet of dark chocolate KitKats from her bag and put them in Sian's snack drawer. That more than covered up for the two fruit Club biscuits and the Mars bar she had eaten the day before. As she returned to her desk she remembered something. She took over from Rory to look into Ryan's past. He must have come across Malcolm Preston during his search. Then it dawned on her. He had. He mentioned it at the briefing in the boardroom at Starling House.

She went over to his untidy desk and rummaged through his notes. It may have looked a mess but he had labelled each piece of paper at the top with the inmate's name. She flicked through his notes on Ryan Asher and there is was – Malcolm Preston's name circled and a question mark next to it. Further inspection showed he hadn't followed it up. His notes on all the inmates were extensive and full of conjecture, but none of it was relevant to solving Ryan or Jacob's murder.

The double doors burst open. Faith jumped and immediately slunk back to her desk. Matilda entered followed by the rest of what used to be the Murder Investigation Team.

'Ma'am, can I have a word—?' Faith began.

'Not now,' Matilda replied, not stopping but storming off towards her office.

'It's kind of—'

'I said not now.'

The office door slammed shut, the glass rattling in the door frame.

'What's going on?' Faith whispered to Sian.

'It's all kicking off. We've got all of the inmates from Starling House downstairs waiting to be interviewed and a couple of the staff too. You've no idea what they've been up to at that place. Matilda's put in a request to the Home Office that it should be closed down.'

'Bloody hell.'

'Exactly. So, what's the problem? Anything I can help you with?'

'I hope so.' Faith filled Sian in on the Malcolm Preston case and how Ryan Asher fitted into it. 'So what do you think? Do you think someone close to Malcolm could have killed Ryan?'

'It's possible. It's definitely worth checking up.'

'How can I, though, without going back down to Norwich? I doubt the ACC will budget for another trip.'

'Probably not. Look, leave it with me. I'll have a word with Matilda in a while. Good work though, Faith.'

'Shit,' Matilda cursed herself. She rummaged in her bag for her tablets and found a battered box at the bottom. She knew she shouldn't take them like this, as and when she felt like it, but there was something psychological about taking an antidepressant that seemed to work. It worked for Matilda anyway. She dry-swallowed two and waited to see if they would take effect.

She closed her eyes and leaned back in the leather office chair. She could hear life going on as normal outside her tiny glass box: phones ringing, people chatting and laughing, computer keyboards being hammered, the heavy footfalls of sensible shoes.

Life goes on.

Everybody had told her after James died that it would get easier, that she would eventually remember the good times, the happier memories, and return to functioning normally. Eighteen months later and she was still a physical and emotional wreck. She missed James on a daily basis. The house was empty without him, and it would never feel the same again. Life didn't go on. It was a ridiculous and patronizing saying. Life would never go on. It would just meander in its current state until she eventually withered and died.

Optimistic as ever, Mat.

She remembered a few breathing exercises from her therapist and eventually she began to calm herself. Matilda sank into her chair as her muscles relaxed. Her heart was no longer racing and trying to break out of her chest. She felt calm. Well, calm for her.

Matilda picked up the phone and dialled a number from a Post-It note she had stuck to her computer screen the day before. It took a while for the call to be answered and she almost gave up and replaced the receiver.

'Hello?'

'Hello. My name is Detective Chief Inspector Matilda Darke from South Yorkshire Police. Am I speaking to Belinda Asher?'

There was a sigh. 'Yes,' was all she said.

'Thank you for getting in touch.'

'From what my sister said, I didn't have much choice.'

'I'm guessing you've already heard the news about—'

'Yes,' Belinda snapped.

Why did she interrupt? What didn't she want Matilda to say – her son's name or her calling him her son?

'Mrs Asher—'

'That's not my name anymore.'

'I'm aware that you and your husband have changed your name. If you want me to call you by your new name—'

'No. I'm sorry, but no. Look, we've moved on as best we can. I intend this conversation with you to be my only one. I think I am capable of getting through this with you calling me Belinda Asher but I won't be giving you my new name.' Her voice was fragile and breaking. She was taking deep breaths, trying, but struggling, to hold onto her emotions.

'I understand,' Matilda said. 'Before we go on, is there anything you'd like to ask me?'

'Like what?'

'Like how Ryan died maybe?'

'No.'

'You don't want to know?'

'No, I don't. I'm not interested. Please, ask your questions.'

'OK. Mrs Asher, can you tell me what Ryan was like as a child?'

Belinda burst into tears. 'We tried our best. We did everything we could. We were always there for him. He wanted for nothing. I wanted another child. For some reason I always wanted two but it never happened. I don't know why Ryan ended up the way he did. Maybe I was too protective of him and he rebelled against us, I don't know.'

'His home life was incident free, you'd say?'

'Yes, I would. Until he was twelve he was never any trouble. He was well behaved; he always came home when we asked him to; he cleaned his room and always went to school.'

'So what happened? Did he fall in with the wrong friends?'

'Yes. You probably won't have heard about it in South Yorkshire, but there was a gang in Norwich he got involved with – quite a well-known gang. They damaged cars, stole from shops, terrorized the local kids. Then it escalated. I think one of them got involved in drugs. One of the gang ended up getting stabbed. Anyway, Ryan started asking us for money, ten pounds here, twenty pounds there. At first, we gave it to him but then he started asking for more … '

'Was he involved in drugs?' Matilda interrupted.

'I don't think so. He wasn't taking any but he may have been buying for others. I'm not sure. It all escalated quickly. He started smoking. I could smell it on his school uniform. I told him to quit but he got quite volatile.' She started to cry again. 'I thought that maybe once he'd left school and was away from that gang he would improve. I had no idea things would turn into … he killed my mum and dad,' her words were replaced by heavy and loud sobbing.

Matilda waited until the crying began to subside. 'I'm sorry to bring all this up. I won't pretend I know what you're going through because I don't.'

'It's OK,' she sniffled. 'Just ask your questions.'

'What did Ryan's school say about his change in behaviour?'

'They were useless. At first, they didn't notice a difference in him at all. It was only when I contacted them that they realized he'd changed. They said he was a lot quieter in class and he didn't work to his usual standard.'

'So if he had made new friends they were outside of school?'

'It would appear so.'

Matilda remained quiet. She wanted to ask more but also wanted Belinda to take the lead and offer the information.

'We talked about moving away but we couldn't with our work. Then, the Malcolm Preston incident happened.'

Matilda hadn't heard of Malcolm Preston but felt she should have done. She quickly scribbled his name down on a notepad but didn't say anything. She waited for Belinda to elaborate.

'I often search the internet for Malcolm's name to see if there's any news, but he's still in a coma. The police, the school, even Malcolm's parents, they all knew it was Ryan who attacked him but there was no evidence,' she took a deep breath. 'We knew it too.'

'How did you know?'

'He withdrew completely. He went to his room as soon as he came home and was out the next morning before we both got up. We hardly saw him.'

'It must have made your home life very difficult.'

'It did. Stu … Paul and I were arguing. He wanted to send him away. There are special schools that deal with disruptive children, but I didn't want to. Ryan was my son. I wanted to be able to help him myself, but I couldn't. I tried everything. I failed him.' The tears came fast and she struggled to breathe. 'I should have listened to Paul. If I had, my parents would still be alive.'

Matilda waited for Belinda to regain control but she was in for a long wait. Eventually, a man came on the line.

'My name is Paul Asher. I'm sorry but I don't think you should continue with this conversation. I don't see what use it will be to your investigation.'

'Mr Asher I'm very sorry to have upset your wife but at the end of the day Ryan Asher is your son.'

'No,' he snapped. 'He stopped being my son when he burned his grandparents to death. I want nothing more to do with him.'

'Mr Asher, eventually, Ryan's body will be released by the coroner for burial.'

'Do what you want with him. We don't want him back. Now I would appreciate it if you didn't call this number again. Thank you.'

Before Matilda could say anything, she found herself listening to the dial tone. She wasn't surprised by the result of the conversation. She typed the area code 01806 into Google and found Paul and Belinda Asher were now living in Shetland. They really had wanted a complete change when they left Norwich. She couldn't blame them.

FIFTY-FOUR

Craig Hodge was sitting in an interview room in South Yorkshire Police HQ. He never thought he would be back in a room like this answering questions after spending so long in Starling House. He thought his questioning days were over.

Sitting opposite him were DS Sian Mills and DC Scott Andrews. Sian had informed Craig of his rights and told him the interview was being recorded and videoed. He'd looked up to the camera in the corner of the room and smiled at whoever was watching him. Sitting to his right was an appropriate adult – a woman brought in to monitor the interview to make sure Craig was dealt with fairly by the police, not put under any unnecessary duress and treated with respect.

'Craig, I want you to tell us what's been going on with Richard Grover,' Sian said, starting the proceedings.

'Why?'

'Because we need to know.'

'He … gets us things.'

'What kind of things?'

'Anything we want. Food, chocolate, magazines.'

'What kind of magazines?'

'You've seen what kind of magazines,' he replied, nodding and smiling.

'Pornography?'

'Yep,' he leaned back and folded his arms.

'How long has this been going on?'

'For as long as I've been there.'

Sian looked at her notes. 'And you've been there for just over a year?'

'That's right.'

'We only found magazines in your room and Lee Marriott's room. Does he get things for all the boys or just you two?'

'All of us. We hand the mags round. Although you have to make sure Callum Nixon doesn't get to them first as he rips the best pics out.'

'How do you pay for the things Richard gets you?'

He flashed a knowing smile. Looking up at Sian out of the top of his eyes made him look sinister. 'You know what he does or you wouldn't be asking.'

'We need you to tell us, Craig.'

'What's in it for me?'

'I'm sorry?'

'What do I get for telling you all the gory details? Will I get time off my sentence?'

'No.'

'Then there's no reason for me to talk, is there?'

'There's every reason for you to talk, Craig,' Scott spoke for the first time. 'Things like cooperation go down on your file. When you get moved to an adult prison and the guards see how you've behaved they'll treat you accordingly. Piss us off and you won't get a moment's peace until your parole comes up in thirty years' time.'

The smirk on Craig face fell. 'Grover liked to watch us while we … you know… '

'You're going to have to tell us, Craig. For the benefit of the recording.'

'He liked to watch us while we wanked off,' he replied loudly.

'Is that all?'

'No. Sometimes he sucked us off.'

'You sound like you didn't mind?'

'I couldn't give a toss. If that's how he gets his kicks then it's up to him. At the end of the day I'm getting free stuff and I'm getting my dick sucked,' he shrugged.

'You do realize what he's been doing is a criminal offence? You're underage and he is abusing his position.'

'Not my problem,' he shrugged again. 'It's him that's going to lose his job and go to prison, not me. How can things get any worse for me? I'm already locked up.'

Matilda was sitting at her computer watching the interview. Her screen was split in half. On the other side of the screen, Callum Nixon was impatiently sitting alone with a uniformed officer standing guard. His eyes wandered around and settled on the camera in the corner of the room. He knew he was being watched. He sat back in his chair and looked deep into the lens. He smiled. It was a haunting smile that stretched across his face. Matilda felt a cold chill run through her body. Callum Nixon was pure malevolence. He was due to be interviewed by Aaron and Rory. Matilda found Craig's interview difficult to comprehend. It wasn't that she didn't believe him – the evidence of the magazines spoke for itself. It was the nonchalance of an abused teenager that she found hard to fathom. Craig Hodge was being abused, there was no other word for it, and he didn't seem to mind.

'Sian, ask him if any of the other guards take advantage in any way,' Matilda said into the microphone on her computer.

'Is it just Richard Grover who treats you all in this way or are there any others?' Sian asked.

'Well, none have done anything else to me. You'd have to ask the others. Elly Caine once gave Jacob Brown a good kicking and Call Me Fred often looks at you a bit funny, but that's it.'

'In what way does Fred look at you?'

'Like he wants to do something but knows he can't.'

'Don't you think you should have reported Richard Grover to Kate Moloney?'

'Where would I have got my wanking material from then?' He smiled.

Outside the interview rooms in the custody suite, the other boys were sitting uncomfortably for their turn to be interviewed.

'I need a piss,' Lewis Chapman called out to anyone who would listen.

'I'll take him,' Rory said to the desk sergeant.

'You sure? I can get a uniform.'

'No it's OK. I can't do anything yet. Aaron's checking up on his wife again. If you ever hear me mentioning getting married, you have my permission to give me a good hiding.'

Lewis wasn't handcuffed, but he couldn't be allowed to go to the toilet on his own; this wasn't Starling House. When they entered, Lewis looked underneath all the cubicles to see if anyone was in them before going over to the urinals.

'What did you do that for?' Rory asked.

'In *Scream* the killer is waiting for Sidney in the cubicles and then attacks her.'

Rory remembered Lewis's crime – he killed his younger brother while dressed as the killer from the *Scream* films.

'Do you always check under the doors in the toilets?'

'Always,' he replied, looking over his shoulder and smiling at Rory.

'Are you allowed to watch horror films in prison?'

'Sure.'

'What's your favourite scary movie?'

Lewis started laughing. 'You're supposed to say that in a deep menacing voice like Ghostface.'

'Sorry?' Rory said, not getting the reference to the *Scream* films.

'It doesn't matter. I don't have a favourite. I love them all. You can't beat Hannibal Lecter as the ultimate bad guy though.'

'Why did you do it?'

'What? Kill my little brother?' Lewis asked, washing his hands. He shrugged. 'I dunno. Just wanted to, I guess.'

'Had he done something to upset you?'

'No.'

'Was it revenge or to get back at someone, your parents maybe?'

'No, no, and no. I just wanted to kill someone.' He dried his hands on his trousers and walked up close to Rory, backing him up against a wall. 'It's scarier when there's no motive isn't it?' He smiled.

Rory swallowed hard. 'Are you finished?' he asked, quietly.

With Craig's interview over, Matilda sat up in her chair when she saw Thomas Hartley being brought in. She was keen to hear his version of events about the goings-on at Starling House. For some reason, she felt she could believe him more over the other inmates. She hoped Richard Grover had kept his fat, grubby hands off him too. He was a disgrace.

'Thomas, did Richard Grover ever bring in things from the outside for you?' Sian asked.

'Yes,' he replied. His head was down, facing the table, his hands folded between his legs and his voice was barely above a whisper.

'What did he bring you?'

'Chocolate and sweets mostly.'

'You'll need to speak up, Thomas, for the recording. What did Richard Grover want in return?'

Thomas closed his eyes tight and squeezed out a tear. 'Do I have to?'

'Yes, Thomas, you do.'

'He liked to watch us play with ourselves.' He shook his head, embarrassed at what he had been forced to endure. His interview was a complete contrast to Craig Hodge's.

'How many times did he watch you?'

'I don't know. I can't remember.'

'Were you always on your own or with the other boys?'

'On my own.'

'When did this take place?' Scott asked.

'He'd sometimes come to our rooms at night. Or when he had stuff to give one of us he'd give us the signal and meet us in the toilets,' he replied, disgusted he had taken part.

'Did Richard Grover touch you or the others at all?'

'He didn't touch me. I heard he … you know … sucked off Craig and Lee and Mark sometimes.'

'Why those three?'

'They're blond. He liked them because they were blond.'

'Did anything else happen?'

Tears fell from Thomas's eyes. The appropriate adult handed him a tissue from her jacket pocket, which he thanked her for.

'Thomas,' Scott leaned forward on the table. 'Richard has been arrested and is in custody. He's not going to get away with this and he won't be able to hurt you again. You can tell us.'

'He used Lee.'

'In what way?' Sian asked.

'You've seen Lee. He's very blond and slim and he used him as if he belonged to him.'

'What did he make him do?'

'Do I have to?'

'It would help, Thomas.'

'Lee said he sometimes had sex with him.'

Matilda chewed on her nails in her office while she watched Thomas's difficult interview. She was furious. Richard Grover had been working at Starling House for more than four years. How many boys had he abused in that time?

ACC Masterson didn't knock on Matilda's door, she just pushed down the handle and stormed in.

'This station is in chaos—' Valerie began but was silenced as Matilda put up a hand to stop her.

'Richard Grover has been abusing the boys at Starling House.'

'What?' Valerie moved around to Matilda's side of the desk and watched the interview on the computer. 'Who's that?'

Matilda swallowed hard. 'Thomas Hartley.'

'So that's Thomas Hartley. Nice to put a face to the name. Please tell me you have this Richard Grover in custody.'

'We certainly do. He's not going anywhere.'

'Jesus! As if we haven't got enough on our plate with the abuse scandal in Rotherham now we've got it in Sheffield too. How many victims are we talking about?'

Matilda shook her head. 'I've no idea. We've got six downstairs that we know of. We need to look at the inmates who have been at Starling House during Richard Grover's time there. We could be looking at dozens.'

'Oh my God,' Valerie stepped away from the computer. The worried look on her face said it all. It wasn't the abuse of power or the disturbing stories she couldn't stomach, it was what was going to happen to her and her career.

'Could this Richard have killed Ryan Asher?'

'I don't know. If Ryan had been at Starling House for longer than forty-eight hours I would have said it was a possibility, but Richard would have needed to get to know Ryan, understand what kind of boy he was dealing with. After all, these are convicted killers. They're not your usual timid boys you can warp.'

'You will be questioning him about Ryan's death though?'

'Of course.'

'Matilda, I want some order brought to this station. You're not the only detective investigating a case here. Have you seen how disruptive these boys are being downstairs?'

Matilda pushed herself out from her chair and followed Valerie out of the office. The computer was still playing the interview with Thomas Hartley. On the other half of the screen the interview with Callum Nixon was about to begin with Aaron and Rory leading.

Matilda really should have been watching that interview.

FIFTY-FIVE

There were four inmates from Starling House in the custody suite and they were all being purposely difficult. They knew the abuse that went on at the hands of Richard Grover, but none of them ever talked about it. Now it was out in the open they wanted the gory details from each other.

'It's Lee he fancied the most,' Mark said, nudging Lee and winking. 'He knew he could mould you and get you to do anything he wanted.'

'Piss off, Mark,' Lee said. There was no force behind his warning. The timid boy sat in the corner, shoulders shrugged, head down, looking like he wanted to cry but couldn't.

'You know why he liked Lee best, don't you?' Lewis teased. 'Because he was good at it. He's been sucking cocks all his life.'

'You can piss off as well,' Lee said.

'I bet you've got a right stash of stuff in your cell. Not just food. Games, iPad, mobile ... '

'En suite bathroom, curtains, rugs,' Mark laughed. 'Fitted wardrobes, Jacuzzi bath.'

'A balcony outside the window,' Craig joined in. 'A maid to turn down his bed at night.'

'I think Lee would prefer a manservant to turn his bed down at night,' Lewis winked.

Shrinking further into the corner, Lee clenched his fists together to hold in the rage he was feeling. He hated the fact he was different to the other boys and always tended to keep his head down and not draw attention to himself. With the other three teasing him, loudly, everyone who walked past kept looking in his direction.

'Come on, Lee, give us the details. What else did Groper Grover do to you?'

'Leave me alone.'

'Did he make love to you?'

'Oh God, can you imagine his sex face?' Craig laughed.

'I bet he looked like he was having a heart attack.'

'While he was screwing you did he ask you to call him daddy? Did he pretend you were a girl—?'

Lee snapped. He raised his fists and punched Lewis in the face so hard he was knocked off balance. Lee took the opportunity to pounce.

It was at that moment Matilda and Valerie entered the custody suite. Two boys were brawling on the floor, the other two were jeering them on and there wasn't a single uniformed officer in sight.

'Aaron, there's a phone call for you. It's Katrina. Again'

'Shit. I'm doing to have to take it. Do you mind?' Aaron asked. The look of worry was back on his face.

'No. Go on, we haven't started yet,' Rory said.

'Am I all right to pop to the toilet then, before we start?' the appropriate adult asked.

'Of course. Turn left just before the double doors and it's your second on your right.'

'Thank you.'

Rory closed the interview room door behind him and looked at Callum Nixon sitting at the table. They were alone.

'Can I ask you a question?' Rory asked, sitting down.

'Don't you need to wait for the others to come back?'

'This isn't part of the interview. I just want to get something clear in my head.'

'Shoot,' Callum replied, sitting back and relaxing.

'I've looked at your file, read about what you did to end up at Starling House. I want to know why you did what you did, basically.'

'You mean, why I killed those teachers?'

'Yes.'

'Why?'

'I'm interested. I want to know what makes somebody, a child, kill another person.'

'Why? You got a few victims lined up for yourself?' he sniggered.

'No. Like I said, I'm interested.'

'Well, if you must know, they pissed me off. They were horrible teachers. High and mighty. Thought that just because they were adults and we were kids they could do what they wanted, and we just had to suck it up and go along with it.'

'But you could say that about all teachers. There were a few at my school I didn't like.'

'I got suspended. For something stupid. I wasn't having that. You don't suspend me.'

Rory guessed correctly Callum Nixon fitted into the narcissistic role of a killer. 'But being suspended is part of a school's policy. It's not something they do lightly. They obviously thought they had a reason.'

'Maybe they did, but I didn't.'

'They were their rules, though. Not yours. You have to abide by the rules set down by the school.'

Callum smiled. 'If I don't like the rules, I don't abide by them. I stand up to them.'

'And that's why you were suspended.'

'And that's why I killed them,' he grinned.

'But what made you think killing them was the ideal situation?'

'What other solution was there? They wouldn't listen,' he said, raising his voice. 'They wouldn't see my side of things. I was always the bad guy. So if they wanted me to be the bad guy then I was going to be the best bad guy ever.' His smile changed into a smirk. He looked at Rory out of the top of his eyes.

'Are you sorry for what you did?' Rory asked after a beat of silence.

'Fuck, no. I did the world a favour. Two dickhead teachers in a shit school.'

'Nobody has the right to take another life, Callum. It's not your place to judge.'

'It's not yours either. So don't go looking at me like I'm a piece of shit on your designer shoes.'

'I'm not judging. I want to know why you thought killing someone was the only way out of the mess you found yourself in.'

'I wasn't in a mess. Those teachers needed to pay for what they did to me.'

'Why not just vandalize their cars or something?'

'Because I wasn't eight years old,' Callum scoffed.

'Surely your parents taught you right from wrong and instilled in you the fact you don't fight your battles with violence—'

That was the trigger. Rory mentioning Callum's parents and the way they brought him up was the catalyst. Rory saw the change in Callum's eyes before he finished speaking. What happened next was a complete blur as Callum leapt from his seat and jumped over the table.

FIFTY-SIX

'I will not have that kind of behaviour in my station,' Valerie shouted at the boys of Starling House once the fight was broken up. 'And where were you lot?' she asked the uniformed officers who had come running into the custody suite once they heard the commotion.

There was nothing they could say.

'We need to arrange for them to be moved elsewhere. They can't go back to Starling House. They'll have to go to other institutions,' Matilda said.

'Right, leave it with me. I'll make a few calls. In the meantime, they'll have to be placed in the holding cells.'

'You can't do that we haven't done anything wrong,' Craig Hodge spoke up.

'You're a convicted killer. You've done everything wrong.' Valerie said. 'Sergeant, clear the cells wherever possible and get these boys locked up. I'll deal with why there was nobody watching over four murderers later.' She turned to the boys. 'Don't worry, it's nearly lunchtime, you'll be fed and well looked after. God forbid we infringe your human rights.'

Valerie took Matilda by the arm and led her to the corner of the suite. 'Matilda, get Richard Grover interviewed. I want names, dates, and details of everything he's ever done to the boys at Starling House past and present. Then get him charged and get him out of here.'

'I was just about to do that.'

'No. I want you to solve this Ryan Asher case by the end of the day. Have you seen the amount of press that's building out there? In fact, have you seen today's papers? I do not want South Yorkshire Police in the spotlight for all the wrong reasons again. Let DI Brady interview Grover. You find out who killed Asher and Brown. Understand?'

'Yes, ma'am,' Matilda said, walking away.

'Oh, and Matilda? I want you to call me every hour with a progress report. I don't want you slacking off and looking into the Hartley case. Do you understand me?'

Matilda took a deep breath and bit down hard on the inside of her mouth. 'Loud and clear.'

Valerie was about to add another warning, her finger came up to point at the DCI, but an alarm sounded that caused everyone to stop dead in their tracks.

'Interview room two,' shouted a sergeant behind the custody desk looking down at his monitor.

Matilda and Valerie led the way with uniform backing them up. Matilda pulled open the door to the corridor and saw the red bulb flashing above the second interview room. Without thinking of what mayhem she could be walking into, she depressed the handle and threw the door open with her shoulder.

Rory Fleming was on the floor with Callum straddling him raining down blow after blow with each fist. He was relentless.

With all her energy, Matilda grabbed Callum by the shoulders and lifted him off the DC, throwing him to the other side of the room. She crouched down and looked at the unconscious detective. There was so much blood, so much damage. It was difficult to make out his features.

In the corner of the room, Callum sat perfectly still, licking the blood from his knuckles. 'You might want to get him to hospital a bit sharpish – I'm HIV positive,' he smiled.

FIFTY-SEVEN

'Why was he on his own in a room with a double murderer?'

'I've no idea, ma'am.'

An ambulance crew arrived quickly, tested Rory's vital signs and made sure his breathing was regular before they dared to move him. He was unconscious and unresponsive by the time he was loaded into the ambulance. As Valerie questioned one of the paramedics before he left, he told her they would perform an MRI to check for damage to his brain. There were no signs of life when they flashed a light in his eyes but his breathing was stable.

Valerie was in her office pacing back and forth behind her desk. Matilda was sitting down. She had accepted Valerie's offer of a coffee but it tasted foul. It wasn't the caffeine; it was the image she had of her young DC. Rory was a good detective. He was hard-working, popular, funny, and good-looking.

He's not dead.

'Not yet,' Matilda said to herself.

'Sorry?'

'Nothing. Just thinking aloud. Look, I will find out why he was left on his own. I will sort this.'

'Is there any truth in what that little bastard said about him being HIV positive?'

'I don't know. Sian is on the phone to Starling House now to get his medical records.'

'I don't understand,' Valerie said, scratching her head. 'Rory's tall, he's fit, how could he let a teenager overpower him?'

Matilda shook her head. 'Callum Nixon is a very volatile young man. Maybe Rory struck a nerve.'

'I want these killers out of my station, Matilda.'

Matilda put down her coffee and quietly left the office. She felt sick. Valerie had offered to call Rory's family and Matilda accepted. It wasn't a conversation she relished.

On her way back to CID, Matilda was asked by almost everyone she met how Rory was doing. She didn't reply to any of them.

'Are you all right?' Sian asked from the doorway of Matilda's office.

'No.' She was sitting in her chair, head in hands, praying and hoping to anyone who would listen that Rory would be all right. 'What did they say at Starling House?'

'Callum is not HIV positive. He was playing with us.'

'Bastard. It's horrible to say this about a teenager but I could happily smash his face in and not think I'd done anything wrong,' Matilda said, struggling to keep her emotions in check.

'You can't blame yourself for bringing them all here. They needed to be formally interviewed.'

'Why was he on his own, Sian? That's what I want to know.'

'Ah,' she said, looking out of the window. 'Just before the interview was due to begin, Aaron received a phone call from Katrina. Rory told him to go and they'd start the interview afterwards. Fortunately, the cameras were switched on and we've caught what happened in the interview room on video. Rory was asking him about his crimes when he killed those teachers. It sounds like he wanted to understand why he became a killer.'

'What about the attack?'

'Callum snapped the second Rory mentioned his family. He was like a man possessed. Rory didn't stand a chance.'

'Oh God, Rory. He wouldn't let it drop, would he?'

'He was desperate to find out how a child can kill. He saw his opportunity to interview Callum on his own and went for it. Everyone is asking if there's any news.'

'Not at the moment. Scott's at the hospital. He texted saying that Rory's in theatre. He's got internal bleeding on the brain. It doesn't look good, Sian,' Matilda said, biting back the tears.

'Have you called his family?'

'Valerie's doing that.'

'What do you want us to do?'

Matilda looked past Sian and out into CID. Everything was muted. Hardly anyone was working as solemn faces looked down at untidy desks.

'Crucifying Callum Nixon would be a great start.'

'He's been charged. He's locked up.'

Matilda turned her chair to look out of the window. The dark clouds had gone and were replaced by wispy white ones. The sky wasn't a brilliant blue but it was pale and the low sun was shining. She hoped it was an omen of better things to come, though she doubted it.

'I want Richard Grover interviewed. I want to know the full extent of his abuse over the years. I don't think he killed Ryan or Jacob but we need to know. Also, I want Fred Percival interviewed too. Again, I don't think he's the killer but he has a history of inappropriate behaviour towards young boys. He should not have been working at Starling House. What the hell was Kate Moloney thinking when she hired these people?'

'Well, leave Richard and Fred to me and Christian. We'll interview them. Why don't you go for a coffee or something? Or maybe go and see Adele?'

As she came down from the adrenaline rush of the emergency, Matilda's emotions raced to the surface and tears started to fall. 'I don't want to be on my own,' she cried.

Like everybody else Matilda was human and had the same emotions. However, she saw it as a sign of weakness if she showed those emotions in front of her detectives. She was their leader, and as their leader she had to be stoic and strong in the face of adversity. When everything else was crumbling around them, Matilda had to rally them into some semblance of order.

When she started to cry, Sian quickly closed the door behind her and stood in front of her so nobody outside could see. She had known Matilda long enough to understand she wouldn't want her weaknesses made public.

When the tears stopped, she dried her eyes and walked out of the room with her head down, not making eye contact with anyone. She managed to make it to the car park without being accosted and drove away before the swarm of press could notice.

Adele looked up as the swinging doors to the mortuary opened. She saw Matilda and went back to putting a lifeless body in one of the fridges. She closed the door with an echoing slam.

'Matilda, excellent timing. I was just about to call … what's wrong?' She saw the pale look of anguish on her best friend's face.

'Rory's been beaten. It doesn't look good,' she replied, barely audible through the tears.

'Oh God, no.'

Adele loved Rory. He was the adorable member of Matilda's team, who was always there with a joke or sarcastic comment. It was never annoying. It helped that he was gorgeous too.

'What happened?'

Matilda filled Adele in over a strong coffee and a packet of Jammie Dodgers.

'I know Starling House has always been shrouded in secrecy but I never expected abuse and bullying,' Adele said. 'I bet Val's kicked off, hasn't she?'

'She certainly has. Once this gets out she's going to be in serious trouble for allowing it to go unnoticed all this time. I doubt she'll be here by Christmas.'

'That's not fair. I like Val. She's been a good ACC.'

'She's put up with a lot from me. Anyone else and I'd have been out when I screwed up the Carl Meagan case.'

'Look, if you can solve the murder case and get Thomas Hartley out then that'll go for you and for Val. Imagine the story when it's revealed there was an innocent man sentenced to a crime he didn't commit, and you, and Valerie, against all the odds, managed to get him released.'

'That's all hit the fan too. Val found out I was looking into the Hartley case and warned me off. She doesn't want an argument between forces.'

'But if he's innocent … '

'"If" is the right word. There's only me who thinks so and I don't have proof.'

'Then get proof.'

'How, when I'm not allowed anywhere near the bloody case?'

'Since when has that stopped you?'

'Adele, I've let Thomas Hartley distract me from what I'm supposed to be doing. If I hadn't then Callum fucking Nixon would not have beaten Rory half to death.'

'You don't know that. For Christ's sake, Matilda, you can't be responsible for everything that happens in that station. Rory is a grown man. He knew he was alone with a double killer. He made that decision. Not you. Now, I'm sorry he's been hurt and I really hope he makes a full recovery, but I'm not going to sit here while you go all maudlin again over something out of your control.'

'I'm not being maudlin,' she said.

'Yes, you are. You're feeling sorry for yourself. I love you to pieces, Matilda, you know that, but you need to stop this. Look at me,' Matilda continued to look into her empty coffee cup. 'I said, look at me.'

Reluctantly, Matilda looked up. Her eyes were full of tears.

There were white lines down her face and dark circles around her eyes. She looked as if she had aged ten years since entering the mortuary.

'First of all, you look like shit.'

'Thanks.'

'You're welcome. Secondly, stop whining and do something.'

'What?'

'Well, for a start you can listen to my report on Jacob Brown seeing as nobody could be bothered to turn up for the post-mortem this morning like you said they would. Then, after that, you and I are going to have something to eat—'

'I couldn't stomach anything.'

'Well, I could and you're bloody going to eat for a change. Then, I'm going to phone Pat Campbell and all three of us are going to Manchester to find out who killed Thomas Hartley's sodding family.'

'That's not going to happen. I could lose my job.'

'Do you think, hand on heart, that Thomas Hartley is innocent?'

'Yes,' Matilda replied quietly.

'You hesitated. Are you sure?'

'I'm not sure about anything anymore, Adele.'

'Jesus. OK, I know you're not going to rest until you know the truth, one way or another, are you?'

'No.'

'Well then; if you're going to lose your job, wouldn't you rather lose it knowing you've done everything in your power to free a potentially innocent man?'

'Yes.'

'There you go then.' Adele handed Matilda a box of tissues. 'Now dry your eyes, and blow your nose.'

'Jacob Brown did not die from hanging,' Adele began. She was now sitting at her desk with a fresh cup of coffee, and a file balanced on her lap. 'He was strangled first with a different kind of rope before being hanged. It was obviously made to look like suicide but it was so sloppy a boy scout could have noticed.'

'Maybe it was rushed,' Matilda said. She too had a fresh cup of coffee. She also had a balled-up tissue in her hand which she kept dabbing at her nose.

'I think it was. He was strangled from behind. The rope was thrown over his head and around his neck. There is evidence under Jacob's fingernails that he tried to grab the rope. There's fibres and skin cells under his nails.'

'His own skin?'

'Yes.'

'How can you tell he was strangled from behind?'

'Because of the direction of the indentations in his neck from his own nails. He seemed to put up a struggle too as there are plenty of burn marks and abrasions around the front of his neck caused by the rope.'

'Jacob wasn't a short lad so are we looking for someone taller than him?'

'Not necessarily. If you look at his clothing, the knees on his trousers were badly stained with mud and they were torn. All the killer needed to do was surprise him from behind, maybe a swift kick to the back of the knees to bring him down then go at him with the rope.'

'But, if the killer strangled him, why not just leave him on the floor of the woods? If you're not going to hide the body, why make it look like suicide when it was an obvious murder?'

'To be honest, Matilda, I have no idea. You said yourself it looked staged. The first murder looked staged. This is obviously the way the killer likes to communicate – by showing off his crimes.'

Thinking aloud, Matilda said: 'So we have a killer who doesn't care how his victims die, it's how they look to others. Ryan looked like he was laid out in a coffin, and Jacob looked like he was hanging from the gallows. We have a killer who is celebrating their deaths.'

FIFTY-EIGHT

'Am I going to be in trouble?' Aaron asked Sian.

'I doubt it,' she replied.

They were both sitting at their desks facing each other. Just a few days ago Aaron was all smiles at the wonderful news his wife was pregnant, now his dour expression was back firmly imprinted on his face.

'I had no idea Rory would have started the interview on his own.'

'Aaron, you're not to blame. He didn't start the interview either. He wanted to know what made Callum a killer in the first place.'

'I'll never forgive myself if he doesn't pull through.'

'Sian, sorry to interrupt, but did you manage to have a word with Matilda?' Faith asked. She had obviously been crying as her make-up had run, and, despite trying to rectify it, she hadn't done a good job.

'I'm so sorry, Faith, I haven't. Everything sort of went mad for a while there, didn't it? Tell me what you've uncovered and we'll sort something out between us.'

Faith told Sian and Aaron about the Malcolm Preston case and how everyone in Norwich seemed to know Ryan Asher was responsible, including the police, despite there being no evidence.

'What happened to Malcolm's parents?'

'His mother died of breast cancer shortly afterwards. His father keeps a bedside vigil.'

'Any brothers and sisters?'

'No.'

'We could really do with interviewing the father. Leave it with me, Faith. I'll have a word with the ACC. I doubt one of us will be able to go down because we're short-staffed as it is. However, someone from Norwich could go and have a chat with him.'

'Thanks, Sian. Oh, Aaron, I had a note on my desk about Elly Caine. Weren't you interviewing her?'

'Oh fuck! I forgot all about that.'

'Please tell me you've interviewed her, Aaron,' Sian said.

'Yes, I have. I just haven't done anything about it. I'm sorry.' He looked genuinely upset that his mind was no longer on the job he loved so much. Rightly so, he was putting Katrina first, but he should still be committed to his work.

'Does she have an alibi for Monday night?'

'Yes. She hasn't been anywhere near Starling House since she left. It was a dark time in her life by all accounts. Her husband left her and sold the house without telling her. She was practically homeless. She asked her cousin, Richard Grover, to get her the job at Starling House as she was desperate – for work and a place to live. She's now working as a barmaid at a pub in Derby. She works six nights a week and was there on Monday night. She hasn't spoken to Richard Grover since she left either. He kicked off when she beat Jacob Brown up saying she'd betrayed his trust. They had a huge fight and she hasn't seen him since.'

'She betrayed his trust?' Sian scoffed. 'That's rich coming from him. What about all this abuse that's been uncovered. Did she know about that?'

'Well, I didn't know about any of that myself at the time. However, she didn't mention anything about it. She said the staff were quiet, kept themselves to themselves. They didn't talk much.

If she hadn't been sacked she would probably have left anyway as she didn't like the atmosphere. It was depressive.'

'Did she say anything about Kate?'

'All she said was that Kate needed to take that metal rod out of her arse.'

'Such a lovely way with words,' Sian smiled.

Christian Brady signalled to Sian from the other side of the room. He was ready for them both to interview Richard Grover.

Richard Grover was wedged in behind the desk in interview room one. He was a large mess of a man with greasy hair, unkempt stubble, and dark beady eyes. He had a permanent sheen of sweat on his forehead.

'Richard, you have been charged with causing a child to engage in sexual activity and aggravated assault by abusing a position of trust. Do you understand those charges?' DI Brady began.

'Yes,' he replied, his voice constricted by heavy breathing.

'You've waived your right to have a solicitor present too, is that correct?'

'Yes.'

'Do you deny the charges?'

'No.'

'So you admit abusing Craig Hodge, Lee Marriott, Lewis Chapman, Mark Parker, Callum Nixon, Thomas Hartley, and Jacob Brown?'

'Yes.'

'Are there others?'

'Yes.'

'Going back how long?'

'I started at Starling House in 2012.'

'So you've been abusing boys in your care for more than four years?'

'Yes,' he replied indifferently.

Christian turned to look at Sian. She had children the same

age as the boys in Starling House. The look of disgust on her face showed how difficult it was to hear of a man admitting his grotesque crimes in such a cool and calm way.

'If we get a list together of all the boys who were at Starling House while you worked there, would you be able to tell us which ones you abused?'

'Yes.'

'You brought things from the outside for the inmates, in return for sexual favours. Is that correct?'

'Yes.'

'What did you bring them?'

'Chocolate, magazines, games, anything they wanted.'

'Why did you do it?' Sian asked. It was the first time she'd spoken, and her question was loaded with rage.

'Because I was able to,' he replied calmly, as if anybody would have taken advantage of the position he was in.

'Is that it?'

'What do you want me to say? Would you like me to tell you I was abused as a child, that I was bullied at school, that I've always struggled to meet women? Sorry, can't help you there. I had a wonderful childhood; I was the school bully, and I've been married once and had three serious relationships with women since my divorce. If you're looking for some psychological reason why I did it, you're out of luck.'

'So you abused them just because they were in your care?'

'You keep using the word abuse like I'm some kind of paedo, I'm not. They consented. Yes, I bought them things, but I didn't force them to do anything.'

'Consented? Did Lee Marriott consent to you having sex with him?' Sian asked, the look of disgust on her face.

'As a matter of fact, yes, he did,' Richard sniggered.

'Why? What did you bribe him with? And why only Lee?'

'You've seen him. He's timid, frightened of his own shadow. I could have asked him to do anything.'

344

'You're disgusting,' Christian said, allowing his feelings to get the better of him.

Sian jumped in. 'Lee Marriott was a vulnerable—'

'Vulnerable?' Richard laughed. 'You're joking surely! They're killers, each and every one of them have committed murder. Their victims were vulnerable; they're pure evil. They're manipulative, lying, deceitful bastards. I was just giving them a taste of their own medicine.'

'Did that also include murdering them?' Sian asked.

'What?'

'Did you kill Ryan Asher and Jacob Brown?'

'No, of course not.'

'Why "of course"? You said yourself you were giving them a taste of their own medicine; Jacob Brown was found hanging in the woods – he raped and murdered his girlfriend in the woods. Wouldn't it be justice if he was killed in similar circumstances?' Christian asked, leaning forward on the table.

Richard Grover was visibly sweating. The cocky grin on his face as he defended his actions had fallen, to be replaced by angst and worry. 'I didn't kill them, honest.'

'Why should we believe you?' Sian asked. 'You've readily admitted, on record, that you've abused boys in your care since you started work at Starling House in 2012. That's four years of abuse. You've lied, betrayed, and manipulated for four years. Do you honestly expect us to believe you didn't kill them too?'

'But I didn't,' the panic in his voice was evident. Richard was almost out of his chair. His sweaty hands were clenched tight as the anger raged through his body.

'What do you think, Sian?' Christian asked. 'For four years he's lied, abused, manipulated, betrayed, isn't murder the next step?'

'I'd have thought so,' she agreed.

'NO! Look, I'll put my hand up to the abuse. I've already told you. I'll give you names and everything, but I'm not a killer. You have my word.'

'Your word means nothing, Richard. Interview terminated 14:27,' Christian said, turning off the recording and standing up.

'What happens to me now?'

'You'll be locked up and thrown to the wolves,' Christian said.

The arrogant Richard Grover who had strutted into the interview room was now a shell of a man as he sat back in his chair and thought about what he had done.

'Lady,' he called out to Sian as she was halfway through the door. Sian turned to look at him. 'Have you got kids?'

'Don't answer him,' Christian replied quickly.

Sian mused over the question. Richard Grover didn't frighten her. He was a pathetic waste of space. 'Yes. I've got four.'

'I'll get off. The jury will believe me over six convicted killers. When I do, I'll come and find you, and your kids. I'll enjoy fucking a copper's kid.'

'You sick, fu—' Sian lunged forward but Christian grabbed her and pulled her out of the room, slamming the door behind him.

'I told you not to answer him.'

'Bastard,' Sian said, wiping the tears from her eyes. 'When he's locked up I'm going to make sure everyone knows what he's done, and I hope they fucking crucify him.' She walked away, head down, hiding the flow of tears. It took a great deal for Sian to get emotional, but any threat against her family and nothing would stand in the way of her revenge.

FIFTY-NINE

'Why do I have to sit in the back?'

'Because it's my car and I'm driving.'

'Why can't I sit in the front?'

'Because I get sick if I sit in the back of a car.'

Matilda leaned back and folded her arms liked a spoiled child. The fish and chips she had been forced to eat were lying heavy and giving her a severe attack of heartburn. The fact the windows in the car were open as they drove steadily along the motorway meant Matilda couldn't hear any of the conversation between Adele and Pat in the front so she had to sit and be quiet.

The vibration of an incoming text message gave her something to do. She had texted Sian and told her to make her excuses to the ACC if she wanted to know where she was. The reply:

I told Val you were ill. She's fine.

She breathed a sigh of relief. She put her phone away and quickly brought it back out again and started texting Scott, hoping he would be still at the hospital.

Any news on Rory?

He came out of theatre about 10 mins ago.

And?

No idea yet.

Are his parents there?

Yes. Amelia has come 2.

How are they?

Not gud.

Keep me informed.

Will do.

Despite what Adele said to her in the mortuary, Matilda would blame herself if anything happened to Rory. He was a member of her team, and he had been injured whilst on duty. Therefore, by default, she was to blame, and no Jammie Dodger therapy would change that.

She closed her eyes and could see the stricken detective on the floor of the interview room. His once handsome face was a swollen mess of bruises and cuts where Callum's fists had struck. What had he done to deserve that? Nothing, apart from doing his job, which is exactly what the teachers had been doing when Callum callously murdered them. That boy was pure evil.

'We're here,' Pat said, turning around in the front passenger seat.

'Where's here?' Matilda looked out of the window at the row of depressed-looking terraced houses.

'We're seeing Debbie Hartley.'

'Oh. Yes. Of course,' Matilda replied as if she had been in a daze for the whole journey, which wasn't far from the truth.

'You came back! That's great. I'm so pleased. Come on in,' Debbie said. Her face lit up the second she opened the door and saw Pat Campbell standing on the doorstep.

'I've brought a couple of friends, I hope you don't mind.'

'No, of course not. The more the merrier. I have a sofa and two armchairs. There's enough for us all to sit down.'

Debbie beckoned them all in and led the way into the living room. Again the television was off. It was as if she had been waiting for someone to arrive.

'Take a seat wherever you want.'

'Debbie, let me introduce you to my friends,' Pat said. 'This is Adele, she's a doctor, and this is Matilda, she's a detective. The one I told you about.'

'Oh my God. You're Matilda?' she asked, as if she had been introduced to an A-list celebrity. 'Are you the one who tried to find little Carl Meagan?'

Matilda smiled through the pain she felt every time she heard his name. 'Yes. That's right.'

'I bought the book this morning,' Debbie said. She grabbed it from a coffee table beside her armchair and held it aloft. 'I remember Pat here telling me about you, and when I saw this in Sainsbury's I had to buy it. It was half price too. Will you sign it for me?' She handed the book out for Matilda.

'What?'

Adele stifled a laugh and tried to turn it into a cough.

'Go on, please. For me. I've never met anyone famous before. Well, I walked past Carol Vorderman in town once but that's not the same thing, is it?'

'I didn't actually write this book, Debbie.'

'No. I know, but your photo is inside it. You could sign your picture for me. I won't put it on eBay, I promise.' Debbie began frantically flicking through the pages to the photos section.

'Debbie, I don't really think it's appropriate for Matilda to sign a book about a missing child, do you?' Pat said, leaping to Matilda's defence.

'Oh. No, you're probably right. It is a bit morbid, isn't it? I'm sorry. I hope I didn't offend you.'

'No. That's fine,' Matilda said, smiling through gritted teeth again.

'I'm not a very fast reader so it might take me a while to finish it but it's started well. I hope he gets found in the end.'

Matilda looked at Pat with a frown. Could Debbie really be relied upon as a vital witness to get Thomas out of prison?

'Debbie, is there any chance we could have a drink? It's really cold outside.'

'Oh, I'm so sorry,' she replied. 'Where are my manners? You can tell I'm not used to having company, can't you? I'll make us all a nice hot chocolate. That'll warm you up. I've got plenty. Sit down and make yourselves comfortable.' She ran out of the room like a child eager to please.

'Her heart's in the right place,' Pat said quietly by way of an excuse.

'If the Hartley case gets reopened she will get slaughtered on the witness stand,' Matilda said.

'You should have seen your face when she asked you to sign the book,' Adele laughed.

'It's not funny.'

'It is. I wish I'd taken a photo.' Adele picked up the book and flicked through the pages. 'She really thinks this is a story, doesn't she? Bless her. Oh dear, Mat, not a very flattering picture of you here.'

'Mat, look in that drawer over there. That's where the passport was in a different woman's name.' Pat whispered. She went over to the door and kept a lookout for Debbie returning.

Matilda opened the drawer. It was full of old bills and bank statements.

'Next one down,' Pat whispered loudly.

The next drawer contained letters and receipts. At the bottom she pulled out a passport. She opened it at the back and saw the name Catherine Downy written in block capitals. The date of birth was 12th March 1977. The photograph showed a chubby, blonde-haired young girl who looked like she was trying her hardest to suppress a smile. The passport had expired years ago.

'Catherine Downy,' Matilda said.

'Who's that?' Adele asked.

'Catherine Downy. Catherine Downy,' Matilda repeated to herself. 'Why do I know that name?'

'I've never heard of it,' Adele said.

'I have but I can't think where from.'

'She's coming back,' Pat said, running from the door to the sofa.

Matilda quickly threw the passport back in the drawer and returned to the sofa just in time as Debbie kicked open the door. She carried a tray with four mugs of hot chocolate topped with whipped cream, chocolate shavings, and tiny marshmallows.

'I thought I'd give us all a nice treat.'

SIXTY

The sleuthing team of Matilda, Adele, and Pat walked silently back to the car. Matilda didn't moan about having to sit in the back. As soon as they pulled away from Debbie's house, Matilda took out her phone and began scouring the internet. It didn't take her long to find what she was looking for. She told the others and they asked her to read aloud.

IDENTITY OF MYERS KILLERS FINALLY REVEALED

The identity of the killers of 13-year-old Felix Myers can now be revealed after a judge lifted a reporting ban.

Felix Myers was beaten, mugged, and stabbed before his body was set on fire last June in an unprovoked attack which shocked the country. His killers were caught following an extensive search of CCTV footage within the area and pains-taking work from police forensic officers at the scene of the murder.

In a trial that lasted six weeks, the court heard how Felix was subjected to a prolonged and sustained abuse by two boys in his class at school.

The trial was delayed on several occasions due to a juror

fainting upon hearing the forensic evidence and the breakdown of the police officers giving evidence. The jury eventually took just forty-five minutes to find the two schoolboys guilty.

At the time, Mr Justice Kent said identifying the killers was not in the public interest and would lead to their families receiving adverse publicity. However, the national press has lobbied for their names to be made public, arguing that people living locally already know the identity of the killers and officially revealing them would stop the worldwide press from making the lives of locals difficult.

After months of court wrangling, the boys can now be identified as Wesley Brigstone and Thomas Downy, both thirteen at the time of the killing. From St Austell in Cornwall, they were well known in the local community as being bright and friendly boys. Their acts came as a complete shock to everyone.

Brigstone and Downy were sentenced to life in prison to serve a minimum of twelve years.

Cornish Guardian, Wednesday 4ᵗʰ June 1986.

FELIX MYERS' KILLERS RELEASED EARLY

The killers of 13-year-old Felix Myers have been released early from Youth Detention Centres.

As the release date of killers Wesley Brigstone and Thomas Downy approached, family members of Felix Myers called for their sentence to be increased, particularly in light of stories in the press about the luxury they lived while in prison.

Earlier this year we exclusively revealed that Thomas Downy, now aged 22, had received one-to-one tutoring, gained four A* passes at A-Level when he was 17, and received a first class degree in English Literature.

The date that Brigstone and Downy were released has not been revealed but it has been confirmed by the Home Office.

'Thomas Downy and Wesley Brigstone were released from detention earlier this year. They were sentenced to life in prison and will remain on licence for the rest of their lives. They will be closely monitored and will return to an adult prison to serve the remainder of their sentence should they commit any further crime.' A Home Office spokesperson said in a statement.

A representative for Felix Myers' family said: 'It is inconceivable they have been allowed an early release. We find it disgusting that we were not even informed of this decision. They have only served nine years and if the stories in the newspapers are true they've hardly suffered for their crime in that time. We're still living in agony. Our lives have been ruined by those two evil boys.'

Wesley Brigstone and Thomas Downy have been given new identities upon release. However, there are strict instructions to which they must adhere. Neither of them are allowed to contact family and friends from their former lives, they are not to contact any member of Felix Myers' family, and must not return to St Austell in Cornwall where both were originally from and where they committed their crime.

Brigstone and Downy are now free. Aged just 22, they can return to normality and rebuild their lives. The Myers family continue to suffer.

The Sun, 10th August 1995.

WHERE IS CATHERINE DOWNY?

Mystery surrounds the "disappearance" of Catherine Downy who has not been seen since July.

Catherine Downy is the younger sister of Thomas Downy, who was released three years early from a twelve-year prison sentence for the brutal killing of Felix Myers in 1986.

When Thomas was convicted with Wesley Brigstone, the Downy family moved to Birmingham to be closer to their son. In the nine years Thomas has been in prison, both of his parents have died – father Robert died in 1988 aged 45 from lung cancer and his wife, Wendy, died three years later from a heart attack aged just 44. Catherine lived with friends until she was old enough to live alone.

Jilly Sanders, a close friend to Catherine said: 'Catherine lived for her brother and visited him as often as she could. She has been counting down the twelve years until his release. When she found out he was to be released early she was over the moon. I've never seen her smile as much. She talked about Thomas being given a new identity. The thought of not seeing him again was very difficult for her.

'I last saw her on 15th July. She was going into her flat and we spoke briefly. She seemed happy and everything was normal.'

West Midlands Police have said they have received no missing person's report for Catherine Downy and are not investigating her whereabouts.

The Sun, August 12th, 1995

'Catherine seemed to have disappeared around the time her older brother was released from prison in 1995,' Pat said.

'So Debbie Hartley is really Catherine Downy?' Adele asked.

'Yes. The photo in that passport is definitely of a young Debbie. You could see it in the eyes,' Matilda said.

'So her brother was Thomas Downy who murdered Felix Myers,' Pat said.

'It would appear so.'

'And when he was released he was given the new identity of Daniel Hartley. He killed an innocent little boy – his son, Thomas Hartley, killed too. Maybe some people can be born evil,' Adele mused.

'We don't know Thomas is guilty,' Matilda said, sounding less convinced now.

'So, Thomas Downy was given the new identity of Daniel Hartley. He broke the rules of his licence straightaway. He left Birmingham and moved to Manchester and contacted his sister to join him. She changed her name to Debbie Hartley and they continued as brother and sister,' Pat summed everything up.

'What I don't understand,' Adele said, 'is why did Daniel Hartley then went on to get married and have kids and have a decent job while Debbie continued to live in the shadows?'

'Well, she's not exactly playing with a full deck of cards, is she?' Pat said. 'It sounds like she needed her brother in order to function. Without her parents she latched on to Daniel and spent her life waiting for him to be released.'

'She must have thought all her Christmases had come at once when he came out three years early.'

'Don't you think it's a bit sick that Daniel named his son after his previous identity? It's a bit like sticking two-fingers up to Felix Myers and his family. I don't think I would have liked Daniel Hartley,' Pat said. 'He sounds cocky and, well, to be honest, a complete shit.'

'But he didn't deserve to be hacked to death. Neither did his wife and daughter.'

'I think we can discount Debbie as being the killer though. Her life was her brother and his family. Without them, she's nothing.'

'You're quiet in the back, Matilda. What are you thinking?' Adele asked.

'I'm thinking that I'd love to know what happened to Wesley Brigstone.'

The car fell silent. They were all thinking roughly the same thing – If Thomas Downy, now Daniel Hartley, immediately broke his licence and contacted his sister, did he contact his partner in crime too? If so, was he in Debbie's life now without her knowing it? She could be in danger without realizing it.

SIXTY-ONE

Matilda asked Adele to drop her off at the Northern General Hospital. She had sent a text to Scott on the way back from Manchester but he hadn't replied. She wanted to assume he had simply turned his phone off as he was in the hospital, but her overactive mind had a life of its own. She was worried Rory had died from his injuries, and Scott was dealing with the aftermath all on his own.

Matilda battled the stiff breeze and light drizzle as she walked up the steep hill to the main entrance of the hospital. By the time she reached the doors she was windswept and soaked.

She was directed to ICU, where she found a shattered-looking Scott pacing in the corridor just outside the unit.

'Scott, what's happened?' Matilda asked, reading his tired expression.

'I'm just having a breather,' he replied.

'How's Rory?'

'He's fine. They thought he might have swelling of the brain but he hasn't and there was very little internal bleeding.'

'So he's going to be OK?'

'It seems so. They're going to run some more tests when he wakes up but they think so.' He gave a brief smile.

Matilda sighed and visibly relaxed. She would have jumped for joy if she hadn't been so emotionally drained. 'Where's his family?'

'They're through there,' he pointed to the double doors. 'His parents are livid. They want to know how he managed to be attacked in a police station. I've told them to contact the ACC but to wait until Rory is conscious and their emotions aren't all over the place. I think I've managed to calm them down.'

'Scott, you're a star.'

'I'm bloody knackered.'

'Look, I'll get off home. I don't think my presence will help if they're still at the stage where they're looking for an argument. Tell them you're going home too and get some sleep. I'll get a uniform to come and spend the night here.'

'Are you sure? I don't mind staying.' Scott was obviously worried for his friend and colleague but he looked dead on his feet.

'I'm sure.'

Matilda left the unit and was crying before the lift reached the ground floor. Relief. She was thankful the rain was falling heavier as she left the hospital. It would disguise her tears. She stood in the car park and looked for her car before remembering she had been dropped off by Adele.

Matilda was sure the taxi driver had been trying to make conversation but she hadn't registered. He dropped her off outside the police station and she passed a ten pound note through the gap in the partition. He didn't give her any change, not that she waited for any.

There were very few staff around as most of the offices were shrouded in darkness. Matilda made her way along the quiet corridors to the CID suite. She turned on the lights and listened as they clicked and flickered into life. She surveyed the open-plan office: the mess on the desks; the mismatched chairs; the dying pot plants; the damp patches on the ceiling, and the nasty, stained carpet tiles. It was still more welcoming than an empty house.

Her small office was cold so she kept her jacket on. She powered up her computer and looked through the messages left on her desk. She read a brief note from Faith Easter in her scribbled handwriting about a boy called Malcolm Preston (a name she had heard before, but couldn't remember where) and put it to one side.

Matilda looked at the blank computer screen and had no idea where to begin. She wanted to know what name Wesley Brigstone now lived under and where he was, and she needed confirmation Debbie Hartley really was Catherine Downy.

She looked up at the loud, ticking clock on the wall. It was almost midnight. It was going to be a very long night.

SIXTY-TWO

'Have you been here all night?' Sian asked, shaking Matilda awake softly by the shoulders.

Matilda opened her eyes and sat up in her chair. Every bone and muscle in her body ached from being bent over her desk for the past few hours. She noticed drool on a sheet of paper in front of her and quickly hid it away.

'What? Yes, I think so,' she replied, dazed.

'Here, have this,' Sian placed a large takeaway latte from Costa in front of her.

'Sian, you're a lifesaver. I owe you one.' She took off the lid and inhaled the creamy coffee. Ambrosia.

Sian went over to her desk and took a Twirl from her snack drawer. 'It's not the healthiest breakfast snack in the world, but it will give you a sugar rush.'

'Thanks.'

'You're going to make yourself ill. You need to have a proper night's sleep.'

'I know. I didn't intend to spend all night here. I went to see how Rory was and just ended up back here.'

Matilda saw the pad in front of her computer where she had written down everything she had found out about Debbie

Hartley's brother and his former partner in crime. As much as she trusted Sian, she didn't want her involved in this, so quickly closed the pad and placed it in her drawer. 'It's a bloody mess in here,' she said by way of an excuse.

'How is Rory? I texted Scott this morning but didn't get a reply.'

'He was at the hospital until late. I suppose he's still asleep. Rory's going to be fine,' she smiled.

'Oh that is a relief. I hardly had any sleep last night worrying about him.'

'What time is it?' Matilda asked, noticing daylight coming through the slats in her venetian blind.

'Almost eight o'clock.'

'Shit. I need to speak to the ACC first thing.'

'She won't be in yet.'

'No. I'll have time to go home and shower first.'

'Good morning, ma'am, any chance of a word?'

An hour later and Matilda was poking her head around Valerie's door. She had taken a taxi home, had a long shower and a change of clothes, a strong black coffee, and a brief chat with James, telling him all about her maybe breakthrough in the Thomas Hartley case. As she left, she stuck two fingers up at the treadmill and closed the door firmly behind her. A shower and a coffee; that was all it took to give Matilda a fresh perspective.

'Matilda, of course. How's Rory?'

'He's fine. His recovery will take a while but he's heading in the right direction, which is the main thing. Callum Nixon will be on his way to Sheffield Magistrate's Court this morning.'

'What about the other inmates at Starling House?'

'They're still in the holding cells. We're waiting on the Home Office.'

'So what can I do for you?'

362

Matilda sat down at Valerie's desk without being offered a seat. She swallowed hard and braced herself for an onslaught.

'Do you remember me talking about Thomas Hartley—?'

'Matilda, please don't tell me … '

'Wait. Thomas's father, Daniel Hartley, was really Thomas Downy.'

'Thomas Downy?'

'When he was thirteen, he and Wesley Brigstone murdered Felix Myers in St Austell, Cornwall.'

'I remember.' It was obvious Matilda had piqued Valerie's interest but her tensed jaw and thin lips were evidence she was annoyed at Matilda for going against her wishes to leave the Thomas Hartley case alone.

'I want to interview Wesley Brigstone.'

'What? No. That's not happening.'

'Why not? I'm sorry, ma'am, but this obviously shows the original case was flawed. They assumed Thomas was guilty and refused to look elsewhere. If they'd have explored all angles they would have found out Daniel was really Thomas Downy and found the real killer.'

'Do you have any idea how this is going to look to Greater Manchester Police?'

'Isn't this supposed to be about justice and not reputation? Besides, only the other day you were worried about South Yorkshire's reputation. This is bound to win us some brownie points.'

Valerie looked at Matilda's pleading face and sighed. 'Leave it with me. Stick to the Starling House case for now.'

There was nothing more to be said between the ACC and the DCI. Matilda quietly walked out of the office and silently closed the door behind her. She was surprised Valerie hadn't erupted and suspended her on the spot – she had been expecting that. She wasn't allowed to investigate the Thomas Hartley case herself but it was being looked into. That was a major turning point, wasn't it?

SIXTY-THREE

'How's everything with the house?' Matilda asked Sian as she approached her desk with a replacement latte.

'We've lost all the downstairs carpets, and the sofas are ruined. I'm not sure about the dining table until the wood dries out. The fridge, washing machine, and dishwasher are all broken. It's a nightmare.'

'I'm sorry, Sian. If there's anything I can do,' Matilda said.

'Thanks.'

'Look, if you or the kids need a place to stay you're more than welcome to use a couple of my spare rooms.'

As soon as Matilda offered up her home she immediately regretted it. As much as she loved Sian and wanted to hear life in her home again, she wasn't sure she was ready to share her space with anyone other than James.

'That's very kind of you, Matilda. Fortunately, the kids are loving just having the upstairs to live in. It's like camping. They may change their mind in a week or too. If they do, I'll let you know.'

'Well, it's an open offer. As and when.' Meaning Matilda didn't need to offer anymore and, hopefully, Sian would be too polite to bring it up.

'Am I OK to have a word with you about Ryan Asher?' Faith

asked entering the open-plan office. This morning her hair was tied back in a ponytail which reminded Matilda of Kate Moloney. She wondered how she was coping with the unrest. A small article in the newspapers this morning stated Starling House was to be closed down while an inquiry was taking place into its conduct over the years. Matilda doubted it would ever reopen.

'Of course you can, Faith. What have you come up with?'

Faith told Matilda and Sian all about Malcolm Preston and Ryan Asher seeming to get away with putting a teenager into a veritable persistent vegetative state.

'Now, according to the couple of nurses I've spoken to at Norfolk, Malcolm's father used to keep a bedside vigil. The last couple of months or so he hasn't been there much.'

'Any reason?'

'Well, the consultant was getting worried about him as he was losing weight and hardly sleeping. They had a counsellor talk to him who basically said it wasn't healthy to be spending every day by his son's bedside. After that he started missing the odd day and now it seems he's stopped coming completely.'

'Maybe he's decided to take a holiday and gather his thoughts,' Sian suggested.

'You're not convinced, are you Faith?' Matilda asked, looking up at the stern expression on the young DC's face.

'I'm not, no. I think this whole Ryan Asher case is bizarre, and now we have a person going missing. From what the nurses have said, John Preston's life revolved around his son. He wouldn't just stop visiting without saying something.'

'Faith, give Norfolk police a ring and ask them to send a couple of uniforms around to this John Preston's house. If he's not at home, ask them to have a word with the neighbours.'

A smile spread across Faith's lips. 'I'll do that right now. Thank you, ma'am.'

Faith turned and bounced away, her ponytail swishing with every step.

'I think MIT merging with CID has been the making of Faith,' Matilda said. 'She was a bit of a fish out of a water in the Murder Room but in CID she's come into her own.'

'Well, I'm glad someone's seen a benefit from it.'

'Are you still not happy?'

'I'm not happy that we're cramped into the corner as if we're something to be ashamed of, and I'm not happy that some thieving bugger is nicking stuff from my snack drawer.'

'You know what, you're right. It does look like we've been thrown into a cupboard, doesn't it? When we get some free time I think we need to open this place up a bit. Get rid of a few of the filing cabinets and really merge with the CID. We need to be one unit.'

Scott dragged himself into the office looking just as tired as when Matilda had left him at the Northern General the night before. He slumped into a chair and made no apology for being late.

'Any news on Rory?' Sian asked before Matilda could.

'I went to see him on my way in. He's looking a lot better. He's awake and sitting up in bed. He's not happy he's had to have his head shaved.'

'That's a shame, he's got gorgeous wavy hair,' Sian said. 'It'll soon grow back though.'

'He'll make a full recovery then?' Matilda asked.

'It looks like it, yes,' Scott smiled.

'That is good news. Seeing him unconscious in that interview room yesterday covered in blood; my heart almost stopped,' Matilda said. 'I never want to see any of my team in that situation again.'

'He wanted to try and understand the inmates better. This case has really got under his skin,' Sian said by way of an explanation. She turned to Scott. 'How are things with him and Amelia? Any chance of a reconciliation?'

'No. I think this has actually given him a bit of a confidence boost … '

'Yes, that's just what Rory needs, more confidence,' Matilda laughed.

'I was talking to his mother and she said Amelia felt guilty for neglecting Rory while she was studying and would like to give it another go. Rory just turned around and said no. He said it was definitely over. If she'd have said that before he was attacked, I think he would have jumped at the chance of them getting back together.'

'Good for Rory. Why should he make her feel better? She shouldn't have taken advantage of his good nature,' Sian said, ever the protective mother.

'Well, I'm going to grab myself a coffee. Have I missed the briefing?'

'You have but never mind. You can go with Sian back to Starling House and interview what is left of the staff there. I can't believe none of them knew what was going on,' Matilda said.

'Apart from that, the inmates of Starling House are still locked up downstairs waiting to be scattered around the country. Richard Grover is waiting to go to magistrate's court, as is Callum Nixon, and Fred Percival has been released without charge as he hasn't done anything wrong. He immediately tendered his resignation and plans to go back to … I can't remember where he said he lived,' Sian added.

'Oh, well I might grab a bacon sandwich while I'm at it if there's nothing to rush back for,' Scott added.

'Don't go slacking; we've Sian's chocolate thief to hunt down,' Matilda smiled.

'I get the feeling,' Sian said once they were alone, 'that you're sitting here running out the clock. What's going on?'

'I'm waiting for some information from the ACC, and I want to be here when she calls before she changes her mind.'

'Sounds ominous.'

'It is.'

'But you're not going to tell me?'

'It depends. Do you have a dark chocolate Bounty in your drawer?'

Adele sent Matilda a text just after midday saying she would be unable to meet for lunch as two elderly residents at a nursing home had died within twelve hours of each other and she was helping Claire with the Digital Autopsies. Matilda was relieved. She wasn't in the mood for small talk and the endless questions from Adele about her well-being. She knew she had her best interests at heart, but, for one day, she wanted to be alone.

The irony wasn't lost on her. At home she hated the loneliness and the silence but when company was offered she tried everything to get out of it.

You really are weird, Matilda, do you know that?

The phone on her desk rang before she could answer herself.

'DCI Matilda Darke?'

'Yes,' Matilda confirmed reluctantly.

'I'm Emma McDermid ... ' began a thick Scottish accent. Matilda wondered if she was any relation to Val McDermid, who was rapidly becoming her favourite crime fiction author. Suddenly she remembered she was on the phone and hadn't been listening to the conversation.

'I'm sorry, can you repeat that? It's a bad line.'

Emma spoke louder and slower. 'I'm Emma McDermid. I'm a reporter with the *Daily Mail*. As I'm sure you're aware the book about Carl Meagan written by his mother has been released and is selling very well. I was wondering what your thoughts on the book were. Have you read it?'

Matilda's blood ran cold. Before the book was released it felt like she was the only one to have a copy and nobody else but her would ever read it. It seemed like the private thoughts of Sally Meagan had been written just to torment Matilda. Now it was on the shelves, anyone could get their hands on a copy – family, friends, neighbours, colleagues, even journalists. This would be the first phone call of many.

'I'm sorry Ms McDermid, but I have no comment to make.'

'DCI Darke, you must have some thoughts on the book. Were you consulted at all during it being written?'

'I had no input into the writing of the book, and I haven't read it,' she lied.

'I'm just over halfway through it, myself. I have to say, you, and South Yorkshire Police, don't come across as very competent. Given the negative press the force has received in recent months, are you worried for the future of South Yorkshire Police?'

'I'm not at liberty to answer any question on the future of the force—'

'What about your own future?' the journalist interrupted.

'I'm going to hang up now, Ms McDermid. I'd rather you placed any further questions you may have through the press office.'

Matilda hung up and found her hands were shaking. Her palms were sweating and she could hear her heart beating rapidly. She took a deep breath to control her breathing but it didn't seem to work. She felt hot.

'Sir Robert Walpole, Spencer Compton, Henry Pelham … ' she began reciting the names of the British Prime Ministers, which was an exercise she used whenever she felt a panic attack coming on that was taught to her by her therapist. She hadn't had an attack for months, and she hadn't needed the support of the Prime Ministers for a very long time. 'Thomas Pelham-Holles, William Cavendish – don't start all that again, Matilda, for fuck's sake,' she chastised herself.

She kicked back her chair when her phone started to ring again. She wanted to ignore it. She wanted to rip the phone off the table and throw it out of the window. Unfortunately, her new office in CID had glass walls and she could be seen by anyone who happened to look up from their work. At the sound of her phone ringing three times, four, five, people had started to take notice. She could already feel their eyes glaring at her through the glass.

'Yes,' she said quietly into the phone.

'Matilda, I'm glad I've caught you. Can you come up to my office when you've got a moment?' ACC Valerie Masterson said.

'Sure. Not a problem,' Matilda said, trying to sound relatively normal – feeling anything but.

SIXTY-FOUR

Starling House often had an eerie air of the macabre about it. Maybe it was the gargoyles; the turrets; the high ceilings and gothic windows; the history going back hundreds of years; the long, echoing corridors. Or maybe it was the fact it housed the most dangerous boys Britain had ever known.

With the inmates no longer there the building took on a darker tone. The boys may have left but it felt like the evil they embodied remained. For twenty years, Starling House had been home to murderers, rapists, and arsonists. Their crimes, their dark personalities seemed to have leeched into the fabric of the building.

The remaining staff felt self-conscious. They were in limbo and didn't know if their jobs were safe or if they had all been made redundant. Until a representative from BB Security arrived from Ireland they had to continue as normal. Normal? Nothing about this place was normal. Every sound, smell, creak, and groan had a hidden meaning. Fear and danger lurked around every dark corner. There was a permanent sense of foreboding. Two inmates had been murdered, and despite the killers being removed the atmosphere at Starling House still felt incredibly bleak.

Kate Moloney was silently walking through the corridors. There was nothing for her to do apart from wait to be told her twenty-year career with BB Security was at an end. It was sad it had come to this. She had enjoyed her time here. It hadn't been an easy job. Some of the staff had been difficult, the inmates less so, surprisingly, but it had been interesting and she had relished the responsibility and freedom given to her by head office.

She walked along A corridor, where the inmates had their rooms. The doors were open and the light from the small windows came out into the usually dark corridor. Kate didn't bother locking the gates behind her. What was the point? This was no longer a prison. It was a shell.

Kate stopped outside Callum Nixon's room. She stood in the doorway and surveyed the mass of belongings he had accumulated. She entered the room and smiled at the Liverpool FC posters on the wall. His bed was unmade so she tidied up the duvet and plumped the pillows. She'd disturbed a smell. It was Callum Nixon's scent. She lifted the pillow, held it to her face and took a long, lingering sniff. She smiled.

Further down the corridor was the room Ryan Asher had been allocated on Monday morning. It was difficult to believe all this started less than a week ago. It was Ryan's arrival, and someone who thought he should be sentenced to death, that had kicked off a chain of events that led to Starling House being closed.

With Richard Grover being charged and Fred Percival handing in his notice, the staff at Starling House were small in number. The cooks and cleaners had been dismissed and told their services would no longer be required. The guards were also free to leave if they wished, and some of them couldn't pack and get out of the building fast enough. The ones who remained had very little to do.

Oliver Byron entered the staffroom and found Rebecca Childs and Peter McFly having a quiet chat over yet another cup of coffee.

'Is this a private conversation or can anyone join in?' he asked, helping himself to a coffee from the pot and digging deep into the biscuit tin.

'You're more than welcome to join us, Oliver,' Rebecca said. 'We were just wondering what's going to happen to Starling House. It's a gorgeous building.'

'It is. I wouldn't be surprised if a property developer didn't turn it into apartments. It would be a shame if it was. Maybe a nice country hotel?'

'After twenty years of housing child murderers, I can't see anyone wanting to spend time here.'

'I don't know,' Peter added. 'It could be very popular hosting those murder mystery weekends. Or maybe ghost hunting.'

'So this is where you're all hiding is it?' Gavin Ryecroft said entering the room.

'I thought you'd gone home,' Rebecca said.

'No. I drove through the night from Norfolk and spent the last two days trying to sort out all this sodding security crap for the police. I was knackered. I've just been having a lie-in.'

'I don't know how you can,' Rebecca shuddered. 'I'm finding this place creepy with hardly anyone around. I wasn't keen on sleeping in the building when the inmates were here. Now they're gone it seems worse for some reason. I put a chair under my door handle last night. I didn't do that with murderers sleeping below me.'

'It certainly seems strange without them, doesn't it?' Gavin said, sitting down next to Rebecca. 'Do you reckon we're all out of a job then?'

'It's beginning to look that way.'

'I wonder which one of them did it?' Rebecca said, refilling her mug from the coffee pot.

'Did what?'

'Killed Ryan and Jacob. Obviously one of the inmates did it. I wonder which one.'

'The way that DI was talking when I was taking him through

the security system, they thought it might be one of us,' Gavin said, blowing on his coffee.

'What? That's absurd.'

'The boys were locked in their rooms when both murders took place. The only people with keys are sitting in this room.'

'And Richard Grover and Fred Percival,' Oliver said. 'I can't believe Richard abused his position like that. And who would have thought Fred was a paedophile? It beggars belief, it really does.'

'Fred has been released without charge,' Rebecca said. 'He hasn't done anything. Well, not here, anyway.'

'I never really warmed to Richard,' Gavin said. 'I liked Fred though. He was a good man, very intelligent. I had many a long conversation with him. It just shows you don't really know a person, do you?'

'Did that DI say who they thought was the killer if they thought it was a member of staff?' Peter said.

'He's hardly going to say that now, is he, son? He just said they couldn't rule anything out. They like to keep their options open, don't they?'

'But it could be any one of us,' Peter said, worry etched on his young face.

'I think it's more likely to have been Richard,' Rebecca said. 'If they thought it was one of us remaining the police would be here guarding us.'

'They are. There's a couple of cop cars on the drive.'

'Oh.'

'Anyway, Rebecca, you said yourself you slept with a chair under your door handle last night. You obviously still think the killer is here.'

'No. I just said it felt spooky, that's all.'

Peter stood up quickly, tipping his chair over. 'I think I'm going to go.'

'Go? Where?' Oliver asked.

'Home.'

'I don't think the police will like that. Kate certainly won't.'

'I don't care. I'll resign then she can't stop me. I'm not staying here another night with a killer waiting to strike again.'

'Peter, you're being silly,' Rebecca scoffed.

'Really? Are you telling me you're not going to put a chair under your handle again tonight?'

'I … well …' Rebecca flustered.

'You can't. You're just as scared as I am.'

'Peter, sit down. Let's all be rational about this,' Oliver said.

'No. I'm not staying here a minute longer than I have to.'

Oliver stood up and went over to Peter by the door. He placed his hands on his shoulders to try and calm the young guard down, but Peter shook them off. 'Don't touch me, Oliver. I'm sorry. I can't trust any of you.' He turned and ran out of the room.

'Well that was a performance,' Gavin said.

'Do you think I should go and talk to him?' Rebecca asked.

'He's probably best left on his own.'

'What if he's right though? What if one of us left is the killer? Shouldn't we all stick together?'

'I think you've been watching too many horror films, Rebecca,' Oliver laughed.

'Really? Then where has Kate been these last couple of hours?'

SIXTY-FIVE

'Every time my phone rings I expect it to be someone from Greater Manchester Police wanting to tear me apart,' Valerie said as soon as Matilda was sitting comfortable in the seat opposite her desk.

Matilda didn't say anything. Everything she thought of would sound shallow and placatory. She needed Valerie on her side and knew she was going against her own judgement so didn't want to annoy her any more than she already had.

'I have some information for you about Wesley Brigstone. You're not going to like it.'

'Is he dead?'

'No. He's back in prison.'

Bang goes my theory.

'He was released from HMYOI Stoke Heath in August 1995, three years ahead of his official release date, and given the new identity of Samuel Bryce. He was moved to Leicester where he found it difficult to cope with life back in the real world. He couldn't get a job, fell into alcohol addiction and he received treatment at various facilities in the local area. He seemed to turn his life around in the early 2000s but lost his job at a packing factory in 2009 just after the economic crash which forced the factory to close. He turned back to the drink and, this time, to drugs too.' Valerie was reading all this from a printed sheet of paper in front of her.

'When did he go back to prison?'

'September 2014. He won't be coming back out.'

My theory is still alive.

'The Hartleys were murdered in January 2014,' Matilda said. 'I'd still like to talk to him.'

Valerie let out a sigh. She knew Matilda wouldn't give up. 'There is a DS at Leicester who monitored Wesley Brigstone while he was out. I've had a very discreet word with the Chief Super at Leicester and he has agreed for you to meet with DS Amy Stringer, who will take you to Wakefield Prison to have a chat with Samuel Bryce.' Valerie spoke slowly as if each word was causing her a great amount of pain to say. They were probably sticking in her throat, making her feel sick. She was going against every instinct in her body. 'Nobody in Manchester knows anything about this. If it goes tits up, Matilda, you're on your own. Do you understand?'

'Yes. I understand perfectly,' Matilda said.

'I want you to know I'm not doing this for you, Matilda, I'm doing it to salvage the reputation of this force.' Valerie tore a piece of paper from a notebook in front of her. 'This is the number for DS Stringer and everything I know about Samuel Bryce.' She was about to hand it to Matilda but pulled her hand back. 'I don't want you heading straight there, though. I want the Starling House murders solved before you even touch this case. Thomas Hartley isn't going anywhere. There's no great rush to get him released if he turns out to be innocent.'

'That's fine,' Matilda said, not taking her eyes from the sheet of paper Valerie was gripping in her right hand.

'I've gone out on a limb for you here, Matilda. I hope you realize that.'

'I do, yes. Thank you. I really appreciate it, ma'am.'

'What are you going to do if Thomas Hartley is guilty?'

'Then I'll drop it.'

Valerie frowned. 'What about your gut feeling?'

'I'll put it down to indigestion.'

Neither of them laughed, not even a smile. Their eyes remained locked on each other. They were trying to read each other's facial expressions but both were masters of the poker face. Reluctantly, Valerie handed the paper across the desk. Matilda wanted to snatch it from her grip and jump for joy, but she managed to restrain herself. She folded it immediately and placed it in her jacket pocket.

'Thank you, ma'am,' Matilda said, standing up.

'If that information gets out, if Samuel Bryce needs to be given a new identity, I swear to God, Matilda, I'll crucify you myself. Is that clear?'

'Perfectly.'

Matilda couldn't get out of the ACC's office fast enough. As soon as she was clear of the door she pulled the paper out of her pocket and read the information written in Valerie's neat and tidy handwriting. Upon release in 1995, Wesley Brigstone and Thomas Downy took very different paths. Thomas did all the right things – job, wife, family – whereas Wesley couldn't find his place in society. Did that make him resentful, angry, bitter? Did that make him want to track down his former partner in crime?

An alarm sounded somewhere in the station. It was muffled, coming from several floors down. The door behind her leading to the ACC's office was thrown open and Valerie stormed out.

'What's going on?' Matilda asked as her boss charged past her.

'Another assault in the holding cells. What are those sodding inmates still doing in my station?' Valerie shouted without stopping.

Matilda ran after her and caught her up at the stairs.

'We're still waiting for them to be transferred to other Young

Offender Institutes,' Matilda said by way of an excuse. 'They're considered category A prisoners, and not many institutes are suitable for them.'

'Not my problem.'

By the time they reached the holding cells the alarm had stopped ringing and everything appeared to be calm, despite the blood on the desk sergeant's shirt.

'What the hell happened here?' Valerie asked, hands on hips.

'Thomas Hartley was attacked by one of the other inmates.'

'What? Badly?' Matilda asked looking worried.

'Not overly, no. He'll have a shiner and a split lip but he'll be fine.'

'I thought they were supposed to be in separate cells?' Valerie asked.

'They are, ma'am, but we're really short-staffed. I can't look after them, the other prisoners, and feed them all at the same time. I've got Flash Gordon in again for frightening women in the NCP, and Alan Barney faked a fit to get out of going to magistrate's court. I had to put some of the Starling House inmates together. I didn't think it would have kicked off like that.' The desk sergeant was obviously flustered. His face was red and his hair an unruly mop from where he had run his fingers through it.

From the corridor, Thomas Hartley was brought in, flanked by two uniformed officers. He was holding a bloodied tissue to his nose. To Matilda, he looked more frightened and vulnerable than when he was in Starling House. She almost ran over to hug him, but stopped herself just in time. She could feel the burning gaze of the ACC on the back of her neck.

'Leave it with me, I'll have these boys removed by the end of the day,' Valerie said. 'Matilda, I assume you'll be needed back at Starling House.' It wasn't a question; it was an order.

'Yes, ma'am.'

Once Valerie was safely out of hearing distance, Matilda dug the piece of paper out of her pocket and dialled a number on her mobile. There was no way Thomas Hartley was going to another Young Offenders Institute. Not if she could help it.

'DS Stringer, I'm DCI Matilda Darke from South Yorkshire Police. I believe my ACC has been speaking to yours with regards to Samuel Bryce.'

'That's right. I didn't expect to hear from you so soon. You're wanting to meet up with Samuel, I'm guessing.'

'Yes. When would it be possible for me to see him?'

'Well, I'm not sure. I can call the prison and ask when they can have him ready to be interviewed. When were you thinking of?'

'This afternoon if possible.'

'Oh. Leave it with me. I'll see what I can do.'

SIXTY-SIX

'Now, the nurses at the hospital where Malcolm Preston is say John Preston hasn't visited at all for at least four weeks. And I've spoken to a lovely DC at Norfolk,' Faith said as she flicked through her notebook, 'who has been to John Preston's house. It looks like he hasn't been home for about that long either.'

'What have the neighbours said?' Matilda asked.

'They haven't seen him. The bloke next door used to notice him drive home late at night and go back out again early the next morning, but he hasn't seen him for weeks.'

'Does he know the exact date he last saw him?' Matilda asked, scratching her head. She felt as if her brain was itching. This case was growing more and more confusing with every additional layer.

'He just said a few weeks.'

'Maybe he's committed suicide,' Sian suggested. 'His son is in limbo, his wife has died, maybe he can't cope with it any longer.'

'No. When you love someone who's ill,' Matilda began, immediately thinking of James, 'you stay with them until the end. You put all thoughts of yourself aside as you need to be strong. When they've gone, when they're at peace, then you think of yourself and decide what you're going to do next. Until that time, your life is virtually on hold.'

'Anyway,' Faith said, trying to bring the conversation back to topic, 'there is no missing person report for John Preston. He seems to have just disappeared.'

'There's no missing person report because there is nobody to miss him,' Matilda said. 'All he has left in life is his son, and he's hardly in a position to report his father missing.'

'So where do we go from here?'

'Is there any sign of life at all from his house?'

'DC Jacobson had a good look round. It's a bungalow in a cul-de-sac. He looked in all the windows, and he said it was clean and tidy but unlived in. There were letters piled up inside the porch, and the gardens were in need of mowing.'

'I suppose we can't just break his front door down in the belief that he's lying dead in the bath or something,' Sian said.

'Not yet we can't. Faith, check the PNC, see if there is a car registered to that address. If there is use the ANPR to track its last movements. Once we locate the car we'll go from there.'

'Yes, ma'am,' Faith said, heading back to her desk.

'Are you all right?' Sian asked Matilda, lowering her voice and leaning across the desk.

'I'm fine. Why?'

'You went all wistful there for a moment.'

'I'm fine,' Matilda repeated, offering a weak smile. 'I think I've got a headache coming on.'

'Would you like a couple of paracetamols?'

'No. I think I might pop out for some fresh air for an hour or so. I need to have a think.'

Slowly, Matilda pushed back her chair and left the CID. She could feel Sian's eyes burning into her so she put her head down and pinched the bridge of her nose. She dragged her feet on the ground and paused as she left the room, as if wondering which direction to turn. She turned left and headed for the stairs. It was only when she knew she wouldn't be seen by anyone that she stood upright and increased her pace.

Matilda needed to get to Wakefield.

SIXTY-SEVEN

'Has anyone seen DCI Darke?'

DS Sian Mills signalled to DI Christian Brady to come over to her desk. The rest of the officers in CID went back to their work.

'She wasn't feeling too well,' Sian said in hushed tones as Christian bobbed down next to her desk.

'What's wrong with her?'

'I think she's feeling a bit … you know … '

'Not really, Sian. Are you trying to tell me it's her time of the month?'

Sian laughed. 'No, nothing like that. I think she's a bit over-whelmed. Every once in a while she remembers James and she gets a bit down. Grief is a very strange thing. I think she just needs a few hours on her own.'

'Oh. Does the ACC know about this?'

'About what?'

'Matilda taking a few hours off whenever she feels like it?'

'You make it sound like she's bunking off work to go shopping. She's grieving.'

'Hasn't it been more than a year since her husband died?'

'Well, yes, but you don't just get over the death of someone you love in the space of a few weeks. It stays with you. It's something you have to learn to live with.'

'It doesn't sound like Matilda has learned to live with it though, not if she's taking random hours off in the middle of an investigation.'

'Christian, you're not going to say anything to the ACC are you?' Sian asked, a worried expression on her face. 'We stick together in the Murder Room. We're a close-knit team and we help each other out. It's what we've always done.'

'Sian, the Murder Room no longer exists. We're one big team now, and we all need to pull our weight to get the job done. We all need to be on the same page. Is that understood?'

Sian was hoping it was a rhetorical question but Christian stared at her and wouldn't leave until she replied.

'Yes,' she said reluctantly.

Christian picked up the mug of tea he'd placed on top of a file on Sian's desk (leaving a ring mark behind) and headed for his office.

'That's the last time I let you have the last Snickers out of my drawer,' Sian said under her breath.

Detective Sergeant Amy Stringer was a short woman with long, dark hair. There was nothing memorable about her appearance. She was slim and sensibly dressed, plain-looking, and wore thick-framed glasses that didn't suit her. She was already in the car park of Wakefield Prison when she saw Matilda's Ford Focus pull in. Amy climbed out of her car and buttoned up her coat. There was a cold wind blowing around the building. She recognized Matilda immediately and held out her hand for the DCI to shake.

'It's nice to meet you DCI Darke. I've heard a lot about you.'

Matilda hated it when people said that.

'Nice to meet you too,' Matilda said. Amy Stringer's handshake was firm and confident.

Amy headed for the main entrance but Matilda stopped her.

'What can you tell me about Samuel Bryce before we go in?'

'What do you want to know?'

'Why did he end up back in prison?'

'Life didn't seem to suit him on the outside. As sad as it sounds, I think he's happier now he's back in prison. He has a short fuse—'

'He's quick to anger?' Matilda interrupted.

'No, I didn't mean it like that. Whenever something goes wrong, he just gives up. He doesn't look for a solution. When he lost his job in 2009 he took it as a sign that he wasn't meant to improve his life and was always going to be a loser. He started drinking heavily again.'

'Did you try and help him?'

'Of course. I put him in touch with a rehab facility in Leicester, which seemed to work for a while. He was in therapy too. He found himself a girlfriend as well, which I thought would be a turning point for him.'

'But it wasn't?'

'No. He didn't tell me at the time but I later found out she was also a recovering addict. Only, her addiction wasn't alcohol, it was drugs.'

'And she got him hooked on drugs?'

'She certainly did. Nothing heavy at first, cannabis, a bit of coke. Then he went on to crystal meth.'

'Bloody hell! So what happened for him to get sent here?' Matilda asked, nodding at the imposing building in front of her.

'He started dealing. And he was eventually caught in Manchester.'

'Manchester?' *Where the Hartleys lived.*

'Has anyone seen DCI Darke?'

It was the second time that afternoon Sian had heard that question. This time, she was reluctant to answer.

'What's the problem?' she asked as Faith came over to her desk.

'Not a problem as such. Well, it may be a problem. I'm not sure.'

'You're not making much sense, Faith. Have a seat.'

Faith pulled up a chair and perched on the edge. She flicked her hair back and began. 'John Preston has a silver Vectra. Registration number VF51 CJS. He doesn't have a garage and keeps it on the driveway. According to his neighbour, it hasn't been outside his house for about a month. Anyway, I've had the number run through the ANPR and it was last seen here in Sheffield just over a week ago.'

'Where?'

'The A6102. Bochum Parkway.'

'Please tell me he was travelling out of Sheffield.'

'Sorry. He was heading for Sheffield.'

'Starling House isn't far from Bochum Parkway.'

'That's why I was looking for the DCI. If John Preston has been in Sheffield for the last few weeks or so, then surely he's a possible suspect for the murder of Ryan Asher.'

Sian thought for a while. 'Do we have a photo of John Preston?'

'I don't believe so.'

'Try and get one. Let's see who we're supposed to be looking for.'

SIXTY-EIGHT

Matilda had visited Wakefield Prison many times in the course of her career. However, the sense of the occasion was not lost on her. It was the same with hospitals. Whenever she entered one she thought of James; the many scans and sessions of chemotherapy he'd had to endure. The memories came flooding back. As she entered the prison, she thought of the cases she had worked on over the years; the suspects who had been found guilty and sentenced. She knew some of them would be here in Wakefield Prison. She often wondered about them. Another reason for her sleepless nights and heavy mind.

For security reasons, Matilda and Amy had their phones, keys, wallets, and anything else in their pockets locked up in reception and were then shown into the Legal Visits Room. As Matilda saw her phone being locked away she wondered if she doing the right thing in putting Thomas Hartley before the Starling House case. What if she was needed urgently? She wouldn't know of anything happening until she left the prison.

Minutes went by slowly, which did not help Matilda's anxiety at all. Anything could happen in a prison, and, knowing Matilda's luck, it probably would. Her mind was charging full speed ahead as it conjured up the many dangerous scenarios – a riot, fire, explosion, lockdown, revolt. She wanted to recite her list of Prime Ministers. She needed the comfort of banality to settle her nerves but she couldn't allow a detective sergeant she didn't know to see how fragile and pathetic she was.

Matilda looked over at Amy whose face was blank. She was chewing her bottom lip – was that her way of controlling her own anxieties or was she just bored of being kept waiting?

Pull yourself together, for crying out loud.

The door was unlocked and in walked Samuel Bryce, formerly known as Wesley Brigstone. He was followed by a female prison guard who showed him to a seat opposite Matilda and Amy. Once he was sitting, she unlocked his handcuffs from behind his back. He placed his hands on the table and knitted his fingers together.

The only photograph Matilda had seen of Samuel was taken more than thirty years before when he was still called Wesley. Then, he was a fresh-faced thirteen-year-old boy wearing his school blazer and smiling his cheeky smile directly to the camera. The blue eyes were bright, his cheeks had dimples, and his hair was soft and flowing. Now, time, alcohol and drugs had ravaged his body. He had the harsh look of a man on the edge of life. His dull blue eyes had sunk into his face. He looked tired and drawn. His once shiny hair was lifeless and cut short. His uniform of navy trousers and sweater were old and stained and at least one size too big for his skeletal frame. He looked more than a decade older than his forty-four years.

Amy cleared her throat and introduced them both. The silence returned. It was time for Matilda to take over and begin the interview.

'I'd like you to tell me about what happened once you were released back in 1995.'

'She knows,' he nodded in Amy's direction. His voice was quiet and gruff as if it physically hurt his throat to speak.

'I'd like to hear it from you.'

'There's nothing to say.'

'OK. What about from 2009 when you lost your job at the packing factory in Leicester?'

'I didn't lose my job. I was made redundant. I'd worked for them for more than ten years. I got a good payout.'

'So what happened?'

'There weren't any jobs going. People were being laid off, left, right, and centre. Companies weren't hiring as they were scared by the economy. I managed to survive for a while; I had my redundancy money, but it didn't last long. I had a few temp jobs, working behind a bar, as a postman at Christmas when they needed extra staff, then a milkman, but even they dried up eventually.'

'It sounds like you wanted to succeed though. You didn't want life to beat you.'

'I didn't. At first. It was the bloody Olympics that did it.'

Matilda frowned. 'How's that?'

'While the whole country was pissing themselves about the Olympics, saying how brilliant it was going to be for Great Britain, how the mood of the nation was high, I couldn't get arrested.' He laughed and showed a set of brown, broken teeth. 'Actually that's not true. I probably could have got arrested if I'd wanted to. I had to go and sign on. I've never done that before in my life. Do you know how degrading it is having to beg for a bit of money just so you can pay the rent? I had some snotty cow behind a desk asking me what I'd done to find work. What work? There was nothing out there. I ended up having my benefits stopped. I couldn't even afford the bus fare to get food from a food bank. How bad is that?'

Matilda started to feel sorry for Samuel. Had he been let down by the system or was he doomed from the day he was born?

'So what happened?'

'Around September 2013 I started getting into drugs. I met this woman in a pub and I went back to her place. She had some coke and we had a pretty heavy night, if you know what I mean.

Anyway, we met up a few more times, and it was always the same thing: coke, drink, and sex. One night, she didn't have any coke and I had no idea where to get some from, but she said she knew a guy so off she went. She came back and said she had something new she hadn't tried before but was told it was the bollocks.'

'What was it?'

'Crystal meth.'

Matilda had to bite her tongue. Crystal methamphetamine was one of the most powerful illegal drugs available. Commonly known as the 'club drug' it is addictive from the very first hit. The first experience may involve some pleasure and act as a stimulant to party all night, but it would already have begun to attack the body and change the user's life.

Samuel noticed the look on Matilda and Amy's faces. 'You know what it does. At first I thought it was brilliant. It gave me so much energy. I was happy. But it doesn't take long to bring you down. I was getting depressed. I stopped eating, lost weight, and the only way to stop yourself from feeling down is by taking more meth. I sold everything I had to buy more. I lost my flat, everything. I ended up moving in with Caitlyn but it wasn't her flat to begin with. It was just a squat.'

'Was Caitlyn supporting your habit?'

'Yes. To begin with.'

'Was she working?'

'She was,' he smiled. 'But it wasn't the sort of job you put on your CV.'

'She was a prostitute?'

'And a bloody good one too. The problem is the dealers know how much you need the drug so they keep putting the price up. You can't afford it but you need it, so you'll do anything to get it.'

'What happened?' Matilda was engrossed in Samuel's story.

'Caitlyn was going out more and more to get money. She started doing riskier stuff if it meant getting more cash. She didn't like it.' Samuel genuinely looked disgusted as he relived his darkest days.

'What was she doing?' Amy asked.

'Trust me, you don't want to know. You'll be shocked if you knew what sick things some men like to do. I liked Caitlyn. I genuinely had feelings for her. It was horrible seeing her change into a shell. She stopped talking to me. She stopped eating, and she was crying all the time. Then I remembered.'

'Remembered what?'

'I remembered I had a friend ... Thomas Downy.'

SIXTY-NINE

'Christian, any chance of a word?'

Sian and Faith were standing in the doorway of his office. They looked pensive.

'You can have as many words as you like if it's going to distract me from these sodding overtime sheets.'

'Faith's been trying to track down John Preston all day. She's run his car through the ANPR and it was last seen a few weeks ago here in Sheffield, despite John supposedly keeping a vigil at his son's hospital bed. We've got a copy of his driving licence and … well … ' she handed him a printed copy of the licence.

'That's not John Preston,' Christian said, studying the printout.

Sian and Faith exchanged glances.

'I called the hospital that Malcolm Preston is in and spoke to one of the nurses,' Faith said. 'I sent an email of the driving licence and asked her to confirm that it's John Preston. Six nurses all confirmed it.'

'This makes absolutely no sense. What does Matilda say?'

Sian looked everywhere apart from at Christian Brady. 'She's not back yet.'

Christian blew out his cheeks. He would have to step up to the plate and make a decision. He hoped he would make the right one. If he did he would make sure the ACC knew it was him who solved the Ryan Asher case and not Matilda Darke.

'Well … ?' Sian prompted.

'We need to visit Starling House. Someone is either a very good actor or everyone has been lying to us the whole time.'

'The first thing you were told upon being released from prison was that you must never contact Thomas Downy,' Amy said quietly yet firmly.

'I know that. But when you're desperate you'll do anything.'

Matilda was reminded of the inmates of Starling House and the crimes they had committed. Some of them found themselves in desperate situations and felt murder was the only solution. It could happen to anyone. That thought sent a chill straight through her. Was she capable of murder given the situation? She hoped not.

'How did you know where to find him?' Amy asked.

'He was in the newspaper. I can't remember the story, something about a protest over immigration. There was a group of people standing in front of a banner. I recognized him straightaway.'

'But you hadn't seen him since you were both thirteen. You went to different Young Offender Institutes. Surely he'd changed?'

'It may have been thirty years but some things don't change. The eyes never change,' Samuel said. He was smiling. He seemed to be enjoying his audience.

Amy was disgusted. 'The newspaper wouldn't have given his address though.'

'No. The protest was in Heaton Park in Manchester. The picture that went with the article had the names of the people in it. He was calling himself Daniel Hartley now. He wasn't too difficult to find.'

'So what did you do?' Matilda asked. 'Did you just knock on his door and ask if he wanted to reminisce about old times?'

'No, nothing like that. I had to do my homework. I found him, followed him, worked out his routine. He'd done all right for himself. He was married, had a nice house, new-ish car, two kids. He was fit and healthy, wore designer clothes, cufflinks, the latest mobile phone. To look at him you wouldn't have thought he'd helped butcher an innocent child.'

Samuel's words were making Matilda and Amy uncomfortable. They tried not to make it obvious but it was difficult. He was revelling in his captive audience. He appeared to have no remorse over the killing of Felix Myers and would probably have given them an intricate account of the gruesome murder if they'd asked. He really was a disturbed individual.

'One evening he pulled up outside his house and got out of the car. I'd been waiting for him all day. I was freezing. I called his name, his new name, and he turned around. You should have seen the look on his face when he saw me.' Samuel laughed as he relived the memory. 'He recognized me straightaway. It's like I said, the eyes are a giveaway.'

'What did he say?'

'He was full of questions: What do you want? How did you find me? What are you doing here? He was stuttering and sweating and practically pissed himself. I told him I wanted to talk, that it was important. He told me to meet him at the bus station in an hour.'

'Did you?'

'Yeah. We went for a drive. We were driving for ages and didn't say a word. I could see he was seething; he was itching to ask me all kinds of questions but he didn't know where to start. We drove into the middle of nowhere. I think we were on the moors or something.'

'What did you talk about?'

'I told him straight – I needed money.'

'What did he say?'

'He asked how much, and I told him a grand a month would

be good to start with. He said he couldn't afford that, and he saw no reason why he should give me any money at all. I told him he had three good reasons – his wife and two kids. He called me a few names, which I won't tell you as they were pretty harsh. He said he'd give me two grand right there but I had to promise to fuck off and not come back.'

'Did you agree to that?'

'Two grand's better than nothing. We went back to Manchester. He went into a bank and got the cash. He drove me to the bus station and practically threw me out of the car.'

'Please tell me that was the last you saw of him,' Amy said. She was still in blind hope that it was the extent of Samuel's breaking of the rules.

'Not exactly.' he grinned. 'I went back a few weeks later.'

SEVENTY

While Faith concentrated on driving through another heavy rain storm, Christian and Sian were busy with their mobile phones.

Christian had tried to call Matilda three times; each time it went straight to voicemail. On the fourth attempt he left a message. His voice was terse and there was anger behind his words. 'Matilda, it's Christian. I really need to talk to you. It's urgent. Call me immediately.'

In the back seat, Sian was feeling guilty. She should have lied and pretended she had no idea where Matilda was. Why did she say she was still grieving over her husband? She thought she knew Christian. She thought he was one of the good guys who would understand what Matilda was going through. Surely, he wouldn't use her fragility to further his career? With nervous, shaking fingers, Sian sent Matilda a series of text messages. All of which went unanswered:

I told Brady you were taking some time out. Thought he'd understand. Typical bloke he doesn't. Sorry.

Brady has been trying to ring you. He's pissed off. Think he might go to ACC.

You need to ring me, Mat. We've found John Preston. You're not going to believe this.

Brady, me and Faith are going to Starling House. Brady is seriously pissed. You need to get here Mat. Where are you???

As the car turned into the grounds of Starling House, Sian looked at her phone one more time. It was five o'clock and almost dark. There were still no messages from Matilda. She looked around the headrest to see Christian also staring at his phone as if willing it to ring. Was he worried he would mess up without Matilda or was he angry she had abandoned him when the case was finally getting somewhere?

Starling House looked deserted. There were no cars or vans in the car park at the front of the building, and the windows were unlit.

'Drive round to the back,' Christian instructed Faith, who had already parked.

She turned on the engine and slowly made her way to the back of the building. The car crunched on the gravel of the sweeping driveway. All three were looking up at Starling House, trying to see some sign of life.

The car park at the rear of the building was for staff only, and there were three vehicles parked in random spaces. They recognized one straightaway. The Vauxhall Vectra belonging to John Preston.

'VF51 CJS,' Christian said, checking the Post-It note from his pocket.

'Should we call for backup?' Faith asked. It wasn't long ago when Faith and Sian innocently knocked on the door of a witness and ended up being held at gunpoint. The memory was still raw for Faith; she had bad dreams about it from time to time. She hadn't mentioned it to Sian but she looked at her in the rear-view mirror. Was she going through the same panicked emotions?

'No. I think John Preston may actually be relieved he's been found out,' Sian said.

'Really?' Faith was surprised. 'Why?'

'He's not a cold-blooded murderer. He just wants vengeance for his son.'

'You sound like you have sympathy for him.'

'I'm a mother of four. If anything happened to them at the hands of someone else, I'd want justice to be served.'

'I agree with Sian,' Christian said, suddenly thinking of his own two children.

'So are we just going to sit here or are we going to go in?' Faith asked.

'We're going in.'

SEVENTY-ONE

Manchester. December 2013

'Dad, you've got a visitor.'

Ruby Hartley bounded into the kitchen. Her father, Daniel, was sitting at the table tapping away on his laptop. He looked up and his smile dropped as he saw Samuel Bryce standing in the doorway.

'What are you doing here?' he asked. His voice had dropped and was shaking.

'Daniel, that's no way to speak to a visitor,' Laura said. She wiped her hands on the tea towel. 'Hello, I'm Laura, Daniel's wife. I must apologize for my antisocial husband. His manners appear to have taken the evening off.'

'That's quite all right,' Samuel said, smiling without revealing his teeth. He had purposely spruced himself up for the occasion. He'd washed and flattened down his knotted hair and managed to find some old clothes in a bin at the back of Primark to make himself look halfway decent. 'Daniel and I go back a long way. I'm used to his moods.'

'You're an old friend of Daniel's? That's nice.'

'Yes. I'm visiting Manchester for the Christmas holidays and thought I'd look up an old friend while I'm here.'

'Well isn't that sweet. Would you like a drink … ?'

'Samuel. Samuel Bryce. And a drink would be lovely, thank you.'

Daniel watched on in horror as his wife was innocently having a charming conversation with a killer. She had no idea who she was inviting into their lives.

'Ruby, go and shout Thomas down to say hello to an old friend of your dad's.'

'Actually, love,' Daniel said, jumping up. 'Let me just have a few words with Samuel on our own. I'll take him into the living room.'

He practically pushed Samuel out of the kitchen and manhandled him into the lounge. He closed the door behind them with a slam.

'What a beautiful Christmas tree,' Samuel said looking up at the seven-foot spruce.

'What the fuck are you doing here?' Daniel spat with venom.

'I've come to see your family. I've come to wish you all a very merry Christmas. I've come for my present.'

'Present?'

'Yes. I thought you'd like to give me a couple of grand in the spirit of the season.'

'I told you the last time I don't have that kind of money,' Daniel hissed.

'Really? I think you're lying; but then you were always good at lying, weren't you? Let's see,' he said, walking around the large living room. 'That TV must have set you back a few grand, and I know for a fact Bang & Olufsen aren't cheap either. Was that an Apple Mac you were playing with in the kitchen?'

'Come off it Wes … Samuel, that isn't fair. I've paid my dues. I served my time and I made something of myself. You could have done it too. Why should I help you because you couldn't be bothered to create a decent life for yourself?'

'Don't you dare!' Samuel said. He walked up close to Daniel, who took a step back in fear. 'You have no idea of the struggle I've had to cope with. I've tried to make a life for myself. I've tried to get a career, a house, and a job, but I've always fallen at the final hurdle. Do you know why? This,' he tapped the side of his head. 'I can't get Felix Myers out of my head.'

It was the first time Daniel Hartley had heard Felix's name since his trial, and he recoiled at it was spoken.

'Unlike you, I have a conscience,' Samuel continued. 'You've obviously been able to put it behind you and move on. Did you think serving nine years was enough? Did you think that made everything better? Well it didn't. I couldn't just turn my mind off and carry on as normal. I've had Felix Myers living in my head for almost thirty years, and it's fucking killing me. You may have been able to shut him out but I haven't. So yes, I think you could afford to give me a few quid to help me out.'

'No way. I'm not giving you anything,' Daniel tried to sound confident but it wasn't working. 'I'm going to call the police and say you've broken the terms of your licence. You'll be straight back in prison, and you'll never see daylight again.'

'And what will that do? Do you honestly think you'll be safe with me behind bars? I know where you live now. I know your name. I can write to your wife. I can look your kids up on Facebook and let them know all about their precious daddy.'

'You're a sick bastard.'

'I'm sick? That's rich. You named your son Thomas after your old life. Now that's sick. I bet if you'd had another son you'd have called him Felix, wouldn't you?'

'I want you to leave,' Daniel said with all the hatred he could muster without raising his voice.

'I'm not going anywhere without some cash.'

'I've already told you I don't have any.'

'Then I'm going to go back into that kitchen and have a lovely chat with the lovely Laura and tell her all the lovely things about her lovely husband. I wonder how she'll react when I tell her the man she sleeps with every night crushed the fingers of a thirteen-year-old boy with a pair of pliers, or that she's had two children with a man who set fire to an innocent teenager and laughed while he watched him burn.'

Daniel was stuck against the back wall in the living room. His left hand was clamped to his mouth and tears were streaming down his face as the whole nightmare came flooding back. He had tried so hard to forget it, to block it out, to build a life for himself, and his family, but it was always there. Now, the full memory was back and it was eating away at him.

Daniel fumbled in his pocket for his wallet and opened it. There was eighty pounds in cash which he shoved into Samuel's hand. He lifted out his bank card and pointed it at him. 'The PIN is 1191. There's about three grand in the account. Take the lot. Only, do me a favour; whatever it is you're taking make sure you give yourself a killer dose because, I swear to God, if you come back here again I'll beat every ounce of life out of you and I won't be able to stop until I've pummelled you to death. Do we understand each other?'

Samuel took the blue plastic card in his dirty, grubby hands.

Daniel turned away, opened the door and found his son standing on the other side.

'Is everything all right, Dad?' Thomas asked.

'Everything's fine, son. Samuel's just remembered he needs to be somewhere else.'

'That's right. Thomas. Sorry I can't stay. Wish your family a merry Christmas from me. I hope you all get what you deserve.'

SEVENTY-TWO

'Did you ever see Daniel Hartley again?' Matilda asked Samuel Bryce.

'No.'

'When did you find out he'd died?'

'The thing is, I don't really remember much about that Christmas, or afterwards. I cleared his bank account like he said I could. It took me a couple of weeks to empty it. I had to write the PIN on my arm in case I forgot it.'

'Did you blow the lot on drink and drugs?' Amy asked.

'Certainly did. Best Christmas ever, from what I remember.'

'Did you go back to Manchester to see Daniel Hartley or his family in January 2014?' Matilda asked, raising her voice slightly.

'I honestly can't answer that. We kept buying more meth and we'd lose days, sometimes a full week. I didn't know what I was doing.'

'Where's Caitlyn now? Could we speak to her?'

'Not without holding a séance. She died in February 2014.'

'Overdose?'

'She needed it. The bloke who sold us the meth said he had a few mates who'd pay her a grand to spend the night with them. She didn't want to, but I talked her into it. We didn't have much of Daniel's money left and needed everything we could get. The night she left I told her I loved her for the first time,' Samuel's voice broke and his bottom lip began to wobble. 'She said it back to me too. The next morning, I found her in the living room. She'd been beaten black and blue. She wouldn't talk to me. It took me all day to get it out of her. They weren't a couple of his mates, there was a whole gang of them. She lost count of how many there were. They did anything they wanted with her and she just had to take it. They kicked her out when they'd finished and didn't give her a penny.'

Samuel was crying. He had genuine feelings for Caitlyn and he'd encouraged her to go out that night. He'd sent her to her death.

'I cleaned her up. I told her it would be all right. We'd move away, start a new life. She'd given up though, I saw it in her eyes. She said it was too late. No matter where we moved it would always be with her, in her head. She told me she couldn't live like this any longer, and she wanted to go to sleep. I let her.'

'Did she give herself the overdose?' Amy asked.

Samuel nodded. He couldn't speak. There were genuine tears of sadness pooling in his eyes.

'What happened after that?'

'The next day I took her to the park and left her in the bushes. She was found later that day. I saw a story in the newspapers a few weeks later saying the police were still appealing for witnesses to come forward to identify her. They're probably still waiting.'

'I'm sorry about Caitlyn, Samuel,' Matilda said.

'So am I.'

'Where was this flat you lived in?' Amy asked.

'Near the train station in Leicester. Just off Wellington Street.'

'Samuel,' Matilda asked. 'Going back to Daniel Hartley. Is it possible you killed him while on crystal meth and not remember doing it?'

'I've no idea.'

'Daniel's son, Thomas, is currently serving life in prison for killing his father, mother, and eight-year-old sister, Ruby. He's maintained his innocence from day one, and I believe him.'

Samuel shrugged.

From her inside pocket, Matilda took a photograph of Thomas Hartley. It was the standard photo taken at school. He was flashing a toothy smile, head up high, back straight, grinning to the camera. He was a handsome boy, smart and tidy. He looked nothing like that now. The life had been torn out of him. Matilda pushed the photo to Samuel.

'This is Thomas Hartley. You met him, briefly. Look at him. Young, happy, good-looking, intelligent. He's got his whole life ahead of him. He could be anything he wants. Instead, he's languishing in a Young Offenders Unit for a crime he didn't commit. I think you went back to Manchester while you were high on meth, and you killed Daniel and Laura and Ruby when you couldn't get any more money out of Daniel.'

Samuel looked at the photo. He didn't touch it, he leaned over the table and stared, analysing the picture.

'You're in here for the rest of your life anyway, Samuel. Is it really worth ruining another boy's life by not owning up to what you've done?'

Samuel couldn't take his eyes from the photograph. The clock at the back of the room ticked away a painfully long minute. Eventually, he looked Matilda in the eye. 'I'm a killer. I killed Felix Myers for no reason. I'll admit that as I know, hand on heart, that I did it. Killing is in me. Crystal meth gives you a rush of confidence and energy. It makes you believe you can do anything you want. I've no idea what I was doing around the time Daniel and his family were killed. But when I read about it in the papers, when I saw the way they died, I knew it was me. I knew I'd done it. I just couldn't prove it. Not even to myself.'

Inside, Matilda was cheering. She'd just secured Thomas Hartley's release from prison.

SEVENTY-THREE

Kate Moloney was walking past the back entrance to Starling House when she saw the three detectives approaching. She pulled opened the door and let in a torrent of rain. She shivered against the cold stiff breeze.

'What are you doing here?' Kate looked dreadful. Her hair was tangled, her face was make-up free and every wrinkle and line was on show. 'Don't you think you've done enough damage?'

'We need to talk to your staff again.'

'You're joking, surely. You still think one of the staff killed Ryan and Jacob? Bloody hell, it's no wonder Matilda Darke couldn't find Carl Meagan when you're constantly looking in the wrong direction.'

'Where are your staff, Ms Moloney?' Christian said, ignoring the remark about his boss.

'I have no idea and I'm not in the slightest bit interested.'

'Is the representative from BB Security here yet?' Sian asked.

'No. They've had storms in Ireland too. No planes out until tomorrow at the earliest.'

'Do you mind if we have a look around?'

'You can do what the hell you want. I'm past caring.' She turned and headed off back down the corridor.

'Kate, how long have your staff been working here?' Sian asked.

'Does any of that matter now? We're all out of a job.'

'Humour me.' Sian stared her out.

Kate took a deep breath and let out a huge sigh. 'Peter McFly has only been here a few weeks. Rebecca Childs about a year or so. Same for Gavin Ryecroft. Oliver Byron, a few months, maybe—'

'None of them for very long then?'

'We were all new at some point. Now, if you'll excuse me,' she said. She turned and headed down the corridor.

'Ms Moloney, I'd like you to come with us if you don't mind,' Christian said.

'Why?'

'Please.'

'I'll be glad to see the back of you lot,' she said under her breath but loud enough for them to hear it.

Oliver, Gavin, Rebecca, and Peter were all in the staffroom having a sandwich. The atmosphere was tense and the conversation was stilted. They were making pointless small talk just for something to say, to take the edge off the situation.

'Would anyone mind if I closed the window?' Rebecca asked.

'I would. The smell of whatever it is you're putting in your sandwich is turning my stomach,' Gavin said.

'Fine. I'll freeze to death then, don't worry about me.' She purposely made a performance out of zipping up her jacket and took her sandwich and mug of tea to the table.

The door opened and Kate entered with the detectives following her.

'Here they all are. Which one do you want to accuse this time?'

'What's going on?' Gavin asked, his mouth full of a cheese and pickle sandwich.

'These detectives have put all our names in a hat and pulled one out at random and whoever they've chosen is going to be framed for Ryan and Jacob's murder. Isn't that right, detective?'

408

'There really is no need for that attitude, Kate,' Sian said, slowly losing patience with her.

'Isn't there? You come in here and blunder your way through a murder investigation and allow another inmate to be killed under your noses. Thanks to your ineptitude you've probably managed to get this place closed down and all of us fired. Don't you think we have a right to be slightly pissed off?'

Christian Brady ignored her and stepped forward. 'Oliver Byron, we'd like a word in private.'

'With me?' he asked.

'Yes. If you'd like to come with us?'

'Why?'

'If you could come with us we can talk about this in another room.'

'Don't worry about it, Oliver,' Kate said. 'They'll blame you for half an hour then they'll change their mind and try and pin the murder on Rebecca. Then it'll be Peter's turn.'

'I don't understand,' Oliver said.

'I think you do, John.'

The room fell silent. Christian and Oliver stared at each other. Neither one of them wanting to flinch first.

'John? Who's John?' Rebecca asked.

'You know?' Oliver looked up with wide eyes.

'We know,' Christian said. It was evident he was taking no pleasure out of this. Nobody who had children would relish taking another father into custody for protecting their own child. 'John Preston, I'm arresting you for the murder of Ryan Asher and Jacob Brown. You do not have to say anything; but it may harm your defence if you do not mention when questioned something which you later rely on in court.'

'What the hell is going on?' Gavin protested. 'Who's John Preston?'

'Would you come with us, please, John,' Christian said.

'No. I'm sorry, no. I'm not going anywhere.' John started to back away but the staffroom was small and already full to capacity. There was nowhere for him to go. His eyes widened and darted around the room as if looking for a way out. He saw a large knife on the counter and picked it up, grabbed Rebecca by her hair and lifted her out of her chair. She screamed as he gripped her firmly in his left hand and held the knife to her throat.

'John, this is not the way to solve this,' Sian said, stepping forward. 'Put the knife down, let Rebecca go and we'll talk about this.'

'No. I've nothing to say.'

'It's over, John. We know everything. We know about your son in hospital. We know what happened.'

The heavy silence enveloped the entire room. Kate, Peter, and Gavin were struck dumb by the unfolding drama. Rebecca, tears streaming down her face, was fearing for her life, and Oliver Byron, or John Preston, was panicking, as he knew the end was near.

'I had no choice,' he began, swallowing hard. 'Everyone knew Ryan Asher beat my son to a pulp. Even the police knew it, but there was no evidence so they couldn't arrest him. The only person who could point the finger was my son, and he's in a coma and destined to be in one for the rest of his life.

'A part of me wanted to hunt Ryan down and knock him over with my car or give him the same beating he gave Malcolm, but I didn't. I sat by my son's bed day after day after day thinking of ways to make Ryan pay for what he'd done. Then I read in the newspapers he'd killed his grandparents. I went to his trial. I made sure I sat near his parents so that every time he looked up at them he'd see me too … '

'Were you the man who made the scene?' Faith interrupted.

John Preston grimaced. 'I'm afraid I allowed my emotions to get the better of me that day. His mother was crying. I thought, how can she weep for a monster she brought into the world? I decided not to go back after that. I couldn't face it. I did my homework though. I knew he'd end up at Starling House when he was found guilty so I went along for a job interview. At first I thought it was serendipity that there just happened to be a position available – until I started working here. There's always a position available. Nobody wants to work here.'

Kate looked at the ground as if everything that went on at Starling House was her fault.

'The last day of the trial was my day off. I was glued to the television just waiting for the breaking news. When the guilty verdict came through I was delighted. It was the first time I'd smiled in years. Ryan Asher was coming to Starling House.'

'Did you kill him yourself?'

He looked away from Christian. 'No. Like I said, I'm not that type of person. I didn't need to be though; I was surrounded by killers. I knew what that pervert Richard Grover was doing to the boys, so I used it to my advantage. I heard some of them saying how he made them feel physically sick. Jacob Brown was one of them. I took him to one side and made him an offer he couldn't refuse. If he killed Ryan Asher for me, I'd break him out of Starling House.'

'Oliver!' Rebecca exclaimed.

'He fell for it?' Sian asked.

Oliver tightened his grip on Rebecca's hair and she cried out. 'Well, I had to sweeten the deal a bit more. I offered him some money so he could start afresh somewhere and I said I'd have a car waiting for him outside. He just wanted out.'

'How did you get Ryan from his cell to the recreation room?'

'We don't call them cells,' Kate said weakly.

'Oh give it up, Kate,' John snapped. 'It's that kind of pussy-footing around that's made this country the joke it is. We can't call them cells; we must give prisoners the right to vote in an election. Why not send a prostitute to each cell every Friday night and give them all an hour's fun? They're criminals, Kate. They're killers. They should be locked up for the rest of their lives without any privileges.'

Everyone was silent while John's rant had the chance to settle. He continued. 'I messed about with the CCTV on A corridor, and unlocked Ryan's door. I told Jacob to tell him that it was some kind of initiation as it was Ryan's first night here. I don't know what he said to him but he must have been convincing as they were soon in the rec. room. I was hiding behind the bar. I didn't want Ryan recognizing me as soon as he walked in. You should have heard Jacob,' John laughed. 'He had the patter down perfect, telling him to lie on the pool table and close his eyes. He told him not to be nervous as nothing bad was going to happen to him; it was just going to be a bit of fun. The next thing I heard was a groan as the knife was plunged into his stomach.'

'You didn't kill him yourself?'

'I couldn't. I'm weak. I wanted to, but I couldn't,' he said, looking down. 'As soon as I heard the first stab, I came out from behind the bar and went over to the pool table. Ryan looked up at me, his eyes pleading, then he recognized me. He knew who I really was. I told Jacob to stab him again, which he did. I wanted twelve stab wounds. I was Ryan's jury. I was his executioner. I think he died after the fourth of fifth stab. I don't care how long I live for but I'll die a happy man knowing Ryan Asher's final thought was about Malcolm.'

The room fell silent once more as they took in what the man they knew as Oliver Byron had done. The look on the faces of the staff was one of disbelief.

'Surely Jacob Brown would have been covered in Ryan's blood. What did you do about his clothes?'

'I had Jacob change out of them in the rec. room and gave him a fresh set. After I'd locked him back in his cell I cleaned the knife and put it back in the kitchen and put his clothes in a bag and hid them in my room.'

'We've searched your room. We didn't find them,' Faith said.

He smiled. 'There's a ledge outside my window. The wood is rotten. If you lift the top off there's a nice gap between the roof and the wall of the building. I wedged the bag in there. I was planning on taking it home to burn when I got off shift.'

'So what happened with Jacob?' Sian asked.

'Jacob was a loose cannon. All the next day he kept badgering me about when I was going to get him out, how much longer would he have to wait. When the storm came I knew that was the perfect opportunity. I sneaked him out, smashed the window in the rec. room to make it look like he'd escaped, and got him through the gates at the top of the drive while everyone else was at the back of the building looking at the broken window.'

'Did you need to kill him?' Rebecca asked.

'Don't feel sorry for him. Why are you all so shocked? The boys in here are all convicted killers. Jacob Brown was a rapist and a murderer. Ryan Asher killed his grandparents and set them on fire. He beat my son so badly he's in a persistent vegetative state. Why should they get your sympathy? If you should feel sorry for anyone it's Malcolm, it's his mother, it's me who has had to endure this agony.' The tears were coursing down John's face as he sought to find someone who would be on his side.

'You're not arresting me for doing this country a favour. Those killers were still teenagers. Do you have any idea how much money the tax payer was going to have to waste on those two evil bastards? You shouldn't be arresting me; you should be giving me a medal. I've saved you all a fortune.'

'John, put the knife down,' Christian said, his hands raised. 'Come on, you don't want to hurt Rebecca. You've worked with her for months; you like her. You're colleagues, friends.'

'No. I've been playing a part all these months, a means to an end. Oliver Byron was Rebecca's friend, but I'm not Oliver. I'm John and I need to get out of here.'

'That's not going to happen, John. Now put down the knife, let go of Rebecca and we can talk about this down at the station,' Christian said. He tried to sound soothing and placatory but judging by the steely look in John's wide eyes it didn't seem to be having any effect at all.

'No, here's what's going to happen. You're all going to move away from the door, and Rebecca and I are going to walk out of here. I'll drive off and release Rebecca when I'm far enough away.'

'No!' Rebecca screamed. 'Please don't let him take me anywhere.' She started to squirm and wriggle free from John's grasp.

'Stand still you little bitch.'

'John, let her go. Put down the knife.'

'Oliver, please let me go. I've got a child, a baby, she's not even a year old yet. Please,' Rebecca cried. She grabbed at his arm and tried to push it away from her throat but he was too strong for her. 'Oliver, you're hurting me.'

'John, stop this right now,' Sian screamed.

Rebecca slammed her foot down on John's foot. He called out in pain. He swung his right arm out to regain some balance and Rebecca went limp in his arms. He looked ahead at the shocked expression on the faces of everyone in the room. He lifted his arms up and Rebecca fell to the floor with a thud, the blood gushing out of the large slit in her throat.

SEVENTY-FOUR

By the time Matilda and Amy left Wakefield Prison it was dark and the temperature had plunged. The sky was cloudless and an infinite number of stars and a full moon lit their path to the car park.

'Well that was certainly eye opening,' Amy said.

'You can say that again. He was unburdening himself, wasn't he?'

'It seemed like it. Nobody has asked him about the Hartley killings before, so he probably thought it wasn't worth mentioning.'

'The trouble is, we only have his word for it. If he gets himself a decent solicitor he'll get off with it. We need physical evidence.'

'Such as?'

Matilda fished her mobile out of her pocket and turned it on. 'I'm going to get onto your DCI in Leicester. I want a full forensic search of the flat he and Caitlyn shared. I know it's going back a few years but it if was basically a squat, which it sounds like it was, it may have been left abandoned. Also, could you track down Caitlyn, get her formally identified and sort out a burial?'

'Sure,' Amy smiled.

'Jesus Christ!' Matilda exclaimed, looking at the brightly lit screen of her phone.

'Problem?'

'I'm not sure,' she frowned. 'Look, I'll give you a call later. Thanks for this afternoon.'

Matilda saw the many texts from Sian, the several missed calls from Christian and a voicemail from Valerie waiting for her. Something had obviously happened in Sheffield that warranted her attention, and she had been in Wakefield. The fact her hunch paid off wouldn't be enough for the ACC. She had told Matilda to wait until the Starling House case had been dealt with, and she had gone against her wishes.

'Matilda, it's Christian. Sian tells me you've taken a couple of hours off. Any chance you can give me a quick call please?'

'Matilda, Christian again. Look this is getting a bit urgent now and I'm not sure how to approach this. I could really do with some advice. Ring me.'

'Matilda, I know you're going through some personal shit but this is serious. I'm going to have to go to the ACC.'

Matilda couldn't blame Christian for going over her head. She had left him in charge, but, despite him being an excellent DI, he often needed clarification for the decisions he made. It was as if he was afraid of doing anything on his own. It was something he would need to work on if he wanted to gain promotion to DCI but, right now, he needed her help and she hadn't been there for him. She hoped he had decided to sit tight and wait for her call.

'Matilda, it's ACC Masterson here. I'm guessing you've gone to Wakefield Prison despite the fact I told you not you. We will discuss that another time. I need you back here right now.'

As soon as Matilda hit the M1 she floored the Ford Focus and tried to get as much speed out of the dated car as she could.

'Shit,' she said under her breath.

Matilda changed lanes to get around slow-moving vehicles like an expert on a Formula One track. It wasn't the other drivers going slow; it was Matilda breaking the speed limit. She didn't care if a traffic camera flashed at her or if she was stopped by police. None of that mattered.

With one eye on the road and one hand on the wheel, she placed her phone in the hands-free cradle and dialled a number from the phone book. She called Sian but there was no reply. Christian's mobile kept ringing out. What the hell was going on back in Sheffield?

Rebecca Childs was in shock, her whole body shaking as the life drained from her body. Faith leapt forward and dropped to her knees. She grabbed the roll of kitchen paper from the table and pulled off several sheets to press against the gaping wound in Rebecca's throat. The paper quickly soaked up the blood.

'Give me your jacket,' Faith said to Gavin.

'John, drop the knife,' Christian said. His eyes darted from John's stricken face to the bloody knife in his right hand. He wished he hadn't left his baton in the car. He looked over to Sian. He could see the outline of a pair of handcuffs in her back pocket but that was it. How had they not realized they'd be entering such a dangerous situation? He doubted Matilda would have made such a monumental error.

'I'm sorry,' he said, his voice suddenly calm. 'I didn't mean for that to happen. I like Rebecca. You saw what happened. She struggled. She … the knife … it just—'

'Put the knife down, John.'

'I just want to leave. I want to get out of here.'

'I can't let that happen.'

John's breathing grew in intensity as his mind thought of a new scenario for his escape. His facial muscles ticked and pulsed. 'You, bitch copper,' he said, calmly, pointing the knife to Faith. 'Move away from her.'

Faith looked up into the desperate eyes of her captor. 'If I release my hands, she'll bleed to death.'

'I don't care,' he struggled to get the words out. He obviously did care.

'She has a baby. She needs to survive for her baby.'

'She has a husband. She has a family. They'll bring it up. Move away from her now.'

Faith seemed to think about it before saying: 'That's not going to happen. I'm not leaving this woman to die.'

John turned his attention back to Christian. 'If you don't stand out of my way, I will stab whoever I have to so that I can leave this building. I'll start with the bitch copper here.'

'Shit,' Christian said under his breath.

'Ok, John, calm down,' Sian said. 'Take some deep breaths. I know you don't want to hurt anyone else in this room. You know them. They've done nothing wrong, have they?'

'No.'

'Exactly. So, like I said, take deep breaths.'

John breathed in slowly through his nose and out through his mouth. His entire body was shaking with adrenaline.

'This is what's going to happen,' Sian said, her voice low and soft. 'We're going to stand to one side and we'll let you leave. As soon as you've gone, though, we'll be calling for an ambulance for Rebecca, so you'll need to run fast. Do you understand?'

Christian stared at Sian. He couldn't believe what she was saying. Was she really allowing a killer to walk free.

'Yes. I understand. Thank you,' he gave her a weak smile.

'OK. We're going to move nice and slowly.' She looked at Christian and nodded for him to do what she said.

'No funny business,' John said. He held the knife firmly in both hands and edged towards the exit.

'Scott, it's Matilda. What's going on?' She shouted into her mobile in the cradle on the dashboard. She was hurtling down Bochum

418

Parkway swerving around cars and ignoring the beeps from fellow drivers.

'I've no idea. Why?'

'I've called Christian and Sian and neither of them are answering. I've also rung Starling House about four times and nothing. Who's in there with you?'

'Nobody.'

'Where's Sian and Christian?'

'They said they were going back to Starling House. Apparently, Faith had a breakthrough with this John Preston guy.'

'Shit. OK. Scott, I want you to stand by your phone. We may need backup.'

'Why? What's going on?'

'I don't know. Just a feeling at the moment. Pick a lane you stupid bitch.'

'What?'

'Not you, Scott.'

'Where are you?'

'I'm heading for Starling House. I should be there in a few minutes.'

'Do you want me to meet you there?'

Matilda wiped away a tear. 'Scott … I'll … I'll call you back.' She tore her mobile out of the cradle and threw it on the passenger seat. 'FUCK!' she screamed.

The sky was dark with heavy low-lying clouds. The wind whipped at John Preston as soon as he opened the back door and was hit in the face by a whirlwind of rain. He took a deep breath and ran out of Starling House. With a bloody hand, he fumbled in his pocket for his car keys. He dropped them as he tried to keep hold of the knife and select the fob to unlock the door. He had to be quick. He needed to get out of the grounds and onto the motorway. It wouldn't be long before an ambulance and more police would turn up, then a manhunt would be launched and the whole country would be looking for him.

He climbed in behind the wheel and slammed the door shut. It echoed into the cold night. He had only run a few metres but he was soaked to the skin. He stalled the car in panic. His hands were shaking; he was cold and wet, and he couldn't seem to control himself at all. Eventually, the car started and began to reverse out of his parking space. As he looked up at Starling House he saw Sian in the window of the staffroom talking on her mobile phone.

John slammed his foot down on the accelerator, kicking up gravel from the driveway. He headed for the open security gates. There was no reason for them to be locked with no inmates to keep from escaping.

He didn't slow down as he turned right out of the drive. Accelerating to forty miles per hour, he took the tight corner, and scraped the side of his Vauxhall on the wall. He just needed to get to the motorway. Once he was on an open road he could go anywhere.

At the first bend he tried to turn the steering wheel but his sticky bloody hands lost their grip and he moved over into the next lane of oncoming traffic. He leaned forward to try and see through the blur of rain on the windscreen and the battering of the wipers. Coming in the opposite direction he saw a speeding silver car heading towards him. It beeped for him to get out of the way.

But there was nothing he could do.

The silver Vauxhall and the silver Ford Focus made contact. One left the road and slammed into a tree, the other flipped and rolled twice before crashing into a drystone wall.

SEVENTY-FIVE

Matilda wasn't sure which hurt most – the actual crash or the impact of an airbag to her face. It took her a while to find her bearings. She could see the ugly image of Starling House just ahead. Her head felt fuzzy; she was dazed and confused. She tore off her seatbelt and stumbled out of the car.

Ahead, two shapes came running towards her. She recognized the small woman with the red hair as Sian; the man alongside her was a mystery to her blurred vision.

'Matilda, are you all right? Can you hear me?' It sounded like Christian Brady but his shape seemed all wrong.

Matilda placed a hand to her forehead, and it came away wet with blood. She felt as if she was falling yet there was ground beneath her feet.

'Sian, call for an ambulance.'

'I already have. It's on its way. She should lie down; she looks unsteady.'

'I think she's in shock.'

'I'll stay with her. Maybe you should check on Oliver, I mean, John.'

'Good idea. Try to keep her awake.'

Matilda heard the words spoken by her colleagues but they

421

made no sense to her. Were they even talking about her?

Sian's blurred form came back into view. 'Mat, I want you to sit down, OK? You're looking a bit wobbly.' Her voice was slow and controlled. 'Mat, how many fingers am I holding up?'

Matilda tried to focus. She couldn't see any fingers, never mind count them. She felt sick. She could feel bile rising up her throat. She opened her mouth and out came a torrent of vomit. Her legs gave way and she fell to the ground.

'Christian, what's happening?' Sian screamed, the panic in her voice was evident.

Sian held Matilda in her arms as her boss began to convulse. Her entire body tensed and shook violently.

Christian turned around at the sound of Sian calling out to him. He was standing by the mangled Vauxhall trying to find a way in to check on John's condition, but it was impossible. The driver's side of the car was tight against the damaged stone wall. Smoke was rising from the engine. Fierce heat radiated from the car.

He crouched down to look through the shattered windscreen. Was John alive? It was difficult to tell. His face was covered with blood. He couldn't see his nostrils flaring with breath, and his eyes were tightly closed.

'Christian, I need your help,' Sian again, screaming at him this time.

He turned from the car. There was nothing he could do here. This situation needed a fire engine to cut through the quagmire of mangled metal.

He headed back to Matilda and Sian. The look of horror on her face was disturbing to see. Sian was the unflappable one; the one who remained calm in a crisis. To see her looking so distraught was worrying.

'What's happ—?' The explosion from the Vauxhall lifted Christian off his feet and threw him to the ground. He heard a scream coming from Sian and then nothing as he lost consciousness.

EPILOGUE

Matilda required a two-day stay in hospital, mostly for observation. The head injury caused by the crash wasn't serious and at the scene she was suffering from a mixture of shock and concussion. The only way for her body to make sense of what was happening was to simply shut down. All the scans and tests had come back clear and she was discharged into Adele's care.

Christian suffered concussion and minor burns. He stayed in hospital for slightly longer than Matilda until his wounds started to heel. She visited him before she was discharged.

'I'm sorry,' she said from the foot of his bed.

'What for?'

'For not being there. I should have been. Sian told me everything that happened in Starling House; the stand-off with Oliver … John. I'm sorry. You should never have been put in that position.'

'It's part of the job, though, isn't it? Tell me, would you have done anything differently if you'd been there instead of me?'

Matilda thought for a while. 'I don't think so. I wouldn't have wanted him to leave the building either. Sian knew what she was doing, though. I think we both owe her a lot.'

'I'll buy her a box of Maltesers,' Christian joked.

Matilda laughed and quickly stopped as she held her right arm over where her ribs hurt. Christian winced too as he laughed.

'I'll come and see you when you're at home,' Matilda said.

They both smiled and nodded. Everything was fine between them. As Matilda made her way down the corridor she realized how much she valued Christian. He was a good man, a dedicated copper, and definitely someone she wanted by her side during these more complex cases. It was time to allow him into her inner circle more.

Adele had wanted to take Matilda straight home but at the request of ACC Valerie Masterson, Matilda was sent to her office. Things needed to be said, and they couldn't wait.

Matilda sat uncomfortably and listened as Valerie laid into her in a tirade which seemed to last hours. The ACC was disappointed in Matilda's conduct throughout the whole Starling House investigation. She was appalled at the lack of respect for her fellow officers for allowing them to enter a dangerous situation, for abandoning them when they needed her the most, and for her complete disregard of authority.

There was nothing Matilda could do but take the vicious character assassination. With her head down she thought of how the hostage situation in Starling House could have ended so tragically had Sian not been there and taken control of it. By allowing John Preston to leave she had saved the lives of everyone in there. It could have resulted in a bloodbath. She hoped the ACC would make sure Sian received the necessary commendation for her actions.

'Matilda, look at me,' Valerie said. She was standing behind her desk, arms firmly behind her back, lips pursed, a stern expression on her face. 'I'm giving you a week off. I don't want to see you in this station at all. During that time, you will think about how you've behaved during this investigation and you will change your behaviour. If you cannot put the lives and safety of your team before your own agenda then there is no place for you in South Yorkshire Police. Do you understand?'

Matilda nodded. Right now, she had no energy to fight.

After two days off work Matilda was already beginning to climb the walls. She had finished reading *Carl* by Sally Meagan, but had no idea what to do with the book. Matilda's phone had been busy as Sian filled her in on everything that was going on in CID, and she found herself missing the place.

Rebecca Childs was recovering in hospital following an operation on her trachea. She had lost a great deal of blood and needed two transfusions. She wasn't out of the woods yet, but the signs were good.

Rory Fleming was still recovering well. He was in a great deal of pain but he was more worried about bruising and if he would be scarred. Now that he was single he wanted to make sure his looks remained intact. This made Matilda laugh and she promised she would visit him in a day or two, maybe take him some concealer.

On the third day of her leave, the phone rang. Matilda muted the television and answered. She was surprised to hear from the ACC.

'Matilda, I'm not going to say I owe you an apology because I don't believe I do. However, it would appear you were correct.'

'I'm sorry?'

'I've had a call from the Chief Superintendent at Leicestershire Police who tells me DS Amy Stringer and a forensic team have spent the last two days searching a squat. I'm guessing you know something about that.'

'Yes, ma'am.'

'The flat has been untouched for a number of years and an extremely thorough examination took place. An item was found beneath floorboards in the living room wrapped up in a bloody rag. I'm also guessing you can tell me what that item is.'

Matilda found herself smiling. 'Would it be the murder weapon used to kill to Thomas Hartley's family?'

'It most certainly would. I spoke to Superintendent Spicer at Greater Manchester Police and he has confessed to knowing all about Daniel Hartley being Thomas Downy, though not until after Thomas Hartley had been convicted.'

'Why didn't he do anything about it?'

'Because he had been given promotion to DCI on the back of his speedy success of the Hartley case. If the whole backstory had come out, he would have been in serious trouble for not looking deeper into Daniel Hartley's life.'

'I hope Pat Campbell's son will be getting his suspension revoked.'

'He's already back at work, and Superintendent Spicer will be making a statement later this week in which he will resign for personal reasons.'

There was a long silence on the phone while Matilda took in everything that had happened.

'Matilda, I cannot condone the way you went about this, but you have saved an innocent teenager from a lifetime of imprisonment. You should be incredibly proud of that.'

'I am. Thank you, ma'am,' Matilda said. She felt a smile growing on her lips and a warm glow from deep within.

The process to release Thomas Hartley was not a quick one and Matilda was back at work by the time the CPS decided his conviction should be quashed and Samuel Bryce charged with his role in the murders.

Pat Campbell wanted to be there when Thomas was released. She had returned to Manchester to explain everything to Debbie Hartley in person, and on the morning of Thomas's release she went to collect her and bring her back to Sheffield, so she could welcome her only surviving relative when he was finally freed.

It was a bright October day. The sky was blue, there wasn't a cloud in sight, but it was chilly. Winter was slowly arriving.

In the car park at HQ Pat and Adele sat in the front seat with a nervous Debbie in the back.

'Where do you go from here, Debbie?' Adele asked, not taking her eyes from the back entrance.

'He can come home with me for as long as he wants. I'm sure he'll want to leave Manchester eventually, start his own life, and I'm fine with that. As long as he stays in touch.'

'And what will you do?'

'I don't know. Just carry on as normal I suppose.'

The doors opened and Matilda walked out with Thomas Hartley following. He was experiencing the fresh air of freedom for the first time in almost three years. The cold sun was on his face; the breeze ruffled up his hair. He stood still and took a deep breath.

Debbie opened the car door and leapt out. 'Thomas,' she called.

He looked up and saw his aunt running towards him with her arms wide open. She threw herself around him and grabbed him tight. At just over six feet tall, Thomas towered over Debbie. With her head buried in his chest her speech was muffled. Only Thomas could understand what she was saying. When she released him there were tear stains on his shirt.

'I'm sorry I didn't believe you. I'll never forgive myself.'

'You don't need to be sorry. There were times I didn't believe myself either.'

He looked up and saw the three smiling faces of the women who had secured his release staring back at him.

'I've no idea how to thank you.'

'You don't have to,' Matilda said. 'Just promise me you'll enjoy your life to the fullest.'

'I intend to.'

'I've booked a train to take us back to Manchester. I've made a room up for you too, and I hope you still like Super Noodles.'

Debbie was so ecstatic her words were falling over each other as she spoke.

'I certainly do,' he smiled.

Thomas thanked Matilda, Pat and Adele in turn and gave them each a hug.

'I feel all warm inside,' Adele said. 'Are you crying?' she asked Pat.

'No. It's this bloody hay fever.'

'In October?'

'Shut up, Adele.'

Pat turned away and Adele looked in her bag for a tissue.

Thomas took Matilda to one side and lowered his voice. 'I really don't know what to say. Thank you doesn't seem enough.'

'Like I said, you don't have to say anything.'

'You believed in me straightaway. I'll never forget that.'

'I always trust my instincts,' she smiled.

'"A guess is either right or wrong. If it is right you call it intuition. If it is wrong you usually do not speak of it again." Hercule Poirot.'

Matilda smiled, not quite sure what to make of that.

Thomas held out his hand for Debbie to take. Instead, she threw her arms around him once more and gave him a tight squeeze. Matilda smiled as she saw the final two members of the Hartley family reunited. Thomas made eye contact with Matilda. He had the look of gloating triumph etched on his face. Then something happened. His smile faded but he held eye contact for longer than was necessary. It may have been the wind but Matilda felt a cold chill run right through her.

ACKNOWLEDGEMENTS

There are so many people I would like to thank for all the help, encouragement, and information which has gone in to making this book become real. Firstly, Finn Cotton, Sarah Hodgson, Lucy Dauman and everyone at Killer Reads and HarperCollins for taking great care of me, and offering so much support. Writing is a very lonely process. It is a comfort to know I have such reassurance at the end of an email.

Claire Walker, Chris Howard and everyone at iGene Global for answering my questions on Digital Autopsies. Kim Suvarna for meeting with me and giving me an insight into what Adele Kean's office would look like. Simon Browes for the medical research – thank you for answering my texts.

A belated thank you to Jon Appleton for informing me of Killer Reads in the first place all those years ago.

My unnamed police contact is invaluable to me. This book would be full of procedural errors if it wasn't for him. Any that remain are all for story-telling purposes and not due to lack of research. This is a work of fiction, after all.

Many thanks to everyone at Agatha Christie Limited for permitting me to quote from *The ABC Murders*.

Also, a huge thank you to my copy editor Janette Currie and to Sarah Baxter for legal advice.

As always, a big hug for my mum, and a hearty northern handshake for Chris, Kevin, and Jonas for the support.

A final thank you to Woody. I'm not sure where I'd be if you hadn't saved me. Sleep well, sausage.